The Spare

S.K. Presley

Paperback Cover Design: RJ Creative

Editing and Proofreading: Traci Burns Tlmburns0107@gmail.com

Contents

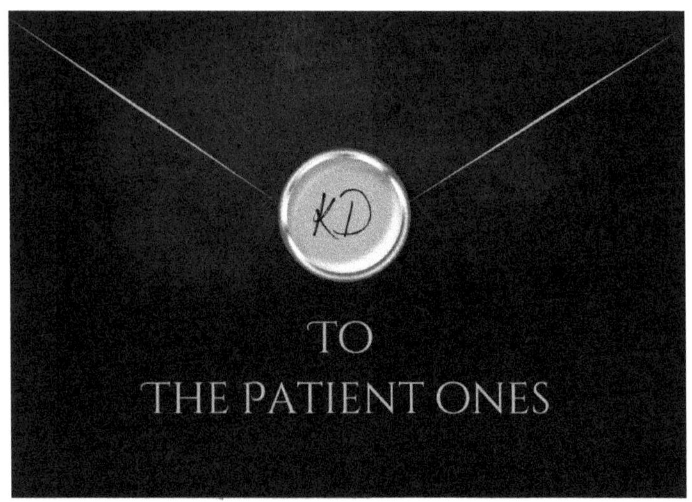

Dedication

To Ashli, Jess, Tracy, and Mari.

And for those of you who believe love wins.

PLAYLIST

Rain -Sleep Token

No One Else – Chris Brown

Royalty -Egzod, Maestro Chives & Neoni

Constellations -Jade LeMac

When I'm Small -Phantogram

Oh My God -Adele

You're In Love -Taylor Swift (Taylor's Version)

Paint It Black -Ciara

Skin -Rihanna

Love Story -Indila

Always Been You -Chris Grey and Josh Makazo

Chokehold -Sleep Token

Eyes on You -SWIM

Author's Note

Dear Reader,

Thank you for joining The King Dynasty bandwagon! I am so happy to see you.

Unlike The Heir, which focuses more on the love story of Hendrix, the elder son in the King family, The Spare takes off in a slightly different direction; through the POV of a tormented and damaged alpha hero, we'll be tackling tough subjects such as family secrets, a convoluted sense of belonging, and parental emotional abandonment. Through our beautifully lost heroine, we will see her struggle to cope with her feelings of loss of autonomy, lack of self-identity, parental loss, and mistrust through self-harm (though no thoughts of suicide), and emotional isolation.

We will be tackling all of this as well as, of course, our two MCs entering into an intense sexual relationship, finding healing and solace in one another as their relationship shifts from one of friendship, to romance.

Though ultimately this is a book (and series) about redemption, we cannot have redemption without seeing the gritty, dirty, and raw aspects of life that our characters have to tackle.

I knew going in that if I was going to write a series about a powerful family such as the Kings, that I was going to put a heavy emphasis on how a lifestyle such as theirs can affect the family members in different ways. Astronomical wealth also comes with a heap of familial expectations, tensions, problems… and in The Spare, we dive deep into how oppressive that can really become within a world such as theirs, and what a person is willing to sacrifice once they've had enough.

I hope you like it, and I hope you stay along for the ride because there's more to come.

Best,

SK Presley

Mentions of child abandonment (emotional)

FMC self-harm (intentional self cutting, only mentioned, not depicted, and unintentional starvation due to stress)

Abduction

Breath play

Degradation

Stalking

Flashbacks of Family Suicide

Murder

PTSD symptoms

Parent/Child verbal and emotional abuse

King Dynasty Appdx

Within this archive, each King offspring agrees to record the whole and undiluted truth of your union for the purpose of documentation for the King Family Marital Archives. In doing so, the subsequent generation promises to uphold the tradition set forth by their predecessors. In the event that a family member refuses to uphold the traditional marriage set forth within the familial contract, they agree to forfeit their inheritance, and they will document their reasoning by their sixty-fifth birthday, or, in the case of a spousal death. All records will remain sealed, only to be opened upon the death of both spouses. In agreeing to the rules set forth, proceed to the next page where you will *carefully* sign your name within your spot on the King Dynasty family tree.

King Dynasty Official Family Archives

Prologue

Mason and Melody's First Meeting

At King Compound, I lean my head on my fist and tear my eyes from the two story windows showcasing the dusky evening, watching Isobel go to her knees in front of my mother and take baby Vi into her arms. I'm *utterly* bored, itching to be anywhere but here. In my peripheral, Hendrix's eyes snap to mine, waiting for me to acknowledge him, but I don't, averting my eyes.

I greet his ass every week. He'll be okay if we skip one.

I do, however, give Isobel a small smile when she turns her head to me and says hello. My beef isn't with her, just her fucking husband.

Hendrix sits down on the couch near Isobel, and gets this look on his face that informs me he's completely whipped. Bending my elbow, I look at my watch on an eye roll just as Father leans towards me.

"Mason, have you thought any more about the talk that your brother and I had with you about the family business?" I slowly turn my head to the side, and as I meet Father's blue eyes, I find myself searching for even a hint of something that I'm more than just a work horse for this family's reputation. A futile effort as usual, because there's nothing.

All his affection is reserved for Mama, Teresa, and now Isobel, apparently. Typical Richard King.

I hesitate answering because this is bullshit. I could be on a beach in Bora Bora right now with my friends for two weeks, but Father forced me to cancel my trip because we're supposed to be meeting Isobel's family. Now, why *I* have to meet them makes no sense to me. They're not my in-laws; they're Hendrix's. But, as the Golden Child, the world will continue to evolve around him.

"Well?" Father says, arching an eyebrow as he takes a sip of his whiskey.

"I'm interested in the finance aspect-" I cut my words off at the disgusted expression that slides over Father's features, looking away from the familiar stern stare that lets me know I should have just kept my mouth shut, because it doesn't matter what I want. It never has.

"I thought I'd told you that I'd already given you my answer regarding that, Mason. To put you over the King Dynasty financial future after you've done nothing to earn that spot isn't going to fly. No. Find something else."

A surge of anger rises up in me, so vicious that my eyes narrow. "But this *is* what I'm good at, Father. There is nothing else."

Not for me.

"Anything else," Father stresses as his brow pulls low in that all-too-familiar stare that lets me know I need to rethink how I push back at him. "Just find something that doesn't involve you in the forefront of billions of dollars of our company and client's assets," he says sternly. "It's not exactly a hard request, Mason."

A muscle ticks in my jaw at the request because finance is the *only* thing I'm good at. Numbers, stocks, bonds; the green shit that makes the world go around.

It's why I wanted in with Balducci. The money I could have made there, the *connections,* would have been unlimited. Helping the underground families further their financial interests would have propelled me even higher than Richard King's status, and would have aligned me with the world's most powerful. I wouldn't have been limited to Richard King's Dynasty.

I could have had my own.

And the fact that I was foiled at every attempt burns my ass up in a way I can't even verbalize, so I keep my mouth shut for the most part. Not a hard feat, as they never want to hear from me anyway. I'm the family's black sheep. I wonder how they'd take it if I *baaed* at them instead of talking.

Maybe I'll bleat at Hendrix next week, instead of saying hello.

Just then, my parent's butler comes into the room announcing the presence of Isobel's mother and sister, Donna and Melody. Thankful for the distraction, I look up, seeing a beautiful African American woman with tiny, intricate locks that are twisted up in a rather elegant crown on top of her head. Some escape out to frame her face, hanging past her breasts. My first perception of her is, simply put, *shocking.*

She's *young.* Maybe around forty or so? Whatever her age, Donna does not look near old enough to have a child Isobel's age.

My interest piques just about as high as my brows raise as I take in the woman's physique; her skin gleams, showcasing delicate collarbones that flow into impressive arms of steel. She's dressed in a lavender dress and sandals. This is not what I expected Isobel's mother to look like, honestly.

"Hello, everybody!" Donna greets us all with a reserved smile.

She must think we're all idiots because we're all struck rather dumb at the statuesque woman, and no one says anything at first. Suddenly, a movement behind her draws my attention. As my eyes cut to the flash of blue fabric, both the blood and common sense leaves my body as I lock eyes with the most beautiful woman I've ever seen in my life who *has* to be Melody.

I can't think straight.

She doesn't look like her sister.

Whereas Isobel has light skin, cat-shaped hazel eyes, deep auburn hair, and a curvaceous body, Melody has hip-length dark-brown hair, darker skin, almond-shaped eyes, and freckles all over her face. My eyes tear from hers, dragging down her body to take in her slender arms. Her mid-thigh length dress showcases the toned legs of an obvious athlete. She's got an inverted A-frame body type with breasts on the smaller side.

And she looks...shy.

She hasn't said a word yet, which is fine because neither have I. My eyes snap back to hers, seeing she's blushing furiously.

Suddenly, Hendrix's infuriated face steps into my eyesight, and he snatches me up roughly by my elbow. I rise fluidly from the chair, looking past him to catch her eye again. Her head turns to keep my eye contact, and a grin tugs at my mouth as he pulls me behind him, moving to the other side of the room and well out of the ear shot of our families.

"Hey, Hen. *Let go of me!"* I snap tugging against his hold, but it just makes him tighten down even harder as he jerks me around to face him.

"What the fuck are you doing?" he says roughly. "She's *sixteen,* Mason!"

Irritated, I throw his hands up and take a step back, getting some distance between him and me. Seriously, it's too much after my conversation with Father. I need them to leave me the fuck alone.

"Nothing, Hendrix. *Goddamn, you are such a fucking killjoy.* I thought being married to Isobel would calm you down a little because you're finally getting laid on a regular, but nope, still just as uptight of a dick as ever," I snap, snatching my arm away on a frustrated grunt and narrowing my eyes at him.

He narrows his eyes back, pointing a finger at my face. "Stay the fuck away from her, Mason. She's *underage!"*

"All I did was look at her! Goddamn, bro. Can you mind your fucking business *for once?"* I clench my jaw hard as I avert my face and fold my arms, leaning a shoulder against the wall. Across the massive room, Melody is taking a seat on one of the leather couches, away from the others. She pulls a throw pillow to her chest and hugs it.

"No," he snarls. At his violent tone, I drag my eyes from watching Melody, and see he's clenching his fists. Good, I hope he tries it. My eyes slowly slide back to his.

"I want her."

He shakes his head and pinches the bridge of his nose. "Ohhh, Jesus. You have really lost your goddamn mind." He takes a deep breath.

I guess it'd be too much to ask that he hold it till he passes out for once.

My eyes slide back to Melody, uncaring of what he thinks about me. I've pretty much given up ever receiving approval from him or Father.

Melody shakes her head as Teresa offers Vi to her to hold, and the soft, apologetic smile that graces her face does something to me. My heart tugs at the way her doe-shaped eyes can't quite maintain anyone's eye contact, and she doesn't try to take up any more space than she has to.

Instead she works to make herself smaller. As far away from the spotlight as possible. She tucks her hair behind her ear, shaking her head no once again as my father offers her a water.

Her movements are insular, graceful.

I feel a connection to her I can't explain. My eyes slide back to Hendrix, seeing him staring at me with a perplexed look on his face.

"No, Hendrix. You don't understand, *I want her."*

As we stare each other down, his eyes widen.

"No!" he says sternly, shaking his head and taking a threatening step towards me. "I forbid it! *She's too young.* Stop thinking with your motherfucking dick! She's not a conquest, Mase. Not one of your back alley whores you pick up at the strip club. That's my wife's sister, and I won't hesitate to fuck you up if you hurt her."

My eyes narrow, because I haven't even thought once about fucking her.

"I didn't say I wanted her *today,"* I stress quietly. Turning my gaze back to Melody, I continue to watch her, fascinated. As I think, I tap my hand nice and slow against my bicep. "But in any event, I'll wait. *Say,* what do suppose you call your sister-in-law if she's also your brother's wife?"

Melody crosses her long legs, and though she's in a skirt that goes to her knees, the action causes it to ride up showing plenty of thigh. Heat crawls up my neck at the sight. Hendrix scoffs, turning on his heel to walk to her, snagging a blanket off the back of a leather chair and draping it over her legs. She looks up at him, arching an eyebrow.

Pulling out my phone, I type out a text.

Fuck you, Hendrix. -Mase

Hendrix pulls out his phone, before being distracted by something Donna says to him. I walk over to join them, deciding I'd like to get to know her. I sit down directly next to her, ignoring Hendrix's face turning pink. The first thing I notice is her smell. She smells sweet. Innocent.

I hate she's tainted by this family. She deserves to be free.

My phone pings.

I'm going to haul you to the backyard to beat your fucking ass. Go sit somewhere else, NOW!- Hendrix

I'd like to see him try. I'd lay his ass out so quick he wouldn't know what hit him.

Thoroughly annoyed with my oldest sibling, I throw him a filthy look before shifting my stance; I spread my legs and cross my arms, grazing Melody's thigh with mine. She shoots me an innocent look and smiles, shifting herself to where she's facing me a little bit more head on and pulling her leg away.

I give her a smile, looking back at my phone to text Hendrix back.

No, I don't think I will. Is this how you felt when you first met Isobel? -Mase

Looking up I give him a sly grin before turning to Melody, who's clueless.

"Damn, you got some legs, girl!" I tease in a lighthearted voice that's in direct contrast to how I currently feel on the inside. The longer she looks at me, the more the room falls away. Leaving just me and her. "You a runner?" I ask, striving for nonchalance.

Her head tilts a little and a bright smile almost splits her face in half.

She's got a wide, endearing mouth that's warm and welcoming. And the fact I just made her smile like this chases some of that resentment away that's always there regarding my relationship with my family, and it causes this sudden yearning for her to deepen.

Nothing, so far, has worked to pull me out of this pit of hate that's been my home for so long that I can't even remember when I first fell into it. My eyes roam her face, enamored with the fact that an innocent girl with doe eyes, a wide smile, and twenty three freckles managed to do with one smile and twenty seconds what countless experienced whores across four continents haven't been able to accomplish in seven years.

"Yeah, I'm in cross country," Melody says, her soft voice reeling me in the rest of the way. With that tone she's got me hook, line, and sinker. I'm gone. "I can run ten miles without stopping."

"Jesus," I drawl lazily, running my gaze across her face. "That's impressive. Sounds like you have some stamina. My name's Mason; I'm Hendrix's brother." I hold out my hand but don't move to actually shake hers, merely wrapping my fingers around her slender fingers and squeeze gently, content to have her skin against mine.

"I'm Melody. Pleased to meet you too, Mason." Melody deftly plucks her hand out of my grasp, and my eyes flicker to her lips for a hot second.

When she looks away back towards the baby, they go even lower to pause on her breasts before flickering back up to her eyes. I give her my most devilish smile in an attempt to catch her attention once more, and pleasure fills me as her face goes bright red.

"No, I'm pretty sure the pleasure's all mine, Mel," I say.

"Baby, are you *pregnant?"*

Donna's voice breaks our spell, and we turn our head in unison to where she sits across from us staring rather hard at Isobel, who's tucked under Hendrix's arm looking like a deer caught in headlights.

"Yes, we just found out yesterday," Isobel says with a sheepish look on her face. "I wasn't going to say anything because it's Vi's day and we didn't want to dim her shine."

Curious, I glance at Melody who's oddly silent, making me wonder if she knew. Something tells me she didn't, though. When she clutches the pillow to her chest even harder, I lean into her, sliding my palm to her back as I whisper in her ear.

"Seems we're going to have so many kids to spoil, huh, Auntie?" I whisper conspiratorially. "Congratulations."

"Get your hand off her," Hendrix says quietly, giving me a narrow eyed look. I roll my eyes, turning my attention back to Melody, who's frowning at Hendrix.

She's so intriguing.

"It was nice meeting you, butterfly," I whisper, pressing my hand slightly harder into her lower back before pulling away and standing up to walk over to my father, who's sat back down in his chair after fawning all over Isobel.

Blatantly ignoring Hendrix, I straighten my spine, aware of Melody's eyes on my back and make my decision. I'll claw my way to the top if it means I get to have her, I don't care who's in my way. Family or *no* family. Bending down into Father's ear, I put my hand on his shoulder. He turns his head slightly, his eyes finding mine.

"I'll do it without you," I say coldly, turning and striding out the door, only giving Melody one last look as I head out.

Playtime is officially over. By the end of the week I've secured a two million dollar loan from Uncle William, and I'm firmly on my way.

CHAPTER 1

You're The Problem

Five Weeks Later

I HATE WE'RE SITTING around dissecting my love like this, I think.

However, I keep quiet, letting my family take the lead on the current situation: discussing whether or not to put Melody in a rehab facility due to extreme weight loss. I press my lips together, hands in my pockets, floundering. Digging the paperclip under my fingernail in a bid to remain in control and helplessly watch them decide amongst themselves what to do with Melody.

"She won't eat. She won't *move,*" Donna, Melody and Isobel's mother, says tearfully from her spot at my father's desk. "I don't know what to do anymore. She needs help."

The office lights up with a flash of lightning, the thunder shakes the house as if to lend her words precedence and strength. My lips tighten, as do my arms folded across my chest. The desperation in Donna's voice is almost enough to send me over the edge.

An edge I'd just sharpened to an unbearable point with my recent admission to my family.

To Hendrix...

We're packed seven deep in my father's office at King compound: Hendrix, myself, Teresa, Donna, Father, Mother, and Father's estranged younger brother, William. My eyes meet his across the room.

We've a shared disposition, he and I, as their relationship mirrors mine and Hendrix's relationship. William was the black sheep to my father's status as a golden child.

Thirty years have separated the two men to near irreconcilable levels, and he's only here because I'd called him out of desperation and his love for Hendrix. Otherwise, he'd never have known what happened to Isobel had I not informed him.

Father extended a guest room to Uncle William; however, that's it. And since he's been here I haven't seen him say more than two words to him. An ice cold energy has entombed this house, and made space for the intense grief that currently gives life to the expansive walls that I used to call my childhood home.

Madre leans over to place a tissue in Donna's hand and places her hand on her back.

"Donna, we're here, honey," she says. "I promise we will do everything in our power to see to it that she is taken care of."

My eyes glance over their attire. Both women are dressed in funeral black out of respect to Xavier, Isobel and Hendrix's bodyguard we'd just buried not three hours ago.

My gaze now slides to Hendrix who stands at the fireplace with an arm leaned against the mantle. Every muscle in his body is tight with tension, and worry reflects in his blue eyes. A fact I know, even if I can't currently see them. In three weeks I've witnessed my confident brother slowly be eaten away into a shell of himself, and in the twenty minutes that I've shared my hand in Isobel's disappearance, he's turned his back on me.

And kept it there.

My brows pinch as worry fills me anew, but not enough to edge out this sickening guilt that's sat on my chest like an iron weight. Refusing to be moved even now that I've confessed that it was my friend within the Balducci mafia who'd given away Isobel's location to her father, Claudio. Resulting in her abduction, and Xavier and two others' deaths.

The room fills with the roar of the great fireplace behind my father's chair and the sharp pitter patter of rain against the two ten-foot tall window panes on the western side of the room. As if the heavens are also mourning, it's rained almost every day since her abduction.

And as the rain washes away bits and pieces of the Earth, it also mercilessly carries away parts of the man who used to be my brother.

And viciously corrodes what's left of Melody's sanity.

"I'm so terrified that she's next," Donna cries, clutching her hand to her chest as tears stream down her face.

Her shoulders shudder as she fights with everything in her to stem the fervor of her cries, but not one of us would blame her if she completely broke down. Isobel's been gone for three weeks now, and we're no closer to getting her back than we were the first day she was taken.

Hendrix just gave the order for my friend to be captured, and we're awaiting more information.

My father leans forward now, reaching for Donna's other hand across the table. "Donna, we won't let anything happen to her. The two of you will stay here at King compound-"

Stepping forward from my place against the sidewall, I tilt my head. "Hold on, why do you think she's next?" I ask, daring to interrupt my father.

"Because of who her father is," Donna says, wiping her eyes.

Father and Madre share a carefully concerned look.

"Our security team is very skilled, Donna..." Madre says, putting her kind eyes back to Donna, who's now shaking her head, looking thoroughly tired.

"I don't understand why Maximus would have anything to do with this?" Father says, frowning, apparently referencing Melody's father, as well as a conversation that I must have missed somewhere along the way, because this is the first time I'm hearing about a Maximus, much less him being Melody's father.

"Because Maximus and Claudio are rivals, Richard!" Donna says loudly. "If Claudio found Isobel, then he no doubt has found out about *Melody, and he will kill her for no other reason than to get back at Maximus!"*

The room goes quiet.

Placing a hand on his jaw, Father heaves a slight sigh, scrubbing his hand down the short hairs there. "I thought Maximus was dead, Donna," Father says softly.

Donna sniffs. "Yeah, I thought he was dead too, for a while. Max is the only reason I was able to get away from Claudio in the first place.

He secured me time to get Isobel out of Claudio's and my home in the middle of the night, and gave us the money we needed to procure new identities. For a few years, money would appear, and things would randomly show up that I needed, but Max never showed his face until almost eight years later. We got together, and I became pregnant with Melody, but I...." she trails off, looking to the side as her features contort on a wince.

Hendrix turns his head slightly, gifting me with his profile as he moves the smallest amount. The only proof that he's listening, and not trapped in his head.

The tension thickens to an acute, almost painful level before she turns her eyes back to my father's. A crack of lightning throws her vulnerable, eerily youthful features into sharp relief, and for a moment, I see the terror of the girl she was back then. Helpless and alone.

"And then?" Madre asks softly, rubbing her hand in soothing circles on Donna's back.

Donna takes a deep breath, rocking in her seat in a self-soothing motion reminiscent of Melody and Isobel's anxious mannerisms.

"Claudio hunted us down and found us before I could tell Maximus that I was expecting Melody."

My father's posture visibly tightens, and the energy shifts once more. My eyes flit, seeing Father look sharply at Uncle William whose lips tighten, but he doesn't tear his eyes from Donna. Donna continues speaking, effectively bringing my attention back to her.

"He broke into our home one night, and attacked Maximus while we were asleep. And, while I was fleeing with Isobel *-again-* I heard a gunshot. I didn't turn back. I was too scared, and Max was yelling for us to run." Donna blinks, rolling her lips as an embarrassed expression graces her features.

She squeezes her eyes shut, and though I find myself sympathizing with her pain, my mind races, winding through the hallways of my parent's home to where I know Melody's bedroom is. The fact she's been alone for this long doesn't sit right with me, but Donna begins speaking again, bringing my attention back to her.

"The years crawled by, and I didn't hear from Max. Not one time. I'd assumed he'd died, until a couple weeks before Isobel's eighteenth birthday. A note showed up at my door instructing us to move to New York into the Balducci territory. It wasn't signed, but I could tell from the handwriting it was Maximus..." she goes silent as she brings the tissue up to wipe at her face. "But he never came back."

"It was probably a good thing you did, and got under the protection of the Balducci territory. It bought you a few years until you had the resources to fight back." Uncle William's voice rings out, drawing everyone's attention. "You were smart to come here."

My eyes go past Donna to the leather sitting area where my Uncle sits half in shadow on the opposite side of the wall from me.

He'd been silent this entire time, unsure of how his presence would be tolerated. But his gaze remains hard on Donna, where it's been since he first laid eyes on her.

Donna shakes her head rapidly. "You don't understand!" she says, turning in her seat to throw half-crazed, red-rimmed eyes at Father. "He will steal Melody just to get back at Maximus! I'd always told her he was dead. It was easier than trying to explain all of this to her. How could I explain she had a father that I couldn't find and wasn't even for sure that he was alive?" She takes a deep breath, bowing her head. "I couldn't even wrap my *own* head around it, much less find a way to tell her." Her eyes flick back up to Father's, who continues to listen with a quiet, reserved expression on his face. "But these people are dangerous, Richard. I don't think it's going to stop with Isobel."

Father sits back in his seat, scrubbing his hand across furrowed brows. Mine lower as well. King stays unmoving.

I speak up from the other side of the room. "Donna, you need to tell Melody."

Hendrix turns to face me now, the lines in his face etched deep with grief, his blue eyes are narrowed, causing my heart to skip a beat, freezing me in place.

"You. Will. Be. Quiet." The threatening growl in his dangerously quiet tone sends chills through my body, and I dig that paperclip just a bit deeper. Pain explodes through my finger, but I keep my expression impassive. "You have no fucking right to an opinion about any of this. *We* will decide what is shared and what is not. *I* will decide when you can have a goddamn say in a*nything* from now on."

An uncomfortable hush falls over the room as Hendrix and I keep our eyes locked. Father doesn't stand up for me, not that I really expect him to, but his emotional abandonment of me is highlighted even more in this moment. I continue to stare into Hendrix's eyes as pain fills me, because though we've had our differences, in the back of my mind Hendrix was always my protector, even if I didn't like how he went about it.

The man in front of me now isn't Hendrix. This isn't my brother.

This is a man who despises me.

I avert my gaze, ashamed of myself. Knowing that unless a miracle is granted to us, if Isobel never comes back to this family, then neither will I. Everything hinges on if we get her back. My chest tightens as a different type of terror fills my heart now to live alongside the grief that cripples me to the point I don't feel like I have anything worthwhile to give.

Useless, just like they've been calling me for years.

Madre turns in her seat to meet my eyes, but even she quickly averts her face to wipe her eyes, making me feel truly alone.

Overwhelmed, I push off the wall and pivot on my heel, pushing through the door and heading to the staircase which I know leads to Melody. I just need to check on her. Keeping my eyes pinned to the rug in front of me, I ignore the family portraits mounted on the walls as it's too painful to look at, not knowing if I'll ever be sitting for another one.

Somewhere along the way, before I was born, Uncle William stopped appearing in our family pictures, so I know it's not far-fetched that it could also be my future. The last one he'd sat for was when Madre was pregnant with Hendrix, almost thirty-eight years ago.

I nod at Stephen, Melody's security who is stationed outside the tall walnut door, and turn the knob. Letting myself in, I shrug off my jacket, hanging it up on the discrete hook and kick off my shoes in the tiny foyer that leads to the apartment sized guest wing of her suite.

Squinting my eyes against the dark, I walk deeper into the space and pause at the slight lump of her body in the king sized four-poster bed.

Gauzy white curtains hang down from the posts, partially obscuring her view from me as I walk further into the room. My steps hesitate when I hear a sniffle, and the closer I get to her, the tighter she curls in on herself. I feel a crack start in my heart, one I know might be permanent.

I pause just at the end, taking a deep steadying breath.

"Melody?" I call quietly. She doesn't answer. I bend forward, feeling along the covers until my hand grasps her foot and I squeeze, but she still doesn't respond. "Come on, butterfly. It's Masey." My breath hitches, but I don't have the pride anymore to care I'm emasculating myself. She needs me.

I need her.

At her continued silence, I glance behind me at the dark foyer and the heavy door that leads to the hallway, knowing at any moment one of our family members might come through. But I take a chance anyways and say fuck it. What are they going to do if they catch me alone with her? Kick me out of the family?

If Isobel dies, I'm as good as gone anyways.

Forgiveness isn't for men like me and Uncle William, I don't think.

I walk to her side and sit, reaching forward and clicking on the bedside lamp to the lowest setting and bend closer to see her buried in a cocoon within the sheets. Her eyes are red-rimmed and swollen from crying, as are her lips.

My heart tugs for my little butterfly.

"Hey, you," I reach forward to caress my knuckles down her wet cheek. "Move over," I whisper.

Not even asking permission, I tug the sheet free of her body and slide in next to her, pulling her tightly into my arms and pressing my lips to the top of her head as that crack in my heart gets a little wider. She smells like she hasn't bathed in a while, and her usually groomed hair is limp and lifeless.

I caress a hand down her hair, and pull her closer with my other around her waist trying to comfort her the best I can. I try to keep my movements slow, but my fingers slow when I feel her waist.

Jesus, she's skin and bones. I try to be inconspicuous as I probe her delicate ribs beneath my fingertips, feeling a self-loathing rise inside me swift and mercilessly. My throat convulses on a hard swallow, and it's everything I can do to not break down as her slight body molds into mine, lending me comfort I don't fucking deserve.

I don't deserve her.

I truly hate myself. For doing this to Isobel, Hendrix, Donna, and Melody. I squeeze my eyes shut as pain flows through me. If Isobel dies,

I may as well kill myself, too. I could never live with myself knowing I did this to them. I won't.

"You need to eat, sweetheart," I say quietly, swallowing against the lump in my throat as her tears soak into my shirt.

"I-I don't want to e-eat," she sobs. "H-How can I eat when they're p-p-probably k-killing her right nowww!"

She cries a long tortured sound into my chest, making my own eyes well up with tears. Her cries of sorrow echo throughout the room, and I sniff, bringing a hand up to wipe a tear away, and clear my throat.

"I know," I say, my voice low, and rough with grief that I'm only now able to acknowledge. I didn't dare to in my father's office. I had no right, as Hendrix said. "I know. But you've got to, honey," I say harshly, putting both my hands on either side of her head and pulling her away. I keep my eyes tight on her tear-stained face, letting her know how serious this is. "Otherwise, they're going to send you somewhere where they'll force you." My voice shudders with emotion, and I know the color is high in my face; I feel it. "Mel, she needs you strong."

Melody's face contorts as she breaks apart between my hands.

Lowering one, I fist the material of my shirt, bringing it up to wipe the tears away and to wipe her nose. I crush her to me, our hearts beating erratically as I begin to fall apart too. But I keep her face to my chest so she can't see.

Pulling her even closer I swing my legs off the side of the bed, hoist her bridal style into my arms, and stand up. Carrying her out of the bedroom and down the hallway towards the kitchen.

Once inside, I keep the lights turned off and head to the refrigerator where I open it and sink us both to the floor, nestling my back against the door. I reach up, and rummage around in the drawers, snagging down a bag of grapes and placing it by my hips. I meet her tired eyes while I work to maneuver her limp body so her head is against my bicep and her body is nestled between my spread legs.

"Open up," I say, her face swims through the tears in my eyes.

"N-Nooo," she says, closing her eyes and shuddering through a series of body wracking sobs.

She begins to dry heave, and I pull her forward so she's bending over her knees. When she's done, I lay her back over my arm.

"Open, Melly," I whisper, pressing the grapes to her lips.

She's not relenting, so I put it between my teeth and bite it half, then smearing the juice onto her lips. She moans, looking at me weakly through glazed eyes.

"I'm not going to let them take you away," I say harshly, pressing harder.

This time she relents, parting her lips enough to let me push the grape through, but she just lets it sit there. Narrowing my eyes, I move fast, digging my fingers into her tummy. Her eyes fly wide as she jerks hard, biting down on the fruit. Her eyes meet mine as she chews and then becomes more desperate as the taste floods her tongue.

She swallows it on a gasp, panting weakly against me.

"He came for her," she suddenly says, her lips trembling. "He came for her and took her away, and didn't take me *too.* Why didn't he want *me?* Why am I never good enough?"

Shock fills me; however, I fight to keep my expression neutral. Aware in her half-starved state she's probably slightly delusional, but there's a sorrowful tint to her voice that lets me know her words come from some place true. A place of hurt so deep that you wonder why you aren't worthy. Why one sibling was deemed good enough to be abducted, to be the chosen one, and you weren't.

I understand that hurt.

To the bone, I understand that pain.

Seems Melody and I swim in the same waters.

"I get it, sweetheart," I say softly. Rocking her in my arms, I place my lips to her neck and nuzzle her, taking a deep breath. "I know what it's like not to be wanted." My head raises as she sniffs, meeting my eyes warily. "And if you think no one wants you, Melody, that's *bullshit. I* want you. I need you here. So, you need to eat."

I reach in the bag for another grape and hold it to her lips.

Her eyes stay wide on mine, and seeing she's unmoving, I bite the grape in half again and press it to her lips where she bites into it gently, pulling it from between my fingertips.

"Good girl," I murmur, reaching for another one. "You got this. Come on, let's have another one. We can get through this together."

In the light of the refrigerator, I spend the next hour slowly feeding her grape after grape until the bag is gone, and I know without a doubt that Isobel's coming home. She has to. Because I won't suffer a life without Melody.

I won't tolerate living a life without my love.

Or my redemption.

CHAPTER 2

Meeting The Don

One year, three months later. Los Angeles, California.

Shifting my body weight in the back seat of the armored car next to my private security guard, I put my unease at the back of my head, scrolling through my phone aimlessly as we make our way to the Scognamiglio mansion.

I wasn't allowed to come on my own. Lucien Scognamiglio sent this vehicle for me, and I was heavily searched before I even got in. Lucien's accompanying guard did everything but stick his hand up my ass.

He's sitting in the passenger seat all innocent, like he didn't just take his sweet time learning my dick size.

I frown as a text comes through. Disappointment fills me as I see it's not Melody.

Hey bro, so guess what? -Henny

What? Mase

Lucien brokered an arranged marriage between his younger cousin and Joaquin ANYWAY! –Henny

I roll my eyes, and call him.

"Hey, Mase-"

"Sooo, does that fucking mean I don't have to do this?" I interrupt him.

The driver and security guard both turn their heads to glance at me in the rearview mirror.

"What?" Hendrix snaps. "No. He summoned you. Take that meeting, Mason. Besides, you're already there."

I hang up on him, and turn off my phone, glancing up and arching a brow as we roll onto a massively secluded gated property. Driving under palm trees that flank a double gate attached to an eight-foot tall fence, I'm pleasantly surprised when we are suddenly transported to Tuscany, Italy.

Cypress trees and raised gardens juxtaposition sunken gardens with granite fountains. Birds fly around, and to be honest it's nothing like how I'd thought a mafia don would be living. Where's the guard dogs, and barbed wire fence with-*oh...*

There's a couple men walking the perimeter of the fence with AK-47s, speaking discretely into walkie talkies. My eyes rise to see another man hidden in the trees.

I only see him because we're driving damn near under him, but he's there.

We don't go to the front; rather we pull around the side of the house, through a stone archway leading to a separate entrance. Two intimidating men with guns flank the walnut door. The driver jumps out and opens my door, and I give him a nod of thanks as I step out onto the cobblestone drive, jerking the lapel of my tailored suit jacket.

I pull out my cigarette tin, packing it and then lighting one quickly. Whoever this man is can wait a minute for me to chill out before our meeting. When I'm done, I put the half smoked cigarette back into my tin and then nod at the guard. Ready.

One of the guards opens the door wordlessly with an impassive look on his face. Pausing just inside the threshold, I cast a curious look around the courtyard, seeing more guards in the shadows. My ears prick at the muted sound of a walkie talkie coming from somewhere in the heavily landscaped garden about a hundred yards away.

Turning back to the door I walk on in. A different guard on the inside leads the way, and one trails me as we make our way deeper into the home.

I wish I could say I'm impressed by the interior, but I'm not.

Years of mansion parties, lavish vacations, and having access to untold wealth has worn down my ability to find pleasure in these things, but I guess it's a good space, considering. Tasteful.

Taking stock of my surroundings, I keep my expression impassive at the obviously expensive art on the walls, eyeing priceless vases that are scattered about in aesthetically pleasing places on the floor. The walls are stucco, the sconces are dark pewter, the floor is terracotta, the chunky beams are exposed.

Tick, tick, tick. I mentally check through the list of stereotypical features found in Italy. This one sure enough fits the bill, but to top it off, several maids scurry around, trying but failing to be discrete. I keep my gaze averted from theirs. It all comes with the territory of wealth, mafia or not, and it does much to make me feel like I'm at home, lending me what I believe is a false sense of security.

I'm ushered though another wooden door, and into a study where Lucien Scognamiglio sits behind his desk, flanked by two security guards. The ones that brought me through the house retreat, stationing themselves just outside the opened door.

"Mason King," Lucien drawls in a lazy voice, looking up from his stack of papers. He throws down his pen and slides the stack to the left of him, gesturing to one of the three leather seats on the other side of his desk. "How are you?"

I cross the room taking the one in the middle, directly across from him, crossing my legs and settling back in the seat, not offering my hand.

To put it mildly, I'm not exactly pleased that I'm to be summoned like a fucking dog.

"I'm a little shocked that you're not sequestered in some stone castle somewhere, Scognamiglio," I respond wryly.

I can't help my tone. A few minutes in this man's presence won't cure me of a lifetime of obligation, forcing me to adopt bored, aloft mannerisms that I can't shake no matter how much behavioral therapy I've attempted.

He chuckles, sitting back himself and not offering his hand either. I note the amused expression on his face, and he tilts his head curiously. Obviously assessing me just like I'm assessing him.

So assess we shall.

"I have almost one hundred men on the property at all times, Mason," he says. "I come out of pocket in order to appear as harmless as possible to the outside world when I'm out and about. But trust and believe, no one is getting on my land unwanted. If they do, they come to me with a bullet in their skull, because I'm not the type to ask questions."

I nod my head, glancing around his room before even going so far as to look over my shoulder, being overtly obvious about how I'm judging his place. However, there's not a flaw to be found.

I like it.

It's nothing like Father's study. It's a nice set up. Intimate, comfortable, and warm. Another surprise, because according to what I've observed so far, Lucien seems sort of like me: not fussy about being overly lavish or pretentious. My interest in him is piqued; however, I don't let that be overly obvious either. I keep my head turned, driving home how thoroughly I'm assessing his dwelling.

A man's home is a reflection of himself, you see.

A bar with sparkling crystal glasses and decanters sits adjacent to us. Top shelf liquor fills a miniature cellar within the bar with a tasteful, yet sparse selection informing me he's a picky drinker, and the clear window pane beyond shows me a rather pretty view of the landscaping on the East side of the grounds.

"I'm sure you must also pay a shit load for gardeners," I say, bringing my gaze back to his before falling on an interesting ceramic of a rabbit on the fireplace mantle behind him. It's not a professional piece; no, it looks like something a kid would put together. The ears look funky, too. I frown, because it looks so out of place. "What's *that?"*

It's the ugliest thing I think I've ever seen.

He turns to clock what I'm talking about. "Oh, that?" He turns back around, rubbing his hand near the base of his thumb. "That's a rabbit. To remind me to be humble, you see."

I raise a brow. "Can mafia Dons *be* humble? Is that even in your DNA?"

Lucien barks out a laugh, and the guard behind him to his right even gets a shadow of a grin; however, he kills it quickly. "Well, a good Don knows when to be humble because there's a time and a place for everything, Mason. As you'll soon know."

I roll my eyes. "How do you know I don't already know that? Don't be an assumptive dick *already.* I just met you."

Lucien pauses at my words, quickly hiding a shocked look before chuckling. "Hm," he says. "You're interesting, Mason."

"Thanks, I'll choose to take that as a compliment."

"Good, because it was." He clears his throat, leaning forward and swiping a hand through his thick brown hair.

He's not too much older than me, roughly mid-thirties, maybe. Little lines grace the corner of his eyes when he laughs; other than that he looks like he could have stepped off the runway with Teresa's husband Brody. He's got a distinctive nose, though not too big, and chocolate eyes that feel warm, but I know better. He's a Don for a reason.

"I'll dare assume your brother told you why I wanted you here?" he asked, his eyes roam my face tightly. Curiously. Never as curious as I am, though.

"Si. He mentioned you wanted me to be your new finance guy. But you took long enough to call in your favor."

None of us are pleased with him regarding that.

He nods. "Yes. I need you to handle the finances of my business."

"Money laundering." *I knew it.*

"No," he corrects me quickly. I frown at his answer, confused.

"Stacking your stocks?"

Lucien smiles. "What a lovely criminal mind you have. No," he says. "I need you to take financial control of my non-mafia business dealings and make a name for me outside of-" he waves a hand around the office, *"this."*

I shift in my seat, rubbing my fingers along my jaw as I just stare at him. "And your stocks?"

"Correct."

"How many businesses?"

"Four. One art business, two jewelry-"

I grunt, because jewelry is what made the King name; however, no one owns a jewelry business, much to my father's discontent. That's what he thought Teresa would get into, but she steered towards fashion instead.

"And a few nightclubs," he finishes.

"And you don't want me involved in the actual day to day dealings of your criminal organizations?" My tone drips disbelief, laced with a touch of confusion.

"No." He gifts me with that smile again, making me uneasy. "Unless you want to, that is. But no pressure."

"...... So my brother was correct. I'm not to be *in* the mafia, but I'm in with *you?"* I huff out a laugh, treating him to a disdainful look. "I thought you lied to him, wheedled him down enough to get me here so you could offer me a real position."

"What the hell gave you the impression it's not a real position?" he asks coldly, arching a brow.

I arch mine back, not intimidated. "Is it?"

"This is a real position, and one I take just as serious as if you were in with me." His brows raise. "I'd never lie to a King, Mason."

I snort on a humorless laugh, glancing to the side in amusement. "I didn't realize our influence ran quite this deep, to be honest."

"I wouldn't admit that outside of these walls," he says in a serious tone, bringing my eyes back to his.

"Hmm..." I hum, because honestly I could care less about the King Dynasty influence. I never abused its power, or really used its influence one way or another. That would call for a very rare occasion. But I guess for Hendrix's sake I'll maintain the front we're a perfect family.

Even if Luca knows we aren't.

"So, what? Am I not good enough to be in your ranks?" I drawl, feeling a touch put out honestly.

He chuckles, his face lighting up with humor. "Quite the contrary. I want you within my ranks very much. I think you're clever, smart, articulate, capable. Trilingual-which seems to be asking *a lot,* these days for some reason," he says sarcastically, flipping his pen again. "But your brother's wrath is-" he looks to the side and whistles. "Actually, it's not so much *your brother,* honestly. It's the pesky little fact that he's got *Frank Jackson* on his side."

I fold my arms, vaguely remembering Frank as the man who handled Isobel's father's execution. "And why are you waxing poetic about him?"

He points the pen at me, lowering his brow. "The man is a beast. Slippery as an eel and stealthy as they come. He's managed to evade mafia, cartel, *and* governments all over the world. He's *lethal.* And we *all* in the underworld know not to get on that man's bad side. So, no. If your brother asks me to not invite you in, then I'll respect that. But, to make myself crystal clear, Hendrix King is about the only man in the entire world who gets that privilege."

My eyes snap to his, and I tilt my head as he continues to watch me quietly.

"But if you want in, all you gotta do is ask," he smiles, making me shake my head.

It's like the carrot is to be forever dangled in front of me, but I'll never be able to attain it for anything. There was a time I'd salivate for this opportunity. Cut off my left *arm* to have an in like this. But now?

Now it comes with a heap more risks than it did before, because I don't want Melody hurt, and I don't want her close to this.

I sigh heavily, rubbing the bridge of my nose with my fingers. "I don't get it. All those years my brother fought like hell to keep me away from the mafia, and look, he seemingly has no problem just laying me at your front door like it's nothing."

Lucien's eyes glitter in the firelight as he just stares at me, not offering any input one way or another.

Clearing my throat, I switch tactics. Wanting a taste of his inner mind. "Why me?" I ask roughly. "Why not deal with King, hm? *He's* the golden boy, not me."

"Ahhh." Lucien shakes his head on a rather long suffering exhalation of air. *"Golden boy.* Do you hear that, Blane?" he says disdainfully, throwing a look to the guard behind him who just stares stoically ahead. When he turns his gaze back to me, a wicked smile curves his lips, and he half scoffs, waving a hand dismissively. "I didn't want the golden boy. *Everyone* always underestimates the spare. And in my experience, with spares in particular, there's always a wealth of talents overlaying the abyss of a stifled persona which isn't usually tapped into."

My brow raises. "Well, damn," I say. "You're a right poet, Mr. Scognamiglio. Who'd have thought?"

He chuckles. "Call me Luca. If I have to hear you butcher my last name again I might shoot you. I think I'd suffer the wrath of your brother."

I laugh. "Sure. Luca. Well, I hate to have to tell you that I will be declining your offer."

I contemplate for a few, drawn out moments. However, despite the great temptation, I couldn't haul Melody into this lifestyle. I just couldn't.

No dice.

His next words almost make me get shot, for real.

"Okay," Luca says in a hard, matter-of-fact tone and turning his attention back to his paperwork in a dismissive move that sets my blood on fire. "Well, tell Hendrix I'll be coming to collect Melody, then. He needs to have her ready for me by no later than Tuesday next week."

He grabs his pen and begins to sign the stack of papers to his right.

The laughter dies on my tongue as my blood pressure skyrockets.

"The fuck you are!" I say in a nasty tone, uncaring of his status, or the way the two armed men behind him tighten and train their gazes on me. *"You lay a hand on Melody, and I'll kill you myself."*

Luca's head snaps up, furrowing his brow as a disbelieving look crosses his face so fast I barely see it. He holds a hand up to halt Blane when he takes a step forward, but his advance doesn't phase me. Luca needs to understand I'm not playing around. He wants me in his mafia so bad, he's going to need to understand a few important facts about me: one being, I don't play about Melody.

Period, point blank.

"You mean, your precious brother didn't tell you?" he asks slowly, his gaze turning curious as he, again, sees way too much.

Father would murder me himself if he saw what was going on right this very second and how I'm challenging California's most notoriously dangerous, and *lethal,* crime boss.

"Tell me what?" I growl, leaning forward in my seat.

His men take another step forward, but I couldn't care less. My eyes stay trained on the ruthless Don in front of me who meets my stare with a calm confidence that would probably terrify any other normal person. However, ruthless or *not,* I'll go toe-to-toe with him over what's mine *any* day of the week.

"That it was either you or Melody. He instinctively picked the woman's side and offered *you* up instead." He smiles. "Just like a fucking heir would."

Yup. By his words, he's already clocked the discontent between Hendrix and I somehow, making my lips tighten.

Suddenly the door bursts open, causing me to half turn in my chair to look over my shoulder to see what's going on. A petite brunette Italian woman comes through, looking distressed.

"What do you mean you're marrying me off?!" she cries. She stumbles as she strides to the desk, forcing me to shoot out a hand and quickly grab her arm so she doesn't fall. Her arms flail as she tries to catch herself on the back of the chair, not even sparing me a glance.

A man comes in behind her, looking like he's getting ready to pull her back; however, Luca just gives him a tiny head shake and a dismissive flick of his fingers. He steps back, adopting a watchful stance against the wall. My eyes go back to hers, seeing her eyes unnaturally dilated, and she's squinting. She must be on one hell of a drug. The bandaid in the crook of her arm is telling.

"Amelia," Luca says in a soft voice, causing my eyes to raise with how tender he is with her. "Calm down. Where's your glasses my love?"

"You know I don't like to wear them!" she says in a distressed tone.

Luca keeps his voice calm. "Amelia, you know after your appointments-"

"I don't want to talk about my eyes, Luca!" she snaps. I frown. I guess I got the drug thing wrong, maybe."I want to talk about you marrying me off to the first man you can think of to get rid of me!"

"Amelia, you have to, sweetheart."

But she sniffs, trembling as she stands near me. *"No!* I don't even know this man, Luca!"

Her hand trembles as she brings it up to wipe her eyes again. I avert my face, not wanting to embarrass her by overtly staring.

He sighs, looking weary. "His name's Joaquin Balducci-"

"I don't care what his name is!" she cries, holding her arms folded across her stomach timidly. Her big eyes swim with tears. "How can you do this? How can you send me away knowing what I'm going through?"

He stands up, walking around the desk and turns her gently, tucking her under his arm and slowly walking her back out the way she came. Her hand skims the wall as they walk, letting me know that she's having pretty bad issues with her eyes. The security guy follows her, and the room falls silent. Leaving me and the two security guards still standing against the wall on the other side of Lucien's desk.

After a few minutes, he walks back in, tugging his suit jacket back and smoothing a hand down it as if he's in a desperate bid to pull himself back together. It's in this moment I feel for him; the human piece of me sympathizing with the human piece of him. But, I can't forgive his comment about Melody.

My eyes narrow. *"No,"* I say simply.

"No to what?" he tilts his head as he sits, keeping his brown-eyed gaze steady on mine.

Ignoring his question, I narrow my eyes. "Why do you want Melody?" I begin to sweat as my neck heats up.

His smile turns into something a bit sadistic. He shrugs a shoulder, sitting back in his seat. "What can I say? Didn't I just tell you I have this thing about spares?" As I stare blankly at him, understanding lights his eyes. "Ohhhh," he hums, twirling his pen in an impressive, practiced movement and points it at me. *"You* want the girl."

My throat convulses on a swallow, and I fight to snatch the pen from him and shove it in his eye.

"Am I right?"

I stay silent, not sure how much to divulge here.

He leans forward, putting his hands together and bracing his elbows on the desktop. "Tell you what, you can do all your advising from New York, and there's no need for you to be heavily involved in the criminal side of things. I just need you to oversee my businesses and financial networking in the civilian world." His eyes roam my face. "This way, the girl doesn't have to be involved either. *If* you say yes," he adds, sitting back in his seat. "However, if I take Melody, she becomes a mafia queen. She'll bear my heirs, and be heavily tied into the crime world. Forever a target. And by the look on your face, I don't see that going over too well with you."

My lips tighten. I literally didn't go into this life because I wanted to spare Melody that risk. I can't do it.

I have to accept his offer. Which is why I'm sure he played it this way.

He knew, somehow.

Biting the inside of my cheek, I hold my hand out, and when he takes it, I see a circular discolored scar three or four inches from the base of this thumb. Frowning, I give him a firm shake and raise my eyes to his. "Someone putting cigarettes out on you?"

Lucien looks down at his hand, getting a wry look on his face before pulling his hand away. "No, just a wound from an old friend," he says curtly.

"A man friend?" I ask, arching a brow, not believing that the Lucien Scognamiglio would let a friend wound him and then wax poetic about it later in life. I hit the nail on the head apparently, because he clears his throat and leans back into his seat.

"Woman," he says dismissively, raising a brow. "You're dismissed, Mason."

I bite the inside of my cheek. There's definitely a story there. "Okay then, *boss.* You or one of your men will need to give me a listing of what you expect me to get started on. I can't promise the numbers; as you know, stocks are a finicky thing."

"That shouldn't be too much of a problem for you," he says, giving me another smile. Except this one has a slight warning to its curve. "You've made quite the reputation as a miracle worker in the finance game, so I'm told."

I scoff, scrubbing a hand across my jaw. "Well, don't hold me to it, friend," I say in a cheeky tone.

Lucien gets a ghost of a smile on his face but doesn't answer or move to correct me. Rather, he looks amused, and instinctively I know that there's a story there, too.

I stand up, brushing my hands down my thighs. "Well, it was great meeting you, Luca."

Not even bothering asking for next steps, I turn on my heel, making my way through the door. But before I could walk through, Luca stops me. "Oh, Mason?"

I turn as he looks up from his paper with an amused grin. "You'd make a hell of a right hand man. The way you took it in stride that I told you I wanted your woman and didn't leap across this desk at me to kill me shows strength and restraint that I could use within my inner circle. Let me know when you're ready."

Turning dismissively, I round into the hallway right as an older Italian man in his mid-fifties walks by with a set of security guards. When our eyes meet, my skin erupts in goosebumps. He looks oddly familiar, but I can't place where I've seen him before.

I shake the shiver off and keep going, sliding back in the car. The driver takes me back to the airport, and I shake my head in annoyance.

This could have been an email.

CHAPTER 3

M. Brookes

Dear Diary,

I went running today for the first time since Isobel's been back home. Mason made me. He showed up at the house at 5am, knocking on my bedroom window with my favorite green juice and drove me to the track by my house.

While we were stretching, he told me his Uncle loaned him two million dollars to start his own business. Which makes no sense to me, because I thought the King Dynasty was his family business.

When I asked him why he didn't just use his own money to invest in his start up, he said he didn't have any money because he won't come into his inheritance until he marries. He lives off a monthly allowance gifted to him by his brother.

I don't understand this family at all. Their dynamic is fucked up. I wonder why. Bet it's in those archive's Isobel told me about.

Anyway, I could only run 3 miles. I'm rusty. But I'll try again tomorrow, I guess.

M. Brookes

CHAPTER 4

SIDE EYES

One and a half years later

MY EYES POP OPEN at four forty-five on the dot, fifteen minutes before my alarm. I look over, thankful to be in the tastefully decorated bedroom at my sister's house instead of the drab dorm I live in during the week at the college. Not because it particularly excites me to be here, but because at least while I'm here I don't have my security guy so obviously tailing me all the time.

I sit up and swing my legs over the side of the bed, stretching my arms above my head. I reach over and turn the lamp on, and then pull my bonnet off as I work to roll my neck. The curls tumble down my back and I shake my head, fluffing them out slightly. It's day three, the best natural hair day for me.

Yawning, I grab my workout gear laid out on the ornate, one-person desk on the other side of the room along with my phone, seeing a text notification already from Mason, my brother-in-law's brother.

The man I'm hopelessly in love with.

I read it as I pad barefoot across the cool hardwood floor to the en-suite bathroom, rubbing the crust out of my eyes.

Are you up yet butterfly? Would you like a ride to King Compound? -Mase

King Compound, or affectionately dubbed 'KC' by Mason and I, is the hub of the family.

You miss too many of those weekend breakfasts then you'll get treated to a phone call from Richard King *himself*. Not having had a father, Richard and I have become particularly close and disappointing him makes me uncomfortable, so I go to keep the peace. I tend to keep to myself during these visits.

I eat, say a couple words, and then hightail it to the nearest sitting room or library, claiming I have homework, where I hide out until it's time to leave. It's the only thing that Henny asks of me: that I make it to these brunches.

But his father, oh boy.

Though he's sweet on me, that first year getting to know Richard King was quite something, especially when he'd laid into one of the men for even a slight transgression. The man has a snappy temper that will scare even the most rebellious person straight. Look at Mason; he's sure been reformed.

Though, there's still a bad boy in there sometimes when he lets it out. Which is never.

He's done a complete one-eighty transformation from the man I met just four years ago.

Since then, he's joined his brother's business, moved onto a floor in the King Dynasty building, and bought his own penthouse. The last I heard, his finance business garnered King Dynasty an added three hundred million in profit this year alone, and we have a few more months to go until the New Year.

See? Mason's miles away from the fuck up -as Richard and Henny used to call him- that he used to be.

I barely recognize him anymore.

He's morphed into this almost untouchable persona of who he used to be. Though he's still quite clever, he's got a sexy hint of danger to him that only seems to inhabit men who have unlimited amounts of money.

The Mason of today wouldn't want me. And I don't even know why I entertained thoughts that he would for as long as I have. Wait, yeah I do; I'm foolish. And so, I've pulled back on how much access I let him have when I do hear from him. Today though, I'm feeling generous.

And besides, if I ignore him now, he's only going to be up my ass about it later when he sees me. That's something that *doesn't* change.

I throw my clothes on the nearby bench in the bathroom, flicking the light on and blinking sleepily.

It's a beautiful space with a heated marble floor, freestanding soaker tub, a shower big enough for at least three people and stocked with expensive, high quality hair products. The window looks towards the East grounds outside. My room faces the tennis court, looking down on Mariah's life-sized dollhouse and her playground. But of course you can't see it because it's still dark outside.

The property is currently illuminated by strategically placed lights that highlight the admittedly stunning landscaping.

Turning from the window, I sigh as I pull my hair into a high bun and reply back.

I don't think my sister would appreciate that very much. I'm at Hendrix and Isobel's this weekend. -Mel

Brushing my teeth, I watch the text bubbles appear, fighting off the anxious emotions I feel when I talk to him. Butterflies erupt in my stomach just like it does every time he messages me. I spit and rinse my mouth as it comes through.

Ohhh. Lucky you. You're not at your mom's this weekend? -Mase

I shimmy out of my pajamas, kicking them to the side and wiggle my toes on the warm floor.

She's in the Bahamas for the weekend with her friends, remember? – Mel

Starting the shower, I put a playlist over the speakers and think about Mason. Though we were close the first couple years of Isobel and Hendrix's marriage, he's thrown himself head first into his business, and these last two years he's become increasingly unavailable the more successful he gets.

Except for when I see him at the infamous King family brunches their parents host every Sunday, and roughly two times a month when I beg him for soda. I roll my eyes and bite back a goofy grin at the reminder.

I lost a bet years ago, and now, the only time I can have my favorite soda is when he sees me in person. And he always makes me get on my knees for it.

I wonder if he realizes how sexual that looks. I honestly don't think it's ever crossed his mind.

Ah. Was hoping to have some time to catch up without our family there. Is there any juicy gossip you can share? -Mase

I smirk and lean my hips on the vanity to reply. Mason loves dishing and collecting all the dirt going on in the family. It's part of what's kept us close, especially in the beginning.

So close that I developed feelings for him like an idiot.

Feelings that at one point I'd thought had been reciprocated, and I foolishly harbored hope that Mason would come for me. But my eighteenth birthday came and went, then my nineteenth. And with my twentieth birthday in two weeks, I've all but given up.

I sigh and look down at my phone, typing a reply. A harsh reply...but Mason will understand.

He always does.

Other than the fact that Isobel seems to be more overbearing with this pregnancy than she was with Mariah, and King's turned into a little Isobel worshipping pussy whipped bitch? No. -Mel

Honestly, I gave up hope a while ago, and tried my hardest to move on and forget how I feel about Mason. But every man I've involved myself with over the last almost two years winds up disappearing.

Now, I've developed a reputation at NYU as that girl that no one wants to date because you'll be doxed, like I'm cursed or something. I was freaked out for a quite a while, thinking that I was being targeted like Isobel was. But King assures me that my security has my safety in hand.

Isobel wouldn't even let me switch schools so I could have a fresh start.

So, here I am, about to turn twenty, still a fucking virgin. At a school where everyone talks about me and with no love life to speak of. It's depressing. I can't even work so that I can make my own money to leave.

I have no autonomy.

No. That all ended the day I fell into King at the running trail almost four years ago.

I'd pay you so much money to say that to their faces. -Mase

I arch a brow, snorting. I might have a chance at a getaway after all.

How much? -Mel

Fifteen grand. -Mase

My brow arches. Steam fills the bathroom, reminding me I'm supposed to be getting in the shower.

Tempting, but have you ever pissed off a pregnant woman before? It's not worth it. See you at K.C. -Mel

I put the phone down and step into the shower, rushing through as I lost precious minutes texting. When I step out, I towel off, pull on my workout gear and walk back out in the bedroom to pull on my sneakers. Putting in my headphones I stride out of the bedroom and into the hallway. Smack dab into Marianne.

"Hey, Marianne. Good mornin'!" I greet Isobel's head maid who is setting up a ladder, preparing to dust the chandeliers that illuminate the space.

I shake my head. Chandeliers in hallways. Who would have thought that'd be our lives?

Not me.

"Hey, Mel! Good to see you, girlie!" she calls out to me, grabbing her feather duster and stepping on the rung. "Have fun on your run."

I swing my head to the side, making sure that someone's there in case she falls. Relaxing when I see Gustavo a couple doors down the hallway switching with the night shift outside of Mariah's bedroom door.

Hitting the playlist I want, I break out into a light jog, making my way to their in-home gym and then hit the treadmill hard. I do nine miles before I call it quits and then bake in the sauna for twenty minutes so I don't get cramps.

It's a luxury I'm not afforded at school so I take advantage of it when I'm here. As I sit, I think about school and what I can do to get Isobel to be okay with me going to work. The fact that I'm well into adulthood and can't even make my own decisions is a prison I'd never thought I'd find myself in, and I need a way out.

Sometimes I think I'd even kill for it.

"Is that what you're wearing?" Isobel says.

I fight like hell not to roll my eyes as hers drag judgmentally down my body.

"What's wrong with it, Izzy?" I ask in an exasperated tone, folding my arms and looking to the side.

We're standing on the concrete steps outside the front, waiting for Hendrix to wrangle Mariah in her car seat in the back of the car.

Isobel's eyes snap to mine. "Jesus. Did you miss your run this morning or something?" She rubs her swollen belly, rocking side to side.

"No. I did nine miles. Why?"

"Because you're acting like you found out someone shit in your cheerios this morning," she says, gingerly making her way down the steps as Hendrix motions for us to come on.

I take a deep breath and follow her, putting my hand on her elbow. "I'm just bored, Izzy. I want to talk about me getting a job."

"Melody, you know you don't need to work." She gives me a pointed look as she slides into the back of the car, making room for me to get in behind her. "You have a credit card for anything you need."

I wait patiently as Henny gives his instructions to the driver before continuing to speak. "That's not the point. I want to work."

Henny looks at me now. "Melody, take the time that you could be working and focus on your math grade instead. You need to focus on *school.* You know that's all we ask. We've got everything else taken care of. Enjoy the freedom of not needing to hustle just yet and figure out what you want to major in." He arches his brow. *"Have* you decided what you want your major to be yet?"

Now I really do roll my eyes.

Snapping my seatbelt on and folding my arms again, I look out the window, going silent. Maybe I would know what I wanted to do had they let me get a job and gave me some room to figure out what I was passionate about. But nope. In the reflection of the window, I see him throw Isobel a concerned look, but she just shakes her head and slides on her sunglasses, going quiet.

The rest of the drive is filled with awkward silence. Because we're at a standstill. The same standstill we've been in for months.

Soon, we roll up to the massive gates at King Compound, and as we make our way through, I entertain thoughts of doing something completely mundane. Like taking a walk in Central Park by myself. Hopping on a plane to start a new life in Hawaii, maybe selling surfboards out of a shack on a beach.

Getting out from under Isobel's thumb.

We pull up next to Mason's Ferrari, and a little thrill courses through me at the sight. I step out of the car and make my way in, eager to get out from Isobel's suffocating presence, even if it's just for a minute. I nod at the butler and make my way through until I hear the unmistakable chatter of the family emitting from the dinning room.

I round the corner. The maids are still setting up the sideboards with the buffet and placing pitchers of mimosas on trivets on the walnut table. My seat has water, as usual. Maribel, Teresa, her husband Brody and their daughter Vivian are already sitting, talking and laughing. Mason's spot is empty.

I frown, my eyes roaming until I find him.

He's standing in a corner next to the big picture window that overlooks the back gardens, speaking with his father. Mason's back is turned towards me, and I let my eyes roam for just a second. Beating back familiar, lustful feelings.

Desperately forcing myself to forget any romantic feelings I harbor for him.

But it's hard when he's looking this delicious.

My heart races, and, as if he was right next to me, I inhale deeper at just the mere memory of his smell.

He's in all black today. Button up shirt with the sleeves rolled up and tucked into a pair of black pants that grip his ass just right. His pants are tailored perfectly, showing me the barest hint of black socks hidden by leather dress shoes. His chest is broad, and his arms are thicker than even the last time I'd seen him, filling out the sleeves of his shirt.

My mouth waters. His forearms are thick with prominent roping veins that cause my pussy to clench at just the mere thought of him working out.

Fuck, I love watching a sexy ass man do arm day in the gym.

My brow raises at the sight of his expensive watch glinting in the sun when he raises his hand to rub across his jaw. He used to laugh at Hendrix for stuff like that. Not now, I guess. Now, he's embracing everything he used to sneer at.

Mason screams money, and here I show up in a frumpy black shirt and Dollar General leggings. The whole outfit probably cost half the amount of one of his shoes. Teresa's obviously judging me, her brow raising when she sees me, though she keeps quiet. The only time I ever let her touch me is for an event.

Richard turns his head and pins me with his eyes, breaking out into a fond smile. At his father's distraction, Mason's speech ceases, and he turns his head slightly to no doubt see what's distracted his father.

Our eyes lock, causing my heart to begin to bang out of control, but I keep going.

Breaking our eye contact, I head to the table to take my usual seat across from Mason and smile politely at everyone. Ready to get brunch over with and leave.

Isobel and Hendrix finally make their way in. Vivian, Teresa and Brody's daughter, races over to fling her arms around Mariah, thankfully distracting everyone. However, there's always one person who manages to keep their eyes on me.

Mason's mom Maribel, leans over and gives me a wink. "Hello, beautiful." She greets me with her softy accented voice. "How are you?"

"Ohhh." I smile back and reach for my glass of water. "Not much has changed since last week other than I'm now seven days older since the last time I saw you, Maribel."

I inwardly panic as a broad smile curves her lips and a spark enters her eye. She waits until Richard sits down and Mason pulls his chair out, obviously trying to catch my eye, but I keep my gaze averted, picking at my nail as the chatter escalates while everyone finds their seat at the table.

Just when I think I'm in the clear, Maribel leans forward again.

"Dearest," she says, bringing my eyes back to her where I give her a closed-lipped smile. "Speaking of getting older-"

Oh no.

-"I was speaking with Isobel. And, well, because she's so close to the end of her pregnancy, she graciously relented to letting me host your twentieth birthday party this year!"

My brows raise. *"Oh, Maribel. There's no need for-"*

My words die, obliterating to nothing as Isobel leans over, gushing over Maribel and thanking her and Richard for being so amazing and helping her out. Offended, I sit back in my chair and sip my water again. Not even bothering to speak up. It doesn't matter anyways.

It never does.

Mason's stare burns a hole into the side of my face, but I keep mine on Mariah and Vivian, dedicating myself to a life of no children. Because there's no way in *hell* I'd subject a child to this kind of life. A life where you have no autonomy and have no say over anything.

A life you can't live for yourself.

His stare is unrelenting, so I turn my head to meet his gaze head-on while I take another sip of my water, almost jumping in my seat when I feel his foot press into the side of mine. He gives me a cheeky smile and a wink, not saying anything. But Mason and I rarely talk in front of our family. Instead, we leave our discussions to the four walls of Richard and Maribel's study, or my dorm, or the park when we run.

They don't know how close we are.

I press my toes into the top of his foot before giving him a playful little kick. His brow arches and he tilts his head as he puts a bite of pancake in his mouth. We hold each other's eye contact. His eyes flick across my shirt, and I can virtually hear him teasing me about my outfit without him even having to open his mouth.

Teresa's voice breaks through my bubble, though, but Mason can't tell.

Or *won't* tell. It's hard to know with him sometimes.

"Your sister's talking to you," I say simply.

He blinks, turning his face to the side to see Teresa scowling at him. *"What's up?"* he says in a bored tone.

"I said how's work going, jerk?" Teresa asks, rolling her eyes. "Jesus. Why even come to breakfast if you aren't going to talk to any of us?"

His eyes slide back to mine, and I blush, looking down at my plate of food. Chasing around the diced potatoes as his foot presses just a little harder against mine, and I foolishly let myself imagine he comes to these breakfasts for me.

"Work is going well. Thanks, Teresa," he says in his smooth voice.

I drop a potato on my shirt, smearing ketchup on it. "Damn," I mumble, but honestly, it's the perfect excuse to leave. "Excuse me."

I stand up, placing my napkin on the table and walking off towards the hall that leads to the bathroom. I clean up, and when I make my way to the study, Mason's right there, watching me out the side of his eye.

CHAPTER 5

Desires of The Heart

"Hey, Mason. What the fuck are you doing, bro? Do you ever *not* work?"

I studiously ignore him, refusing to look up.

"What are you looking at?"

I glance up sharply from my phone as Benny, one of my finance friends, playfully lurches forward and tries to snatch my phone from my hand. I jerk my hand out of the way, sinking a bit deeper in my seat, clicking the power button and turning the screen black.

Cutting off the feed of something a lot better than what everyone else is currently entertaining themselves with.

"Nothing, Ben," I say, throwing him an annoyed glance as he tosses a few hundred dollar bills on the stage in front of me, making my skin crawl.

"Hey, baby doll," he calls to a nearby stripper. "Give my friend here a lap dance."

The other members at our table trade glances and chuckle, their mirth deepening at my obvious discomfort.

I pick up my bottle and take a deep swig, moving my head out the way when the brunette comes up to me and puts her hands to the side of my head and scrapes her fingers through my hair. Her perfume is obnoxious, as are her fake boobs.

Propping my elbow on the seat, I block her from trying to drag her hand down my chest and stomach. Irritated, I cut my eyes to Ben, who takes a drag on his cigar and narrows his eyes at me through the smoke, gleefully watching me push away the stripper they hired for our table.

I cannot stand these private mansion parties. Fuck.

"You know, Mason," Joseph, the groom-to-be at this ridiculous bachelor party I was forced to attend, catches my attention. "Maybe next time we should hire some chippendales?" he says suggestively, trading a look with the two other people at our table. "Seems like they might be more your speed."

Scoffing at his audacity, I meet his eyes for a second, seeing genuine curiosity within his pea colored irises, reflecting the size of his dumbass brain, no doubt.

I look down, picking up my own cigar and busy myself crossing my ankle over my knee while I light it. I take a comically slow drag, blowing out a big smoke ring while they all wait for my response. I'd be an asshole if I just up and left after just getting here.

The purple and pink strobe lights illuminate the moody interior of the private club of one of the most powerful wall street brokers here in

New York. Father does business with him, and his son Joseph is getting married this weekend. I was *supposed* to be landing a major client for King Dynasty here tonight.

But apparently not tonight. And the thought upsets me.

In the effort to continue to attempt to repair mine and Father's relationship, I've spent the past almost four years straight filling my evenings and weekends with dinners, lunches, parties, and vacations; gathering clients and connections to strengthen the financial sector of the King Dynasty empire, as well as paying my dues to the California mafia Don, Lucien.

Doing anything and everything I can to take my mind off of what I can't have right now: Hendrix's sister-in-law.

Melody.

The love of my life, my confidante, and oftentimes, the thorn in my side.

But ultimately, the desire of my heart.

These last almost four years have been the most agonizing blip of time in our love story, and I'm eager to put it behind us.

I clench my jaw and shake the woman's touch off my shoulder, leaning away from her when she goes to nuzzle into my neck.

"Will you get off of me already? Fuck." I snap, irritated. The men all laugh at me again, and I decide I'm out. Father will just have to understand.

Or not, I don't give a fuck.

I firmly push the stripper away, giving her a dirty look before turning back to Joseph, seeing Ben start to shake his head, and rubbing a hand down his jaw. But I don't care if I've offended him. Joseph's seriously touched a nerve, and he's about to pay for it.

"And even if I *was* gay, fucker, what would be the problem with that? *Hm?"* I cock my head. "Because if I *were* gay, I promise you'd know about it, 'cause I don't have nothing to hide, pendejo. Not like *you,* right?"

His eyes go wide, and his nostrils flare as he sucks in a sharp breath. "What the fuck are you talking about?"

A sick pleasure fills me.

"You know exactly what. It takes one to know one, Joseph," I say, standing up and snuffing out my cigar. Leaning forward, I look down my nose at him, feeling the corner of my mouth tilt up. "Tell me, how was it blowing out Tim's asshole last week? I saw him today, and he still don't look like he can walk right yet. Looks like you both had a great time to me."

The men all glance uncomfortably at each other before snapping their eyes to Joseph who gets a rare, evil look on his face. His lip curls, and he wets his lips as he narrows his eyes at me, sitting back in his seat. "I don't know what the *fuck* you're talking about," he says, his voice deepening with tension.

"Send my regards to Cecilia," I say lightly, referencing his intended. "Hopefully she doesn't kill you in about five years when she finds out your secret."

Landon, Cecilia's brother, snaps his head over to Joseph and leans forward in his seat. "What the fuck is he talking about? You fucking around on my sister?"

Joseph cuts spite-filled eyes at me. "You fucking asshole. Who do you think you are, *you piece of shit?"*

I lean forward. "I'm a mother *fucking King.* You'd do well to remember it, too," I snarl, giving him a scathing look back, wrapping both hands around the edge of the table threateningly, and jostle it *hard.*

The men get a surprised look on their faces and scoot back as the pitcher of beer overturns on him, soaking his shirt and spilling into his lap.

Uncomfortable and pissed off at myself for using my name to assert my status, I turn, ignoring the sound of punches being thrown and glass shattering, shoving my hands into my pockets and calmly skirting the various private tables, dancers, and servers carrying trays of drinks. I find the exit door and make my way outside to the valet stand on the side lawn, thankful for fresh air.

"King," I say in bored tone, watching as the valet gets my keys and then runs off towards the hidden parking area. I stand to the side and pull out my phone again, opening the screen I'd been forced to abandon earlier. The real reason for my ire.

I smile as the screen lights up.

She's still there.

Melody moves around the screen of my phone; the image sent to me via a hidden camera I'd paid her dorm's maintenance guy to plant. The camera points down to her bed, showing me a lot of her dorm room, minus her roommate's bed. I'm not interested.

No, the object of my desire has *all* of my attention and affection.

Hence, why I can't focus on anyone else. Nor have I been with anyone else since I've met her.

I couldn't even imagine sinking my cock in anyone else. I think it'd break my damn heart.

Melody's currently crawling around her bed on her hands and knees, tucking the fitted sheets around the mattress and smoothing her pillowcase. She walks the two feet over to her roommate's bed and snatches up her comforter, placing it down before flopping down on her belly to try and shove the thick blanket between her mattress and the concrete wall.

I make a soft noise of amusement, grabbing my keys from the valet who'd just parked and hopped out.

"Thanks, man," I say, handing him a hundred dollar tip.

Sliding into my car, I mount my phone and pull off into the night, headed to NYU where she lives. I text her quickly, needing to see her.

Care for company, butterfly? -Mase

In the camera I see her snatch her phone up off her nightstand and then lean her weight on her left hip. She shoves her curls to the side and then starts tapping at her phone.

Hi Masey! Sure, but I don't have anything to eat here. Or to drink, except water. -Mel

Getting the hint, I swerve when I see a store ahead. Parking illegally, I run in to buy a couple cans of sprite. Getting back in my car, I take back off quickly, glancing in the rearview mirror to make sure my security, Dante, is still on my tail, and we make it to the university in record time. Parking nearby, I grab the cans and shove them under my arm, sauntering past campus security with Dante behind me. He nods at us and then goes back to his book, unconcerned. I smile.

Money really does make the world go around, and don't let anyone tell you otherwise.

We journey up three floors in silence and then veer right down the hallway until I get to room 309 and knock. Melody opens the door with a wide smile and, like always, her face takes my breath away.

"Hey, butterfly," I greet her, leaning down to pull her into my arms.

"Hiii," she sings. Peeking over my shoulder, she calls out, "Hey, Dante. How're you?"

"I'm fine, miss. Thank you," he says curtly, shaking hands with Stephen. They make themselves scarce like they always do when I'm here.

Inhaling deeply, I nuzzle into her temple and stroke my fingers down her back. The smell of her hair oil fills my lungs and makes me feel at home.

"How's it going, sweetheart?" I ask, dragging my eyes down her body as she backs up to let me into the small space.

I can't help the direction of my thoughts at the sight of how delicious she looks, and my lips curve on one side, betraying me. But I can't help it; I never can when I'm around her. She's comfy in a pair of tight, thin gray leggings and a white crop top showing off her small waist. Her hair hangs loose down her back in shiny ringlet curls skimming the exposed flesh, and her face is bare. It's late, so she doesn't have much makeup on right now, and my pleasure grows at seeing her freckles stand out so prettily.

All twenty-three of them.

Reaching forward, Melody tries to reach under my arm for the sodas, but I twist away, grabbing her up by *her* arm in a smooth movement and pull her with me as I walk backwards to her freshly made bed.

"Nuh-uh. What you thinking, girl?" I tease, sitting down and bracing my back against the wall behind me and kicking my feet up on the wooden chair. I heave a deep sigh at her pout. "Now, Mel," I say in a teasing voice, cocking my head. "You already know the only way you get to drink soda with me. Don't fake like you have amnesia."

"Come on, Mason!" she giggles hitting my arm and pouting playfully, but I shake my head staying firm.

"No," I chuckle, feeling better than I've felt all fucking week now that I'm with her.

Due to a bet she lost three years ago, the only time she gets to drink her favorite soda is when I'm with her. I was grasping at straws at the time, but it was a way for me to ensure I can see her at least four times a month. Silly and juvenile, I know, but a man's gotta work with what he can when his hands are strapped.

I arch an eyebrow as she rolls her eyes before getting a sexy grin on her face. "Fine," she grumbles.

"Hmm." Leaning forward, I plant my feet on the floor, placing my elbows on my knees and wait patiently. "You know I don't like to be kept waiting, butterfly."

"Are you *ever* going to bring me alcohol?" Melody complains in an exasperated tone. A little bit more sassy than usual as she's annoyed with me, but that's okay. "Because I'm about to be twenty. One or two shots isn't going to kill me, you know."

"But being almost twenty, is not the same as *being* twenty, now is it?" I say. We agreed for her to have her first drink at twenty, not twenty-one.

She twists her lips, and her body jerks almost like she wants to stamp her foot.

My cock tightens because she's just so goddamn *sexy.*

"Didn't think so. On your knees."

She takes a step forward and then sinks to her knees between my legs. My cock turns stone hard now, twitching in my pants. I clear my throat and reach for one of the cans, snapping open the top. She braces her palms on my thighs, and it's all I can do to not throw her on the bed and fuck her tonight.

Because I'm ready for this insufferable waiting game that Hendrix has forced me into to end. *I'm over it.*

I crook a finger under her chin and tilt her head up. "Open wide," I say.

She parts her lips and sticks her tongue out looking like a seductive sex kitten. Something that stripper who dared to touch me earlier could only ever pray to emulate. I tip the can over slowly and pour a small amount in her mouth.

She swallows, and her eyes dilate with pleasure as she brings a hand up to wipe her mouth, but I grab it quickly, reaching forward to swipe my thumb across her mouth and gather the moisture that's dotted on her bottom lip.

I press my thumb in slightly, making her wait for me until I take my own drink, groaning with pleasure as it goes down. I love sharing a soda with her; it's one of my absolute favorite things about our relationship.

A guilty pleasure of mine, if you will.

"Have you been a good girl, Mel?" I ask, looking to the side as I place the soda on her nightstand. "Passing all your classes for me?"

She rolls her eyes again, her husky laugh making my dick swell even tighter somehow.

"Come on, Mason! First Izzy, mom, Henny, and now *you?"* she sighs, rising off her knees in a graceful movement. I take her arm when she reaches for the chair my feet are propped on, yanking her to sit on the bed next to me instead. "I guess I should expect a call from Teresa, next, huh?" She grabs two pillows and shoves one behind me and then her, getting us comfortable.

"Well, you're barely maintaining your GPA," I say, concerned. "What's up with that?"

"Math," she grumbles, her face pinching up in a scowl.

My eyes narrow at this girl's fucking attitude. She only shows it with me.

Melody folds her arms obstinately, and I cut my eyes at her, kicking off my shoes and drawing a knee up onto the bed to drape my arm over it. Settling myself in to talk about this with her. She and school have been like oil and water, and I need to get to the bottom of it before Isobel inserts herself in the picture. Because, *my god,* as much as I love that woman, I'd rather throw myself to my death head first off the Eiffel tower than deal with overbearing, pregnant Isobel.

Fuck.

God *bless* my brother. He's a saint.

"I told you to call me if you started having problems again, and I'd start back tutoring you, Mel. I'm really not happy that you're failing something that could be easily rectified with a phone call and some extra tutoring time, sweetheart. That doesn't make me feel good."

I feel rejected, actually.

She purses her lips and her cheeks flush as she nibbles on her bottom lip in irritation. "Yeah, well, *you've been busy."*

Uh-uh.

"I'm never too busy for you, *you know that,"* I snap, a lot harsher than I mean to. "I told you I'd always be there for you. All you have to do is call me."

Melody looks over at me and flicks her eyes from mine to my lips and back again. For a second, it almost looks like she wants me to kiss her. My body strains towards her; however, I keep myself in check. Honoring my promise to my brother to give her time.

Goddamn it. Fuck him. I take back the saint comment.

My hesitation doesn't even matter because she turns at the last minute, snatching the soda off her nightstand. The barely there visible muscles of her trim waist ripple with her movement, drawing my eyes down. Her cropped top rides up just a little, revealing the bottom edge of her pink sports bra. It's all very innocent.

For her.

"Well," she stresses, handing me the can. "I know, but..." she hesitates, looking unsure.

"Tell me," I stress. "Don't clam up on me, sweetheart. *Just spit it out."*

She meets my eyes, her speech reluctant. "I overheard your brother and your dad talking about how they'd lost out on a few clients those couple months you were tutoring me, and I figured I didn't want to rock the boat any more than shit already was. I know your relationship with your dad is not..." she trails off, but she doesn't need to say it.

We both know the status of mine and Father's relationship.

There really isn't one. Me helming my own financial sector didn't exactly help like we'd all thought. It's fucked up.

"Melody, I don't give a flying fuck about what they want," I say, shoving a hand through my hair. I look back at her, trying my hardest to hide my irritation. My father and brother, always fucking something up for me. "We made a pact, Mel. You need help, *you call me!* That was the deal!"

She's silent... too silent.

I reach over and pull her to face me. I soften my tone, cognizant of the pressure that the both of us are under regarding our families. "Hey, I thought we said that even if everything and everyone else fell away, that we'd still have each other," I say softly. Her beautiful brown eyes widen, and the can crinkles in her hand. "Is that not the case anymore?"

"Yeah... *i-it is,"* she says in a shaky voice. "That's never going to change. Are you..." her eyes flicker between mine. "Are *you* worried that it's going to?"

"No," I say hoarsely. "The only change I'm concerned with is *yours,* butterfly. I'm dying to see you break out of your cocoon."

The cracks are forming already. I swear I can see it.

"Nothing's going to change, Masey," she whispers, her eyes flicking to my lips again. My cock jerks again. Arousal rises up within me swiftly, setting my skin on fire.

I almost do it; I almost lean forward and kiss her.

My thumb brushes her cheek, I even lean in a bit, but at the last second I pull away, taking a deep breath.

"It better not," I growl through the lump in my throat. Because I can't imagine not ever having her. My whole fucking world would end. I spent too long curating this life for myself so that when it was time, I could pull her into my orbit.

And if my father ruins this for me because he feels like I'm not giving our family business every ounce of blood, sweat, and tears that he and Hendrix did, then I'll never forgive them. Ever.

Especially after me having to also moonlight as a financial advisor to Lucien.

They had *years* to work and focus before their spouses came along.

I didn't have that luxury. Melody and I found each other earlier in life, and I refuse to work myself to death to prove something to our families that I don't need to. I need to save something of myself to give to her.

I change the subject. Listening to her chat about her grades, her teachers, and her irritating ass roommate, while we finish off our sodas. I hug her goodnight, and make my way to my car, already making up my mind.

I pull out my phone and text my brother. Truly over him and my father. They can kiss my ass.

I'm done waiting.-Mason

CHAPTER 6

M. Brookes

Melody King
Melody Brookes-King
Mason and Melody
Mason and Melody Brookes-King
Mason and Melody King
Mason Antonio King and Melody Rachael King

CHAPTER 7

EN GUARD

MY FEET POUND THE pavement littered with damp leaves as I race across the trail as fast as I can. My breath comes out in harsh pants, white billowy smoke accompanied by desperate whimpers escapes past my lips as I hurdle myself through the thick foliage of this unfamiliar place. My thighs are tight, and my arms pump as I strain to push myself harder, faster.

My skin is flushed uncomfortably hot. Sweat dots my brow and my upper lip, trailing down my spine and in between my breasts. Everything burns: my muscles, my lungs, my feet.

I've been running too long this time.

My arms fly up to protect my front as branches and leaves smack my face and arms, tangling in my long hair which has long since lost it's ponytail. I furrow my brow, forcing myself to go even faster and in response the blood rushes in my ears, pounds through my veins. The air saws in and out of my lungs desperately, bringing with it the smell and taste of damp and rain.

"Come on, Mel, faster!" I grunt through gritted teeth as my steps begin to slow. Panicking, I pivot off the pavement and onto the dirt trial headed to where the thicket of trees are denser.

Lightning cracks the evening sky as the heavens opens up and begins to pour down on me, plastering my clothes to my skin and my hair to my head. The trees sway as the wind picks up; leaves swirl around my feet, clinging to my ankles and calves. But still I run, because I can't afford to stop. Not right now. Because I'm not running for pleasure.

No. Now, I'm being hunted.

"It's only a matter of time, Melly."

His deep voice sends a thrill through me. But this time, it's more of an excited thrill than usual. I dig deeper, grinding my feet into the dirt. A second pair of footsteps sound out along with mine, making my heart pound. He's closer. Closer than he's been the last four years he's been chasing me. I've never seen his face, because I've never let him catch me.

This evening is different. This evening I'm *weak.*

"Give up, Melly."

"No!" I gasp.

The strength it takes to utter that one simple word weakens me even further, and to my dismay, I lose a fraction of my speed. Which, if anyone knows anything about running, is all it takes. Especially when the other person is still going full speed ahead.

I throw a look back over my shoulder, my eyes going wide as I see him almost right behind me, and whimper in fear.

Dressed in all black, his zip-up jacket encases a tight muscular torso as he pounds across the dirt floor inching closer and closer. The hood of his jacket is pulled low over his head, his face hidden by shadows. Black gloves, thick arms, muscular chest, powerful thighs. So powerful that he's able to keep up with me, and that's not an easy feat.

My feet slip on the wet leaves and I slide, stumbling as my feet seek purchase against the slippery ground to no avail. My arms flail, and as I pitch to the side he snatches me up by my arm and roughly yanks me around to face him. Our momentum is such that he slams into me, and I pitch backwards now. He suddenly twists us in midair, buffering me against his hard body.

His arms tighten around me, tucking me into him as he curls his body around me and absorbs the impact of us hitting the ground. We roll several times across the wet leaves and dirt before coming to a dead stop with him on top of me.

I tremble. His hard body is pressed against every inch of mine, and his hips nestle intimately into the space between my splayed legs where his erection settles against my pussy. The rain pounds down on us, and I blink against the droplets that fall into my eyes. His face is still cloaked in shadow, and all I can see is the hint of his jaw.

Could it be him?

My breath saws in and out my lungs, making my breasts heave against his broad chest.

He slaps his palms to the ground on either side of my head and tilts his. Without seeing his face, I can tell he's grinning at me. I raise a shaking hand to the hood of his jacket and grip it, surprised he lets me. My heart races as I pull it back slowly, and my eyes widen with shock as I unveil my chaser.

"Mason?" I whisper, feeling my heart pound into overdrive.

His brow lifts, and he narrows his eyes. "Didn't I tell you I was going to catch you?"

"Yes."

"And what did I tell you I was going to do when I catch you?" His hips nudge me firmly, causing me to become slick between my legs.

My brain whirls, remembering the things he'd taunt me with as we'd run while he chased me down over these last four years. "You said when you caught me, you'd...*you'd..."* I trail off at the look of absolute hunger in his eyes.

My God, he looks *ravenous.*

His head dips down, and he brushes his lips ever so softly against me. *"I said I was going to fuck you,"* he whispers against my lips, before sealing his mouth to mine in a deep kiss.

Gasping, I jerk out of my dream and sit straight up in bed, drenched with sweat and panting hard. The flesh between my legs throbs; my inner thighs are slick with the evidence of my excitement. I blow out a breathe and hold a shaky hand to my head, squeezing my eyes shut. This is the first time I've actually seen his face in my dreams in four years.

Leaning over, I flick on the bedside lamp, casting a glance at Karissa who's fast asleep under the covers and reach for my diary in my nightstand to get out my feelings. An hour later, I feel a little bit better, and I pull out my cell, sending out a text. I drop it to the bed on a frustrated huff, irritated at seeing it immediately bounce back as undelivered.

"What's the matter with you?" Karissa asks from her bed, still laying down.

I shake my head. "Howard's messages won't go through," I say irritably, referencing my latest love interest. If you could even call him that. It's been two weeks without a single word from him.

Just like the other four men who've mysteriously come and gone out of my life.

She scoffs, flopping back on the bed and rolling to her side to face me. *"So?* Stop trying and move on to the next one."

My mouth parts at how dismissive and rude she is. "Karissa," I admonish, narrowing my eyes at her. "All my boyfriends keep disappearing. Can you show a little sympathy, please?"

She snorts, covering her hand with her mouth. "I'm sorry, Melody, but can you really call them your *boyfriend* if you've never even slept with any of them? Come on, now. That's cute."

I roll my eyes. *"Rude."*

"No, I'm a realist. Now, forget about all them fucks and go find yourself a real man *and actually crawl under him, please.* I'm tired of you being a virgin."

My jaw drops. *"Karissa!"*

"What?" she whines, sitting back up. "Melody, you're missing out on so much! It's killing me. We're in our prime!"

I heave a sigh and shake my head, lamenting at my free-spirited, albeit very self-centered best friend. "I don't have time for this today. I have to go."

"Fence with daddy?" she says sarcastically. "Damn, I feel sorry for you."

Her words pierce me right in the heart, and I look at her sharply. *"Don't,"* I snap as hurt fills my being. She knows how bad it hurts I don't have a dad, and how sometimes going to these fencing spars with Richard helps keep the pain away. Why she'd so carelessly say something so hurtful is beyond me.

Karissa's eyes go wide and a wince crosses her face. "I-I'm sorry, Mel. You know I didn't mean it like that."

Sure she didn't.

Scooting off the bed, I head to my closet and grab my usual uniform of leggings and a plain t-shirt. "Gotta go, Karissa."

"Oh, Mel," she says in a sad voice, sitting up and giving me a pleading look. *"I'm sorry! I didn't mean to-"*

Picking up my phone, I hoist my bag over my arm and slide my feet into a pair of sandals. "It's fine. Talk to you later."

Every other Saturday I fence with Richard, his way of bonding with me. He fences, and I was curious enough to pick it up as a hobby. He has his own thing with each of us girls. We fence, he travels around the world shopping for interior design furniture with Isobel, and he sits for all the fashion shows that Teresa drags him to.

I feel like an asshole for admitting that though Richard puts forth every effort, he's no replacement for what I've lost. It doesn't stop him from trying, though. He's very involved with us women. His sons, not so much.

It's weird, and I can't for the life of me figure it out even after three straight years of sleuthing. There's a missing piece of the puzzle I just can't find.

Every family gathering I sneak off to the library to delve into the journals that are locked up within The King Dynasty archives. There's dozens of meticulously documented accounts of relationships, marriages, families... but, I haven't gotten a clue to *Richard's* past. His parents' journals are missing for some reason, and something tells me they hold the answers to the questions I have regarding why Richard is so mistrusting of men, to include his own sons.

"Allez!" the coach shouts, and I spring forward, attempting to tap my foil to Richard's lamé.

Our foils collide as he lets me advance, parrying every strike. I dip and lunge, trying to find my way in, but he knocks me away at every attempt. Sweat trickles down my spine beneath my lamé, and my breaths sound loud in my mask. But I don't relent, using every bit of stamina I have and strength in my legs born from thousands of hours of running and training my muscles.

And I don't want to lose in front of Mason. He came today.

He's seated over on the bottom rung of the three tier bleachers in the sparring room, suited up in his own white fencing outfit, lounging with his legs spread and his elbows resting on his knees watching us closely. Mask next to his hip. Waiting.

Not to fight against me, I hope.

My heart beats wildly as Richard becomes more demanding with his attacks, showing me that he's used up the bit of fatherly patience he tends to exercise with me and is ready to declare a win. Unfortunately the pure, raw energy emitting from Mason suffocates me and distracts me enough to make me panic, and I retreat until I step off the strip, forcing the coach to call a loss.

Richard pulls his mask off, breathing hard. "What a shame, Melody," he says, looking me up and down. "You almost had me. What's wrong?"

"Nothing."

As if I'm about to spill my pain over not having a father all over the strip for everyone to see. No thank you. They'd probably go straight to Isobel and she'd find a way to dig even deeper up my ass than she already is.

"You sure?"

"Yeah, it's nothing. Promise."

Pulling off my own mask, I clock a wince pass Mason's face as I wipe the back of my glove on my forehead and roll my lips.

"You did well, Mel," Richard says. "You're getting faster. I just wish you'd learn to trust yourself a little more. Otherwise you'll be like your sister, and you see how hard she's fighting to overcome the perils of not leaning into her intuition. You don't want that for yourself."

Unexpected tears well in my eyes. The pain deciding it wants out after all. "I'm sorry, Richard. I just-"

"No need to apologize, butterfly," Mason interrupts, stepping to the strip and giving me a devilish smile that causes my tears to dissipate, my heart rate to pick back up, and my palms to go damp. "Because you're about to go again."

I snort. "Uh-huh. With who?"

"With me."

I scoff on a half laugh. *"Yeah, right."* I slide my eyes to Richard who's busy pulling off his glove, not paying us any attention. "Wait. Are you serious?"

In the three years we've been fencing, Mason has not come to a single spar between Richard and me.

"Hmhm. Serious as a heart attack," Mason answers. "Put your mask back on." He shoves his over his head, adjusting his glove in a rough, sexy move that causes heat to curl low in my belly and my thighs to tighten. Even my toes curl when he turns his head slightly to look back at me. *"En guard!"* he says sharply.

So sharp I know I'd better listen.

I chew my lip nervously, giving Richard a jerky nod of my head as he walks off the strip, bypassing the bleachers and going off with the coach, leaving Mason and I alone.

I pull my mask back on and take my place opposite Mason. He inclines his head at me politely, and waits for me to reciprocate before putting his arm behind his back, the tell that he's skilled at the sport. I bend my knees and raise my foil, holding my other arm up behind me as I take my own stance.

"Allez," Mason's voice is sharp, in a direct contrast to how he stands there patiently; however, my feet cement in place as my nervousness paralyzes me to the point I can't move. He steps forward and flicks his foil, tapping mine in a couple warning raps that jar my wrist and wake me up.

I inhale sharply, flicking my foil back in a parry, taking a hesitant step forward and repeating the movement. Mason doesn't retreat, only parries my flicks with his own. Considering this a potential weakness, I lunge hard, flinging my arm forward in an attempt to poke his lamé, but he steps smoothly out the way and hits my foil so hard I feel the impact vibrate up my arm.

He tilts his head as I panic and step back a couple feet, not even resuming my stance.

"Stop running, Melody. This isn't track. Advance *forward,* or you'll step off the strip and forfeit a point. Come forward at me, even if you're scared. *Even if you're doubtful.* You can't ever know what you're capable of unless you jump in even while you're afraid. Now, *en guard!"*

I damn near chew a hole through my lip as I obey, sliding back into my stance and then slide into position.

"Don't hold back, Melody. Give me all you've got. *Allez."*

I lunge forward, flicking and even laughing as we twist and turn around each other.

Though I'm not getting a tap in, I'm holding my own, and it makes me ecstatic. At just the last moment, I step forward when he hesitates for a second, and I tap my foil to his chest. He stops, his mask lowering to see the point sticking into his lamé.

My eyes widen in shock as I just stare, not believing I tapped him. His head raises, and with a flick of his arm he flicks my foil away, taking two steps forward and picks me up, hauling me against him on an excited shout.

I squeal, dropping my foil to the mat and laughing with real joy as he turns me around, joining in my laughter. Our masks touch as he lowers me to the ground, and it's only then I realize how intimate of an embrace we were just in. He puts a finger to my chest, keeping his mask pressed to mine.

"Have faith in yourself, butterfly," he says quietly.

I pull back, ripping off my mask and shoving my hair out of my face breathing hard. "I did it," I pant, feeling my chest tighten.

He pulls his off as well, giving me a wicked grin. "You did."

"I did it." My lips quiver as tears prick the back of my eyes. *"I did it,"* I repeat in a thick voice, bringing my gloved hand to cover my mouth. The tears come unbidden as suddenly Karissa's daddy comment hits me full force.

For all my accomplishments and the things I want out of my life, I'll never have a father to share the highs and lows with. No father to protect me, no broad chest to curl into when I need to cry or feel loved when the world is being nasty, and I just want to feel safe. I sniff, trembling, trying to give Mason a shaky smile through the tears.

Mason's face falls at the sight of my tears.

"Mel?"he says, dropping his mask and his foil, pulling me to him not saying another word. He doesn't need to. He knows how I feel, just like I know how he feels. Things usually don't need to be said when it comes to the two of us.

I rest my head against his lamé and cry.

Cry for myself, and cry for the things that I want that I probably won't have.

And therefore, I have nothing to share with said 'father' after all. And the knowledge breaks my heart.

CHAPTER 8

NEW ROLES

OPENING MY EYES I grimace, lamenting my sour mood as I apparently wake up on the wrong side of the bed. It's a drizzly Friday morning, and there's not much to see out the window of my bedroom.

It's been two days since I've seen Melody at the fencing venue, and I'm desperate to see her. Knowing it'll make myself feel better, I pull out my phone and take a peek through the hidden camera in Melody's dorm, and as if it's just working out to be a shitty day all around, it seems she's not her best self today either.

She wakes up fifteen minutes late, and she's back from her run a lot earlier than normal which means she didn't do her usual nine miles.

To make matters worse, an accident en route to King Dynasty makes me almost an hour late and causes me to miss the early market, but once I'm there, I take an astonishing half a million dollar loss in one of my personal stocks. However, Melody's goes up almost thirty grand, so that's good news.

I'm sitting at the leather seating area in my office around noon, clutching a crystal tumbler of scotch and contemplating calling it an early day when Hendrix comes strolling in the office looking rather haggard-if I may say so myself. I eye him warily.

Damn, has everyone been dealt the shit end of the stick today or what?

Oddly enough, a spark of sympathy flickers to life where annoyance usually dwells.

"Hendrix," I say slowly, tilting my head and giving him a thorough assessment. Jesus, he doesn't look right. "To what do I owe the honor?" Other than his weary expression, though, he looks like his usual put together self. His three piece suit is impeccable as always.

He heaves a deep sigh, walking over to the drinks cabinet and pouring himself a whiskey. I take another sip and force myself to be patient as I'm not exactly jumping with joy to go back to the numbers after sustaining such a heavy loss.

"Mason, I hate to ask you to do this, but I need a favor."

"Oh, fuuuck," I growl as that sympathy flame effectively snuffs out. I wanted to go home and work out some of this stress, have a decadent dinner, then pleasure the rest of it away and go to bed. "What is it?"

He sits heavily in the chair opposite and groans, grabbing a hand to his nape and rolling his neck hard.

I grunt. "Isobel finally try to break your neck or something?" I chuckle, remembering the time she slapped him when she was pregnant. He deserved it that time, though.

He throws me an annoyed look that I return. *"No,"* he snaps. "I've barely slept in a week."

I squint, taking a closer look. His eyes are bloodshot, and the expensive suit might actually be the only thing holding him up at the moment. Hendrix tosses back the drink, downing it all in one go. He coughs once, rubbing his hands harshly down his face and leaning forward to put the crystal tumbler to the table with a thump.

"Yeah, you look like it, too," I say.

"Isobel has been so miserable lately that she can't sleep which means I can't *either.* I'm up all hours of the night, rubbing her back, her feet, her hips. I just fucked up my drawing for the building on eighteenth street. And she just called me in pain."

"Damn, brother." I swallow the rest of my scotch and suck my teeth. "Sounds bad. Why can't she go get a massage, or have Marianne do it?"

His eye's snap to mine and I feel my balls shrivel tight. "Are you fucking kidding me right now? This is *Isobel,* Mason. You know better than that."

I tilt my head on a grimace, because, yeah, I certainly do. Poor guy. "So what's the favor?"

I need a smoke.

"I need you to go to tonight's Charitable Hearts Foundation in our place."

"Awwww," I groan, tossing my head back. *Fuccck. "Hendrix, please-"*

"I don't want to ask you, I really don't. But King Dynasty needs to be represented somehow-"

"What about Father and Madre?" I ask.

"Father just had his colonoscopy this morning, remember?"

I bite my cheek. Unfortunately, I hadn't.

"Did you call Madre to see how it went?" I ask.

He frowns. "No... I figured she'd let us know if something was wrong."

I blink. "Hm. Thought you two were closer than that."

He raises a brow. *"Madre would let us know if something happened,"* he repeats slowly, letting me know he's really not in the mood.

I leave it alone.

Hendrix heaves another deep sigh. "Mason, you know I don't ever ask you to do these appearances. I know you hate them, but to sweeten the deal, and because I'm desperate, you may bring Melody."

His eyes narrow in obvious displeasure at the smile that curves across my face, but my glee is so delicious I don't have a prayer at trying to hide it. My brow arches.

"Really?" I say sarcastically. "Man. Desperate must be right." Standing up, I head to refresh my drink with a pep in my step, suddenly refreshed. "I graciously accept."

Hendrix grunts, pinning me with a stern look that eerily reminds me of Uncle William when he gave me the terms of paying his loan back. "As long as you remember our agreement-"

"I remember our fucking agreement, pendejo. Now go." Rolling my eyes I turn and lean my hips on the counter, raising my glass and taking another sip. "Go home and get some fucking rest before you do something stupid in your sleep deprived state that causes you to get a phone call from Father."

That bit of arrogance seeps through the exhaustion as he regards me. "Might I remind you he's a silent partner now, not the head?"

I scoff. *Like that means anything.* "You need not remind me, brother. I am well aware of how convoluted your and our father's power dynamic is. Truthfully, I feel sorry for you," I admit. "But that's a conversation for another time. Go home to Izzy and get some rest. I'll text you later and let you know how the night goes."

"Alright. Try to have fun tonight? If not for yourself, then try to make it bearable for Melody." He stands, rolling his neck again.

I give him a pat on the back and walk him to my office door. When he's gone I pull out my phone and message Teresa, seeing if she could get something to Melody in time for tonight, and verify that Father is in fact doing okay, and then I message the beautiful woman herself.

Hey Mel, we've been summoned for a mission tonight. -Mase

Her response is almost immediate.

Oh? -Mel

Yes. Our presence is required at the Charitable Hearts Foundation ball. You're going as my date. -Mase

Fuck. It felt so good to say that.

But Mason, I don't have anything to wear! -Mel

Don't worry, I've already messaged Teresa. She'll have something to you in a couple hours. I'll be there by seven to pick you up. -Mase

I grab my things and then head out to prepare for tonight's ball. As I'm sliding into my car, my phone dings twice.

But you know I can't stand anything she dresses me in! –Mel

And what about my hair? -Mel

I scoff as my fingers fly over the keys on my phone. Though she can't stand dressing up for these events, she looks incredible every time.

Don't worry about your hair. Wash and wear it natural tonight. And smoke out your eyes. -Mase

My cock jerks in my pants at imagining the vision I no doubt will be staring at all night, and I rev the engine hard, pulling out of my spot and setting course to a jewelry store where I pick her out a diamond necklace that costs a small fortune and a matching diamond bracelet.

Still not satisfied, I walk over to the ring section to find her a simple diamond. A princess cut wedding ring snags my attention. The thought of sliding a token of ownership on the woman I've wanted for what feels like my entire life makes my body warm, and I fight a plethora of emotions as I stare at the glass case, wondering which one she'd like.

Knowing Melody, she'd want a ring she wears everyday to be simple, and I see just the one. It's perfect for her.

I motion the clerk back over.

"See something else, Mr. King?" she asks politely.

"That princess cut ring on the fourth row. How much is it?"

She pulls it off its stand and glances at the little tag. "Seventy-thousand, sir."

I nod, glancing at the other options. "And what about that singular infinity diamond?"

"Fifteen grand." She peeks up at me through her lashes, utilizing her seduction skills to try and garner more commission.

"I'll take them both. I need them sized, though. She's a six."

She nods, taking the rings to the back. And by the time she comes back I've picked out my wedding band. Feeling significantly lighter in the pocket, I pay for all the pieces and am back on the road headed home.

If I thought this morning was a torturous one, it's *nothing* compared to how I feel right now. I'm in my own personal brand of hell being choked out by a little something called lust. It wrapped itself around me in an unyielding, merciless grip the moment she opened her dorm door dressed in a strapless baby pink floor-length gown with a sweetheart neckline.

A matching shawl graces her elbows, her skin gleams, and her eyes are smoked out perfectly. They drag slowly down my body, setting me on fire and causing my already stiffening cock to harden to the point of pain.

"You look.... amazing," she says, licking her bottom lip.

"And you look good enough to eat, butterfly," I say with a smirk. "All innocent in that pink."

She blushes, faffing nervously with the skirt. "Well, Teresa says I can't keep it. It's on a loan."

"Hm. What a shame," I retort. "Now, will you please let me in so I can give you your presents?" Her eyes snap to mine before landing on the three boxes in my hand and she opens her door further, stepping to the side so I can walk in.

I place the bracelet and jewelry boxes on the little side table and turn back to her.

"Mason," she chastises me. "You know you don't have to-" her words trail off, and her eyes go wide as saucers when I open the box with the diamond necklace. The tiny light inside illuminates it just right, making it sparkle. Her breath catches in her throat. "Oh my God, *Masey...*"

Though she typically can't stand clothes, she's a slut for jewelry.

I arch my brow, taking the necklace out and placing it carefully around her neck. I bring out the bracelet and clasp it around her left wrist, then pull out the ring. A gorgeous cushion cut diamond.

She holds out her left hand, but I tsk, shaking my head. "The right one, please." As she switches, I cradle her hand delicately in mine and slide the ring ever so slowly on her ring finger. It's a perfect fit.

As she holds it up in front of her, her hand trembles. "Wow," she breathes.

Grasping her chin with my fingers I turn her to face me. "The dress might be on loan, but the jewelry isn't. So when we're done having a good time, I'm going to take these home and put them in my safe. But they're yours whenever you want them. Okay?"

She nods, her eyes sliding back to her hand.

"It's beautiful, huh?" I chuckle. I can't wait until she sees her wedding ring.

She giggles, her gaze catching mine. "You know I'm a sucker for a good piece of jewelry, Mason. What can I do to repay you?"

I pause, not expecting her question. I clear my throat, stepping away from her and dragging common sense back into the game of mental gymnastics that's currently taking place in my mind. "You know I love to spoil you when it comes to these things."

It's not a lie.

Two hours later we've mingled, ate, politely conversed with all the powerful people in New York, and have even shaken hands with a Prince. Melody looks weary, and I am ready to go. But we're caught in a horrendously boring conversation with a doctor who will not shut up about her art collection.

A young man comes up to Melody's side, tapping her gently on the arm and causing everyone at the table to quiet their conversation.

"Excuse me, miss." He smiles brightly at her. "But you caught my eye from across the room and I wondered if you might care to dance with me?" he asks, flicking his eyes across her face with true curiosity that has me clenching my fist on my thigh. If I didn't know any better, I'd think this was the look of first love.

My brow rises, and I cut my eyes at him in disgust.

He's about mid-twenties, dark chestnut hair, chiseled features, and full of so much charm it makes me nauseated. The cigarettes burn a hole in my pocket, as does my craving for stress relief. I smoke to help keep myself from wanting to fuck, but it's ability to stem those lustful thoughts are starting to wane, and I've noticed I can go through a tin in two days if I'm not careful.

My brother's request for me to lay low plays on a resounding loop in my head, and it's the only thing that's keeping me from leaping forward and punching him straight in his fucking too-bronzed face.

Melody's eyes flick to mine for a beat too long and then back to him again. "Sure, I'd love to."

I stiffen as he holds out his hand. Melody takes it, walking with him to the dance floor where he pulls her close, and they sway to some slow song. A muscle clenches in my jaw, and my mood sours.

The doctor leans forward, with a conspiratorial wink. "They look beautiful together, don't they? Whoever manages to bag her is going to be one lucky man." She sits back with a giggle and takes a sip of her wine. "As a matter of fact, I have a nephew that I'd love to introduce her to if they don't-

Nasty, hate filled energy swells inside me at her words, and she trails off at the stare I level her with. And I can only imagine what my face looks like because she purses her lips together, suddenly turning her attention to the couple next to her.

Fuck Hendrix's rules. I'll behave when I feel like it.

I stand up, weaving between tables and servers, striding to the dance floor. Melody's eyes are bright, and she's laughing quietly at something he's saying.

"Excuse me," I clip in a stern voice. "You can give me my date back now."

The man turns to look over his shoulder, as does Melody, who meets my eyes with a confused expression on her face. "The dance just started-" he says.

Arching a haughty brow, I raise my voice slightly. "Do I look like I give a fuck?" The man's face flushes as he sputters like an idiot, and Melody blinks rapidly at my nasty tone, but it's true. I honestly don't give a fuck. "I said I'd like my date back. Now. *Unhand. Her."*

His eyes widen, but he lets Melody go immediately, turning to face her and nodding his head. "It was a pleasure, Mel. I hope to see you around."

As soon as he's out of earshot she turns furious eyes to me. "That was embarrassing," she grits through her teeth. "Explain yourself."

"Sure. I'd love to." I reach forward and grab her wrist, pulling her along with me. "Come on, let's go take a breather and talk out on the terrace."

I take her hand and lead her across the room to the glass double doors and hold it open for her, jerking my head to let her go first. Her eyes meet mine as she steps over the threshold, and then turns her head as the wind blows, molding her dress tight to her legs and the perfect round globes of her ass.

My fingers itch to run my hands down them.

My cock jerks as I follow Melody into the night breeze, enchanted by the scent of her perfume and something deeper that's inherently her. I whip off my jacket and place it over her shoulders, leading her to the far corner of the terrace where a little lake sparkles in the moonlight off in the distance. Pelicans float on its surface.

A sort of serene calmness blankets the grounds below us in stark contrast to the tumultuous envy and longing that wars inside me for dominance.

I crowd her in the very corner. The parapet almost comes to her chest, highlighting how delicate and small she is. I step all the way to her, just shy of pressing my front to her back. She settles her hands on the concrete, nervously playing with her new ring. Content with the silence between us, I reach into the inner pocket of my jacket and pull out the small tin I store my hand rolled cigarettes in, tapping it roughly a few times.

She turns to face me with a curiosity that's intriguing. "I didn't know you smoked."

"There's a lot you don't know about me, butterfly," I murmur.

Like how good I can fuck. How much stamina I have. And she does too.

It's going to make for some really fun, *long* nights.

Opening the tin, I pull one out, putting the cigarette between my lips and flicking the lighter, keeping my eyes on hers the entire time. Her eyes nail themselves to the orange tip when I inhale, and I groan low in my throat at how good the burn is and the sexy curiosity in her eyes.

Keeping my eyes on her, I hold the cigarette out as I blow out the smoke, smiling when she scrunches her nose and shakes her head.

"Good girl. I wouldn't have let you anyways."

"Oh, like you couldn't let me have an entire dance with that man back there, huh?" she retorts sarcastically. She turns, putting her back to me again.

"Exactly," I take another puff, groaning because it's just so good.

"What does it matter, Mason?" She turns her head slightly, tossing the question over her shoulder. "We're not together. You don't have to act like that."

"No, we're not together," I say simply, blowing out another plume of smoke as my eyes rake down the creamy skin of her neck and the divots in her collarbone. The gentle swell of her cleavage.

God, how would her nipples feel against my tongue... how creamy would she taste in my mouth? I raise the cigarette to my mouth again with trembling fingers, inhaling slowly, relishing the taste as it rids me of her torturous scent for a moment. Though it's immediately back as she's right there, so close I can press my lips to the sensitive skin of her neck.

I blow the smoke out slowly, catching the gaze of a middle aged woman on the other side of the terrace who is staring curiously at us. I turn my head dismissively, placing my hand back on the concrete parapet next to hers and tilting the cigarette away from her so the ash doesn't fall on her hand by accident.

Every time she exhales, it affords me a deeper look into the neckline of her cleavage. My cock strains against my pants when I see the merest hint of the edge of her light brown areola.

Her fingers clench when my thumb twitches, and I chuckle at how strung tight she is. I inch my thumb closer, rubbing it along the thin skin of her hand and the fragile bones underneath. But that's all I allow myself. Her breath catches in her throat, but she remains silent. My thumb strokes slowly, until it makes its way to the ring finger of her left hand.

She turns her head and looks over her shoulder, our height difference so much that she has to tilt her head to meet my eyes.

"What are you thinking about?" I smile, taking another drag.

"Nothing," she lies.

Lies.

I stiffen, partly because there's a whole lot of something swirling in those pretty brown eyes of hers, and also because I can't stand the word *nothing.* It brings back sickening memories of the first time Father called me that. *Nothing.*

Useless. Worthless. Pathetic.

I tear my eyes from hers and wet my lips, flicking the cigarette over the balcony and stepping away. "Time to go."

Melody turns and cranes her neck back, folding her arms across her tummy. "What's the matter with you tonight?" she whispers.

"A whole lot," I quip back.

"Oh, it's definitely something," she bites back.

"Not anything you need to concern yourself with, trust me."

"So *you* can insert yourself into *my* life, chastise me when you don't like the look of something, but I have no right to know why you're acting like such a pig-headed, short-tempered *asshole* all of a sudden? Fine. I'm sorry for asking. Take me home," she snorts, shaking her head and checking me with her shoulder as she walks by.

I snatch her back by her elbow, ignoring her eyes flashing and her struggling against me as I lean down.

"If you must know, I have had one hell of a shitty day. I lost a shit ton of money this morning, Hendrix required my presence here, and you were the only reason why this was bearable in any way, shape, or form to me. So, if you must know, *no,* I didn't like you running off to go dance with that piece of shit when I would have preferred for you to be by my side for *all of it."*

"Selfish," she whispers back, panting lightly against my ear.

"Oh, you don't know the half of it, woman. I am *very* selfish. Exceedingly so."

Pulling back, her eyes fall to my lips. Fire races up my spine, and arousal dominates every emotion at the moment. If Melody and I had been officially together, I would have crowded her behind the plants in the private area of the terrace, hiked up her dress, lifted her leg, and slammed my cock into her with my hand over her mouth to keep her quiet.

But I can't.

So, I put my hand on her lower back, and escort her home. Only walking away with a hundred thousand dollars worth of jewelry tucked under my arm. Miserable, because I want it to be her there instead.

CHAPTER 9

M. Brookes

Dear Diary,

I took my first shower since Isobel's disappearance thanks to Mason. Mother called him to come over because he was the first one who got me to eat, and he threatened to strip me down and throw me in there himself.

"You smell like ass." He'd said, then bribed me with a bottle of this beautiful French perfume that'd I'd never let myself get. I only had fifteen hundred dollars saved of the allowance Hendrix gives me, and I didn't want to waste a quarter of it on the stuff. But I got in while he and mom stood outside the door like I'm a child.

But I do feel much better. Good enough to take the braids out of my hair and letting my mom straighten it for the first time in weeks. Sometimes I wonder if Mason doesn't have the cure to everything. He certainly seems to when it comes to me.

M. Brookes

CHAPTER 10

GREEDY GIRLS

A WEEK LATER, I'M in the dorm's rec room with Karissa, taking advantage of some down time and attempt to get ahead on my math homework. A hard feat as all I can think about is the way Mason picked me up in joy, and then held me while I cried right after our fencing match. And how close he was at the night of the charity event.

"This is the *fifth* student that's randomly gone missing on the campus in the last *two* years, and everyone is beginning to wonder if it's due to the infamous King Dynasty family's very own Melody Brookes. A second year student here whose ties to the family's oligarch Richard King, and her brother-in-law *Hendrix King*, seems to have brought on a string of bad luck to the campus attendance rates, as well as her love life."

'"Oh my Goddd," I shake my head and groan, leaning over my statistics homework, doing my best to ignore Karissa.

She's flopped down on the couch next to me, reading the school newspaper gossip section. I knew the fallout from my fifth boyfriend's disappearance wasn't going to be pretty, but I hadn't expected for shit to hit the fan quite this bad.

"Karissa, can you *please stop?* I already feel bad enough," I say, hitting enter on the practice question and frowning as it comes back wrong with a big red X.

"Girl, this is juicy fucking gossip. And you need to know what's being said," she says, her nails tapping her screen as she scrolls down further. I look over at her, eyeing her platinum blonde hair and her fake boobs. She's in a tiny dress that really can't even constitute as a dress.

It's more like a napkin.

"I don't care about what's being said," I lie.

"Yeah you do," she says back. "And if you *don't,* you need to start because of this family you're a part of." She pauses, putting her phone down for a second and turning to face me. *"Hey,* what's it like being the sister-in-law of *the* Hendrix King?"

I shake my head, trying to get this question right for the seventh time, but it's no use. I push my laptop to the side irritably.

"It's fine."

She leans forward to grab my hand, yanking my arm and shaking me, "Melody, pleeaasseee? *You never talk about it!* Come on, I had to sign a non-disclosure agreement and *everything* just to be your roommate. I just want to know something, *aaanything!"*

I roll my eyes, but she continues as if she doesn't see me being annoyed.

"Is it glamorous? Is it fun to always be able to buy what you want? Are the parties amazing? Is being filthy rich as awesome as it looks?" Karissa's so excited it makes me nauseated.

"It's *that!"* I snap, pointing to Stephen who sits in a chair by the rec room door, looking stoic as always. "It's always being watched. It's not being able to put a toe out of line because your security guard will run and tell your family, and then they'll jump down your throat. It's not being able to go to the school you want because your sister holds all the cards and is an insufferable, over-protective bitch. It's having to dress up and act like you care about events because your sister might not be able to take her husband. It's always worried about being kidnapped and held for ransom. Or, having every guy you try to touch mysteriously disappear, *apparently!"*

Her face falls. "But the money though?" she says, her tone still hopeful.

I sigh. "The money's fine, Kari."

I don't bother telling her that I only have a twenty-thousand dollar credit card limit.

This appeases her, because she gets a dreamy look on her face and then sits back in her seat. "Your brother-in-law is really fucking hot. I'd do him."

I frown. "Ew."

"So is his brother, the Spanish looking one. Is he single?"

I look up slowly at her words. "I think so," I answer, fighting back a wave of irritation, because I don't know if he is or isn't.

"Can you introduce me?"

My eyes narrow as jealousy easily dominates my emotions. "You've seen him before, Karissa." I say, putting my attention back to my computer and starting my question again. I don't even know why I'm bothering though. I need help. Mason's words enter my head, and I bite my lip.

I really don't want to be a bother.

"Yeahh," she says slowly, "But I mean can you *formally* introduce me? You know," she wags her eyebrows. "Hook a girl up."

I cut my eyes to her. "You're not happy with the ten guys you've fucked this year? And what about Brian?" I say, referencing her newest boyfriend. More like boy toy.

She scoffs and waves her hand dismissively, pinning me with a nosy look. "You ever think about fucking him?"

I pause, feeling really on edge, and put on the spot. Because *of course* I've thought about it. "No," I lie, too shy to confide in her just yet when I've thought about way more than fucking him.

I've thought about kissing him. I've thought about touching him. I've thought about him making me his, just like Henny made Izzy his.

Being his wife.

Being *together.*

I'm obviously dreaming, though. Lost in a perpetual state of delusion I'm starting to be scared I'll never make my way out of. My desire for that seems to be one-sided. Because in almost four years, Mason has not made one move.

My lips twist, he did touch my hand at the charity ball, though. Memories of his thumb stroking the back of my hand and playing with my ring finger assaults me, but I shake my head and scoff, dismissing that thought easily. The Mason I know would have just taken whatever he wanted; he wouldn't have let himself just stroke my hand if he'd wanted more.

Maybe he is with someone. It could be the reason.

My eyes prick hot with unshed tears, and my mood sours completely. I slam my laptop shut, not even bothering trying to finish the problem.

"Oh!" Karissa half shouts, slapping a palm to her forehead. "I almost forgot, Mel. Your toy came!"

I sit straight up, throwing a panicked look at Stephen who's currently scrolling on his phone. "Karissa, shh!" I give her wide eyes, bouncing off my seat and snatching my things. "Let's go." I look over at my security. "Stevie, we're going back to the dorm. You don't need to follow me." I say, hopefully.

But no luck, he stands up and trails behind us anyways.

Walking into the dorm room, Karissa shuts the door on him, leaving him out in the hallway and prances to her bed while I put my things down on the small desk. She grabs the small box off her bed and flops down on it, crossing her legs.

"Here, I got you the pink one. I hope its okay?"

All thoughts of my homework fly out of my head at the cute vibrator bullet.

"Yay! Thanks girl, I owe you one big time," I smile at her.

"No problem."

I start to tear open the box and turn, inserting the cord and plugging it into the wall to charge. I'd never be so open with something like a sex toy with anyone else, but Karissa's my girl.

And I've seen her with cum on her face, so there's not as much timidness like I have with other people. We're close. She loves sending me pictures of her "conquests," as she calls them. I fire my computer back up and attempt this stupid math problem one more time.

I really don't want to call Mason about this if I don't have to.

"Sooo, why don't you buy your own toy, if you don't mind me asking?" Karissa yet again interrupts my thoughts as well as my concentration. What else is new?

"Kari, they pay my bills, they track my phone *and* computer... do you really think I want them seeing I bought a sex toy?" I say wryly.

She frowns. "Well, I'd do it. Small price to pay for being a kept woman."

"You know what, that's it." I say, shutting my laptop I stand up and go to my closet, grabbing a change of clothes and a towel. "I'm going to take a shower." I snatch my air pods, my phone and my vibrator and shove them in a small bag, making my way to the door.

She gives me a teasing smile and a little squeal. "Oohhh, have fun bestieee!"

I pass Stephen, barely acknowledging him as I head to the showers. He stands outside the door and I head in, finding a shower a couple down from one that's preoccupied.

"Ohhhh!" I hear as I walk past with my stuff and pull back the curtains, going inside. The sound of flesh hitting flesh sounds out, echoing around the tiled room.

People are always fucking in here. Hence, the airpods.

I shove them in my ears and turn the shower on, pulling a shower cap on over them so they don't get wet. Thankful, for once, that the raunchy noise of the couple fucking a couple showers over is loud enough to drown out the slight buzzing of my toy.

I turn it on and step under the spray, pushing the toy between my legs and propping up my phone playing a video of Mason from almost half a year ago when he was laying down a floor for a charity organization we all pitched in to donate our time to. We build a house every other year for a family in need.

I stifle a moan as the vibrator hits my clit just right, and I keep my eyes on my screen, eating up the rippling muscles of Mason's arms at work.

It doesn't take long, My belly tightens as my orgasm swiftly takes over. My mouth drops open as the buzzes hit my clit and travel through my body. The sight of his muscled body and wicked grin fills my vision, ramping up my desire to insane heights, made worse by the memory of him having me kneel in front of him the other night.

The phone topples over. *"Shit!"* I curse, lunging forward to grab it quickly so it doesn't fall onto the floor. I leave it screen side down on the little shelf and press the vibrator harder to my clit.

I bite my lip hard as my desire ramps higher.

Squeezing my eyes shut, I bite my lip to contain the moans threatening to break free at how viscously my orgasm hits me.

"You okay, butterfly? You never call me in the middle of the day."

My jaw drops. *"Mason?"* I whimper, not able to stop my orgasm. I slap my hand over my mouth, desperate to be quiet, and confused as to how he's in my fucking ear.

To make matters worse, the couple fucking from the other stall gets even louder, the sound of their skin slapping loudly being amplified by the water. *"Oh fuucckk!"* the man groans.

"Melody, what the fuck?! *Are you fucking someone?"* Mason hisses into my ear, sounding downright pissed.

It's fucked up, but the sound of his anger forces my pleasure even higher, and I whimper as heat spreads through my core and outwards, blossoming on my skin. I'm tearing a hole in my lip as I'm knocked into the hardest orgasm I think I've ever had in my life. So hard a tear slips down my cheek.

The water from the shower hits my nipples, extending out my pleasure, and it just goes on and on, not stopping.

I suck in a deep breath and gasp, jerking the toy away from my clit as my knees begin to buckle. I can never have more than one at time, being too sensitive. Clicking off the toy I shiver as I try to get my bearings. Mason is utterly silent on the phone, and at first I think he might have hung up.

But I hear a door slam, disputing that thought. Because why would it be that easy?

Nah, I'm always finding myself stuck in the most embarrassing situations for some fucked up reason.

"Melody!" he snaps. "Answer my goddamn question!"

"What-" I suck in a sharp breath as another tremor rolls through my body, *"what was the question?"* I lean my head back and pant, fantasizing for a quick second that he's jealous.

"I said, are you fucking someone right now? *What the fuck are you doing?"*

Ohhh he sounds so unhappy, but I refuse to read more into it.

"How did you even get on the phone?" I ask dismissively, letting him stew in his anger. It's a long shot. Wishful thinking, really, but I hope he's suffering.

"Answer my question!" he barks.

My head recoils. "Jesuusss, do you have to yell at me like that?"

"I'm not yelling."

"You are."

"I. Am. Not. *Yelling."*

I squirt some body wash on my loofah and soap up, deciding to fuck with him. "I'm in the shower. I had my airpods in listening to music, and I think I called you by accident."

"I heard a guy." He just won't let it go.

I hum. *"Yeah well... I know a guy who knows a guy."*

"Don't fucking p-"

I roll my eyes in amusement. *"Piss you off.* I know, Mason. But you just make it so easy sometimes that it wouldn't be right of me not to." I tease, grinning as he clears his throat in irritation. I rinse my body and then shut the shower off, grabbing up my towel and then drying off. "You need to see an ENT for all that throat clearing you've been doing, Mason. I'm starting to get concerned."

It's the girl's turn to moan loudly. The man really starts pounding, and Mason goes completely silent on the phone. My cheeks flush as I blush, but I refuse to hang up just yet. Really wanting to rub it in.

"Yes. *Yes, Darren. Yes!"* she yelps before falling quiet.

I giggle. "I think she got her happy ending. What about you?"

"Were you masterbating, Mel, when I answered the phone?" he asks in a deathly quiet voice.

I roll my lips. I thought I might be able to convince him the sounds he'd heard was hers, but apparently it didn't work. I try anyway. "You can't prove that."

"I'm not a fucking *idiot,* Mel. I've been on countless runs with you. I've heard you tired, worn out, moaning in pain. *I know what you sound like,"* he snaps.

"You don't know what I sound like when I'm moaning in pleasure," I throw back, not quite even believing we're having this conversation.

Mason's silent for a few long, drawn out seconds. I take the time to dress quickly. I'm in the middle of pulling on my shirt when his next words cause me to pause and tense up.

"How dare you call me in the middle of the day," he snarls, "whimpering, and damn near crying into the phone and then try to act innocent like it isn't *you.* But tell me, you're the one listening to the couple in the next stall fucking while you do it, so, are you itching to get fucked, too?"

My eyes widen in shock because Mason has never talked to me this way. I go with it in a teasing manner, because I know Mason's not flirting with me. Surely not me?

"Maybe," I giggle, keeping my tone light. "It might help me relax."

"Hmm. Now there's a thought," Mason says. He makes a sound in his throat that causes another shiver to go down my spine. "Need someone to fuck you so you can maybe relax enough to get that math grade up? *Wonder why I didn't think of that."*

My heart pounds wildly.

"I definitely *need* to get my grades up. I'm obviously willing to try anything at this point."

"You sound very needy," he says.

My brows lift. How did we get here again?

"Hmhm. I need a lot of things."

He half laughs. "You also sound very greedy. Girls like that are so fun to break down."

Huh.

"Break down?"

"Hm-hmm," he hums.

I wet my lips, trying for nonchalance. "You sound like you might have some experience in whatever that is. Want to teach me?"

"Experience?" he half laughs. "Girl, I would fuck you into next week," he say sharply.

I blink as my clit throbs. "Mas-"

"You still a virgin?" he interrupts me.

I gasp, feeling my heart stop before it gallops away. I falter, grasping and failing to find words to continue our playful banter that has somehow just turned very serious. I lose my bravado quickly with just a few simple questions from him, so I don't answer, and the silence lingers.

But not for long.

"Keep your legs closed, Melody," Mason says, his voice softening.

My heart skips a beat, but I play off how badly his words affected me. "You're cocky for assuming. Who says I haven't opened them already? Maybe I was going to join them for a threesome, and you answering the phone stopped me."

"I swear to God," he snaps, his voice losing all softness as his anger comes back. *"Let* me find out you're not a virgin, and I'm going to beat your ass into the-"

I hang up on him, finish my business and saunter out of the bathroom, looking at Stephen who has a wildly uncomfortable expression on his face. "No, sir. She was in there by herself. The couple was two showers down. Yes, I'm sure." His eyes slide to me before sliding away. "Yes, sir, I will."

My jaw drops, seeing he's speaking with Mason through his ear piece. *"You'll what?"* I snap, as he hangs up with him.

"Keep a closer eye on you," Stephen answers deadpan.

I narrow my eyes, but he keeps an impassive look on his face. "Want to go on a run?" I say threateningly. His eyes slide from mine.

They purposely hired Stephen due to how fast he can run, a requirement put in by Izzy. I had to have a security guard who could run faster than me.

Stephen just shrugs his shoulders. He runs fast, but he doesn't like long distance. He'll do it, though. I've tested it twice. Once in the pouring rain, even. I don't know what they pay him, but it's not enough.

I make my way into my dorm room and tilt my head back lamenting the sight of my laptop sitting there reminding me of my fucking homework.

I set my bag down and pull out my phone again, calling Mason back.

"What?" he snaps.

"Don't talk to me like that. *I need you,"* I whine quietly, trying to appeal to his gentler side.

"Need what, Melody? *Hm?* What do you need? Tell me."

"I need help with my homework."

"Don't you *ever* hang up on me again," he growls, making a shiver roll down my spine, and my pussy clench greedily. "Do you understand me, butterfly?"

I smile, doing a little dance. "I understand. Oh hey, can you grab us a soda?"

Mason pauses, going quiet. "Already planned on it."

"Yay," I say, throwing myself down on my bed. My hand goes in between my legs, and I touch myself, feeling the tingles of my orgasm still there.

Mason makes a rough sound, and I hear another door close. "I think because you pissed me off I'm going to have you on your knees longer today. I'll be there in an hour."

"That's fine with me," I say, rubbing myself harder. "I gotta go, Mase. I'll see you when you get here." I hang up the phone and arch my back, moaning as I work myself into another orgasm at what just happened between us.

I fall asleep, only waking up when I hear his knock on the door. I pinch my arm, convinced I was dreaming.

By the look in his eyes I'm not so sure. I watch him carefully.

He hugs me a little longer today. His mouth lingers on my temple, and his hand settles lower than normal, curving over the top of my ass, and I eat it up just like the greedy girl he'd called me earlier on the phone.

By the time I'm on my knees looking up at him, letting him pour soda in my mouth while I wish it was something else, I'm damn sure I wasn't, and the phone call actually happened. He doesn't let me up until I drink the entire can.

It takes a bit.

And by the time he leaves, only after making sure I got every question correct, I'm convinced that he wants me, too. But if so, why hasn't he picked me up yet? My insecurities swirl, getting the better of me. Convincing me that I'm not good enough for him.

So, when he calls me later that night, I ignore him.

CHAPTER 11

Don't Let Go

I'm in class the next morning trying to work on this pop quiz our professor surprised us all with when my phone vibrates with an incoming message. I flick my eyes around and sink deeper in my seat.

Opening it, I turn the brightness down in an attempt to be discrete, and I nibble my lip, seeing three missed texts from Mason.

Why didn't you answer the phone last night? -Mase

Hey, why're you ignoring me? -Mase

Melody! -Mason

Oh, you're using your *full* name now on your sign offs? Must be mad at me. -Mel

I'm about to come up there! Pay attention to me. -Mase

I roll my eyes, laughing quietly behind my hand and try to hide my phone behind my purse as I work to reply.

What? I'm in class, Mason! -Mel

I don't care. -Mase

I can't just walk over to my in-office lounge with a drink and scroll and text. I have to concentrate. -Mel

You can spare me two minutes. I have a question for you. -Mase

Whaaattt? Out with it! -Mel

Let's go dancing at that nightclub on thirty-fifth tonight. -Mase

My heart skips a beat, and I flush so warm I look up in a panic, wondering if anyone heard my shocked inhale. What I want to reply is "Why?" but though he said it was a question, he phrased it as a *statement.* So, I decide to take the bone the universe has just given me and say instead:

Sounds like a good time. What time? -Mel

I put my phone away and attempt to focus on my quiz, but truthfully my mind is everywhere and anywhere but on what I need to be focused on.

At the end of the class I check my grade, seeing I've failed the quiz.

Ugghhhhh.

I'm irritated. Pissed at myself that I can't get this man out of my head long enough to pass a pop quiz. However, soon I begin to look forward to going out tonight because I know it'll make me feel better about my bad grade. And I'd do anything to dance with Mason.

Mason gives me a devilish smile as he leans against the side of his red Ferrari, parked illegally of course, as I make my way across the street, being careful of any cars or random students on bikes and scooters. I'm decked out in too-short shorts and a crop top, my hair flows long and wavy down my back, and I topped the look off with a pair of kick-ass heels.

I still barely make it to his chin.

"Hey, butterfly. *Damn you look good,"* he says giving me a whistle, causing me to melt.

I roll my eyes. "You're such a gentleman," I tease, putting a little pep in my step as I get closer. He pushes off the car when I get close and snatches me up, giving me another thorough once over as he pulls me to him for a quick hug.

"Hmm," he hums, running his nose along my ear. "I'm not always gentle, Mel," he says in a sexy low voice, wrapping his arm around my waist and pulling me harder against him. "Remember that."

My heart thumps hard at his words, and my pussy twitches with excitement at what the hell he could mean by that.

"Whatever," I scoff playfully, but I really want to ask him to show me.

I wrap my arms around him, about to risk it all and embarrass myself by asking him, but the way he smells has me captivated as well, and I lean even more into him to get my fix of my little secret.

Our hug doesn't last long, though, before he's guiding me to the passenger side and opening the door for me. The excited energy rolls off him in waves, and there's a spark in his eye I haven't seen in a while. It's nice to see, because I know the tension in his family has been high.

"Oh my god, are you *high* or something?" I giggle, arching a brow at him.

He laughs and then hunkers down, leaning into my ear so close I can feel his breath caress my neck. "I just banked three million dollars today. We're celebrating. The money *and* your upcoming birthday, baby girl," he says in a cheeky tone, slamming my door shut and then sliding across the hood of his car in such a smooth move my eyes go wide.

When he gets back in the driver's seat I snap my seatbelt on and I turn to him. "Three million dollars? *In one day?"* I ask breathlessly.

Because let's be real here; that's so fucking cool, and only something a person tends to read about online, not get to experience.

He glances in the rearview mirror, waiting for Donte and Stephen to flash their headlights before pulling off. As soon as he gets the signal we're off, merging into the nighttime New York traffic and headed to Devotion, a private club that you need a membership to get into.

According to Mason this is the newest addition in a series of clubs sprinkled throughout the city called Club Committed, Club Infatuated, and the newest is Club Devotion, and it looks packed to the brim.

We park and see there's at least fifty or more people outside waiting to get in. However, in true King fashion, we don't wait with the others.

Nope.

We head to the beginning of the line where the mean-faced bouncer doesn't even look twice at Mason. And I bristle, knowing it's because he's been here before. Feelings of jealousy rise hot and fast inside of me, and I cut my eyes to him, wondering if he's taken a girl he's met here home and fucked her.

He's never brought *me* to his house...

"Mr. King," the bouncer says, unclipping the rope and stepping aside. "Have a good time tonight."

"Thanks, Bernard," Mason clips, letting go of my hand and putting his arm around my waist instead, drawing me close to him.

I try not to let that excite me too much and tuck myself closer as the bouncer lets us and our security through, averting my face from the pissed off crowd and ignoring the boos of everyone still waiting in line.

"Yikes. I thought we were going to be drawn and quartered out there!" I exclaim as we enter into bustling nightlife of neon lights illuminating the dark club.

My eyes wander excitedly, seeing women dancing in circular cages hanging from the ceiling, bodies sweating and moving on the dance floor and tons of bottle girls everywhere. It's the type of fun I wanted for myself when I moved to California -which never happened.

Mason's fingers tighten on my waist as we make our way deeper into the club. I don't ask questions, letting him take the lead and soaking in how natural this feels for me to let him. I'm not snippy with him like I am with Hendrix, who I feel like meddles too much.

Of course we go straight to VIP: a curtained area sequestered off in the corner of the club on a raised platform that sets us apart from the dance floor but close enough for us to be in on all the action. I don't recognize anyone as I pass the curtained little areas, but I wonder if Mason does.

"I'm not waiting for a bottle girl," he says, his voice pitched loud over the music as we enter into our own private area. "Stay here, and I'll get us a couple drinks."

"Okay!" I say loudly, throwing myself to one of the plush couches and crossing my legs. His face tightens, but he turns quickly and walks away. I crane my neck to see him wind his way through the crowd, and then disappears behind the bar and pulls down bottles, making the drinks himself. My brows go up.

What the hell?

I turn to eye Stephen who's standing by the entryway.

"Does he work here or somethin'?" I ask loudly in an attempt to be heard over the music.

He turns his head slightly to look at me. "Or somethin'." Then he averts his face.

I blink. *Oh.*

My eyes go back to the crowd again and see him coming back with a small tray of assorted drinks. However, a woman presses up against him, smiling and pressing her boobs all over his arm and smoothing her hand across his chest. I inhale sharply as a hot pang of jealousy shoots through me so fast that I tense up hard enough to strain a muscle in my neck.

"Ow," I whimper, bringing a hand up to rub at it, but I can't look away from the train wreck of this gorgeous woman rubbing herself all over him.

To my horror, tears flood my eyes; although, they go away just as fast when he pushes her off in a firm, no-nonsense movement that's accompanied by a pretty dirty look that makes the woman step away hastily and surprises me with its viciousness. I'm still a little stunned when he sidles up next to me with our drinks and hands me mine.

I widen my eyes at him and blink. "Damn, Mase. What did that poor girl ever do to you?"

Shooting his shot, he places the empty shot glass on the table before tilting his head at me. "Not my type," he answers in a rough, sexy voice.

I scrunch my nose. "I have a hard time visualizing your type, Mason," I tease sarcastically and roll my eyes.

I want to ask him if he's dating someone so bad I can taste it. But I don't tend to like to meddle, and I sort of feel like if he were seeing someone then he'd have told me. That's how close we are.

At least.... I *think* that's how close we are.

I side eye him, feeling irritated and tighten my lips as his thigh brushes mine, and his scent floods my nose. Fuck, I'm so turned on I know I'll need to use my vibrator when I get back to my dorm.

Curiously, I sniff the drink and then take a sip, rolling my eyes in annoyance when I taste it's alcohol free. I snap my head to look at him.

"I thought you said we'd have my first drink together?" I complain.

He gasps appreciatively as he sucks down what I assume is whiskey, looking quite content. "And we will, *on your birthday*. It's not your birthday yet, butterfly." He turns his head to look down at me with a playful look on his face.

I grumble. "Come on Mason! Let me have a sip of that."

"Uh-uh," he leans back, expertly dodging my attempt to grab his drink. "You're not twenty."

"I'm twenty *tomorrow,"* I look at my watch. "In four hours, actually. *Mason, stop playing!"*

"No. *We agreed."*

"I don't care!"

"Too bad, because I do!"

My eyes narrow. "You're an ass for taking me somewhere fun and then drinking in front of me."

He arches a brow as amusement clouds his features. "Oohhh, I love it when you get angry with me, butterfly."

"Stop teasing me." I reach forward, trying to snatch the drink out of his hand again but he's faster, moving it out the way and I fall clumsily against his chest. That spark in his eyes gets deeper, more playful. "Can you at least not drink in front of me then?" I push off him, folding my arms and scrunching my face up showing him how displeased I am.

Though I don't think he cares, the selfish fuck.

He gives me a sly smile, his eyes dragging down my face. "I'm a thirty-year old man, Mel. Who just made three million dollars in *one day.* I'm having a drink to celebrate. I can't help it's not tomorrow yet."

"Come on!" I pout. "You can't even not drink for one night? Even for me?"

"Ohhhh no," he half laughs, shaking his head firmly. *"Nope,* even for you, butterfly. I've already had to give up something really important to me." His eyes smolder as they look down at me, and I find myself holding my breath at the intensity. "And if I had to give up alcohol *too,* I think I might kill someone."

His tongue strokes his bottom lip in a seductive movement that has my pussy clenching greedily, wanting his tongue there.

"Oh, please!" I scoff, hitting him lightly on his arm. *"The* Mason King giving up something? Surely not you. You're the most selfish man I know!"

And he is.

Him blatantly telling me to disregard class because he wanted my attention proves it.

"You wound me, baby," he says, putting a hand to his chest and slumping over to the side. He rights himself quickly, laughing as I giggle at his antics. Anything to not read too much into him calling me "baby" the way he just did, making my heart fall into my stomach.

I get up. "Well, you enjoy your drink. I'm going for a dance."

I need to dance off this frustration so I hurry to the entryway to the VIP section, but I don't even make it through the curtains before he snatches me up by my hand. Feminine pleasure fills me as I clock the slightly pissed off look on his face, because I successfully made him put down his drink in favor of the dance floor.

Smiling brightly, I tug him along behind me as I work my way deep to the center of the carefree crowd. The energy here is infectious, the club goers lost in their race for a dopamine hit. Some people dance in groups; there's several couples grinding against each other.

I let go of Mason's hand and toss my head back, moving my body to the beat and raising my arms in the air, swaying and rolling my hips to the music as it takes me over. I open my eyes and look up curiously at the feel of his hands encasing my hips in a tight grip as he comes close behind me, moving his body with mine.

This isn't the first time we've danced. Mason and I are often partners when we go to a charity gala; however, this *is* our first time dancing like this, and I become even hungrier for him.

I give him a small smile, turn my face back and close my eyes once more, losing myself to the music like everyone else.

But I also lose myself in him, shamelessly soaking up the feel of him against me. Hard and warm as the music transports me into another realm.

A hand leaves my hips to press into my stomach, and he pulls me firmly against him in a rather rough movement that has me gasping and crashing back to earth with him. I raise my arms and sink my fingers into his hair as he presses his lips to my shoulder, and I grind my ass into his pelvic to the beat of the music.

He chuckles sexily in my ear, and his minty, whiskey breath washes over my skin as we sway.

Our hands smooth over each other, and he holds me tighter and tighter until I'm suddenly spiraling again, wondering at what this is between us.

"Butterfly," he whispers in my ear, but before he can say anything else, I feel another body press up against my front and I open my eyes in shock, looking into the eyes of a brown-haired man in his mid twenties. He'd been dancing nearby, mingling with anyone and everyone, seemingly having the best night of his life. But unfortunately, he's *too* uninhibited.

He leans forward, his eyes hooded, getting ready to kiss me. My jaw goes slack, but then there's a hard jerk as Mason moves fast.

His hand leaves my belly to wrap around the man's neck in a rough slap and squeezes in a grip so hard the man's eyes bug out of his head, and he's obviously so stunned he can't react. The man jerks, his body brushing against mine as he attempts to move.

I shrink against Mason's front, crying out in shock, but I'm trapped between the two men as Mason just calmly squeezes.

And squeezes.

My chin quivers as I stare into the eyes of the stranger who's eyes begin to flicker, looking like he's slowly going unconscious.

"Mason! *Mason let go of him!"* I raise my hands and wrap them around his forearm, tugging. The muscles are tight with strain, and when I tilt my head up to look at him, Mason's face is pulled tight in a hateful expression, and his eyes looks a little lost.

I press my lips to his neck. "Mason, calm down. He didn't hurt me. Let him go," I say, feeling my knees buckle.

Mason's chest heaves against my back, but his forearm loosens, and he makes a grunting noise as he lets the man go abruptly and then puts his hand back on my stomach, pulling me somehow even closer. The man collapses to the ground in front of me coughing a sickening, hacking noise that has me taking another step into Mason.

Dante steps quickly in front of me and grabs him up, marching him away from us and off the dance floor.

I turn in Mason's arms, my eyes wide. I'm ready to set him out, but the look on his face draws me up short.

He's standing still. The people dance around us, not even noticing we're in our own world as he stares at me with an ashamed, slightly guilty look on his face, but he's quiet, just waiting for me and my reaction to what he just did. No doubt wondering if I'm going to reject and belittle him like everyone else always seems to.

The crowd next to us doesn't miss a beat, and so, neither will we.

From experience I know that Dante will handle the guy, and he'll probably walk away with a bunch of money after signing an NDA, so he's not my worry.

Mason is.

I bring a hand up and touch his cheek gently before going higher and running my hands through his hair in a slow, soft movement. One I've only ever dreamed about doing. His eyes close, and he takes a slow, deep breath. Though we're in public, it's so intimate that it floors me.

"I'm okay, Masey," I reassure him, stepping into him again and beginning to roll my hips slightly, urging him to dance with me. His eyes open, regarding me with a sad look.

"I'm sorry, Mel," he says in a soft strained voice. So low that I almost didn't hear him. My eyes prick. He looks so tortured, so tense, that I rise to my tiptoes and press my lips to his jaw. Letting myself have this.

He softens immediately, bringing his arms around me and pulling me in close, and I eat that up, too.

"He didn't hurt me Mason, because of you," I whisper against his ear as he relents and begins to move with me. We start off hesitant at first, but soon, he lets the incident go and puts a hand to my hip as we move together properly now, and it's so sexy.

Natural.

I wish like hell our clothes were off, but after a couple of hours he just takes me back to my dorm and leaves.

Leaves me by myself once again.

CHAPTER 12

DON'T PISS ME OFF

"MASON, WAIT..." SHE GASPS. Tossing her head, she stiffens before arching her back on a low, breathy moan. "Mason, I don't know what I'm doing..."

I look up the expanse of her body, seeing her skin shiny with sweat, dotted with goosebumps, and trembling with need.

I indulge myself in another long, slow lick up between the lips of her sex before I pull away and crawl my way up her body. She's panting hard, exactly like she does when she's about three or four miles into a long run. Her breasts heave up and down rapidly; her brows are scrunched together as she stares back at me with a wary expression.

Liquid heat burns me up from the inside out as the blood pumps through my veins fast and mercilessly.

This is the point during her runs when she normally digs deep, forcing herself through the pain. I watch her carefully during these runs of hers, when she thinks she's alone. It's when she's the most vulnerable.

"Do you trust me?" I whisper, licking between the valley of her breasts.

"No," she says, her eyes flickering between mine. Her expression shows me she's dead serious, no hint of playfulness mars her features.

I give her a wicked smile, tilting my head to pull her nipple between my teeth and lashing it with my tongue. "Good girl," I murmur. "Because I taught you better than that. Didn't I? Never trust me when we're like this."

Her head falls back to the pillow and she whimpers, "Yes." The muscles in her arms twitch as she pulls against the rope binding her wrists to the mattress on either side of her head, and I take a second to appreciate her body. She's got a well-defined runner's physique. Except for her hips. They're not super narrow like runners' are. "Especially when you're tickling me."

I press my lips to the curve of her breasts, thinking back to when her sister was kidnapped and the only thing that broke her out of her depression long enough for her to eat, cry, or show any other emotion was to tickle her. I remember those times with her fondly.

It's when we became close.

I kiss up to her collarbone, pressing my lips to the soft skin there.

"Oh sweetie," I chuckle, tilting my head down and kissing her deeply. I stroke her tongue, nipping her lips and tugging, making them swell up and turn a deep red. I pull away and press my body to hers, making sure every solitary inch of me is molded to this woman. "I'm getting ready to teach you what men do to innocent women like you. I almost can't wait."

"I'm not innocent," she whispers haughtily, arching an eyebrow at me. The soft glow of the lamp next to us illuminates her just right, the light spilling across her face, her hair, her chest.

She's breathtaking.

A grin tugs at the corner of my mouth as I let another deep, knowing chuckle escape. She blushes even further, blinking up at me, unsure. I bend down and kiss her lips just once.

"Don't lie to me," I chastise her gently.

She stiffens. *"I'm not lying.* And anyways, how would you even know?"

My eyes narrow, and I feel my face harden. "Because I made sure of it."

Her eyes go wide as understanding shifts her features from sassiness to one of understanding as it finally hits her. *"What?"* she asks. "All those disappearances were because of *you?"*

I nod, rolling my hips against her. Jesus, she's soaking.

"I couldn't have them touching what's mine." I notch the tip of my cock in her entrance, feeling her tighten up again.

"What's yours?" Her nose scrunches up adorably, offensively.

"Yes, what's *mine,"* I emphasize. My back and hips are burning with the effort it's taking not to sink balls deep in her, to finally claim what I've been desiring for so long.

"I belong to myself," she stresses.

I place more of my body weight onto her, tilting my head as she nervously averts her eyes and shifts her hips a little. "Oh sweetie, you haven't belonged to yourself for a *very* long time. You didn't need me to be inside you for you to belong to me. I knew you were mine from the moment I laid eyes on you."

Her eyes snap back to mine and go somehow wider in shock, but I don't soften my words or even attempt to placate and soothe her by taking them back. I never say anything I don't mean. And I meant what I just said more than anything else I've ever said in my entire life.

Her pussy clenches around the tip of my cock, showing me just how much my words affect her.

My hands fist in the sheets and I widen my knees, pushing her legs far apart.

"Keep your eyes on me." I tell her, beginning to sink inside of her.

I'm ripped violently out of my sex dream to the sound of my alarm blaring at five o'clock on the dot. Heart thumping heavily in my chest, I sit up on a curse.

"Goddammit!" Falling back to the bed, I put my hands to my face and scrub hard. *"Fucckk!"* I growl, the sound filling the room loudly, as does my discontent.

The alarm went off right before Mel and I got our happy ending.

*Fuck, t*hat's going to piss me off for the rest of the day.

It takes a second, but eventually my pounding heart goes back to normal. I jerked off for two hours after I got home from dancing last night, suffering as my body was fucking unwilling to let me loose of the absolute manic desire it's trapped me in, and it still didn't help. I went to bed in pain. I don't care what anyone says, it's not normal for a man to go this long without sex.

I actually think my brain is fucked up now.

It was all too much: the excitement of the money, the club, dancing with Melody the way we were, the man trying to kiss her, and then me losing my temper in front of her like I did.

And all I wanted to do was fuck her after she pressed her lips to my jaw, ran her fingers through my hair, and looked at me with so much understanding and...

Love.

She loves me. I wonder if she knows.

Sighing heavily, I sit back up, swinging my legs over the side of my platform bed and snatch my cell off the nightstand, shutting off the alarm and making sure the snooze isn't activated. I hit the button to activate the electric curtains; however, it's still dark out.

Naked, I cup my swollen cock in my hand, ignore the unmade bed, and pad straight to the bathroom where I relieve myself.

I clench my jaw at the ache in my groin as my cock simply refuses to go down. Needing to put my mind elsewhere, I turn to the monitor in the bathroom, turning it on and grab up my toothbrush as the screen flickers to life, showing me Melody's dorm room.

She's bundled up in bed. The swell of her hip makes my cock twitch, but I continue brushing my teeth, ignoring it.

I've learned a lot about control in the last few years, much to my brother Hendrix's happiness. What's his happiness, however, is soon to be Melody's detriment, because I'm going to patiently dismantle her sanity night after night when I finally am able to crawl between her legs.

My body hardens at the thought as desire races through my veins so razor sharp it's a wonder I'm not physically bleeding out my fucking lust all over the floor. I make a rough sound in my throat, trying to get a grip over myself, because once I fall down that rabbit hole, I'm *fucked.* No good for the rest of the day.

Ask me how I know.

Just i*magining* the heaven that's her pussy sends me spiraling, and once I'm there, I won't be leaving for a while.

I mentally plan to let all my clients know I'm soon to be taking two weeks off. I need to let Lucien know as well before Melody and I wake up with a mafia hit man breaking in on our honeymoon time.

I spit and rinse my mouth, swishing mouthwash and narrowing my eyes at the screen, debating swallowing it in an attempt to get rid of my erection.

Why isn't she up yet? She's on the track at five-thirty every morning to get in a run before her classes start. Right now she *should* be getting in the shower. Where I can't see her.

I've never seen her naked. She undresses and dresses mostly in the dorm bathroom out of sight of her roommate, which means out of sight of me. I spit again and tell my bathroom system to call her, pulling out my shaving kit while the ringing fills the space.

Her cell lights up on the nightstand, letting me know it's close by.

Getting the materials laid out, I turn on the black tap and wet my fingers to lather my face with shaving gel and snag up my razor. After the third ring she stirs under the covers, flinging her arm out from under the blanket where she settles back to being still.

My eyes narrow as I get sent to voicemail, and I hang up and call her again. She ignored my call the night before, and I let it slide, considering.

But I won't tolerate being ignored twice in a row. And why the fuck doesn't she have a special ringtone for me, like I have for her? She should automatically know it's me by the tone. My face twitches in displeasure as the phone rings and rings. When I go to voicemail again, I call one more time before I'll contact Stephen to wake her up for me.

The razor strokes along my skin. I can't do a beard like my brother and father. I need my face as neat and orderly as my home. My eyes slide to the monitor, and I chuckle seeing her roommate throw a pillow across the small space to hit her in the head. Melody slaps the nightstand a few times before snagging up her phone and dragging it under the covers.

"Hello," she answers sounding groggy.

I frown.

"Happy Birthday, Mel." I say, rinsing the razor under the warm water I bring it back to my neck and tilt my head at an angle.

I hear her yawn so hard her jaw cracks. "Thank you," she says breathlessly before going quiet.

I give her a second, watching the razor slice through the white gel. For a second, there's nothing but the razor across the roughness of the hairs on my jaw, and the sound of a soft snore coming through the speaker. *"Melody, wake up,"* I say sharply.

"Huh?" she says.

"I said *Happy Birthday,* sweetheart. You're finally twenty-years old now. How do you feel?"

"Mason?" she says, sounding confused.

I recoil my head, sliding my eyes towards the monitor seeing she's sat up in bed and is rubbing her eyes. Displeasure fills me in swathes. However, it dissipates quickly when she slides off her pink bonnet and her hair spills out in a mass of curls.

Fuck, she's so gorgeous.

"I'm sorry, *who else* calls you sweetheart?" I pause with the razor against my cheek, watching her carefully.

She slides a hand down her hair, caressing her collarbone before smoothing her hand over her breasts in a self-soothing motion. Something she does every morning after she wakes up.

Every fucking day I watch her touch herself like this.

"No one," she giggles. Sitting back in bed, she tucks a hand between her legs and rolls onto her side.

"They better not." I breathe quietly, but I know she heard me. I resume shaving. Seeing she's dragging the covers up her body, I clear my throat hard. "No, don't lay back down. *Get up."*

Melody groans into the phone. "But I don't want to." She sits back up in bed anyways, rubbing a hand down her face. *"I want to sleep."*

"You're there on a track scholarship, Mel. Don't slack off. Besides, you're going to have to get used to operating on less sleep, anyways."

I pause, immediately going silent at what I just let slip. On top of all the other slip ups that's happened lately.

"What? *Why?"* Of course she'd catch my fuck up.

Because I'm going to be getting you up earlier than five to start my mornings off fucking you, I think.

"Nothing. I, uh, just figured you might be training harder when you start competing." I clear my throat gently. "Go ahead and get your workout gear on while you're on the phone with me. We can't be having too many of these late night escapades if you're not going to answer my phone call to get you up."

Melody rolls her eyes. "Yeah," she sighs, "it was probably a bad idea to stay out half the night."

She gets up out of bed and walks over to her dresser, looking delectable.

"Well, I don't think so," I say with a smile. "I had a great time."

"How's your hand?" she asks, but I'm too riveted by the sight on my screen to reply.

Her nipples poke out long and thick through her top, and I go still with the razor at my throat so I don't cut myself when my throat bobs hard with a swallow. My neglected cock twitches, the tip dripping with a string of pre-come, and my mouth goes completely dry at the sight of her skimpy shorts and a tinier crop top than what she wore last night.

Holy fuuucck.

It's like a treat. The other day I got to see her touch herself, crying out while she orgasmed so hard her toes curled. Last night I got to feel her hips in my hands, and today she's braless. The creamy skin of her breasts peek out from the hem as she stretches her arms above her head.

I jacked off twice last night to the memory of the way her face looked when she orgasmed.

I want to right now just thinking about it again.

Her eyebrows scrunched together, her breasts heaving as her mouth fell open. Panting short, fast breaths she tensed up, looking down at her hand while she rubbed her pussy hard and fast over her clothes. She rubbed and rubbed. So long that I got my cock out and joined her. My body tightens even harder as I remember the feel of me pleasuring myself at the sight of her orgasming.

Pre-ejaculate spurt all over while I roughly jerked with one hand, using the palm of my other hand to rub circles into the tip of my cock.

Melody jerked hard, looking like she stopped breathing before tilting her head back, licking her tongue along her top lip before hanging there for half a second. Her belly trembled, and she collapsed on the bed, drawing her knees back and then rocking side to side while a wet stain slowly spread across the fabric between her legs.

I came so hard I swear I almost died.

"Mason? Are you still there?"

Her voice jolts me back to reality. *"Yes."* I place the razor down and lean my palms on the vanity, forcing myself to not stare at the monitor and take a deep breath. "Of course my hand's okay." When I feel like

I've got a grip, I resume shaving and chance a peek at her. I tilt my head, eying her through the monitor.

Melody pauses. "You know, I still think you're an asshole for not letting me have a drink last night." She sounds mildly annoyed, which puts a grin on my face as I make the last pass over my jawline.

"Trust me when I say I am so very unbothered."

Finished, I swish the razor under the water and put it to the side, grabbing a towel and wetting it. I wipe my face clean of the little spots of gel and squirt some soothing cream into my hands, smoothing it over my jaw and cheeks.

"'Fuck you," she whispers, making me smile because I think I'm the only one in the family who's heard her cuss like this.

"Good girl. Show some of that temper, birthday girl. You deserve it."

I run a comb and some product through my hair until it's perfect then give myself a glance over in the mirror. My eyes lower to my aching cock. I grab it and give it a little tug, my breath hitches, but I won't pleasure myself right now.

That'll come later.

Turning away from the monitor as she's gone now, I pad back into my bedroom where I grab my phone, switch the call over to it, and look over my stocks. And hers.

I smile at the numbers. "Mel, I'm happy to tell you your stock is doing well."

I bring my phone into the closet and get ready for the day. There's something about the both of us dressing at the same time that feels so intimate. I soak it up with a deep appreciation, not having had that many of these moments.

"It is?" A door shuts on her end, informing me she's in the dorm bathroom.

"Yeah, it's up a few percent. I mean it's not a ton, so don't go all crazy with excitement or nothing, but it's a bit more than it was." I spray cologne on and take a second to pick out my cufflinks. I settle on the ones that say "M," for Melody, though people only assume it's for Mason.

They'd be wrong.

"So that's good, right?" She huffs as the sound of a whisper of fabric whooshes over the phone, letting me know she's taking off her shirt.

"If you consider being a few grand richer good, then *yes.*" An amused smile tugs my lips as I pull on my briefs, then my pants. "So, are you excited about tonight?" The door closes softly again, and I hear her beginning to walk rather briskly through the hallway. "I hope you are, since we had fun last night."

"I actually am."

"Can I pick you up from school?" I sit on the bench and begin to pull on my socks and shoes. My heart beats a little faster as I force myself to wait for her answer, tying the laces and exercise what so far has been hard won discipline over my patience.

"You want to pick me up? That's going out of your way, isn't it?"

I frown, tugging on my shirt and buttoning it up quickly, attaching the cufflinks and tucking in my shirt. A door bangs, and I hear her huffing as she does her warm up routine before her running. "Only thirty minutes. I don't mind."

There's silence for a very long stretch of time as she makes me listen to her warm up without answering me. My neglected cock hardens more, and I seriously wonder how gentle I'm going to be able to be when the time comes for us.

I've waited too long.

I can't wait for her to finish school. It's selfish, but I won't.

It's been three years since I told Hendrix I would, but it was a very obvious lie. In just a month she's going to be moving to her own apartment, so she thinks.

I walk into the kitchen and sit at the breakfast table where my chef has a bowl of oatmeal already waiting for me. It sits steaming, topped with brown sugar, diced green apples, and a small bit of butter. A coffee cup sits to the side, along with a men's multivitamin.

I give a nod of thanks and sit. Setting my phone down on the table, I take advantage of her silence and begin to eat silently.

Eventually Melody goes to speak, but I interrupt her before she can get a word in. She waited too long to give me her answer. "I'll be there at five-thirty sharp to pick you up. Meet me in front of the campus library."

Twelve hours seems so far away, but it hasn't been near as long as these last three and a half years have been, I'll tell you that.

Three years of celibacy. Three years of turning down every woman who's approached me. Three years of having a carrot dangled in front of me that I can't have. Well, enough is enough. Melody won't be moving into an apartment at the end of the month.

No, she'll be coming with me. Where she belongs.

"I might be late. It takes me a little while to do my makeup and stuff," she huffs, beginning to run.

I contemplate her reservation and shyness for a moment. Knowing that's why she's late everywhere. She obsessively makes sure she's perfect before she's seen anywhere, always scared of paling in her sister's shadow.

Her feet hit the pavement, and I hear her work to control her breathing. A muscle in my jaw twitches because she sounds like she's being fucked, and I really want to be the reason why she sounds like that. I grunt, swallowing the last of my oatmeal.

"No, you'll be on time. There's no reason to be late. Your last class ends at *four;* you don't need to spend an hour smearing shit on your face. You don't need it anyways. I want you outside the library at five-thirty, Melody."

"I want you outside the library at five-thirty, Melody," she mocks me lightly. "Fuck, you're so uptight sometimes. *Loosen up."*

"Don't piss me off," I say quietly, frowning, quickly realizing I'm not in the mood for that today, as does she.

My patience is literally hanging on by a thread, and I'm so on edge that I don't think I can tolerate any teasing today like I normally can with her. The silence swells between us, and her footsteps slow just slightly making me feel like an ass at how sternly I just put her in her place.

"Sorry, that was childish of me," she says.

"Well, we're done with that," I say smoothly, getting up from my seat and grabbing my phone, heading towards the elevator of my penthouse.

"What?" she huffs.

"Nevermind. I'll be there at five-thirty sharp."

I hang up the phone and make my way to my area of the parking garage, sliding into a sleek Mercedes and taking off to the office.

CHAPTER 13

HERE WE GO

"UGH!" I GROAN, THROWING my makeup brush onto the small vanity in frustration. I take the makeup wipe and smooth it over my eyelid, praying that it doesn't irritate my skin as this is my fifth time trying to redo it.

"What's wrong?" Karissa, my roommate, walks over to bend down to look at my reflection in the mirror. Her blond brow arches as she assesses my handiwork.

Sighing, I hold the pencil up to my eye again, trying to go slow.

"I keep fucking up my eyeliner," I mumble. The pen slips again, smearing the wing at the edge.

Karissa tsks and takes it from me, rubbing the edge where she starts to carefully draw in my liner with her tongue between her teeth. "Why are you putting on so much makeup anyways?" she asks.

Heat fills my cheeks at her judgemental question. I can't tell her it's because I want to appear more grown up, womanly in front of my sister's brother-in-law. "I just want to start taking better care with my appearance. My sister's in-laws are throwing a dinner party for my birthday today."

She pauses, putting the pen down to look at me. "What? It's your birthday?" My face heats up in earnest now as she glares at me. The room becomes almost as icy as her ice blond platinum hair. "Bitch, why haven't you said anything?"

"I just..." *Because I don't want the attention.* "Because I don't want to make it a big deal."

"Melody, I would have loved to celebrate you!" Her eyes go wide. "Can I come tonight? To the dinner?"

I pause. She must see the look on my face because hers turn pouty. "Come onnn, Melody!" she whines. "I want to help celebrate your birthday!"

"Fine," I sigh.

Pulling out my phone I send a text to mine, Isobel's and Hendrix's group chat, letting them know I'm bringing someone to dinner tonight. I know they won't mind because I never ask for anything. Sure enough, Hendrix texts back quickly, giving me the go ahead.

> Why wouldn't you bring someone? Is it a guy? -Henny

I snort.

I wouldn't dare. The family is strictly forbidden from bringing random love interests into the fold. For good reason, I know, due to all the legal paperwork that goes into drafting NDAs, but it makes me wonder why he'd ask if he knows that's one of the *first* fucking family rules.

"You can come," I tell Karissa, seeing her do a little wiggle dance and shout with happiness.

"Now, what are you going to wear?" she asks. Strolling to my side of the dorm she opens the door then steps back with her hands on her hips. She scans the rows and rows of leggings and tank tops, her frown getting deeper every passing second. Stepping forward, the hangers clack together loudly as she moves it all to the side rather violently to get to the back of the closet, where the pickings are still meager. *"This is all you've got?"*

I bite my lip. "Yes."

Standing up, I clutch the towel I wrapped around me tighter and walk over to the closet with her. She picks out a black dress, but it goes all the way to my ankle and has ruffles on it. It's completely inappropriate for a birthday dinner. Isobel got it for me last year to go to some banquet with her when Hendrix was out of town.

Karissa tsks. "We're going shopping in my closet."

She pivots on her heel and skips to her closet which is stuffed full to the gills with all manner of clothes and begins moving hanger after hanger. I admire her style, but she's shorter than me, so anything she could possibly give me will more than likely be indecent.

My phone dings, and I walk back over to the little vanity where I see Mason's texted me.

It's five o'clock sweetheart. -Mason

I know. I'm trying to find something to wear. -Melody

The bubbles come fast.

"Here, I think these will be so pretty on you," Melody interrupts, draping a couple options over my bed. I look over and cringe, seeing it's just as bad, if not worse, than I thought. She got out options for what looks to be a nightclub, not my in-law's grand estate.

What do you mean you're trying to find something to wear? Melody...-Mason

My brow arches at his obvious slight chastisement of me. His discontent wafts through the phone, and gets my butt into gear. I bite my lip and hurry over to the bed, snatching one up.

"I'll take this one," I say, picking up a rather pretty deep purple dress with itty bitty tassels all over it. It's shimmery and looks good against my skin.

I'm already outside waiting. Don't make me have to come get you. -Mason

"He's here!" I gasp, turning quickly to head to the door so I can change in the bathroom like usual. I'm rushing, and it sets Karissa off, igniting her hyper-excited attitude.

"Who?" Karissa asks, her voice going an octave higher as my panic spreads.

I veer to the vanity and snatch my hair oil off, twirling around like a manic. I don't know why he affects me this bad, but Mason has always been able to dig under my skin and set me off kilter.

"My sister's brother-in-law. The 'Spanish one,'" I air quote her words from earlier. "He's picking me up, and he's already here," I stress, stumbling over a wayward shirt left in the floor.

"No time for that then."

Karissa leans forward and snatches the dress out of my hand and then shoves it over my head. Before I know it, she's ripped the towel off, and, yelping, I clamp my arm over my breasts. I'm left glowering at her while standing in nothing but a black thong and this ridiculous dress around my neck. She ignores me and manhandles me into the dress.

As soon as it's smoothed over my hips I bend down and flip my hair a little, shaking my curls out and spritzing oil everywhere. "It's too fucking short," I complain, tugging on the hem.

"Hang on, I bought some too-big tights last week by accident. See if they'll fit!" She dives for her dresser, pulling out a pair of sheer, black tights. I yank them on carefully, trying to not tear them. Thankfully, they have a lot of stretch, and they work, but they're mighty sheer.

"Here wear these." Before I can stand up straight and get my bearings, she pushes me to the edge of her mattress and picks my foot up where she shoves a black, ridiculously high platform heel on my foot.

"Karissa!" I protest, pulling my foot away, but she just yanks me back, tying the strap around my ankle.

Just then my phone rings. I answer, completely overwhelmed.

"What?" I snap, not even knowing who's on the other end.

"Who are you talking to like that?" Mason says, making me bite my lip.

"Sorry, I didn't know it was you."

"And why not?"

I frown at his irritated tone. "What do you mean why not?"

"Do you need help with cognitive comprehension as *well* as math, Mel? I mean just that. Why not? *As in why didn't you know it was me?"*

"Because I didn't know!"

His voice goes lower. "You don't have a special ring tone for me?"

I arch a brow, and scoff in disbelief. "I'm sorry. I'm gen Z, and we don't even have a ringtone half the time, *selfish."*

He snorts. "Whatever. Well, tick tock, sweetheart, get to moving," Mason growls. I blush, standing up as she gets the last shoe on. "It's five twenty-five. You know I don't like to be kept waiting."

My heart skips a beat at the sound of his voice. It's smooth and elegant, not rough like his brother's. Mason's timbre drips effortless sophistication and arrogance. His slight Spanish accent bleeds through a bit thicker today, and it's so sexy.

"I'm coming, Mason. *Jesus.*"

"Melody, if you get in my car and I see you're late because you have a pound of makeup on your face we're going to have a serious, *serious* fucking problem."

I make a sound and snatch up my clutch, tucking it under my arm. "Just for that I'm not rushing," I lie.

I'm met with silence.

"Text me the address! I'll be there in about an hour and a half," Karissa whispers, opening the dorm room door and waving at me as I run with Stephen in close pursuit, tearing through the hallways. Rushing anyways because I can't help myself when it comes to him. Thank God I'm a great runner. Otherwise, I'd be flat on my face in these heels.

I make it to the library in record time and stop just before the double doors, placing a hand on heart. I know I can't not catch my breath because of running, I run *miles* before I'm affected. It's him. *He* makes me nervous.

"Keep going."

I screech, slapping a hand to Stephen's chest and almost leap out of my skin at the sound of Mason's voice in my ear. He was so silent I'd forgotten I still had him on the phone.

Wrangling a firm grip on my sanity, I push through the double doors and gingerly make my way down the concrete stairs with

Stephen hovering, grumbling about ridiculous stripper heels. Feeling the hair on the back of my neck stand up, I glance up and freeze at the sight of Mason's red Ferrari parked across the street.

He stands there in a navy suit, arms folded leaning against the side of it, staring me down. God, he's *handsome.* Though I've seen this man at least a hundred times since his brother married my sister, it still feels like the first time.

Because he makes it that way.

His eyes bore into mine as I step onto the sidewalk. His hand taps his bicep as he waits patiently in a movement he'd shared that he'd learned from therapy. That familiar heat that plagues me every time we're around one another swamps me again, settling in my core and spreading outwards. His gaze leaves mine to flick downwards, and he tilts his head when he gets to my cleavage then lower to where I'm showing way too much leg.

My eyes lower down him in the same slow perusal.

I bite my lip, seeing the bulge in between his legs twitch. His eyes snap back to mine, but he stands there silently, waiting for me. I immediately blush so hard I feel dizzy and tear my eyes away for a second, needing a moment to get control over myself around him because I've never seen him have an erection before.

Mason's never attempted to hide how attracted he is to me, but today something is different, he looks... *hungrier.*

I wait until a car drives past then walk across the street, unhurried, breaking away from Stephen who turns to join Dante, Mason's security.

Mason keeps my eyes the entire time until I make it to him. I relax my arms, expecting him to pull me in for a hug; instead, he grasps my jaw and tilts my head even further up to him. My heart pounds at the simple action. Even in five inch heels I have to look up to meet his eye.

"You're late," he says, staring into my soul.

I swallow thickly. "Only by a minute or t-two." I blink as he tilts my head suddenly assessing my makeup. I pout, feeling shy and really laid bare. Even more so when his head lowers and he blatantly looks down my body to my legs again. "Can't be in too much trouble since you're taking your time inspecting me like a prized cow."

That draws a laugh out of him.

He leans forward, and I hold my breath as he brushes his lips ever so gently to my cheek. Brushing the corner of my mouth. His arm snakes around my waist, and his hand presses into my lower back, forcing me to close the last two steps between us. My arms twine around his shoulders, pressing my curves against his hardness, and he nuzzles into my neck.

God, he smells so good. His cologne is something deep and spicy, warm.

Even though it's a only a hug, it's incredibly intimate especially out here on the street with onlookers. I pull away shyly, not able to meet his gaze, and spend a second tugging the hem of this too short dress down. I notice the car behind his, idling with our bodyguards who thankfully makes themselves sparse when we leave campus together.

Mason clears his throat gently, guiding me to the passenger side of his car where he opens it and stands back, eyeing me tightly. I stare at the low seat for a second and then tug on my dress again.

Shit, I don't know how I'm going to sit down without flashing everyone.

I hand him my clutch, and he raises his eyebrow at me. He let's out a deep chuckle then sucks in a deep breath, clearing his throat and then stepping into me, closing the door on us and shielding me from the sidewalk.

"Just sit down, Mel. No need to be shy."

I press my legs together tightly, grab the hem of my dress and then sit, picking up my legs and settling into the car. Even an inch higher, the lace of my thong would be showing through the sheerness of the stockings. He leans in, placing my clutch on my lap.

"Thank you," I say, my eyes going wide as his fingers trail down my leg. My eyes slide to his as he squats down, making his pants stretch deliciously across his thick thighs.

"I have a present for you. That's why I didn't want you to be late, I couldn't wait a minute longer to give it to you," he says, reaching forward to the glove compartment.

My belly tightens as his warmth leaves me; my legs shift restlessly, missing the warmth of his fingers. He opens the glove compartment and pulls out a little box.

My eyes go wide, recognizing it instantly.

"Oh my gosh!" I gasp, not able to help myself as a huge smile spreads across my face. "It's the perfume I wanted! How'd you know?"

"Isobel."

He spends a second opening the box. When he gets out the bottle, he grasps my wrist and turns it palm up and spritzes a spray on my wrists, then my neck. Just when I think he's done, he grabs my calf and raises my leg slightly, spritzing a bit on the bend of my knee.

"Why on the back of my knee? That's such a waste," I ask, raising an eyebrow at him. "No one's going to be smelling me down there, Mason."

"I wouldn't be so sure about that, sweetheart," he says.

I blink, staying quiet as he replaces the bottle in the box and puts it back in the glove compartment. "Wait, I want to put it in my clutch," I say, reaching forward to try and grab it before he closes the glove compartment, but to my surprise he snatches my wrist up rather roughly, wrapping his fingers all the way around. *"Hey!"* I complain. "Mason, what are you doing?" I turn my eyes to his, seeing he's standing up out of his hunkered position and looking down at me.

Something flashes in his eyes as they narrow slightly at me. I narrow mine back.

"It's only for you to wear when you're with me," he says.

It's a completely jealous, if not *possessive,* move that burns me up from the inside out.

My thighs clench even harder as the flesh between my legs becomes heavy and hot with need. His eyes burn into mine, as do his words. Mason and I have been dancing this rather precarious, dangerous tango that only he and I seem to know the steps to.

Well, *he* only knows the steps. I have to follow his lead. Problem is, I'm tired of waiting. He hasn't made a move yet, and I'm beginning to be frustrated beyond belief. Thinking maybe I'm only imagining he wants me, and I just spent three years pining for a man who doesn't want me back.

Feelings of inadequacy arises from deep down inside, stifling the desire I feel towards him.

Mason shuts the passenger door and then walks lazily around to the driver's side, sliding in. I watch as he adjusts his long legs beneath the steering wheel, and as he works to make himself comfortable, his suit jacket rides up, revealing his cufflinks.

Every time I see him, he's got the same ones on.

His spicy cologne fills the air and mixes with the muted floral and orange of my new perfume, creating it's own distinct scent that is, quite simply, addicting. It's like it was planned to be perfect together. He stays quiet as he buckles his seatbelt and then puts on his blinker, looking in the rearview mirror to check that security is watching.

He hits the gas, making the quiet engine roar before he smoothly pulls out onto the street and guns it. My fingers twitch in my lap as I stare out the window.

Maybe I'm nothing but his plaything.

A convenient toy to amuse him while he waits for the real person he wants. Maybe I've spent three years imagining this whole scenario between us. That he's nothing more than my sister's brother-in-law, and that's all he'll ever be.

"Penny for your thoughts?" Mason asks, looking over at me while he guides us to the highway. "How's school going??"

"Great," I say lightly, "I'm apartment hunting now."

"I don't know why you're apartment hunting," he says wryly.

I turn my head sharply, raising an eyebrow. "I'm going to tell you the same thing I told Izzy and Henny-"

"Is that so?" Mason interrupts. "That's what you're going to do, huh? Treat me like Hendrix?"

"Yes."

"And what did you tell them?"

"That I want some independence."

CHAPTER 14

A Man In Finance

"Independence?" I say sarcastically with a smile, reaching over to slide on my sunglasses then handing her a matching feminine pair I keep just for her. "What an *overrated* concept."

She gifts me with a rather offended look as she slides them on. "I'm sure it is for *you,* having had it for what... sixteen years now?"

I frown. "Technically twelve. I just turned thirty, Mel, *get it right."*

"Same difference."

I cut my eyes to her. "You know, that explains your math grade a *lot."*

Melody hums a sound in her throat, and it travels straight to my cock making it jerk in my pants. I take a deep breath, seriously regretting not allowing myself an orgasm this morning. I thought I could wait. The breath I just took made it worse.

My lungs fill with the orange notes of her new perfume, and all I can think about is burying my face in between her legs and kissing her in the crook of her knee where I instinctively know her smell is deeper, sultrier.

"You know as well as I do that you'll never have full independence, sweetheart," I say quietly, working to pass a car in front of me. They honk, flipping me off, but I ignore them. "Do you need me to elaborate?"

I keep the car steady on the lane; however, the sight of her brown eyes over her sunglasses draw me back in. She meets them for half a second before turning away shyly again, staying quiet. I stare for a minute, willing her to come back to me, but all too soon my eyes are dragging back down her body to where every fucking inch of her legs are on display.

Torturing me.

My fingers flex on the gear stick as I shift my weight in the seat, willing this goddamn erection I've had on and off since this morning down. Distracting myself from her taut muscles and smooth gleaming dark tan skin, I look in the rearview mirror again. The skyscrapers of the bustling city recede in the background as we head towards my parents' house, a place that, until recently, had been like a prison to me.

Melody and I don't belong there with them.

We belong back *there*. Where there's hustle and bustle, and where we can climb to the highest building and look down, safe with each other in the clouds where no one can touch us.

"Another guy I was talking to went missing..." she says, now bringing her eyes to mine. The air immediately shifts in the car, becoming stifling and tense.

"Did they?" I force myself with everything in me to keep my tone calm and unassuming.

"Yeah," she says. "He's disappeared straight off the face of the Earth. No socials. None of his friends know where he is or what happened. Just like the other four." She looks back out the window, her fingers clenched so hard around her clutch that her knuckles turn pale. "He's the fifth guy since I've been in school that this has happened to. No one's going to want to date me now because I'm cursed."

I make a fake sympathetic hum in my throat as a rush of pleasure flows through me so thick that a drop of pre-come drips from the tip of my cock, wetting my thigh. Though she's obviously bothered, I refuse to acknowledge anything she just said. A tense silence swells around us once more as I make the turn onto the paved drive of my parents' property.

We amble through the gate, and I move my hand over to grab hers and pull it over to me.

I kiss the back of her hand, letting my lips linger as I take the time to enjoy the scent I bought for her. Her natural chemistry mixes with it to create something deeper. Slightly muskier, turning innocence into something sexy and forbidden. I wait for her to pull back from me, but she doesn't.

She never does.

"I'd like you to wear that scent more often. You smell so good," I say quietly, wanting to break the silence, giving her a little more than I usually do. Being a bit more openly verbal with my desire towards her.

"Thanks." Her voice quivers a little. "But you're not letting me take it home, so I can only wear it when I'm with you."

Exactly. *"Hmhm,"* I say, already planning to have a talk with Hendrix because I'm through waiting.

I think I've beyond proved myself to my family.

I pull up behind all the other family members' cars right as the last rays of sun disappear and all the lights around the property pop on. The trees around us light up, the fountain gurgles, and I see my mother has decorated it with Melody's favorite flowers. It's an explosion of lush colors entwined with greenery that would put any party planner to shame.

"Aw, it's so pretty!" Melody gushes, stepping closer and touching one of the flowers. I pluck it off and hand it to her.

Her fingers graze mine gently as she takes it, and that familiar spark tugs at me once again. I know I'm not the only one who feels this.

Placing a hand on her lower back, I lead us to the stairs but stay a step down to watch her legs in this dress. I tug at my collar, feeling extra warm, and be sure to fix my face when we arrive on the landing together and push through the front door.

Soft instrumental music greets us first, along with the warmth of my parents' home. Muted sounds of our family talking and laughing drift from the den to the foyer, informing me they're knee deep in having a good time. So good, I wonder if we even had to show up. Theoretically, I could be deep in something myself.

Knuckle deep.

My parents' butler appears out of thin air, interrupting my thoughts of sliding my fingers in Melody's pussy. "Your jacket, sir?"

"Sure thing, Jefferies." I shrug out of it and then undo my cuff links, sliding them into my pants pocket. I spend a second rolling up my sleeves to my elbow, undoing my tie, leaving the two pieces hanging down. I'm in the middle of undoing the first couple buttons when Melody clears her throat, bringing my attention to her. "Yes, Mel?"

"What the fuck are you doing?"

I grin. "A guy can't get comfortable?"

She rolls her eyes. "You rushed me half to death so you could take your time spraying perfume on me and then undressing in your parents' foyer? Got it."

I smile. "Such an attitude. Why do you only ever show it with me?" I ask, knowing as soon as we get in the den, Melody's going to withdraw into herself like she always does. It's not that she doesn't like them; she's just more like me. Doesn't fit in. Isn't as sure of herself like the others are.

A sentiment I can sympathize with. Because I was a late bloomer, too. Never knowing which direction to go in, never knowing how to trust myself and my instincts.

It took me years to gain confidence in myself. A byproduct of being a younger sibling. Sometimes I wonder if that month I spent helping Melody through the trauma of Isobel being kidnapped meant as much to her as it did me.

Hours I'd spent feeding her, holding her, sitting with her in silence. Letting her cry on me. Wiping her tears away.

The hundreds of Hail Marys I've said over this girl probably needs a case study. They say everything happens for a reason, and though I'll never tell any of them because it's fucking selfish and wrong as fuck to say, I firmly believe that Isobel going through that kidnapping was the catalyst to my personality change. And Melody.

I'm not ashamed to admit to myself that a woman woke my ass up out of the deep pit of spite I'd been stewing in for years, until she came along.

Nurturing her through that month finally broke something inside me that they all spent years trying to chip away at. It made me realize that I could trust myself, if I just allowed myself to be vulnerable instead of spiteful. It took some time, but eventually my displeasure with Hendrix and my family morphed into camaraderie.

And the harder I worked, that camaraderie turned into respect.

"I don't just show it with you," she retorts in a sassy tone, tilting her chin up and looking away.

"Yes, you do." I chuckle, fixing my watch. When I'm sure that I'm put together comfortably I step into her and then place my hand on her lower back and press.

"No, I don't," she whispers at me defiantly.

"Stop talking back," I say, pressing my lips to her temple in a hard kiss. "And let's try to enjoy your birthday with them."

"I'm not talking back!"

I ignore her as we walk into the den, and everyone looks up, greeting us with bright smiles.

"Melody! *Happy Birthday, honey!"* My mother jumps up and almost rushes over to us where she pulls Melody in for a hug. I haven't asked, but she acts like Melody's her favorite out of all of us, almost always managing to get to Melody before her own mother does. I stand next to her while everyone comes up and takes turns giving her a hug and their congratulations.

When Hendrix walks up, he gives me a look while he's bent down hugging her, and I roll my eyes.

"Study," he says.

Before he even gets the last syllable out I'm already headed that way, giving my dad a back clap on the back en-route to the study. Walking past the side table laden down with presents, I step through the heavy ornate oak door and meander over to the drinks cart next to the roaring fireplace.

I'm busy making the both of us a drink when Hendrix steps in.

"We need to talk, Mase," he says.

I clench my jaw as I grab up our glasses and take a swallow of mine while I hand him his. He sits down on the leather chair our father usually sits in and crosses an ankle over his knee, assessing me.

My skin doesn't prick like it normally does when I'm being scrutinized. No, things like that don't hardly get under my skin anymore. Instead, I sit across from him, right on the table and lean forward with my elbows on my knees. "About what?"

"You know what."

"Sorry for being an asshole." I clear my throat, tipping my drink up and swallow, relishing the slight burn. "I know what. I just don't understand what *there is to talk about."*

"Mason, let her get her own apartment." Hendrix eyes me with nothing short of patience. Having a kid has really mellowed him.

I narrow my eyes, curling my lip as that familiar twinge of sibling rivalry fills me. "No, and fuck you for continuing to try to dictate how I live my life. No one tried to control how you got Isobel."

"Mason, she's-"

"A legal adult." I finish for him. I sit back, placing my drink on a coaster next to my hip. I square him with a look and arch an eyebrow. "Look, I did *everything* that was asked of me. I became legit. I got a real job, I solidified myself as a major contributing factor in the King Dynasty business and carved my own sector out for myself. I haven't touched her, haven't fucked her. I haven't so much as even kissed her this entire time you've asked me to wait." I pause, seeing a flash of surprise mar his features. "Yeah, I bet you didn't see that coming, did you?"

That resentment I work so hard to keep under check swells within me, threatening to break through.

"I'm very proud of you, Mase," Hendrix says, looking at me with, in fact, brotherly pride. I stare back, almost afraid to acknowledge it. "You've done us *all* proud."

My lips tighten as I take another sip. "Yeah, well, I know it took long enough."

"Can you give her one more year?" he asks me, tilting his head.

My answer comes back fast and with a quickness, "No. No, I can't."

He sighs, clearing his throat and goes to say something else, but he's interrupted by the doorbell ringing. "Are we expecting someone else?" I ask, standing up and tossing back the rest of my drink.

"Yeah, Melody is having a friend over," he says, but I'm already on my way out the door to see what's going on.

I meet up with Melody, who's making her way to the foyer and grab her elbow. "Hang on, sweetheart, let me go first." I tell her, pulling to slow her down. I wave Johnson away, getting to the door and opening it to her too-blonde, big-boobed, plumped up roommate Karissa. Who has two younger men behind her.

I pause, tucking Melody further against my side. "Who're you?" I say, but Melody pulls out from my side and reaches out and grabs Karissa, pulling her inside.

"Thank you for coming!" she gushes, pulling her in for a hug.

I frown and step aside, making room for the two men to come in behind her. Irritation like I haven't felt in a minute rises inside me, and I visibly bristle. What's worse, I can't even help it.

"Hey, man." The dark-haired man steps forward with his hand outstretched. I ignore it, turning away from him to close the door dismissively. His hand lowers, and he trades a glance with the other man. A blonde who is looking a bit too hard at Melody for my liking.

Karissa's head snaps to me, and her eyebrows raise, her eyes go wide, and her face breaks out in a big smile.

"Hi," Karissa says, stepping into me before I can react and throwing her arms around me. "It's so good to meet you!" I stiffen as she squeezes hard and rocks me, and I keep my hands to myself, not really knowing what to say. My nose scrunches up as the smell of her overly processed hair hits me.

Uncomfortable, I tilt my head back, pulling away from her.

I throw a look at Melody, who's currently shaking hands with the blond. "It's good to meet you too," I say tightly. I feel the old Mason coming back, and I bite the side of my cheek trying with everything in me to keep my attitude in check.

The brown-haired guy named Brian throws an arm around Karissa, and she tilts her head up at him, placing her hand on the side of his face.

The blonde man's name is Leo, and he looks like what the fuck you'd think a Leo would look like, too. He's got blue eyes, dark blue jeans with a polo shirt and converse. My lip curls, seeing how he's smiling at Melody. And when she leans forward to shake Brian's hand, he tilts his head, checking out her ass in her too-short dress.

The way he's looking at her has my irritation spiked to unreal heights.

My lip curls, *"Get your-"*

Right as I'm getting ready to lose my temper, another voice sounds out. "What's going on?"

I turn at the sound of my brother's voice.

Hendrix walks into the foyer, and immediately the other guys straighten up and all the fun sucks out of the room as usual when Hendrix comes around. I've learned by now that he just can't help it. He walks in a room and commands it.

"Hello, sir. I'm Leo, and this is Brian." Leo steps forward, holding out his hand. Hendrix takes it, shifting his eyes to me.

I stand to the side, leaning a shoulder against the wall and just watch. His eyes slide to Melody, who is blushing harder than I think I've ever seen her do before.

"Melody, you didn't say your friend was going to be bringing friends," Hendrix says smoothly, ignoring the men.

"I-I didn't know she was going to," Melody stammers, biting her lip. "Is that okay, Hendrix? They drove all this way."

My eyes narrow, getting ready to kick them out, long trip be damned, but Hendrix turns his blue eyes back on Melody and nods once. "Stay in the den or the dining room, please. No wandering the house. And sign this."

I narrow my eyes at him as Jefferies steps forward and gives them all an NDA to sign.

They all proceed to follow him out the foyer, but I hang back to see what my girl is going to do. Just as they reach the doorway to the den, her steps falter, and she looks back over her shoulder, meeting my eye. I stay right where I am and watch her carefully.

For one long drawn out moment, everything falls away, and it's just me and her.

My heart beats heavily in my chest watching as she half turns, the tassels in her dress swaying with her movements. The muscles in her legs stand out as she pivots easily back around to face me.

"Are you coming?" she asks.

I push off the wall and stalk towards her, stopping when I'm by her side. I turn my face to look down at her, seeing her eyes light up, like she's so innocent. But I know better, we both do.

"You keep your hands off Leo," I say, "Or I swear to God, Melody."

Her brow arches as a disbelieving look crosses her face. "Or *what,* Mason?"

A muscle twitches in my jaw as her eyes narrow at me. I lean forward, snatching her by her wrist and taking her in the opposite direction of the den. I ignore her soft protests as her heels click loudly on the marble floor as I work to lead her down the hallway and to the opposite side of the house where we won't be disturbed.

Opening the door to a random sitting room, I pull her through and close the door harshly behind us. *"You know what,"* I growl, my eyes flash as I spin around to face her. My patience finally snapped. *"You know what the fuck you do to me."*

There's a tense moment of silence where she breathes hard, staring at me. It's like a key sliding into a lock and her eyes narrow. "Mason, what are you *t-talking* about-"

"I want you, Melody," I say harshly, my heart pounding against my ribcage.

An awkward silence ensues as my words echo throughout the room. Her eyes widen, and I take a step forward, effectively breaking her from her spell.

"If you want me, then do what it takes to have me, Mason," she snaps. Her usually soft voice is firmer, but I know her. It's also laced with hurt.

"I do want you," I stress, taking another step forward.

Her eyes well up with tears. *"No, you don't!"*

I grab her by her elbow, pushing her the few feet to the door behind her. Her back hits it with a thump, and a gasp escapes her lips as I crowd her space. I press myself into her body, catching a groan in my throat at the feel of her curves against me.

"Enough," I rasp, looking down into her eyes and feeling a muscle jump in my jaw as I clench my teeth hard. "I've been driven crazy for as long as I've wanted you-"

"No, you don't," she hits back at me, narrowing her eyes. "If you wanted to you would have-"

"Melody, stop fighting this!" I exclaim harshly. "The rest doesn't matter anymore. I want you, and I know you want me; don't try to hide it." Her breathing becomes labored, and she stiffens against me as I tilt her head up with a finger under her chin.

"Mason..." Her breath hitches as the anger melts from her eyes, instead becoming hooded with desire, and I swipe my thumb over her trembling bottom lip. Finally so close to what I've coveted for so long. "Mason, we *sh-shouldn't.* They're all waiting for us-"

"No. I've waited long enough...," I say quietly. "So they can wait, too."

Melody's hands come up to my chest and fist my shirt in her slender fingers while I move my hand to her nape and grip her tightly. Desperately. Forcing her head to tilt up so I can stare in her eyes for a few drawn out seconds before lowering my head, and brushing my lips against hers. Finally.

Her lips move against mine, whisper soft, our kiss hesitant and slightly unsure.

Heat blooms inside of me so hot that I have no doubt she feels it too. My entire *being* lights up at the feel of her lips.

I pull back, catching her eye, seeing her desire mirroring mine.

My heart pounds even harder, and I flick my tongue out to lick her bottom lip before covering her mouth with mine, slanting my mouth against hers and deepening our kiss. Melody moans, her lips parting to allow my tongue to sweep along hers. My skin tingles as she shivers against me, her nipples distending and pressing into my chest, sharpening my desire to a ruthless edge.

My fingers tremble against her. Almost four fucking *years* I've waited for this moment.

Groaning, I tighten my fingers, tilt her head to the side and lick even deeper. God, she tastes amazing. We kiss for what feels like forever, our bodies pressed tightly together, rocking against one another as we explore each other's mouths greedily. My hands sink into her hair and hers grip my neck as we strain together. Trying to get closer.

It isn't until my hand slides from her hair to cup her left breast, and she lets out a needy whimper that I come back down to earth. Cognizant we've been alone for an unusual length of time, I pull away and wait patiently until her eyes open. She blinks almost sleepily, like she's in a daze.

I place my forehead against hers, exhaling a deep breath, squeezing her plump flesh in my hand, and feathering my thumb against her distended nipple.

"You taste like heaven, but God knows you're built for sin," I say roughly.

"It's about fucking time," she whispers, looking up at me with complete trust. "What took you so long, Mase? I thought you didn't... didn't *want me like that."*

I fill with shame. The admission that she wanted me as much as I wanted her all this time throws a dark cloud over our first kiss.

"I'm sorry." Bringing my hand from her breast, I stroke my knuckles down her cheek and implore with my eyes for her to forgive me. "I'm so sorry. I wanted you more than anything. However, you can thank my brother for why I haven't made you mine yet."

She gasps, and much like when Hendrix walks in a room and sucks all the fun out, all the arousal she was just feeling disappears in a nanosecond. The heat between us becomes non-existent.

At least from her end, and I know I just fucked up.

Big time.

Her eyes scrunch together, and her head recoils slightly. *"What do you mean?"* she says shakily, her eyes flickering between mine.

"Hendrix forced me to not take you when I wanted you," I say. "It's because of him I haven't had you sooner. And I've wanted you a long, *long* time, Melody. Since the moment I met you."

And just like that, I watch all the passion drain from her face as a new understanding drapes her features.

Fuck.

CHAPTER 15

AN UNDERSTANDING

"GET AWAY FROM ME," I snap, pushing hard at Mason's chest.

My eyes well up with angry tears, and I step to the side and walk deeper into the room, putting some much needed space between him and me, and get myself away from being trapped against the door. I wrap my arms around my torso, trying to take in what he's just told me.

"Mel," Mason says, hurt sounding as rejection drapes his features.

He'd never quite mastered covering up his emotions like his brother. No, Mason wears his heart on his sleeve. He stands there, sliding his hands in his pockets and regarding me with a serious, albeit sober look.

"No," I turn to face him, folding my arms and shaking my head when he goes to take a slow step towards me. "You don't get to fucking sound hurt. *I'm* the one who gets to sound hurt!" I half yell, taking a step back when he doesn't stop advancing towards me. I hold up a hand, palm facing him. "You and your brother had *no right-"*

"I know," he grits out harshly. "Mel, I *fucking know!* But he-"

"-making fucking decisions for me," I yell, finishing my sentence. I narrow my eyes and take another step back. "That's why you've been waiting so long?" My lips tighten as my eyes narrow at him. "Because of *them?* All they've been doing for the both of us is fucking making decisions about everything! *Everything!"*

Mason shoves a hand through his hair and throws me an exasperated look. "Melody, you know more than anyone that I understand what you're saying because for *years* I felt stifled by my brother and father." He takes a step towards me and narrows his eyes. "But you have to see that he thought it was for your own good-"

"For my own good?" I interrupt, recoiling my head and narrowing my eyes. "For my own good, Mason? I couldn't even fucking go to the college I wanted, and you're trying to tell me that it was for my own good? I can't walk around like a free person, always being followed. I couldn't date for the last three years, because everyone I talk to *goes fucking missing-"*

"Melody, calm down-"

"No!" I snap. "Fuck you, Mason! I've been feeling like I've been going crazy for years because of *you!* My emotions all over the place, up and down. Does he like me? Does he not like me?" I throw my hands to the side and give him a pointed look. "I was so fucking confused that I actually convinced myself I was losing my mind. And then every time I tried to move on, every boyfriend I tried to involve myself with went missing!" I shout, my eyes going wide.

A guilty look clouds his features as he flushes, and I know without him saying anything that it was him. He did this.

"Was it you?" I half whisper, taking a hesitant step forward my anger deepening at the trapped look on his face. "Answer me."

His eyes are equal parts angry and guilty, his hands come to rest on his hips, and a muscle ticks in his jaw. He searches the ground for a minute, but still he doesn't say anything.

"Tell me the truth. Was it you?" My eyes narrow. "Did you make all those men disappear?" When he takes a deep breath, I step forward and gesture an arm at him. *"Dammit, Mason, tell me the fucking truth-for once!"*

"Yes! Okay?" he yells, bring his hands up to grip his hair. "It was me. I paid them off to leave you alone." His hands drop, and he scoffs, turning away from me and beginning to pace.

"Why?"

"I didn't want them touching you. *Obviously."*

"Why?!" I shout, my hands trembling as my irritation sparks.

He throws me an irritated look before turning away, continuing to pace. "I was waiting for you because Hendrix made me promise. Because he wanted me to prove to him that I was serious about you." He turns imploring eyes on me. Eyes that are angry but also filled with sadness.

I clench my teeth, my breath shooting hard and fast through my nose. "Why, Mason?"

"Because I fucking love you!" he shouts, his voice cracking causing my heart to skip a beat. I take a fast step back, shocked at the raw fury in his eyes. "But he was worried that you were just a plaything to me, and that I was going to use you up and toss you aside."

Tears fill my eyes and my jaw drops because the Mason *I* know would never do that to me. And it causes my wrath at Hendrix to burn even hotter.

He and my sister deserve each other.

My heart flutters for more than just the anger I have at Hendrix and my sister. Mason just confessed to loving me. Words I'd daydreamed about hearing more times than I care to admit. I become quickly overwhelmed at the riot of sensations crashing over me, and I know I have to leave. I need to get some space.

I hold up a hand, just over it.

"Say what you want; I'm not interested in hearing any more. Thank you for the truth, but I'm done. I didn't even want this dinner party. I'm out."

I walk towards the door, gasping as I'm spun around hard to face him. His fingers tighten hard on my elbow, pulling at my skin.

"Melody, *I just told you I loved you."* His voice is hoarse as his eyes search mine, pleading.

Wanting something I'm too scared to give him. It's too fresh.

Narrowing my eyes at him, I struggle against him. *"And I said I'm leaving."*

"You're not going anywhere," he snarls. His brow is furrowed and a muscle clenches in his jaw betraying how on edge he is.

I rip my elbow from his grip and look him up and down. *"Says who?* The man who let his brother dictate to him how to go about his business? And then I'm supposed to just sit idly by and wait for someone to tell *me* what to do with *my* life?" Ignoring the hurt that flashes across his face, I take a step into him. "I'm a grown woman, and I'm done letting people make decisions for me. So," I tilt my head as his eyes harden. "I'm going out there, I'm telling our parents thank you, and I'm leaving to go bar-hopping with my friends. I'm done with this, and I'm done with *you!"*

I turn and run to the door, hearing him close on my heels.

"Mel," he bites out, but I walk even faster through the hallway, evading his hands as I cross the foyer and into the den where everyone is mingling.

They all turn their heads to look at me in shock as I bust through the threshold with Mason two feet behind me, slapping his hands away.

I don't acknowledge any of them.

I mean it. I'm done.

"Melody? Are you okay?" Isobel says, struggling to get off the couch with a concerned expression on her face.

King takes her hand and helps pull her up, but I ignore her, finding Karissa instead who's in conversation with Brian and Mason's mother and father. I see Isobel's face drop, turning confused, but I don't have it in me to reassure anyone.

I'm too angry, and they're *all* the source of it.

"Karissa, let's go," I snap.

Karissa turns to me, getting ready to speak, but she snaps her mouth shut quick and raises a brow when Mason appears right next to me.

"Melody, can you please relax and just talk to me?" Mason comes around to my front and tries to catch my eye, but I turn my face from him.

I'm just too caught up in my feelings right now.

"Hey, what's up, Mel... Are you good?" Leo says slowly, standing nearby with a shot of vodka. I eye him for a second before turning my face back to Mason.

"Can you pour me a shot too, Leo?" I address Leo, seeing Mason's jaw clench.

"Sure."

Mason's eyes narrow, and his features settle into something scary.

Dismissively, I turn from him and walk over to Leo, taking the shot he hands me before turning back to Mason, narrowing my eyes back in anger.

"I decided to give *Leo* my first drink."

The air suddenly becomes so chilly that my skin breaks out in goosebumps, but I don't care.

Mason's lips tighten, and he looks so angry that I'm sure he's going to snap at any moment. But he stays quiet, the fury emanating from him letting me know all I need to know about how he really feels, despite him exercising a massive amount of self-control.

Seeing Mason step forward quickly, I tilt my head to shoot it right as he reaches forward to snatch it from my hand. His fingers circle my wrist hard, and he makes a rough sound in his chest as he yanks at my arm to try and stop me.

We grapple against each other for a second. Some of the liquor spills down my chin and drips onto my chest, but most of it got into my mouth, thankfully. His hand tightens on my wrist as he jerks hard, ripping the shot glass away with his other hand, and it clatters to the floor a few feet away. I lash out, slapping him across the face with my free hand.

Everyone gasps, but I turn my head quickly, coughing against the burn.

"Melody! What the hell is going on?" Isobel shouts, but I ignore her.

I swipe the back of my free hand across my mouth, wiping the vodka off before pinning Mason, who looks absolutely murderous at me, with an equally irate look. My eyes flicker seeing a red mark on his cheek where I've slapped him, and I grit my teeth, feeling feral as his fingers tighten even more on my wrist.

"I also decided to not have your bodyguard follow me," I hiss at him. "Because that's not going to be the last *first* I give away tonight."

The room plunges into absolute silence at my admission.

In my peripheral vision I see Karissa's jaw drop; however, my eyes are firmly on Mason who currently looks like he's made of stone. A look I've never seen before turns his face from one of anger to downright evil. He gets in my face, his minty breath fanning over my lips he's so close.

"Over. My. Fucking. Dead. Body," he snarls, making my blood run hot.

"What's happening?" Leo asks, sounding confused.

Mason and I both ignore him. I refuse to answer either one of them.

"You can't stop me," I breathe, my face defiant as I stare at him unblinkingly.

"Are you willing to bet on that, butterfly?" he says just as quietly, his eyes hard as he looks down into mine, letting me know how serious he is. "I'll break your goddamn legs if you spread them for that son of a bitch."

We commence to staring each other down while we wait one another out. His eyes bore into mine intimidatingly, but I hold my ground because a point needs to be proven. Hendrix takes a couple steps towards me, both his brows raised.

"Mason-"

"Fuck off, Hendrix"

He tries to speak to me. "Melody, I get you're upset, but you need to have security-"

"Hey, Henny," I quip, snapping my head over and giving him a nasty look. *"Fuck you."*

Hendrix frowns, looking down at Isobel to whisper something indescribable to her. She mouths 'no' and shakes her head, holding her hand to her belly.

My mom steps closer, worry etched on her face. "Baby, what is going on? *Why are you acting like this?"*

I raise my eyebrow and point at Hendrix. "Ask *him.* Since he knows everything." I turn to Mason's parents, whose eyes are pinging from mine to Mason's, and to Hendrix who's expression changes from confusion to a slightly sheepish and guilty look as it dawns on him that I know. "I'm leaving. Hope you all enjoy *my birthday,"* I grit out, jerking my wrist from Mason's hand with effort, and turn towards Karissa. "Let's go, please."

I walk around Mason who turns smoothly to fall into step behind me as I make my way back to the foyer. "Do not walk out that door, Melody," he says quietly.

"Fuck you," I whisper, breezing through the front door, into the night air, carefully making my way down the stairs and towards Karissa's car.

"Mel-"

"Mason!" I hear Hendrix's deep, stern voice ring out, and I glance over my shoulder to see Karissa, Leo and Brian appear through the door behind him and hurry down the steps.

Mason pauses, turning to look behind him, but I keep going until I'm at the passenger door, jumping in the seat when she unlocks it.

A second later, they all get in with a flurry of questions and slamming doors, but my attention is on the front of the house where Mason is yelling at Hendrix. Hendrix says something back, pointing a finger at Mason, and then Mason hauls off and punches Hendrix in the face.

Karissa starts the car, but she doesn't move to drive, riveted to the fight breaking out. Everyone's quiet for a moment, blatantly staring at the spectacle I so thoughtlessly created.

"Damnnn," Brian says, "Melody, what the hell happened in there when you were talking to Mason?"

"You want to know what happened, Brian?" I say lightly, watching as Hendrix throws a punch at Mason, who ducks quickly, and then tackles him to the ground.

"Yes," Brian says incredulously. "You two look like you *hate* each other. What the hell did he say to you?"

"Yeah," Karissa says, glancing over me quickly. "Everyone wants to know. It was obviously bad, whatever it was."

I turn my face from the sight of Mason's father and Brody tearing the two men apart, and look out the front windshield as we begin to creep alongside the other parked cars and pass the beautifully decorated fountain.

"I stopped giving a fuck. That's what happened," I say, closing my eyes.

There's silence for exactly twenty seconds before Leo leans forward between the two of us in the front seat. "So where are we off to now?" he asks. "Is the night over?" I pry an eye open to look at him. "I hope not," he says suggestively.

I close my eyes again, because I'm not planning on fucking Leo, no matter what I insinuated back there. I was just being difficult.

"Bar One," I answer. "I intend to make the most of my birthday."

"Alright, birthday girl. Your wish is my command." Karissa sings, picking up speed as we leave the pea gravel to the asphalt driveway.

I'M TRYING TO MAKE THE BEST OF IT,
BUT IF I COULD TELL YOU THE TRUTH,
I WOULD LET YOU KNOW-
IT BREAKS MY HEART, STILL, EVERY DAY,
TO LIVE IN A WORLD WHERE THERE'S NO YOU.

M. BROOKES

CHAPTER 17

WELL, FUCK.

WALKING INTO THE FOYER, I turn wild eyes to my brother, who's holding a handkerchief to his cheek where I split it open.

"This is your fault!" I yell, pointing a finger at him. *"Goddamn you, Hendrix!"* My eyes narrow to slits, and I roughly shrug off my father who's put a firm hand on my shoulder to hold me back. *"Get off."* I snap, jerking to the side and putting distance between myself and the rest of my family. *"Fuuuck!"* I shout, losing it.

"Mason, get a hold of yourself," my father says sternly.

Turning away from them, I put my fingers to the bridge of my nose and squeeze as I take a deep breath, more furious than I've ever been in my life.

Turning back, I see mine and Melody's bodyguard hanging out by the powder room, talking. "Hey Stephen," I snap, waiting until he puts his eyes on me. "I don't give a fuck *what* she said. You get your fucking ass on her tail, and do what I pay you to do, *now!"*

"Yes, sir," he says respectfully, nodding at my guard, Dante, who slides his eyes to the wall and keeps them there. Stephen walks past all of us, not meeting our eyes.

"And let me know when you've got eyes on her," I say. "I'm coming to get her later tonight."

"Yes, sir." Stephen slips through the door hurriedly.

There's a tense silence as everyone looks at each other. The only ones who don't have a confused expression would be me and my fucking brother, Hendrix.

Who I hate so very much right now.

I slide my hands in my pocket, gripping the paperclip I keep there to remind myself to stay in control. I dig the sharp point under my fingernail as I catch Hendrix's eye and take a step forward. He eyes me warily, and Isobel steps into his side, arching a brow. "Mason, what's wrong-"

"If you just cost me the love of my life, *I will kill you,"* I say to Hendrix, interrupting Isobel. "Do you understand me, *brother?* I will make her ass a fucking *widow."*

His brows rise, but he stays silent.

"Hendrix," Isobel gasps, her fingers flying to her mouth as her eyes widen in shock, but I ignore her, letting Hendrix know with everything in me I'm dead serious. He doesn't get to have everything *and* his happily every after, while I lose Melody after I just spent the last three and a half years putting my head down and doing everything possible asked of me.

I'll *kill* him. With a smile on my face.

"Son," my father says stepping forward, his own eyebrows furrowing as a shocked expression clouds his features. As does everyone else. Because they didn't know.

No one knew but me and Hendrix.

"I told her I loved her," I say in a choked voice. *"And she didn't even say it back."*

Father lets out a muted curse, putting a hand to his forehead and rubbing on a sigh.

"Mason," Madre says gently, stepping to my side and puts a hand on my arm, but her touch doesn't soothe me. "Mase, you love Melody? For how long?"

"Since the moment I met her," I answer simply, staring my brother down as I work the hardest I've ever done in my life to control myself. There's only one reason I'm not slitting this man's throat right now, and she's in Donna's arms.

Melody's mother Donna puts a hand to her mouth, but she stays quiet as she stands off to the side, holding Hendrix and Isobel's toddler Mariah. His goddamn saving grace.

"I told him to wait until she's done with college before picking her up," Hendrix explains.

Madre turns her face sharply to the side. *"You interfered?"* She inhales sharply, puts her hand to her throat, tilting her head as she glances quickly at father. They trade a look.

Validated, I lift my chin a little higher, maintaining our eye contact.

Father's face is the picture of fury as he turns his head to face Hendrix, his eyes betraying a deep anger I haven't seen come from him in a minute.

"You know better. *You know to not interfere, Hendrix,"* he barks, the color rising in his face. "You know our rules! *You know what's at stake!"*

he says in a rough, harsh tone, pointing a finger at Hendrix's face. "You know something like this can tear a family apart!"

"Oh my God," Madre whimpers, bringing up her hands to cover her nose and mouth. "Richard, don't," she whispers.

Donna looks over at her perplexed, before turning her eyes to Isobel who just shakes her head in a slight movement.

"Father, I did what I thought was best. I'm sorry," Hendrix shoves an agitated hand through his hair and gesturing to me. "You know how I've been killing myself my entire fucking life to make sure that Mason stays on the straight and narrow. Cut me some slack *for once!"* he shouts, the bass in his voice echoing around the foyer.

A hush falls over the foyer so quiet I hear the grandfather clock in the distance ticking away. That's not good.

Anger swamps me at his words; however, heat crawls up my neck as my eyes ping back and forth between the two men, because Hendrix has never dared to challenge Father before, and why he has to do it *right now* has got me ready to kill him for a different reason. The insensitive fuck.

It always has to be about him.

Father's brow goes so low *I* take a cautious step back. *"Cut you some slack?"* he parrots. "Has being married cost you your goddamn sense, boy?"

Isobel goes pale, her fingers digging into Hendrix's arm.

A muscle clenches in Hendrix's jaw. "How dare you speak to me this way after I have given *everything* to this family," Hendrix challenges father in a rough voice, pulling from Isobel's arm and daring to take a step towards him. "I've given everything to *you!"*

Father tilts his head, his lip curling as he takes a step forward now, too. But I'm not having it; for far too long everything's been about them and never me. Currently, I'm hurting.

I'm the one wronged right now.

Seriously offended, I feel my face heat up with anger at the audacity my brother and father have to square off at *this exact* moment.

"I don't need you to babysit me, Hendrix!" I growl, taking a threatening step forward and shoving my sleeves up my arms. About to beat his ass. Both he and father turn their heads to me, but I keep my eyes on Hendrix. "Don't you dare fucking credit yourself with everything *I've* done these last four years, asshole," I pound my fist against my chest. *"I've* put in the goddamn work and made something of myself *by myself,* without either one of you, might I remind you! You fucking *piece of shit!"*

Hendrix gets a shocked look in his eye at my harsh admission.

Isobel's chin quivers as a tear slides down her cheek, and as Donna steps back a few paces with Mariah, Teresa walks over to her and whispers something in her ear. Donna nods, handing off Mariah to Brody who has Vi in his other arm, and they disappear down the hallway.

"I have more than proven myself," I say, narrowing my eyes. My heart pounds, and my eyes fill with tears it almost kills me to fight back. My words come out rapidly and harshly. "I have *more* than earned a place within this family. *A place that wasn't just handed to me!* And all either of you two have done is discredit me, belittle me, and make sure every step along the way *you remind me of how worthless I am! And I am through. I'm done, you hear me? I want nothing more to do with this fucking family."*

Madre starts crying, and father steps to her, pulling her under his arm.

"Now, hold on, son," Father says, a flash of hurt entering his eyes and his voice thickens with emotion. "Just wait a second, Mason. You don't have to-"

"No-" I slash my hand through the air, feeling sick. "I've been holding on my whole life, Father. What don't you fucking get about that? I finally got something to love, something for *me.* And because it had to be on *his* terms, she's gone!"

Father's head snaps to Hendrix. "Explain yourself. *Now! And it had better be good,"* he says to Hendrix in a deathly serious voice that causes the hair on the back of my neck to stand up.

Hendrix's face flushes slightly. "She's Isobel's sister, and I didn't want her to be hurt. Is that not good enough?" He turns sharp eyes on me before facing our parents once again. Madre's curled in on herself, and Father looks as if he's going to lunge at Hendrix. I frown, because that's different. "And in case none of you remember," Hendrix snaps, "Mason wasn't exactly in the best position when they first met. Neither was she; she was *sixteen."*

That's it. My eyes narrow.

"Almost seventeen, and a year after that I could have picked her up *then,"* I snap, slapping my fist into my palm. "She has been waiting for me, and *I never showed up!"* My voice cracks, betraying just how deep this goes for me. "Now she doesn't trust me! I've lost her tonight, Hendrix, in case you hadn't got a fucking clue."

"Wait, I'm sorry... but I'm so confused," Donna speaks up now, walking closer. "Why do you keep saying 'picked up?' What's that supposed to *mean?"*

I let out a curse, forgetting no one formally told Donna how this family procures their spouses.

My sister Teresa steps over to her, taking her by the arm. "Come on, Donna," she says softly. "I'll explain to you in the study. Let's let them figure it out, and we can call Melody and make sure she's okay."

I feel myself deflate with relief that they're going to check on her, knowing Teresa will always step in.

"Mason, *I'm sorry,"* Hendrix stresses, stepping towards me.

"Get the hell away from me. I don't want a fucking apology," I bellow. "I want you to stop interfering, and leave the two of us alone." My eyes slide to Isobel, who's looking at me with a mixture of pity and anger. "Except you, I'd never ask you to leave your sister alone," I stress. Putting my eyes back on Hendrix I stiffen my spine. *"But you?* Stay the fuck out of our business."

He tightens his lips, but wisely stays quiet.

"I'm going to go pick her up, and I would appreciate it if *none of you* call me for a while."

The party effectively ruined, I tear my eyes away and make my way around them to the front door where I climb into my car and take out into the night. I look in my rearview mirror, seeing Dante tailing me. His headlights flash just as my dash lights up with a message.

> She's at Bar One, sir. -Stephen

The location pops up, but I ignore it, calling Dante instead.

"Yes, sir," he answers.

"Dante, I need you to call the maintenance guy at Melody's dorm, and let him know we're coming and need to be let into her room. We're moving her out while they're partying so we'll need to stop by the store and get some boxes."

"Yes, sir, I'll call him now."

"Thank you, Dante. Let Stephen know to inform me when they're about to head on their way back."

"Yes, sir."

I hang up, seeing my phone light up with a text from Isobel.

> Mason, are you okay? -Izzy

I throw my phone in the console, irritated. Turning my radio on and ignoring my phone pinging repeatedly as I speed my way back into the city.

"Here," I huff. Piling a small box housing her makeup on top of the stack by the door, I tape it carefully. "I think that's almost everything, I just have to clear out her nightstand, and I'd rather do that myself. Go ahead and start taking these to the car," I say to Dante, dusting my hands together and looking around the small room.

"Yes, sir. I'll start loading mine up first," he says, grabbing the first two boxes and backing out the door.

I fold my arms for a second, taking a slight break. Not quite believing that I'm getting ready to take her to my home.

To our home.

I hope she likes it. It's a lot different than this bachelorette pad, that's for sure. She had way more stuff than I'd originally thought. Kettlebells and yoga mats stashed under the bed, a small collapsible treadmill, and so many tennis shoes and workout clothes I thought I was going to go crazy after I folded the thirtieth pair of leggings.

I grab a box and make my way to her nightstand, getting a half chubby at the prospect of finding a sex toy or two in there. She'd just got one a few days ago.

I open the drawer, disappointment filling me that all I see is a few pens, some sanitary pads, and sticky notes. A necklace I'd given her for her eighteenth birthday is still nestled in its velvet box.

My eyes go back to the sanitary pads.

I've found several of these all over her side, but no tampons. I wonder why. I begin to load the contents of her drawer in the small box, making a mental note to remember the necklace is in here and wondering if I should ask her about her preference of pads over tampons. Or, is this even a man's business? I don't know. I'll ask Teresa.

I glance over at her pillow, wondering if she stashes her toy there. I run my fingers under her pillow, pausing as I hit something hard. I flip her pillow, seeing a small leather journal. I look back towards the door, hearing Dante come back in and grab two more boxes and leave again.

I sit on the small bed, holding the journal and feeling such a connection with her because I journal as well, and neither one of us knew that about the other. It burns in my hands, begging me to open it and read it.

It's a horrible invasion of privacy, but really, is it any worse than moving a person out of their home without permission?

Rifling through their clothes and intimate things?

I flip to the first page, seeing her first journal entry was almost four years ago around the time when she first met me. Curiously, I begin to flip through the pages only focusing on the dates at the moment. The dates are sporadic, she isn't an everyday writer.

The journal spans three and a half years.

Her handwriting is a beautiful cursive, with cute flourishes.

I go back to the first entry, just needing to know.

September 20th

I met King's brother today, he's so handsome.

Darker skin like mine, Spanish. Thick curly hair, full lips. Smooth as hell accent. Eyes that seem to see into the depths of my soul. He put his hand on my leg and I was so flustered I didn't know what to do.

He's twenty five.

I wonder if he knows how shy I am? How nervous. Or if that even bothers him? I've never even had a boyfriend before. I can't believe I feel this way about someone almost ten years older than me.

So stupid.

xoxo

The joy I felt at her mentioning me dampens at how disparagingly she talks about herself. I frown, turning to the next page and feel my heart squeeze realizing she documented the time Isobel was kidnapped.

Guilt swamps me, and my fingers shake as I try to keep the journal steady.

October 7th

Izzy's gone. Someone took her.

I won't be anything without her. She was my everything.

October 19th

Mason made me eat today. I threw it up almost immediately.

October 29th

They still haven't found her. The only way I'm able to sleep is in Mason's arms. I don't think I'm ever going to see her again. I don't want to run anymore. I don't want to do anything.

I don't want to be here.

The guilt begins to eat me alive. I drag a hand down my face, cupping my jaw for a minute remembering we'd almost had to sign her into a rehab. That was the longest day and night of my life, her pleading and begging not to be sent away.

The next page is a journal entry depicting me getting her the diamond necklace I'd just packed up. I flip and flip, seeing her feelings on not going to the college she originally wanted in California because Isobel and Hendrix wanted to keep her close. As did I.

She was so upset. The page looks a bit stiff in spots from tear stains. I remember the day they told her she had to stay in New York for her safety. I was so torn. I told Hendrix I'd move to California with her to keep an eye on her, but that was shot down, too. He didn't trust me, he'd said.

I tilt my head, my lips curling in amusement at the sight of our names combined together. I run my fingers across the lines, my skin going hot.

Mason Antonio King and Melody Rachel King.

I stare at our names together far too long, thinking they look perfect. I'm glad she scratched out her maiden name, she wasn't going to be allowed to keep it anyway.

The next journal entry Melody speaks about her first boyfriend disappearing, thinking something happened to him. Then by the third boyfriend, she'd begun to believe she was the problem. That they were running from her. Rejecting her. All journal entries after that depict a Melody that I'd personally never seen before.

One who's deeply insecure, and very unhappy with herself.

I look up, thinking.

This is also the time she'd started to wear a lot of makeup.

I flip the next page, inhaling sharply at the depiction of an incredibly detailed sex dream she'd just had recently about me. My cock jerks against the tight confines of my pants, and I groan quietly, putting a hand to the ache and squeezing. Trying to get myself in check.

"Jesus," I mutter.

Hearing Dante come back in, I close the journal and shove it into the box with her things and tape the box shut. I check my phone, seeing it light up with an incoming text, and my blood runs hot with anger as I read the contents.

Headed to you now, should be there in fifteen. I just want to let you know, they stopped by his house for about thirty minutes before making their way back to the university. Her blonde friend left to go to her boyfriend's, so they were alone. -Stephen

Why the fuck didn't you call me and let me know? -Mason

I swear to God he's getting fired.

I did, boss. You didn't answer. -Stephen

Frowning, I scroll up and see he'd also texted me to let me know as well as called me three times, but my phone was on do not disturb because of the incessant ringing from my family members. I shake my head and force myself to take a deep breath.

When I'm wrong, I'm wrong.

I'll admit it.

Sorry, Stephen. Thank you. -Mason

I pocket my phone and grab the last three boxes, shutting the dorm door behind me. A student lingers in the hallway giving me a side eye as she sits on the floor on her phone. I ignore her, stepping over her legs and make my way to the stairwell where I make the short journey to my car and shove the boxes in the backseat.

I try to call Melody, but her phone goes straight to voicemail. Not wanting her to see me, I park further down the street and wait.

About ten minutes goes by before a dark green SUV turns a corner then parks next to the sidewalk. It's her and Leo. A minute later headlights shine in my side mirror before dimming. I look, seeing it's her bodyguard parking behind Stephen's car. Dante pulls out, headed to take Melody's things home.

Melody doesn't get out.

I watch them, seeing what they're about. I don't want to make my move in front of Leo but may have to. My heart begins to beat faster, the blood rushes in my ears, and my skin dots with goosebumps. It's finally time. I strum my fingers on the steering wheel, forcing myself to be patient.

I waited four years, surely I can wait a few more minutes.

I clear my throat. Looking at my watch, wondering what the fuck they're talking about. Ten minutes pass. Then twenty.

Her window lowers and I see her arm dangle out the car, looking like she's getting mighty comfortable at almost midnight.

Leo turns in his seat to face her better, and the brake lights go off as he turns the car off. My lips curl with displeasure as my patience finally comes to an end. I'm not going to sit here and watch them get chummy. I pull out my phone, calling Stephen.

"Sir?"

"I'm about to grab Melody. I need you to make sure Leo doesn't call the police or get in my way. Pay him off, whatever it takes," I say simply.

"Yes, sir."

I open the door, the sound almost sounding like a bullet going off, and make my way down the street to her side of the car, coming up from behind. I clock the side of her profile in the side mirror; her attention is so focused on him that she doesn't notice me.

Neither of them do.

I get to the window. "Time to go," I say sharply.

Her head snaps to the side and her mouth opens in a shocked scream, but I bend down quickly, grabbing her arm before she can retract it and lock down hard on her wrist. "Mason," she snaps, struggling against me. *"Mason, get off me!"*

"What the fuck, man? *What is your problem?"* Leo reaches over and tries to grab her arm, pulling as well. But I'm stronger. I don't bother with opening the door; instead, I yank her out of the car through the window, hoisting her into my arms.

"I said *let's go."*

Melody strains against me as I walk us to my car. Stephen runs past me. Leo's car door slams behind us, but I keep my focus on her. "I was on a date!" she hisses, irate.

Her eyes flash at me, but I give her an irritated look, letting her see the extent of my displeasure. Her eyes lose some of their fire, but not much. "You think I give a fuck about your date?" I emphasize, arching my brow at her. "You turned your back on me earlier. And what's more, you disappeared with him for half an hour while you ignored my phone calls."

"You deserved it!" she yells in my face.

I get the car door open and set her inside, grabbing the seatbelt and pulling it over her body.

"I got-*I got it!"* Melody snaps irritably, jerking it out of my hands and pushing my arm away. She turns, her hands shaking so hard she can't get it to click. I wait for a second before trying to reach in again, but she throws me a nasty look. *"I said I got it!"* she yells.

"Then act like it and snap the fucking seatbelt already!" I yell back, feeling my patience snap. "God, woman! What the fuck!"

It clicks, and she sits back tightening her lips together. Her eyes narrow at me, as I slam her car door, keeping her eye contact the entire time I walk around the car and get into the front seat.

"What?" I grit out, buckling my own seatbelt.

She recoils her head and scrunches her nose, giving me another nasty look. "Where are you taking me?"

"To my house."

"For what?" she snaps.

"You know what!" I growl, seriously hanging by a thread.

Her eyes go wide. She breaks our eye contact and sits back in her seat before turning her head to look in the backseat. "Where the fuck is all my *stuff? I had way more than those three boxes."*

I muffle an exasperated groan, feeling a headache gathering behind my eyes.

I start the car, pulling off. Breezing right by Stephen and Leo, who looks a little shell shocked at our car as we drive past. "The rest of it's in Dante's car; he's gone ahead of us to unload it."

She's silent again.

My fingers are so tight on the steering wheel my knuckles go white. We're both breathing heavily, upset with each other, and it's ten solid minutes into the drive before I dare to break the tension. "What were you doing at his house, Melody?"

"Nothing," her tone is short, too perfunctory for my taste.

"Nothing, huh?" I take a deep breath, blowing it out calmly through my nose. "What does *'nothing'* mean nowadays, Mel?"

Fuck, she knows I can't stand that word.

I'm met with silence.

"Did you fuck him?" I ask.

"It's none of your business."

"Hey, stop playin', Mel. I asked you a question that I want answered," I say quietly, looking over at her.

"And I said it was none of your *motherfucking business!"* she turns to pierce me with a stare so pissed that if it were any other person, they'd be getting jumped in my car. No lie.

My eyes snap to hers as I crawl to a stop at a red light around the corner from my building.

"Look at me," I say, keeping my voice even. It takes everything in me to act calm. I wait until her head turns, and her eyes find mine. "It would be easier for us both if you answer my questions now, because when I get you in the house, if you don't answer my questions, I'm going to *force* them out of you. Do you understand what I'm saying, Mel?"

She blinks, her face flushing slightly. "Maybe."

Her innocence cools me down just slightly.

Slightly.

I take a deep breath and wet my lips, seeing her eyes flit to them then back again. "Did you fuck Leo tonight, Mel?"

The silences stretches between us and the light turns green, illuminating her face. This time, I let her have her silence. I turn to face forward, drive us into the parking garage, and park in my space. I unbuckle my seatbelt, rubbing my hand along my jaw.

"Do you love me?" I ask quietly. Pulling my eyes from the concrete wall in front of us I turn my head and meet her eyes. She's staring at me like a deer caught in headlights. My eyes lower to where her hands lay in her lap, clenched so hard they're turning red. I look back up at her, covering her hands with my own. "It's a simple question, *much* simpler than the other one. But I need you to answer this one. Do you love me?"

"Yes," she says breathlessly. Her chin quivers, and she pulls her lips into an adorable pout, but she keeps my eye contact.

My heart skips a beat, my hand tightens over hers, and I let the warmth melt the ice of my ire before I answer her back. "I love you, too."

The lights in the car go off, and an eerie silence fills the small space. But she still doesn't look away.

I don't either.

I shift in my seat, draping my arm across my steering wheel in a relaxed stance, hoping it'll get her to open up.

"One more time, baby," I say calmly, fighting that anger always swirling deep down inside. "Did you fuck him?"

"What does it matter if I fucked him, Mason?" she whispers. "I'm sure you've fucked plenty of women since I've met you."

I lean forward, tucking a wayward curl behind her ear. "I haven't touched a single person since the day I met you, Mel. How could I, *hm,* when I had you to look forward to?"

"But.. but..." Her brows furrow, and I close the distance between us, pressing my lips to hers. Silencing her.

I kiss her slowly, feeling her hesitancy. Her fingers tremble under my hand, and brush my thumb softly over them.

I kiss her for long minutes, memorizing her taste and how she likes her tongue stroked. Finding out quickly that she doesn't like her top lip nipped, but she does like her bottom lip to be tugged on. Her skin is so soft, like the silk sheets upstairs in our bed.

The bed she's never even seen before but is her bed now. I didn't give her her own room like Hendrix did Isobel. I'm too selfish.

When I pull away from her mouth, she's panting lightly, and her lips are swollen.

I move my hand from her hands and cup her upper thigh, curling my fingers around and squeezing gently. I'm so close to her pussy I feel the heat warming my fingers. I massage her flesh, bunching it up in my fingers before releasing her, letting myself enjoy touching her before we go upstairs where it's no doubt about to become supremely uncomfortable.

Her breath hitches in her lungs; her eyes dilate and go hooded.

My dick is so hard.

I pull my hand away reluctantly.

"Let's go," I clear my throat, opening my car door and stepping out, making my way to hers and opening it. The sight of her long, toned legs in her pantyhose swinging from the car makes my mouth go dry and my dick twitch.

It's going to be a long night.

CHAPTER 18

TAKING IT

MASON GRABS THE BOXES from the backseat, and gestures with a jerk of his chin to proceed before him to the door that leads to the elevators. I walk silently, keeping my arms folded across my torso. I've never been here.

"How come you've never let me come here before?" I ask hesitantly.

"Because." He clears his throat softly. "You were underage when I bought the place."

"Oh," I say. But I can't really blame him, because the truth is I would have let him do whatever he wanted to me back then. And I think he knows that.

My eyes flicker around as I hold the door open for him to walk through and I press the elevator, waiting silently. It dings, and I go in first, followed close behind by Mason who is seething. I can tell.

The doors close and I wait a second. "Which floor?"

"Push the penthouse button," he says gruffly.

I roll my eyes at the *'duh, stupid'* in his tone.

"Shut up," I mumble under my breath, reaching forward.

It lights up as I press it then stand back, waiting patiently as we ascend about sixty floors before it opens into a beautiful hallway with a black and white checkered marble floor. I meet his eyes as the doors open, and he again stays quiet. I walk ahead of him, turning and seeing a white lacquered door at the end of the small hall lit up on both sides with modern lighting.

There's a table opposite the elevator doors with an ornate mirror, plants, and the color is a tasteful dark navy.

We make our way silently until we get to the door.

"Press it," he says, arching a brow and jerking his head to the door. Tilting my head down I look, not seeing what he's talking about. "The keypad on the left. You see the little rectangular box there in the side? Press your thumb to it." I bend down looking closer, seeing a small pad recessed into the trim, almost invisible. I press my thumb to it, hearing a muted beep and the lock click before the door swings open. "Welcome home, butterfly," he says with a ghost of a grin.

A thrill courses through me combating the nervousness. Steeling my resolve, I turn my face from his and walk into a modern foyer.

Mason comes in behind me with the boxes, shutting the door, and I walk a bit deeper into the lush, obviously expensive area. My eyes flicker everywhere, trying to take in this man's sanctuary. According to Hendrix over the last couple of years he's owned this place, he's only been allowed over four times as Mason tends to like his space.

"Take your shoes off," Mason says, dragging his eyes down my body.

This is not how Izzy described Hendrix taking her, at all. She said Hendrix dominated her almost like a lion, a wild animal. Mason's making me feel more like the mouse that gets squeezed to death by it's predator before it gets swallowed whole.

I roll my lips, stepping out of these ridiculously tall heels. I wiggle my toes as my feet touch the cool floor, and I take the lead now, walking through the foyer and into the rest of the penthouse. The lights are motioned-censored, and they pop on, dimming as we advance deeper into the penthouse.

Which is *huge.*

I'm a bit in awe; the smell of his apartment is clean, the air slightly cool.

We make our way into the living room where a large fireplace dominates the far wall, flickering blue-orange flames that illuminate the deep brown leather couches. It's decidedly masculine and Mason's style. He bends, putting the boxes on the floor next to the reclining chair.

"It's nice in here."

I rub my hands briskly up and down my arms.

He straightens and steps to me without a word, reaching out and snatching me up by my hand and pulling me through an archway and down an adjoining hallway. The further we venture down past the various closed doors of the hall the harder my heart begins to race, and I try to think of an excuse to not go to the bedroom because I'm so nervous I don't know what to do with myself.

"Mason," I say firmly, tugging at his grip on my wrist. "Wait, please. I want to see your place."

"I'm not giving you the tour right now. *Right now,* I'm getting some answers."

He turns a sharp right and takes me to the last door which he opens and leads me through, closing it. The snick of the lock causes my eyes to go wide, as does the sight of his bedroom.

His shoulder brushes mine as he walks by me, causing my anxiety to spike so high I feel my throat momentarily stick shut.

"You ready to talk now?" Mason tosses over his shoulder in a deceptively calm tone, almost like he could be asking me about my day. "I asked you a question back in the car that you wouldn't answer."

He meets my eyes for a moment, before walking to the ornate dresser and takes his cufflinks off, putting them carefully in a little holding dish. His watch comes off next. The matter-of-fact movements of him doing something so intimate renders me mute as I focus on his strong hands pulling his wallet out of his back pocket and undoing the leather bracelet on his left wrist.

"I think you know me well enough by now that I don't like repeating myself, nor do I like being ignored."

"Uh-huh." I clear my throat, tearing my eyes away in favor of casting a curious look around the bedroom. "And I think you know me well enough by now to know that I don't like being pushed, Mase."

He turns his body towards me, but I keep taking in my surroundings.

He's got a king-sized bed with the most expensive looking blue sheets I've ever seen, topped with a feather down comforter that's folded over to the middle of the bed almost. A huge mass of pillows dominate the bed by the headboard, and it's flanked by two matching floating nightstands.

A small chandelier hangs from the ceiling over the night stands, casting the area in a very soft, muted white glow. The walls are painted the same navy color of the foyer. There's thick carpet in here that makes it feel so homey, and the far side wall is nothing but floor to ceiling windows offering a beautiful view of the city with a slice of deep green Central Park on the left side to break up the concrete and glass of the city.

A bead of sweat trickles down the valley of my breasts. I nervously clench my fingers together and blow out a calming breath, bringing my eyes back to him. Mason places his hand on the top of the dresser and leans against it slightly, adopting an interesting position that I'm not used to, morphing before my eyes into something dangerous.

Powerful.

It's sexy, and I feel my pussy respond, clenching before becoming slick with need.

"Let's start with something a bit simpler than me asking if he fucked you." He folds his arms, staring hard at me. "Did he kiss you?"

I nod my head, feeling my eyes go wide.

"Hmm," Mason hums deep in his chest, his eyes hard on mine. The sound travels straight to my clit, making it throb with need. "What else did you *let* him have?"

A shiver runs down my spine, my skin flushes hot. Without looking, I can tell there are goosebumps on my arms and chest. I wet my lips nervously, the sexual tension between the two of us unbearably thick causing me to take a hesitant step forward, pleading with my eyes.

"He kissed me-"

"No," Mason interrupts, shaking his head once. A muscle twitches in his face as more of his displeasure comes through his features. "You *let* him kiss you. *Let,"* he corrects me. "Say it."

A thrill courses through me at his rough, stern tone. "Fine. I *let* him kiss me," I admit in a small voice.

My arms come up to cross over my torso, and I rub my thumbs across my sensitive skin, needing to be soothed. My eyes leave his to look anywhere and everywhere but at him. I'm too intimidated.

Too raw.

"Did you let him take your virginity?" he asks. "Because as of your last gynecologist appointment three weeks ago, you were still a virgin. And if you fucked that man tonight, I'm going to fuck *you* up."

All the air is suddenly sucked out of the room.

Out of my lungs.

"You know my *gynecologist* information?" I say incredulously.

His eyes narrow and he leans a little further on his hand. "There's not much I don't know about you, butterfly." Looking very pleased with himself, a devilish grin tips his mouth up, causing my heart to flutter. "So?" he asks. "What's it going to be?"

Our gazes clash, and I see he's dead intent on extracting every piece of information out of me tonight. He wants me bare for him, and I'm just now realizing that while I felt almost invisible for so long, that it was but a respite from the true him.

The wicked Mason.

The Mason who apparently won't rest until he has every piece of me, and then some.

I narrow my eyes, feeling the need to fight back. "You can try."

"Oh, butterfly." He scoffs. "I'm going to absolutely tear your beautiful cunt up *trying,"* he says so smoothly that I almost wonder if I imagined it.

My breath comes back in a rush.

Mason tilts his head and arches a brow as if he's waiting for me to respond; however, my bravado fades.

I tear my eyes from his and train them onto the floor between us, mortified and turned on beyond belief. I can't believe he said it like that, but with his words, he's left me no doubt at all about his intentions with me tonight.

He's planning on taking my virginity.

"M-Mason..." I stutter, feeling myself turning bright red, feeling my panties are soaked.

His head tilts. *"Hm?"*

I take an involuntary step back, then another and another until my heels sink into the plush rug of his bedroom. I keep my eyes down, unable to hold his eye contact any longer, and it's all I can do to keep my knees from knocking together.

I wanted this for so long that now I'm almost petrified that I have it.

I peek over at the bed, then look back to the floor digging my big toe into the carpet, suddenly hit with another dilemma. I don't know what to do with a man. I've never been with one. Sure, I've heard about it and understand it in a technical sense. Have craved it, even, because I couldn't have it.

But being within a man's presence like *this,* especially one like Mason?

I'm a little bit scared.

Mason won't tolerate the space between us because he closes the distance easily, coming close enough so I feel the fabric of his pants brushing against my legs. But still, he doesn't touch me.

"So, let's try this again. *I said,"* Mason emphasizes, weighing every word as he speaks slowly, "did you let him take what belongs to me?"

My belly tightens viciously, as does my throat, because I can't seem to be able to form a coherent sentence to save my life. However, despite my abject nervousness, that defiance that only seems to be present regarding him rears its head.

"It doesn't belong to you," I manage to whisper, bringing my eyes up to his. *"It doesn't be-"*

"I *dare* you to finish that sentence. You said it once; I won't let you get away with saying it a second time."

My breath hitches.

Furrowing my brow, I lash out at him, my voice rising. "Give me one good reason why I should let you fuck me, Mason. *One*. Tell me why I should even trust you?"

His eyes flash with anger so bright I attempt to take another step back; however, I'm hindered by the bench behind me.

"Because contrary to whatever the fuck you think, you belong to me," he growls in a rough voice that sends shock waves through my being.

"I don't bel-"

"Every fucking inch of you for the last four years has belonged to me, Melody!" he interupts me, raising his voice to match mine. "Every goddamn *breath* you take is mine, woman! Every move you make is because I fought for your freedom to have these things," his eyes narrow, and a pissed off look flashes over his face, morphing quickly into a confident expression. "You want to know the truth, Melody? Your sister didn't even *want* you to physically even go to college. She was setting up private tutoring so you wouldn't even be able to live on campus."

My lips tighten with the need to curse out that overprotective bitch.

"I fought for you to go to that school, when they didn't want you to go. *I* pleaded with them to take into consideration how hard you worked for that fucking track scholarship when they wanted you to throw it away because '*we could afford better than that.*'" He mimics Hendrix's voice. "It didn't matter we had the money to send you a thousand times over; I knew it'd make you happy for you to be able to feel like you had contributed to your education." He takes another step forward, pounding his fist to his chest, his eyes flashing. "I fought for you when you didn't have a seat at the fucking table where decisions were being made for you. *For four goddamn years* I've inserted myself

in every aspect of your life, and you didn't even have a clue because I was trying to keep the peace within my family."

"Why?" I ask in a shaky breath, forcing myself to speak through the anger at my sister. *"Why, Masey?"*

"Because I saw how bad you took it when Isobel was gone. And I knew I couldn't hurt you like that by tearing us apart. You fucking belong to me, and you would be wise to not test my patience by insinuating otherwise. So yeah, I'm fucking you. You got anything else to say about it?"

I'm so shocked I can't speak.

The silence stretches taut between us as we spend a long few seconds staring each other down. Anger fights red-hot desire as my pussy clenches greedily. The material of the dress presses into my skin uncomfortably as my breasts, unhindered by a bra, swell with my arousal.

Finding my voice, I stare at him, embarrassed. "Mason, *I-I didn't know..."*

His eyes soften slightly. "I know, baby. I know you didn't. And I'm sorry things have been so hard on you."

At the reminder of just how hard, I nod, folding my arms and cutting myself off emotionally from him. "So, you understand, then, when I say that maybe- *maybe this just isn't going to work."*

The softness dissipates like it never was there to begin with.

My heart begins to pound at the hungry, damn near animalistic look on his face; however, it's *his* turn to go silent. And even though I didn't necessarily mean those words, there's something inside me that feels safe enough to push back with him. All the frustration I've harbored about everything comes out against him.

"You might have done all those things, Mason, but what have you done to prove to *me* that you deserve me? All that shit was done in secret. *Behind my back!* I didn't know any of that was going on."

He arches a brow, pulls his hands out of his pockets and shrugs out of his suit jacket, letting it fall to the floor carelessly. I blink, rolling my lips as he undoes his tie. When his shirt and tie hit the ground I take a step to the side, over this insane tension. Ready to walk around him and out of this room, but he reaches out and snatches me back by a hand to the back of my neck, yanking me back in place.

He makes a low sound in his throat and brings me an inch from his face. His arm jerks hard as he discards his shirt from his left arm, keeping my face in place as it hits the floor with a muted rustle of fabric.

My jaw drops, and my eyes go impossibly wide as they lower to see my *fucking name* tattooed in an arch above his pelvis in big, black beautiful font with butterflies intermixed in the design.

Silently, my gaze travels back up every perfect, hard inch of him until I get to his eyes.

They're swimming in emotion, as they almost always are. Though, sometimes I swear I'm the only one that sees it. *Everything* has always been in his eyes.

And I suddenly want all that pent up *everything* expended upon my body.

"I'm going to explain something to you, Mel," Mason says in a rough voice, causing my nipples to pull unbearably tight at the sound. I don't remember ever hearing him sound like this- this desperate and depraved. "You're going to learn many things about me as time goes on. But your first lesson is when I want something..." He pulls me even closer until my thighs press into his and my breasts flatten against his chest. He narrows his eyes and leans in until our noses touch. My blood sings. *"I take it, regardless."*

He closes the last inch of distance, sealing his lips over mine in a rough, bruising kiss that has me crying out in his mouth.

My knees buckle at the first touch of his soft, velvety skin. But when he deepens it, parting my lips with his tongue, my legs finish holding me up at the first lick inside my mouth.

I collapse with a gasp, and my hands fly to his shoulders, clutching at him.

His hand tightens its grip on my jaw, and with his other hand he snatches me up in a fast movement, hitching my knee around his hip. As my feet leave the floor, I tremble at the feel of his hard body against mine and moan when he bites into my bottom lip and tugs, causing tingles to flood my body.

He's back quickly to my lips, tilting his head and kissing me deeply, groaning into my mouth.

"Come on, baby, kiss me back," he whispers into my mouth, using his hand at my jaw to tilt my head further to the side where he somehow kisses even deeper.

I touch the tip of my tongue to his hesitantly, whimpering as he sucks my tongue into his mouth. We attack each other's mouths hungrily. Instinctively knowing that each of us has what the other needs to calm this fire deep inside our cores.

It's happening. I can't believe it's happening.

He pulls away, our lips smacking. His eyes lower, straight to my heaving breasts. My nipples visibly distend against the fabric, and he licks his lips.

Silently, I put my hands to the back of my dress and undo the zipper. Letting my dress slip off my shoulders, and pool around my waist, still held up by my thigh which is hitched on his hip still. He stares at my naked breasts for a few tense seconds while my heart pitter patters weakly against my chest as insecurity threatens to take over.

I'm not near as well endowed as my sister. I count myself lucky to be a very small C cup, but he doesn't seem to mind, though. I notice his chest expands slightly with his breathing, his eyes dilate, and I'm struck by how needy he looks.

Right now, he makes me feel like the most desired woman alive.

"Do-" my breath catches in my throat, "do you like them?"

He says nothing.

Our eyes meet, and he loosens his hold on the back of my knee, letting me place my foot on the floor. My dress falls the rest of the way, leaving me standing in my thong and pantyhose. The slightly cool air of the room caresses my bare skin, making me hyper aware of my vulnerability, and heightening the stark power difference between the two of us.

He lets go of my jaw, and keeping my eye contact, he sinks to his haunches, hooking his fingers into the waist band of my pantyhose and thong. Lowering them slowly to my calves.

The fabric is soaked, rubbing along my legs as he pulls it down.

My hands immediately cover my pussy, and my gaze bounces from his eyes to the fireplace behind him and back again.

His nostrils flare, and his eyes go hooded. "Hmmm." Warm air puffs over my fingers as he sighs deeply. "You smell amazing."

Before I can think to say anything, he tugs my hands away, then moves forward to touch his nose to my bare mound, breathing deeply. My fingers sink into his hair, and I clutch the strands desperately as he runs his nose across my skin in a soft caress.

I'm so fucking thankful I shave.

"Of course I like them. You're so beautiful," he says. "Every single bit of you is beautiful to me, butterfly. Even this." His lips move to the three inch scar at my left wrist where I had to have a pin put in after I broke it a year and a half ago. "And this." His lips now move to my right thigh where he caught me cutting two summers ago, and I had to have stitches because I went too deep.

Mason's always been there for me. Has always seen and understood my pain.

I bite my lip, lifting up one foot, then the other, when he goes to remove my stockings and underwear. Mason pushes me back until my thighs hit the bench at the end of the bed, and I stumble, sitting on the cushioned fabric with a plop and giggle when he lowers to his knees before me. The fabric of his pants stretch tight against his thick thighs, and I'm struck, amazed at how sexy and just downright perfect this man is.

He's built like a fucking *god.*

The breath catches in my throat as he glances up at me with hunger in his eyes.

We maintain eye contact when he takes both hands and spreads my legs apart. My juices coat the inside of my thighs and trail down my ass with how aroused I am. I go to cover myself again, but he's faster, burying his lips into the bend of my knee. His shoulders rise with how deep of a breath he takes, then he moves his head to my lower tummy.

Licking across the crease of my mound with a low growl.

He licks and nibbles the bare skin of my mound then moves to my inner thighs, licking me clean. He gently bites my vulva, nipping and sucking one side before moving to the other. He ignores my clit for long minutes, sucking and using his teeth to scrape along my skin.

I burn hotter than I ever have. This feeling is worse than a four-mile run in the sun, and the heavy feeling in my lungs is almost like I've been out there for seven.

My clit pinches tight, throbbing incessantly. But every time I think he's going to pay attention to it, he switches tactics.

"Masoonnn," I whine, leaning my head back on the bed. I bring my hands to my breasts and squeeze hard, trying to alleviate the pressure. "Don't tease me. I need more."

"Not yet," he says simply, continuing to torture me. "Did you fuck him, Mel?" he asks.

Completely forgetting he still wanted an answer, I flush as he talks to me from between my legs. I stay silent, torturing him like he tortures me.

He sucks on the vein that runs on the inside of my right thigh. He uses his hands to massage my inner thighs, and his thumbs dig into the outside of my lips and press in, dragging upwards and repeating it over and over again, massaging my pussy.

At the first warm lash of his tongue up the seam of my pussy, my toes curl. When he flicks his tongue hard and slow against my clit, I make a soft sound in my throat, jerking at how good it feels. He eats me slowly. Thoroughly. Really making me feel every lash of his tongue against my tingling flesh.

He licks and licks until my orgasm swells then he pulls away right before I crest, looking up at me. *"Did you?"*

My breasts heave, and at my continued silence he lowers his head back down, licking harder. Getting me back to the precipice over and over again, until I'm drenched with sweat and my heart pounds wildly in my breast. My pussy clenches greedily on nothing.

I don't think I'm going to make it.

I give up. I never can win against him, no matter how hard I try.

"No," I whimper hoarsely as tears flood my eyes. *"You know I didn't, M-Mason."*

Finally, Mason sucks my clit into his mouth, staring into my eyes.

I'm so shocked my hand slaps against my mouth, and I arch my back in pleasure. *"Aaah!"* I yelp. My brows scrunch together, my mouth drops open, and I toss my head back on a sharp cry as I explode everywhere. My hands fly to his head, sinking into his hair. The tips of my nipples pinch unbearably tight, my body heats up and mists with a sheen of sweat as I orgasm hard.

Harder than I ever have before.

"No!" I gasp, flinching as my juices rush out of me, and he keeps sucking. I try to tilt my hips to get away, but he locks his hands hard on my thighs.

"Be still," he says. "Give me your eyes."

I look back down at him, seeing him lapping every drop up before settling his lips back against my clit.

I flinch hard, yelping as my swollen, sensitive flesh is scraped between his teeth. His hands travel up my stomach to my breasts, where he plucks and rolls my nipples between his fingers. His hair scrapes the inside of my thighs, and his breath washes warmly against my skin adding to my pleasure.

So long I've waited for this with him.

"Oh my God," I whimper, feeling my face contort as he keeps me balanced perfectly on the edge.

He settles into a rhythmic sucking that sets my skin on fire. My throat convulses as I swallow hard. I roll my hips, not able to keep still.

"Uhnnn," I moan, panting now as he's nipping, sucking, flicking the tip of my swollen clit with his tongue.

He moves lower, rimming my opening, thrusting his tongue inside shallowly.

We both go still as I stiffen.

"Relax, baby," Mason says, pulling away for a second to look up at me. His lips and chin are shiny with my juices, and his cheeks are tinged a red.

My eyes flicker between his as he moves his hand from my thigh, pressing a finger into me. It feels good.

"Oh," I whimper, feeling my pussy spasm slightly.

Feeling my bottom lip quiver, I bite it. His eyes bore into mine, and my belly clenches as hard as my toes do with nerves. But he advances slowly, despite the nerves wracking my body.

My flesh spreads apart as his finger goes deeper before stopping, and I know without asking that he's hit my hymen. I didn't think I had one after all the running I do.

I wet my lips, and flex my fingers against his scalp. "Can I have more?" I whisper.

"Yes, but you're narrow," he says, keeping his eyes on me.

He removes his fingers and lifts me up bridal style, pulling back the expensive sheets on his bed and laying me down. I'm too nervous to watch as he unbuckles his belt and undresses. I hold the sheet to my breasts and train my eyes to the side, listening at the sound of fabric rustling as he takes off the remainder of his clothes.

He gets in bed beside me, pulling the sheet from me and quickly rolling himself so he's on top, pressing every inch he can into me. I feel myself flush with desire and nerves at the feel of his body on top of mine. It's such a new experience, and I'm glad I waited for him. I wouldn't have wanted anyone else to make love to me for the first time.

Based on the feel of him, he's just as excited as I am. His erection lies hard and heavy against my thigh, and I swallow hard, feeling how heavy he is against me.

"Are you angry with me, butterfly?" he asks, staring deep into my eyes.

"Yes," I mumble, breathing hard. Irritated more like, because our family has convoluted everything.

But it's also a fact that I'm anxious.

So very nervous.

"Good. Then that makes two of us." He grips my chin and turns me back to him. "Don't you ever doubt that I deserve you, Melody.

That's the one fucking thing I'm sure of. Please don't take that away from me."

My heart beats wildly in my chest. Every hard ridge of him is pressed against me, and based by how tightly he's strung, how thinly stretched both of our patience is, I just know our first time isn't going to be gentle, and I don't think I want it to be.

I want us to explode with passion.

Mason leans down to seal his mouth over mine, and I stiffen at the first taste of me on his mouth. However, he takes it slow, stroking his tongue along mine, being patient while I acclimate. When all my taste is gone, his eyes meet mine again. I wish I could say that it lessons my anxiety, but it doesn't.

My tummy flips when he pulls my legs back, opening me further.

"When we fuck, I want you to bend your knees back like this," he rasps. "I don't want your legs flat on the bed. I want to get as deep inside you as possible."

I nod, not able to speak.

He notches the fleshy tip of his cock into my opening, swirling it in my juices before pressing. The fleshy cock head is firm and hot as he touches me. The anxiety within my core spikes high, causing tears to flood my vision and distort the sight of him hovering above me. A slight burning sensation takes over me, but before it becomes too distracting, he lowers his head to my right nipple and licks before sucking me into the warm, wet cavern of his mouth.

I stiffen with pleasure and then buck my hips into him on a moan, inadvertently sending him another inch deeper and causing the burning sensation to spread.

Something touches me cool and hard down there. Two little bumps on the underside of his cock press against my entrance. I clench down on him, resisting him.

"Mason, what is that?" I shiver, bringing a hand down to his cock where my finger traces the underside. He releases my nipple with a small sucking sound as I explore. My eyes go wide, feeling a series of metal bumps in a row.

"I'm pierced," he says, a wicked smile graces his face and his eyes drag down my face and back to my breasts. *"Relax,* sweetheart."

He pins me with a stare, and my eyes roam his face greedily.

His face is slightly flushed and damp with sweat. His wavy hair clings to his forehead in some spots. His eyes are hooded, dilated as he regards me intently. His lips are slightly swollen with how long he's been sucking me. He sinks a bit deeper until he stops at my hymen and then goes still. My gaze lowers, seeing his neck and shoulder muscles tense with strain as he holds himself over me, beginning to saw a few inches in and out. Thrusting shallowly for a while, getting me used to him.

I moan with pleasure, flexing my heels against his hips.

His chest heaves, as do his ribs against my inner thighs which are clasped high on his waist.

His biceps are steel slabs of muscle as he-

"Oh!...." I suck in a shocked breath and shriek as he flexes his abs, sinking into me with one hard thrust, not stopping until he bottoms out. Stretching my tender tissues until that burning feeling spreads everywhere and intensifies.

He splits me apart entirely.

My neck arches, and my mouth falls open, panting lightly. Mason lowers his head, running his nose along mine, his warm breath washes over my lips. My nails dig into his arms, and my heart races at the feel of him inside me. It's hard, thick, and *heavy.* Startlingly so. Curved.

I feel he's entered me at an angle, and it causes an unusual pressure deep inside. My heels unlock, my legs splay open as he moves his hips side to side and then sinks slightly deeper.

"Oh fuck," he groans in a low tone. *"Mel."*

Shocked, I make a rough noise in my throat and slap a hand to my mouth on a grimace. Tears fall out my eyes and down my temple, wetting my hair.

I don't make another sound, and neither does he.

He says nothing, merely laying his temple against mine and goes very still against me. I stare at the celling as our flesh throbs around each other. I focus on my breathing like I do when I run and it gets to be too much.

I spasm around him again.

I blow out a breath and then whimper, wiggling my hips slightly trying to find relief. His hand lowers between us, and he begins rolling my nipple, then lowers to grasp my clit. "Ooooohhh," I moan.

Soon the intense burning lessons a bit, making way for pleasure as he patiently pushes me to another orgasm.

It takes a while, but he focuses on me patiently.

My breathing hitches, and I wiggle again as I become wetter. The sound of him manipulating my sensitive flesh fills my ears as does his breathing. He bends his head down and seals my lips with his, stealing my breath and preventing him from hearing his.

We kiss hard. Our tongues tangling, and our teeth clashing messily, roughly.

Probably as rough as he would like to be taking me right now.

Even when I nudge my hips into his in a silent invitation, he doesn't move. He stays still until I jerk against him with my orgasm, digging my nails into the skin of his shoulders and tossing my head back on a wail. That's when he pulls back to the tip and begins to fuck me.

And he doesn't spare me any mercy. Giving me the passion I crave.

"Yes!" I gasp, meeting his eyes.

He thrusts hard and with purpose. The headboard bangs into the wall, over and over again as he slaps his hips firmly into my sex. The sounds are lewd and echo around the bedroom.

I purse my lips and whimper as the pleasure I felt before is dampened, being overwhelmed by the rough feeling of his body possessing mine, but I don't care that there is too much pressure. I want this. Just like this. So I focus on the feel of his hands clutching at me: one on my nape and one at my hip. I lock my ankles at his backside and hang on for all I've got, staring at him.

Watching his beautiful features contort with pleasure.

"How dare you make me wait so long for this," I gasp up at him, bringing a hand up to grab a hold of his hair. "Harder. Harder, Mason."

He growls down at me, smacking his dick even harder into me. His hair is shiny with sweat. A bead of it moves down his temple, his eyes narrow, his nostrils flare, and a vein sticks out in his left temple. "Baby, I will spend the rest of forever begging for your forgiveness," he says roughly.

I pout. "I want more."

His brow goes low. *"Mel-"*

"More. I don't care if it hurts." I scratch my nails down his back, feral with the need for him to take me over. Make me forget this shit between our families. Us fucking is like something out of my wildest sex dreams, and I'll never forgive him if he doesn't give it to me the way I want. The way I've always imagined.

On and on his hips churn against mine until suddenly his rhythm falters, and a change comes over him; his skin gets hotter, his muscles get harder, and a rough growling emits from his chest as he picks up the pace. My pussy twitches, clenching around him in response to how animalistic he's being.

Oh God, the roughness is the best part.

"Mason," I gasp, feeling my throat bob as I swallow hard. *"Mason..."*

"Yes, love?" he replies, but my eyes narrow as I focus on our joining, not answering him.

His sweat drips onto my chest as he fucks into me; his hips chafe against my inner thighs, and he stares into my eyes the entire time. It's so intimate that I want to turn my face away, but I know he won't let me.

The slapping of our skin echoes around us for long minutes, filling the room as does our erratic breathing and my helpless moans.

The blood rushes in my ears.

I whimper, looping my arms around his neck, and he grunts hard with his last thrust, pushing my hips off the bed with the force of it. He stills as his dick jerks inside me. We pant, our breaths sounding loud and harsh in the quiet of the room. My fingers sink into his thick hair, flexing against the damp roots as lash after lash is released into me.

He groans again, lowering to my mouth and kissing me slow and sweet as he orgasms. Moaning into my mouth.

It's everything I've been wanting with him for four years.

He settles his body weight into me, his chest smooshing my breasts flat, his stomach pressing into mine intimately. We're both shuddering, and I give him a weak smile.

"Are you okay?" he asks me gently. "Oh, Jesus, Mel. Talk to me, baby." His face is a picture of concern as he flushes even more as his eyes roam my face with a sort of satiated curiosity that takes my breath away.

"Yes," I say, taking a deep breath, rubbing the back of my fingers against my lips. "Thank you, my love."

He buries his face in my neck, settling even more into me. It feels so right.

So worth waiting for.

CHAPTER 19

Making a Wife

I press kisses to her sweat soaked neck, her temple, and her lips until I feel her heartbeat returning back to normal. Gripping her hip, I disengage slowly, hearing her make a soft noise in the back of her throat.

"I know, baby; I'm sorry," I say quietly.

I hurt her.

I know she begged me for it but, *Goddamn,* I feel awful right now. Glancing down, I see blood on my dick, streaked on her inner thighs, on the bedsheets under us, and it's a lot.

An interesting mixture of pride fills me, but it's dampened with a tinge of worry. Melody stays quiet as I press a lingering kiss to her lips. "Be right back," I say, "I'm going to draw a bath and then clean us up."

She nods, her eyes blinking lazily as I pull away from her. Closing her legs, she rolls over on her side and then tucks her hands under her chin.

I pad to the bathroom where I start the tub, squirting a generous amount of a ridiculously expensive bubble bath and swish the water around until it's nice and bubbly. Turning, I snatch a washcloth off the rolled stack on the vanity, wetting it with warm water, returning to the bedroom where I see she's trying to nod off.

I say nothing, wanting to let her rest and stay at peace. Reaching forward to pull her legs apart again and gently wiping her clean of the blood, then myself.

Picking her up, I cradle her to my chest as I walk back into the bathroom and see the tub isn't even halfway full yet. I step into the deep soaker tub, arranging her with her back to my front and her head against my shoulder, where we soak in silence for the most part.

I drain the tub, turning on the spray to the detachable handle and rinsing the suds out of her hair.

She sits at the counter, not meeting my eye in the mirror while I blow dry her curls.

She stays quiet from her spot on the couch in our attached lounge, waiting until I make the bed with fresh sheets.

She turns away from me when I lay her down on her side of the bed, curled up on herself.

Switching off the lamp, I leave the fireplace on low and get in on my side. I move to lay against her, but she doesn't relax out of her curled up position.

Worry fills me.

"Mel," I say softly, running my hand down her hair. "Mel, talk to me. What's wrong?" I give her a second, but she doesn't respond and that worry balloons into almost a full on panic. "Mel, please?" I plead hoarsely.

"I'm hurting, that's all," she says quietly in a strained voice. "I'm sorry, I don't mean to cry. I really enjoyed it but the after... hurts," she sniffs.

"It's okay," I say quietly, reaching around to brush my fingers down her damp cheek. "The first time usually hurts, but it won't always." I reassure her, moving my hand down her arm in what I pray is a comforting gesture. When she doesn't respond, I turn her to face me, arranging our limbs together. "I can get you some medicine?"

She nods, and I pull away from her once more to go back into the bathroom, where I grab a couple of pain killers and get a glass of water. I take it back to her and sit her up, waiting until she swallows it before joining her back in bed. I tuck her into the nook of my body and smooth her hair back over and over again.

I replay the last hour over and over again.

Fuck, I was too rough. I feel like an asshole.

I waited so long for this, fantasized about taking Melody's virginity just about every way possible over the last three years, and not one time did it end with her crying.

Pressing my lips to her forehead, I soften my voice even more. "I'll be more gentle next time, Mel," I reassure her.

"No, it was perfect." She shifts a little to straighten her legs, not even wanting to put her leg over mine. But despite her words, I vow to be more gentle, even if she doesn't want me to be.

We relax into sleep together, my thoughts shifting to planning our upcoming nuptials.

***

I get up before her the next morning, and I don't bother hitting the switch to activate the electric curtains. I go to the dresser in the dark and grab my watch, seeing it's five in the morning. I look back at the bed.

Melody's on her stomach. The curve of her ass is enticing, the sheets mold to her perfectly highlighting the plump twin globes, and the divot of her crack in between.

My cock stirs, and I head into the bathroom closing the door behind me. I won't be fucking her today. Starting up the shower, I go in and fist my erection with one hand, and brace the other against the wall. Pumping and pumping. Imagining every filthy sound she made last night until I spill my seed, watching the water wash down the drain.

I shower quickly, shave, then dress in my closet before walking to her side and selecting a simple light gray maxi dress with spaghetti straps and a lace bra and panty set, laying it on my side of the bed for her to see when she wakes up.

I doubt she'll want to go for a run this morning.

Not after last night.

I bend down and kiss her cheek, making my way to my in home study where I sit at my desk and flick on the monitors mounted on the wall. Readying myself for the pre-market.

I check my phone, seeing all the texts from everyone.

Twenty from Hendrix, a couple from Isobel. My mother called ten times, leaving a voicemail each time. Teresa called. Even Gwen. Ignoring them, I put the phone face down on my desk and flit my eyes to the screens, monitoring the numbers.

I work for almost three hours before my chef texts me that breakfast is done. I get up, and head down to the kitchen seeing the spread of oatmeal, fruit, and scrambled eggs with cheese.

Melody doesn't like to eat meat in the morning.

"Thank you," I say, reaching forward and grabbing the tray I'd instructed him to make. I pause, "Um, Daniel. Do we happen to have a small vase somewhere?"

His brow furrows. "No, sir, we only have the big one at the front in the foyer."

I turn quickly grabbing a cup and filling it with water, then go to the foyer where I snag a few of the fresh flowers and put it in the cup. I grab the tray and walk back into the bedroom, seeing Melody has turned on her back, the sheets have slipped down baring her breasts and her entire left side.

I set the tray on the edge of the bed and then turn our beside lights on medium setting. Sitting on the edge of her side of the bed I lean down and press my lips to hers. "Good morning." I say quietly against her lips, pressing a palm to the side of her head.

i pull away as she stirs, wiggling down the bed a little. The sheet falls off almost completely with the intensity of her stretch. She makes a little humming sound, arching her back so hard it pops. I grin, waiting for her to open her eyes.

Melody relaxes into the bed on a sigh and then opens her eyes. She blinks, making eye contact with me and then stiffens on a sharp inhale, shooting straight up in the bed and snatching the sheet to her body. "Mason!" she yelps.

My brows raise. "Yes?"

She's breathing hard, looking around. After a second she calms down and puts a hand to her eyes rubbing. "I thought-"

"You thought?" I press, placing my hand on her calf and rubbing up to her knee where I squeeze.

"I thought that I'd dreamt last night," she says almost breathlessly, giving me a shy look before turning her face away.

I smile. "Do you often have dreams like that?" I tease her.

She bites her lip, blushing.

Standing up, I retrieve her breakfast tray and place it over her lap. She sits back further against the pillows and shoves the sheet under her arms tightly.

"The flowers are pretty. Thank you," she says, reaching forward and grabbing the orange juice first.

I raise my hand and rub my fingers down her cheek. "You're welcome, sweetheart."

Her eyes fall to the foo, and she shifts, looking uncomfortable. "Who's supposed to eat all this?"

"It's for us to share." I lower my eyes, seeing it is quite a lot of food.

Her eyes snap to mine. "Share?"

"Hmhm. Like we do our sodas."

Her eyes go back to the plate and she sets her orange juice down, picking up a spoon and dipping it into the oatmeal. But before she puts it in her mouth her eyes slide to the side and roam the covers. "I've never had breakfast in bed before."

"Really?" I tilt my head. "Not ever?"

She shakes her head, leaning forward to eat the first bite of her oatmeal. "No, mom never let me. She was really strict. Every meal had to be at the table."

I take the spoon from her and eat a bite of my own, followed by a scoop of eggs. I swallow, washing it down with some water. "Well, I say we have breakfast in bed every morning."

"Oh no," Melody says sharply, meeting my eyes. My brow arches at how serious her face gets. "I can't do that," she says rapidly. "I have to run in the mornings. *I have to-"*

She cuts off her speech looking at the nightstand and then over at mine.

"What is it?" I say, scooping up more oatmeal and offering it to her.

"What time is it?" she says, letting me feed her.

"It's eight-thirty."

"In the morning?" Melody squeaks, putting the back of her hand to her lips.

Boy, she will not let that sheet fall. She is clutching onto it for her life.

"Hmhm."

"Mason, *school!"* she says trying to move the tray. "I gotta go to school; I'm missing my first class!" I put out a hand to stop her.

"No school today," I say sternly. "I already called them and informed your teachers that you are out sick today. You'll go back tomorrow. Today, you rest, and we pick out your wedding dress for our wedding on Saturday."

Her head recoils in shock, and her voice goes up an octave or two. "Wedding dress?" Her brows furrow together. *"Saturday?* That's in two days!"

"I know."

We're silent for a bite while we take turns eating with the spoon and fork. She puts the spoon down and then turns her head towards me. Her eyes are big in her face, and it looks like it takes everything in her to hold my eye contact. "Mason, you don't have to marry me just because we..." she trails off, obviously embarrassed.

"Had sex. We had sex Melody."

She averts her eyes. A part of me is pleased she's so shy and timid regarding intimacy. I want to break her walls down brick by brick, baring parts of her to me that no one else has ever gotten to see.

"And besides, a wedding is non-negotiable, baby," I say, leaning forward to kiss her forehead. I stand up, grabbing her tray and then motioning to her dress and underwear at the foot of the bed. "I took the liberty of picking this out for you; I thought you'd be comfortable in it. I have to go work in the study, but I'll be back out at lunch. Daniel's going to make poached salmon and creamed spinach. Your favorite."

"Who's Daniel?" she asks, blinking up at me, still clutching that damn sheet to her breasts.

"Our chef. He comes at breakfast, stays half the day and makes our lunch and dinner. If you want to adjust the menu, please speak with him. I'm not picky and will eat just about anything." I lean down and press my lips to hers firmly.

I pull away and go to walk around the bed to head to the door with the tray, but her next question stops me.

"Do we have a maid?" she asks, raising both her brows.

"No," I say, turning back around to face her. "I normally clean. It's relaxing." I refuse to share with her that it's what I filled my days up with while I waited for her. "Why, would you *like* a maid?" I tilt my head waiting patiently.

She shakes her head no.

"Are you sure?"

"Yes."

I take another step closer, making her arch her head further to look up at me. "If you would like one in the future, please let me know, okay?"

"Okay," she says quietly, her eyes flicking between mine.

I turn and head out of the bedroom, disposing of the tray in the kitchen and rinsing the dishes quickly, putting them in the dishwasher and going back to work.

***

Four hours later we've had lunch and are driving to a wedding boutique in Manhattan. The traffic is abysmal, and my temper is slightly high as the stock numbers were just not in my favor today. My hand is on her thigh, and I'm looking out the window, waiting for the light to change when she brings up another subject that causes the hair on the back of my neck to stand up.

"I need to get on birth control," she says, keeping her eyes nailed to the car in front of us.

I pull off slowly, clearing my throat. "You're not on it already?" I ask, keeping my tone level.

I have not a fucking clue why I didn't think to ask.

"No. There was no need to," she says in a small voice.

I think back to her journal, how every boyfriend she'd ever gotten involved with ended up disappearing. I grunt, thinking about the hundreds of thousands of dollars of my inheritance I'd sunk into bribing those men to leave the city, leave her, and never return.

"I need you to make an OBGYN appointment and get on birth control, baby. I don't want you pregnant at twenty years old." I peek over at her and see her squinting out the windshield. "Can you do that by the end of the week?"

"I'll try," she says.

I leave it alone, not wanting to agitate her.

Turning down a street, following the gps. I find a spot and park across the street from the boutique she'd picked. Thankfully it's a street over from the jeweler I'd been eying.

"You don't have a driver?" she asks, unbuckling her seatbelt.

"Nah, I'm not a pretentious fuck like Hendrix," I quip. Pulling out my wallet I pick out the credit card I'd opened for her and hand it to her. "Here, this is yours."

"Oh," she says, getting a confused look on her face. "I was just going to use the card King and Isobel let me use."

I curl my lip. "Let me see it?" Melody digs around in her clutch, pulling it out and handing it to me. "You don't need to spend their money any more. We've got our own." I shove it in my pocket, holding my card out to her again. She takes it slowly, our fingers caressing as she slides it out of my hand.

"Uhm, how much am I allowed to spend?"

I slide my eyes to her. Four years around my family and it still hasn't sunk in. "How much did you ever put on that card they gave you?"

I'll quadruple the amount just on principle alone.

She shrugs her shoulders looking nonplussed. I'd get a Starbucks coffee with it every once in a while, maybe buy a new workout outfit. Go to dinner with my friends, that sort of thing."

Okay, so quadruple times a million. Got it.

I hold my annoyed sigh in. "However much your dream wedding dress is, sweetheart. Whatever you want."

She nods. "Do you want to come with me to pick it out?"

My brows rise in surprise at her question, and I can't help the smile that spreads across my face. "I'd rather you surprise me when you walk down the aisle. If that's okay. Besides, I have my own errands to run."

"Oh," she says, scrunching her nose. "Of course you do, sorry."

I frown, seeing she's retreating into herself again like she's beating herself up for inviting me.

"I have my own surprise for you," I say, leaning forward I grab the nape of her neck and spend several long seconds kissing her. Trying to get her to relax. "Meet me back here in a couple hours?"

"Yeah." She smiles.

I get out of the car and open her door for her, escorting her across the street and into the boutique where I leave her and go to the jewelers, picking up her wedding band I'd bought the night of the charity event.

Two hours later, I meet her at the boutique and carry the heavy garment bag across the street, laying a three thousand dollar wedding dress carefully in the backseat of my car. She'll learn. Or maybe she won't.

Either way, I'll love her regardless.

CHAPTER 20

WHEN THE SUN GOES DOWN

I SNEAK LOOKS AT him the entire drive back home as the sun sets, throwing his features in beautiful shades of deep tan skin and pretty slashes of gold from the leftover rays of the sun.

He's a really good driver, winding in and out of traffic and perfectly compensating for the security tailing us. I feel like such a passenger princess as he holds my hand, our fingers entwined resting on my lap. Every now and then he'll squeeze my fingers then let me go to turn the station onto a different finance podcast.

I don't understand any of it.

Mason looks at me. "Do you want to listen to something, butterfly? I can change it if you want."

I shake my head. "No, but thank you for asking," I say, genuinely curious about what he's interested in.

What makes him tick.

Shifting in my seat I wince at how tender my pussy feels. He glances at me before letting go of my hand once more to turn my seat warmer on. My fingers fidget in my lap because of the obvious reason why. I sneak another look at him, wondering if he is going to want to have sex again tonight.

By the time we pull into the parking garage a half hour later I'm nice and relaxed. The soreness has lessened enough that I don't feel like I'm limping when we walk back into our home, and I actually feel like eating dinner.

My phone dings right as I put my thumb to the keypad, and I hold the door open while Mason carries my dress through. I shut the door and kick my shoes off, following him to our bedroom, digging my phone out of my purse and seeing a text from Karissa.

Where are you? I haven't seen you all day and Leo said your brother-in-law snatched you through his car window last night. Your stuff is gone out of our dorm. Bitch are you okay? -Kari

I groan, placing my head in my hand. "Oh man..." I sigh.

In all the excitement, I'd forgotten all about my friend.

"What's the matter?" Mason asks, hanging the garment bag up. He turns to face me, crossing his arms and his ankles, leaning a hip against the center island of the closet.

I place my purse on the island. "It's Karissa. I didn't let her know that my stuff is gone or.... or what happened. She's worried, and a little upset."

His eyes shine in the light of the closet as he regards me quietly. "How much are you going to tell her?"

"What do you mean?" I ask, tilting my head. "I'm going to tell her everything."

His brow raises. "Are you going to ask her to be in our wedding?"

Though he phrased it lightly, I can tell he's not too happy about my friend. My belly tightens with nerves, and I shift my weight from foot to foot feeling that soreness come back full force. My eyes leave his to travel down his neck and broad chest, his shirt stretched tight across his arms and even lower to where his shirt tucks into his pants, the belt highlighting how thick his waist and hips are.

No wonder I hurt.

"I, uh, I hadn't thought that far, to be honest. This is all so... so..." I avert my eyes shyly, not really sure what to do now that I'm here. Fantasy is a far cry from reality, let me tell you that.

I wasn't expecting all this intensity.

He pushes off the island and rounds it slowly, forcing me to turn and place my hips against the counter and crane my neck up to meet his eyes. "Sudden?" he finishes for me, placing a hand to the side of my face and stoking his thumb across my cheek.

"Yes," I whisper.

He moves, taking my phone from my hand and dropping it on the counter behind me. He places his hands flat on the counter behind me and leans in. My mouth goes dry, my pussy slickens with need. "It seems sudden, sweetheart, but it was always going to happen this way. You know that, right?"

I nod, at a complete loss for words.

His eyes rake down my face slowly, and just when I think he's going to kiss me, his eyes snap back to mine. It's all I can do to breathe normally. Suddenly a playful glint sparks in his eye. The mischievous one that I'd come to be familiar with.

"What?" I say, feeling the corner of my mouth curving.

His eyes slide behind me, and I turn to look over my shoulder, seeing the garment bag hanging innocently. "I think I'd like a reward for buying your wedding dress," he says.

My head snaps back to look at him and I giggle, putting my fingers to my lips. "Oh yeah?" I tease. "Like what?"

"Your mouth," Mason says, pulling the strap of my dress to the side he leans in to kiss my shoulder.

My heart beats hard in my chest, and my knees begin to shake. He rises to catch my eye, leaning in to kiss me softly, tugging on my bottom lip and nipping it. "My mouth?" I ask, holding back a little giggle.

"Yeah. I think your mouth will do just fine for now."

"But, Mason. *I don't know how-"*

He hardens against my lower stomach swiftly, catching me by surprise. Rather than saying anything, he shushes me with another deep kiss before pulling away again. My entire body flushes with need, and I pant, desperately trying to catch my breath.

"Unbutton my shirt," he says.

I bring trembling hands to his chest and do as he says. Unbuttoning them one by one. I fumble with a couple, but when I get to his pants where the shirt tucks in, I hesitate. Hating how inexperienced I am. Loathing how shy I am. I have friends who have done this for years at this point, and here I am, just now about to give my first blow job.

"I'll walk you through it," Mason says in a patient tone.

Matter of fact, it's the most patient I've ever seen him be.

Steeling myself, I untuck his shirt and then undo his belt, the clanging of the metal breaking the silence in the closet, joining the heavy sounds of our breathing and highlighting how stark of an act this is.

I slide my hands in the waist of his briefs, cupping the smooth globes of his ass and lower them slightly.

Mason keeps his eyes on me the whole time as he steps back, and I walk with him, my hands still against him feeling his muscles flex against my fingers. Playfully, I dig my nails in a little and see him suck in a sharp breath. He gives me another wicked grin.

He sits on the bench against the wall, forcing my hands from his backside, and I go to sink to my knees, but he stops me. "Take your dress off. I want to see you in your lingerie." His eyes rake over every inch of my body, and my eyes lower to his lap as his hand goes to the swell of his cock and squeezes hard.

I wet my lips, anxiety coiling deep in my belly. "Okay." I pull the straps of my dress down and go to shimmy out of it, but he pins me with a look.

"Slow down."

I pause, blushing.

Seeing he wants me to make it good for him, I raise my hands higher to my hair and unclip it, letting the curls fall down my back and across my shoulders. I toss the clip behind me, and he wets his lips, beginning to stroke his cock through his briefs.

I take a deep breath and lower the strap of my dress down one shoulder, pulling my bra strap with it until the top curve of my breast is exposed, but my nipple is still covered. His eyes go hooded and I half turn as I let the dress fall slowly, caressing my body as I do so. When it catches on my hips, I turn my back to him and bend seductively, sticking my ass out and shaking it slowly as the dress finishes falling to my feet.

"Fuck, Mel," Mason groans, and with those two simple words I become bold. I pivot, facing him again and sinking to my knees. Before I lose my nerve, I pull out his cock, and my eyes widen at the size of it.

I sit back on my heels. *"That was inside me?"* I say, holding my breath.

It is in fact curved to the right. And thick. I didn't know it was possible for a man to be this thick.

Mason's lips twitch as he chuckles. But I don't think it's funny. I also didn't know it was possible to be this turned on and scared at the same time.

More of my juices slick down my inner thighs, and I feel my panties are completely soaked.

Seeing me not moving, he clears his throat. "I don't expect you to deep throat it, Mel. For today, just lick it. Suck on the tip. Only go down to about... maybe here." He circles his fingers about five inches down from the tip and squeezes hard. "Use your hands on the rest, and be mindful of my piercings please, my love."

My eyes flicker, taking in his smooth, hairless torso, and his perfectly round balls, also devoid of hair, the thick shaft and mushroom head with a thick vein coursing along the top of his length. I suck in a deep shuddering breath, then take it in both of my hands. My brows furrow seeing my fingers don't touch.

I don't let it deter me, though. I firm my grip, trying to squeeze as hard as he did, and lower my head into his lap.

His smell is amazing, and my mouth waters as his scent begins to take over me. It's a rich musk that's uniquely him with a hint of spice from his cologne.

At the first lap of my tongue across the fleshy mushroom tip his thighs tighten up, and he makes a rough sound deep in his throat. I lap a few more times before I lick all the way from the base of his shaft to the tip and then lower my mouth over him, pulling my cheeks in and sucking as hard as I can.

"Goddamnitttt," he growls, the sound reverberating throughout the room. His hands slide into my hair and grip tightly.

I hear a thump from above me as his head hits the wall behind him.

"Baby, *please,*" he pleads, trying to push me away from him, but I dig all ten fingers into his ass and grip hard. He lets out a choked sound and snatches at my hair. I ignore the slight pain at my scalp, sucking harder and harder with every upswing. *"Mel!"* he growls, flinching against me as I take him until I feel him at the ring of my throat.

I pause before going forward a little more, curiously, realizing my gag reflex isn't bothering me. Happy, I take him all the way down until my nose touches his pelvis, and I whimper at the sheer feeling of him spreading my throat out.

Pure joy fills me.

Over and over I pull off and suck him back in, setting my own tempo.

My throat's on fire. My lips are going numb, saliva drips from my lips, and I shiver, feeling my body break out into a sweat.

I love this.

Love it.

He yanks on my hair again, but I raise a hand and slap at his arm, trying to dislodge his grip. I don't want him to take this from me. I won't let him.

His hips begin to rise off the bench as he fucks into my mouth. Long minutes I bob in his lap. His growling and my sucking are the only sounds in the room.

Suddenly he snarls and then bucks his hips up, ejaculating into my mouth. Or rather, down my throat. I swallow it happily, but my joy is short-lived when he firms his hands in my hair on a shout and yanks me halfway off him.

Irritated, I close my teeth around him at the edge of a set of his piercings and make a warning sound.

His whole body tenses back up, and he begins to shudder. My palms become damp as his body breaks out into a sweat, and I can literally taste his nervousness.

"Mel, let go," he says, sounding breathless. "You gotta let go, baby." I shake my head around him and pull against his grip, taking him a couple more inches down my throat and keep sucking. He's still half-hard, and I'm not ready to stop.

"Uh-uh," I whimper around him.

His thighs move restlessly against me, and his breath is labored. His chest heaves. He begins to pump me on and off him, my face making a dull thudding sound as I hit his pelvis. He jerks in my mouth, swelling again and then jacks his hips off the bench on a loud yell. Orgasming so hard he slides off the bench and crashes to the floor.

I follow him down, trying to swallow every drop. I tug and claw at his hands gripping me, desperate. A woman possessed.

"Melody! *G-Get off,"* he yells. We grapple hard, fighting against each other for a minute before he growls deep in his throat. "I said get the fuck off me. *Now!"*

Digging his feet into the carpet, he pushes hard at the same time he pushes me off him.

I fall back onto my ass hard before toppling to my side, sucking in a deep lungful of air. The ragged noise sounds out loud between us.

He props himself up on a shoulder with a groan, the other hand coming between his legs to cradle his cock. Now soft. His face is flushed dark and damp with sweat, as is his chest.

My breasts heave as I attempt to catch my breath as he stares at me with a wild look. His eyes are narrowed and dilated, his chest heaves, and he shakes his head once as I roll to my hip and move a hand forward to crawl to him. It's a clear warning for me to chill out.

Pausing, I roll my lips, licking my tongue out and tasting the cum smeared on my lips. It drips down my chin and smears across my right breast. Feminine pride swells inside me so full that I can't even care that he looks slightly irritated with me.

I give him a soft smile. Truly happy for the first time in a long time.

He wets his lips and pins me with a no-nonsense look. "Go clean yourself up and meet me downstairs for dinner."

I nod, rising to my feet. He keeps his eyes on me as I walk past him and go into the bathroom where I brush my teeth, take a shower, lotion my entire body, and spray perfume before walking out to another dress laid out on the bed.

This one's orange. It's beautiful.

He didn't bother laying another lingerie set out, so I dress without anything underneath.

When I walk down the steps and turn into the dining room, he's fixed back up with his shirt tucked back in, sitting at the table pouring a glass of wine. Instrumental music plays quietly in the background, the little fireplace inlaid in the wall flickers merrily. Like my heart.

My steps falter seeing a deep blue velvet ring box by my plate of spaghetti.

"Come here," Mason calls out, drawing my eyes back to his. "Don't even think about saying no. Not after the performance you just pulled." His voice is hard, sterner than he's ever been with me. I give him a little smile, rolling my eyes at him in mock annoyance.

If I even wanted out of this at this point, I don't think he'd let me.

"This looks so yummy," I hum, sitting down.

He gives me a little grin and hands me a wine glass, snagging up the box and showing me a *stunning* princess cut diamond.

"Oh that's beautiful," I breathe, feeling my eyes go wide. "Mason, it's *perfect."*

He gets up off the chair, turns me to face him and sinks down to one knee in front of me. "Marry me?" he says, looking up at me with the most sober look I've ever seen on his face.

I wet my lips, biting back a grin, thinking that I want to show him this is as serious to me as it is to him.

"Do I have a choice?" I whisper, leaning further down to look in his eyes.

"Not really. However, I think for *this* I'd like for you to make the decision," he says. I don't know how, but I fall in love with him even harder. *My* decision. It's all I ever needed to hear. *"But* don't tell our family that, though," he chuckles.

I stare at him, feeling tears well in my eyes.

"Will you?" he says quietly. "Can we love each other forever, baby? Not just in secret, but in front of the whole world?"

"Yes," I say, closing my eyes briefly. "A million times over, Mason." I hold out my hand and let him put the ring on my finger. I also let him lift me onto the table, spread my legs and eat my pussy as an appetizer.

And by the time he's done, our dinner has gone thoroughly cold.

CHAPTER 21

Everything is Different

"Good morning, sir," my assistant Taylor greets me as I walk onto my floor at the infamous King Dynasty building.

"Morning, Taylor," I respond, walking briskly past his desk. "It's a great fucking day!"

"Indeed, Mr. King."

I feel absolutely amazing, energized by Melody almost sucking the soul out of my body last night. I smile, because who would have thought she had all that in her? Turning the corner, I'm so busy lost in thought replaying last night while heading to my office door when I see it too late. It's cracked.

I stop dead in my tracks and look up at the ceiling on a prayer for peace, feeling that irritation crawl up my spine because *he's* in there.

Hendrix.

I blow out a deep breath and clench my jaw, trying with everything in me to keep my attitude happy and in check. Pushing through my office door, I walk straight past him where he sits in one of the barrel chairs at my desk, opposite where I sit.

I ignore him, grabbing the remote off my desk, and clicking on the monitors that line the wall opposite my desk.

"Good morning, Mas-"

"What do you want, Hendrix?" I snap, folding my arms and watching the numbers tick across.

"Why do you have to be such a dick, Mason?" Hendrix asks with an irritated look on his face. "I don't understand you sometimes."

"Because," I snap, lowering my eyes to look down my nose at him. "I literally told all of you not to contact me for awhile, and here we are not even a full forty-eight hours later. Not only have you disregarded my request and blown my phone up with about a hundred texts and phone calls, you're now smack dab in my fucking face, *unwanted."*

Hendrix's expression morphs into one that's weary and long suffering as he takes a deep breath, and then holds his palms up. "Mase, we're family."

"Are we, though?" I say, cocking my head to the side and eyeing him.

He recoils his head and throws me a hurt look, making me feel like an asshole. "What the fuck is that supposed to mean!"

I clench my jaw and work to get a handle on my feelings towards him. The resentment has got to go away at some point. "I'm sorry I said that. It was wrong of me."

Tense silence becomes almost suffocating before he finally breaks it. "Mason, what do you expect from me?" Hendrix asks softly. "I'm your *brother*. I've only ever tried to protect you the best I know how."

"Uh, maybe to actually listen to what the fuck I want." I lean forward and narrow my eyes at him. "For *once.*"

He shakes his head, and I see now he looks a little weary. The skin around his eyes is tight, and he's got a harsh set to his mouth. He needs to groom his beard. "I was doing what I thought was the right thing to do."

"Yeah, well, your 'right thing' broke Melody's heart. And hurt *me. It almost cost me everything.*"

"Come on, Mase. Can you cut me a little slack here? Isobel's upset with me that I've kept your feelings about Melody a secret and so is everyone else for interfering."

"You expect me to feel sorry for you, pendejo?" I scoff, pulling out my chair and sitting in it. "Go on ahead and get that notion out of your head because it's not happening."

His fingers drum on the arm of the seat and he clenches his jaw. "So, is she okay?"

I turn on my desk monitor "She's fine. Now get out."

Hendrix stands up, turning to the side and walking to the door without another word. He looks dejected, an expression I don't remember ever seeing before on his face.

I sigh, shaking my head. "The wedding's on Saturday," I call out, seeing him stop in his tracks before turning back hesitantly. His blue eyes meet mine, and I feel bad that I was so viscous with him just now.

I can see he cares; I'm just... hurt.

"Am I still your best man?" he asks in a quiet voice that stuns me.

My eyes freeze on the screen before slowly sliding up to meet his. The fucker knows how to get to me.

My heart strings pull, and I tighten my lips at the feeling. I only like it when Melody does that. "Yes, Henny. Now, please leave me alone so I can get some work done. The market opened five minutes ago."

Some of the dejectedness leaves his features, and his eyes warm up a little. He gives me a respectful nod and then pushes through my door. Leaving me in peace. Not for long though, because my thoughts immediately return to my fiancée.

I pull out my phone, seeing Melody's beautiful face on the screen-saver. It's one I took two years ago on her eighteenth birthday. She's staring up at a flock of birds flying above us, and her eyes look like liquid pools of honey in the sunlight. I'd snuck her out of school that day in her second to last week of high school and took her on a picnic at the park. We talked and laughed all day at everything and everyone. People watching, getting ice cream. Talking about Mariah, Hendrix and Isobel's daughter.

That's the day she told me she didn't know if she wanted kids.

It's also the day she told me she got accepted into California State, and I'd looked at apartments to be close to her because I was going to follow her come hell or high water. It was the day her heart was broken when she was told no.

I think it's also the day the light started to leave her eyes.

Needing to hear from her, I swipe in my password and pull up our text thread.

How's your first class, love? -Mase

Five minutes later, I'm dumping some stock for a client when the text comes through.

Boring, would much rather be back in bed.
-Mel

I bet you would. How many miles did you say you ran this morning? --Mase

She was up before me this morning. I rolled over promptly at five to see her side of the bed empty. A quick trip to my in-home gym room showed her on the treadmill, pounding away at the machine. I immediately got dressed and joined her, lifting weights while she got her cardio in.

I could only manage four today. Not my best. -Mel

I sink deeper in my seat, flicking my eyes to the monitors on the wall and making sure everything's good. I know exactly why she wasn't at her best, so I don't even play coy with her with my response. I'm blunt, letting her know what to expect tonight.

I wouldn't count on you being at your best tomorrow, either. -Mase

The bubbles appear and disappear for five solid minutes before disappearing completely. She doesn't respond. A wicked smile spreads across my face, because I want to dig under her skin and torture her like she did me last night.

I actually think you might need to put it out of your mind that you're going to be at your best for a while, sweetheart. I'm planning on breaking that beautiful cunt in sooner rather than later. -Mase

A knock sounds on my door before it opens, and my mother breezes through. I'm up fast, rounding my desk and holding my arms out to her.

"Madre," I greet, pressing a kiss to her cheek.

"Mijo," she says, flitting her eyes down my body. "I had to come to make sure you were okay."

I place my arm around her shoulders and lead her to the sofa that has the best view of the city. "Do you want a drink, mamá?" I ask, walking over to the drinks cabinet and pulling down a glass without waiting for a reply, mixing her a soda with grenadine. "Have you seen Henny yet?"

"No, mijo, I came straight here," she says, accepting my drink. "I actually came here yesterday too, but your receptionist informed me that you didn't come in."

"No, I didn't. I stayed home with Melody yesterday."

It's only ten in the morning, but I fix a double shot of whiskey, needing it to survive the next hour with my mom. Though my mother is softhearted, I get my emotional streak from her. When I was younger and had a hot-headed temper, she was always the one to seek me out, usually hiding out in a random room of the house.

Where everyone else made it worse, she always knew what to say or do to pull me out of it. Sometimes it took hours, but she never left me.

"You didn't answer any of my calls, Mason. I'm hurt."

And there it is.

She doesn't care that I lost my shit in her home the day before, or that I kept a secret from her at all. She only cares that I cut myself off from her.

My eyes flit to my mother's, who's staring at me with a look of carefully veiled pain, waiting patiently.

Walking over, I sit down carefully on the plush cushioned couch across from her, crossing my legs and taking a sip of my drink. Needing the liquor.

"Por favor, mamí," I say, trying to appeal to her gentler side. It works; her eyes soften just a bit. I look down at my drink. "You know how hard being in this family has been for me at times. It wasn't on purpose. I just was angry, and I needed time. But like everything else, this family never respects what I want. *That* is why I'm so fucking upset all the time, mamà."

My phone buzzes in my pocket, but I ignore it.

Mother puts her drink on the table in front of her, getting up and sinking onto the cushion next to me. She takes a second to smooth her dark blue pencil skirt down her thighs before leaning over so close I can smell her familiar perfume. Memories of hours spent being held in her arms as she comforted me as a child swamps me with just one smell, causing tears to well up in my eyes.

I blink them back.

She's the only one who knows the depths of my pain, always there for me when no one else cared. But even she couldn't get Father to look at me differently.

Her hand covers mine, and she waits until I bring my eyes back to hers before speaking.

"Mason, we are so proud of you. You've come a long way, and maybe..." she trails off, looking to the side a bit uncomfortably. "Maybe your father could do a better job of showing you so that Henny doesn't feel the need to step in all the time."

I grunt, taking a deep drink of my whiskey.

Because honestly, if I had to pick between Hendrix or our father, I'd pick Hendrix every time over our father's wrath. Truth is, I think Father gave up on me a long time ago. It was only because of Hendrix that I was able to stay afloat long enough to manage to garner any success.

I owe him a lot. A lot more than a lot, especially regarding Isobel.

That guilt I carry that's never far rears its ugly head, causing me to tighten my fingers on the crystal tumbler in my hand. A muscle twitches in my jaw as new emotions swamp me, and I feel even worse about how I treated him this morning.

Mother talks, drawing my attention back to her.

"You know deep down that Hendrix loves you, and he's doing the best he can at trying to fill some very big shoes. Shoes that are almost impossible to fill. And he's trying to make sure that he keeps everything together while he's at it," Mother says with tears in her eyes.

Always trying to keep the peace.

"I know, mama," I say, simply tossing back the rest of my drink. "You and I both know you aren't telling me anything I don't already know." We sit in silence for a minute because I'm unsure of what to say. I look over at her. "Madre, is everything set for Saturday? Did you get those roses for Melody?"

She breaks out into a bright smile and pats my hand. "Yes, mijo. It's going to be perfect. You better be glad I know a friend of a friend because pulling a glamourous wedding off in three days is no easy feat."

I chuckle, rubbing the back of my neck. "I'm sorry, mamá. I just wanted to give her the wedding of her dreams, considering we've waited so long and all." I glance back over at her. "How much do I owe you?"

Mother scoffs, rolling her eyes and standing up. "Oh please, your father told me to tell you it was his pleasure. And let me tell you, it was quite pricey, too." She gives me a wink before reaching down and drinking the drink I made her. "Now," she says, handing me her empty cup. "My only request is that you stay at the reception dinner."

I laugh. "I make no promises, mama, but I'll try," I say, getting up and giving her a kiss on the check. I walk her out and watch as she makes her way to the elevator bank, hitting the up button.

Going back to my office chair, I sit back and pull out my phone.

You're going to break me? -Mel

I smile, feeling my dick jerk and swell in my pants.

Oh baby, I'm going to absolutely break you off tonight. All I can think about is your delicious pussy. -Mase

Like I broke you off last night?-Mel

Oh fuck, this woman. I chuckle.

Worse. Way worse. You're gong to pay for your behavior last night. -Mase

You're going to punish me?-Mel

Focus on your class, sweetheart, and get your assignments for tomorrow. You're not going. -Mase

The bubbles pop up quick.

Mase, I can't miss anymore school. I can only miss four days a session. And I already have missed one. -Mel

Well, you're going to miss tomorrow too. -Mase

I put my phone up and go about my day as usual and pick her up from campus at four p.m. on the dot. She tosses her backpack in the backseat and then slides in smoothly.

"Hi, baby," I say, leaning over to give her a kiss. I take her lips thoroughly. She moans into my mouth and puts her hand into my lap, grabbing my crotch. I growl into her mouth, nipping her bottom lip. "You trying to get thrown in the backseat?"

"I don't think you can fuck me right back there," she whispers against my lips.

I pull back. "Is that a challenge?"

Her brows rise, and she flushes, looking nervous. "No."

I smile. "Ah, maybe another time then."

Pulling her hand off my dick, I entwine our fingers as I pull out into traffic. Intent on fucking the shit out of my fiancée as soon as we get home.

CHAPTER 22

For-yesss

He parks and yanks me out through his car door.

"Mason!" I squeal, stumbling behind him as he pulls me behind him. He walks swiftly to the elevator, laughing, and we're pulling at each other. He smashes the penthouse button, dragging me inside when the doors open, and then picks me up, forcing me to wrap my legs around him as he slams his lips onto mine. Devouring my mouth.

The doors shut, closing us inside.

I moan as he presses my back into the wall. "I need you," I whisper, licking into his mouth and gripping the nape of his neck. He thrusts his hips against me, agitating my clit and making me moan louder.

We break our kiss, resting our foreheads together. His eyes catch mine as he rolls his hips slowly and purposefully into me. The hard bulge of his erection presses perfectly against my pussy, and he rolls a little harder this time, stimulating me just right.

He repeats the movement over and over again until I begin to shiver against him. He chuckles low and deep in his chest.

"Oh, fuck, that feels good," I gasp. "Don't stop."

I jerk as his hand smooths up from my hip to my waist and then higher, cupping my breast through the thin fabric of my dress. His eyes bore into mine as he traps my nipple in his fingers and rolls at the same time he gives me another circle of his hips. My mouth falls open, and my brows scrunch together as the air freezes in my lungs.

"Does that feel good, too?" he asks quietly, like he's unwilling to break this spell between us.

"Yes," I whimper.

He tugs on my nipple, and the pleasure shoots straight to my clit where it throbs incessantly. My desire winds higher and higher, until my skin becomes dewy and my cheeks turn red. I glance past him in the mirror, seeing our reflection in the wall behind him.

I tilt my head slightly, seeing my legs wrapped high and tight on his torso. His thick hips continue to circle into me, his arm moving slowly as he plays with my breasts. His head turns as he goes to look up the expanse of my neck.

Goosebumps appear on my arm.

When I go to look away, he brings my face back to his and tilts his head.

"I'm about to make you feel even better," he says, taking the strap of my dress and pulling it down right as the elevator dings and the doors open. He swings me around, carrying me into the foyer where he shoves the big vase of flowers over and then puts me on the table.

The elevator closes with another ping.

He keeps his eyes on mine as his hands shove my dress up my thighs and then grasps my panties, yanking them down my legs and throwing them carelessly to the floor. My fingers curl around the edge of the table as he jerks my knees up then leans down and the licks up the seam of my pussy.

I stiffen and cry out, digging my nails into the wood.

"Goddamn your taaaste," he growls.

My hand slaps over my mouth as he takes both of his hands and spreads my lips wide for him and settles his lips over my clit and sucks.

And sucks.

And sucks.

"Mason!" I scream, wiggling as he mercilessly eats me through my first orgasm. My shoulders fall to the table and my hips slide off the edge as he bears all my body weight on his arms. He cups my ass with his hands, his forearms flexing as he works my hips up and down slightly.

I'm so sensitive I can't bear it.

I sob with my next orgasm.

He rips his mouth away from me with a wet, sucking sound and then stands up, pinning me with a lustful look. "Are you sore from the other night?"

Yes, but I might die if he doesn't fuck me again.

I swallow hard. "N-Not badly," I stammer. At his slight hesitancy my eyes widen. "No, please! Please fuck me. I want it." My voice quivers as I begin to plead so hard my eyes water.

When I hear his belt buckle, my breath hitches in my lungs as he moves me quickly, hauling me off the table and then yanking me down onto his cock on an animalistic grunt.

I throw my head back on a wild scream of my own, digging my nails into his neck and shoulder as he splits me wide open, only getting about halfway in before he stops due to my body's resistance.

I break out into a full body mist of sweat, trembling as he adjusts his grip on me to fist both of his hands into my hip and then pulls me off him before slapping his hips forward into me. My face pinches tight at the pleasure of him spreading me wide.

"You're too swollen," he growls, looking down his nose at me.

Scared he's going to change his mind, I give him a defiant look. "Make me," I whisper. Arching a brow I flex my pussy muscles and tighten down on him. "Make me take it, Mason."

He tilts his head, his eyes falling to my lips.

"Or," I whisper, tilting my head up, goading him. "Or maybe you're not man enough?"

A wince passes his face, and he swings me quickly, placing my shoulders against the wall before he lets one of my hips go and then presses my face to the side, against the wall, palming the entire side of my head. I firm my leg around his hip, letting him know I'm with him.

Mason pulls all the way out then rolls his hips against me, smoothing his dick through my pussy lips, getting it wet before notching back into my opening. "Ready?" he asks. He leans a little to the right and then drives forward all the way into me until his balls slap against my ass, shoving me up the wall several inches and making me scream in earnest.

The muscles of my legs tighten as my knees dig into his ribs.

"Not man enough?" He pulls back again and sets a firm, fast tempo. "Is that what you want, huh? To show you what a real fucking man can do to you?"

I feel my orgasm gathering deep in my core, winding tighter and tighter with every thrust into my sensitive body. He grunts roughly, keeping my face pressed to the side leaning into my ear to whisper like the devil.

"You're going to think twice the next time you challenge me, aren't you, Melody?"

I whimper, feeling my nipples draw so tight they hurt. He fucks into me over and over until I'm covered in sweat and move my hand to his wrist, tugging. He grabs my jaw and jerks me to face him, capturing my lips with his and licking into my mouth just as thoroughly as he's fucking me.

"Oh Mason," I cry out biting my lip and screeching low in my throat as my orgasm begins to unfurl.

He moves hard against me. Fucking me like he's got all the stamina in the world. I throw my head back, feeling his lips wrap around my nipple and nip at me.

My skin flushes warm, and tingles erupt everywhere as I jerk, screaming against him.

"That's riiiggghhttt," he groans.

Chuckling, he lifts his head up and cups the back of my head, making me look at him while I orgasm. I moan, breathing hard and thrashing against him as his thrusts draw out my pleasure. But he doesn't stop slapping against me tirelessly.

My toes curl, and I toss my head back on another orgasm, but he tightens his fingers against my scalp and keeps my head still, staring deep in my eyes.

"Don't you fucking look away from me," he snarls.

"Mason," I flinch when he gives me an expert circle of his hips that nudges my clit just right, and I let out a small scream. Squirting on him.

I fists my hands in his shirt, yanking as I fight against him, but he just laughs and thrusts somehow even harder, making me bob up and down, counteracting his thrusts.

My orgasm burns. Sweat drips down between my breasts, and I whimper helplessly.

My pussy spasms hard, and heat fills me from the tip of my head to my toes as he works to make this the most intense orgasm of my life.

"It's not stopping," I sob, trying to jerk out of his grip on my hair, but he tightens down even further on me, slowing his thrusts now from the hard slapping to slow, purposeful movements that have my eyes going wide. I flinch again. "Uhnnnn," I moan, biting my lip so hard I break the skin.

"You like it deep, huh?" he says, getting that wicked smile on his face.

Suddenly the elevator doors open and my eyes slide past him right into the eyes of Hendrix and my sister, whose smiles drop the second they see us, and their eyes go wide. Hendrix takes a fast step back and then turns to the side, but it doesn't matter, the elevator's mirrors reflect everything.

I'm dying, but there's nothing I can do about it. I can't stop it.

I can't even close my eyes I'm so stuck.

Isobel's brows rise as her eyes drag down our bodies before she turns too, and then covers her mouth with her hand.

I can't speak past my orgasm, and Mason's so lost in me he doesn't notice they're here. "You thought you were going to get away with challenging me? What did I tell you about that? You're never going to win against me, Melody."

I suck in another breath and sag against him, pressing my lips into his shoulder and biting down hard. He thrusts three more times and then comes with a growl, grinding against me.

His breaths puff warm against my neck, and I let go of my hold around his shoulder. "Mase, let me go," I whisper. "Your brother..."

Mason stiffens against me and tilts his head to catch my eye. *"My brother?"* His head recoils.

Hendrix chooses at that moment to clear his throat loudly, and Mason's head snaps to the side, clocking them still standing with their backs to us in the elevator. "What the fuucckkk?" Mason breathes, his eyes narrowing in anger "Are you fucking serious right now, Hendrix?" His head turns back to me and then disengages, lowering me, and placing my feet to the floor. "Can you stand?" he says quietly to me.

I nod. "Yes." I keep my eyes averted and hurriedly try to pull my dress back up onto my shoulder and cover up my breast. I am utterly mortified, but Mason is *pissed.* His movements are jerky and rushed as he tucks his cock back in his pants and fastens everything, tucking his shirt back in.

"Go open the door, baby," he says.

I turn to walk, thankful to be out of sight of our siblings even if it's for just a couple seconds.

"What the fuck is wrong with the two of you? You get off on watching people have sex?" Mason hisses, snatching my purse and panties off the floor. "Nothing in you thought to close the elevator and leave?"

His eyes flash angrily as he turns away from them and then walks over to where I stand holding the door open. His features are tight as he shakes his head angrily, then stands next to me, pulling me further into our house.

I want to sink into the floor and die.

"Well, come on," Mason barks, annoyed.

Hendrix and Isobel step out of the elevator. Hendrix keeps his eyes averted from me as he walks past me into the house, but Isobel meets my eyes as she sidles up to me.

"Damn, girl. I'm impressed," she whispers, carefully maneuvering her belly past me.

Mason waits 'til she's in the door before he closes it and leans down into my ear. "Go get cleaned up, baby. I'm sorry we were interrupted. I'll make it up to you in the bath later when they leave." He presses a kiss to my lips before turning to head after his brother.

I take a minute and press the back of my hands to my burning cheeks. We haven't even been together three full days yet and we were already caught having sex. How embarrassing.

Isobel gives me a little smile as I make my way to her where she's waiting by the threshold to the kitchen, where Mason moves around there with Hendrix, taking out a bottle of wine and a decanter of whiskey. "Hey," she says, giving me a shoulder shrug. "At least it wasn't mom that caught you."

I roll my eyes. "That's not helpful," I say sarcastically.

Fuck, I need to lay down.

Sit down.

Something.

I feel a trickle of Mason's semen make its way down the inside of my thigh. "Two seconds," I say to Isobel, walking past her, but she's hot on my heels.

"Nuh-uh, Melly," she waddles next to me, refusing to give me any privacy. "We need to talk. *You and Mason?"*

I roll my eyes and push my way into our bedroom, not stopping until I'm all the way in the bathroom where I take a towel and wet it. "Can you at least turn around so I can fucking wipe up?" I snap.

She turns her back to me, tapping her toe to let me know she's incredibly impatient. "When did this happen, Melody? And why didn't you tell me?"

"I don't know, Izzy. 'Cause maybe I thought it was just a stupid teenaged crush?" I wipe my face with the warm towel, cleaning the sweat off my neck and chest before reaching under my dress where I clean myself up and then toss the cloth into a hamper.

"Have you two been fucking this entire time?" she asks, turning her face slightly.

I scoff, walking past her and then head to our closet.

She follows me, and I make her wait while I open my intimates drawer and grab a change of underwear, yanking it up my legs. She sits on the same bench I blew Mason on, glancing around the space curiously. I make her wait, taking my dress off, standing in my underwear and snatch a clean dress off a hanger.

"Melody!" Isobel hisses as I pull the dress on.

"What?" I snap, turning to face her and crossing my arms.

"Were the two of you fucking each other this whole entire time?" she stresses, giving me an inquisitive look.

"No!" I say, throwing my arms to the side then letting them hit my hips with a little pop. "There, are you fucking happy, sis? He wasn't fucking me. You didn't fail in your pursuit to protect me and smother me half to death. Is that what you want to hear?"

"Melody, please don't be like that. I think we deserve some answers, considering."

I recoil my head, scrunching my face up. "Considering? Considering *what?"*

"Oh I don't know, Melody," she says sarcastically. *"How about everything King and I have done to keep you safe these last four years?"*

Her eyes flash at me, but I take a step forward and meet her ire with my own. "Safe or in a prison? I couldn't even go to the fucking school I wanted to go to, Isobel."

She gets off the bench, cradling her stomach in her hands. "You know why we said no, Melody. *It was too far-"*

"It wasn't your decision to make!" I yell at her, letting it all out. "And I wanted to be fucking free of it all. Did it ever cross your mind that I was going half out of my mind being followed every two seconds, not having any privacy? Not even being able to choose something as simple as a college to go to? I wanted freedom."

She scoffs, nodding her head and pointing her finger at the door. "So your solution to get that hard earned freedom is to *fuck* and marry King's brother, *huh?* Because you want *freedom* so much, Mel?" She shakes her head. "Make it make sense, Melody. You'll *never* have freedom in this family. Ever. So stop deluding yourself. I can't believe you're so fucking ungrateful-"

"Isobel, get out of my closet," Mason's voice sounds out, startling me. "You may be able to run your mouth off to Hendrix, but that won't fly in my house."

I turn, seeing Mason standing there looking like he's going to blow a gasket. He walks a few steps in, followed by Hendrix who looks at me warily before stepping around Mason, the center island, and over to Isobel who's eyes narrow into slits.

"Izzy, you really need to calm down-" Hendrix says, but Isobel's head tilts to the side, and I shake mine, already knowing it's about to get bad.

Downright ugly, knowing both of Isobel and Mason's tempers.

"What the *fuck* did you just say to me, Mason?" she says, her face contorting in anger.

"Mason, I think we-" I start; however, he interrupts me, holding a hand up. I snap my mouth shut, letting him have the floor.

I throw a worried look at Hendrix, who meets my eyes and shakes his head no slightly, telling me to stay out of it. I know I'm mad at him, but right now he's probably the best one to handle the two of them. They've never gotten into a fight before that I know of.

"I said the other day that I'm sick of you all interfering, Isobel. And right now, it sounds to me like you're trying to talk Melody out of marrying me, and you know this isn't how this fucking works."

CHAPTER 23

Coming to Terms

I'm so irritated right now I could choke the living daylights out of Isobel.

She and Hendrix not only had the nerve to interrupt, damn near *watch,* the hottest fuck I've ever had in my life, but now they're taking it a step further and testing me in my own motherfucking home?

In my *closet?*

I narrow my eyes, taking a deep breath and will my feet to stay planted on the carpet. All the pleasure I'd felt just ten minutes ago dissipates almost as if it were never there, leaving a teeth-grating annoyance in its wake that rivals just about any other time I'd lost my shit on Hendrix or my father.

But this time it's Isobel causing it. *Pregnant* Isobel.

"I wasn't trying to talk her out of anything, Mason," Isobel quips, folding her arms and glaring at me.

"Really?" I scoff, eyeing her up and down. "Because that's exactly what the fuck it sounded like to me."

"It's not what I meant!" she yells back.

Hendrix puts his hand on her arm, but she shakes it off, taking another step towards me.

I feel my anger begin to take me over, turning my face into stone. "Well it's what the fuck you just said!" I raise my voice, ignoring Hendrix who gives me a warning glance. "So maybe you need to start being more careful with how you say things, Isobel, because it sounded like you were insinuating she shouldn't marry me!"

"Well, I wasn't," she snaps. "I just wanted some answers."

I tilt my head to the side. "She's twenty years old. What makes you think you're owed an answer about Melody's sex life? Her love life?"

I know I'm one to talk, paying off the various boyfriends in her life to disappear and all, but still.

She frowns, "Because this has been going on under our noses, and we-," she emphasizes, gesturing between her and Hendrix who looks at me and gives me a 'not me' look that's quite perplexing. "-Wanted to know if y'all were fucking while she was underage," she continues.

My annoyance instantly goes a notch higher.

"And what if we were?" I ask.

The room goes eerily quiet as everybody seems to hold their breath. Her head snaps to Melody who purses her lips together, her gaze flickering between the two of us; however, she stays silent.

"What if we were, Isobel?" I repeat myself, getting her attention back on me. "What are you going to do about it?"

Isobel blinks, looking put out. "Well, I-I-" she stammers.

"Is that what you think of me?" I ask, recoiling my head. "That I'd do that? Like a fucking pedophile? I know we butt heads a lot, and I can have a temper but honestly, do you two *really* think that little of me?" My eyes flick between her and Hendrix. *"Well?"*

"Not at all, Mason. We know you aren't like that!" Hendrix says, his voice is strong enough to put me more at ease.

"Apparently *she* doesn't," I say, bringing my eyes back to Isobel, whose face tinges pink. Her lips purse together, and she throws another look at Melody, the worry plain as day in her eyes. I see then that this is about control to her.

Or rather, the lack of it.

She's been like a second mother to Melody for so long that she doesn't know how to let go.

Well, she's going to have to because I'm about to make her.

"Hm, Izzy?" She turns her eyes back to me, and just stares. "If we *were* fucking when she was sixteen, what are you going to do about it *today? Seeing as you just saw me fucking her outside our home. Where we live together,"* I say slowly, pinning her with my eyes.

Isobel's eyes well up with tears, but I don't care. She needs to understand her role from this point on.

"Are you going to lecture me? Put me in my place?" I shake my head, seeing a pinched expression on her face. "Nah, you got a husband for that. And he's standing right next to you." Turning to the side, I push the door all the way open and hold out my arm, narrowing my eyes. "Out of my closet. Now."

Melody's brows rise, and Hendrix goes to move, but Isobel speaks, making him pause. "Mason, I'm sorry."

I nod. "Apology accepted. Now, let's go. This is my personal space, and I don't want you guys in here. We can finish this up in the living room."

"Mason," Isobel frowns, wringing her fingers. "Uhm, I want to see her dress."

My brow rises as I just stare.

The fuck?

Hendrix clears his throat, giving me another long-suffering look. It hits me then why he's acting so differently right now. She's pregnant, and he's in self-protective mode. *Damn.* The memory of Isobel throwing a knife at him four years ago comes to mind, and I shake my head.

Not able to help myself, I let out a humorless chuckle. Isobel can be so self-centered. Worse than I am, ironically.

"Not right now you're not. Not until we get some shit out on the table and come to an understanding really quickly." I look at my brother who could be awarded the Dalai Lama medal of peace right now for being as much of a saint as he is acting. Because really, who is this guy? "Henny, get your wife out of my closet, please. We'll talk in the living room. Go on, I need to speak to Melody for a second."

King takes Isobel by the arm and whispers into her ear. She throws me an irate look, but I just shrug my shoulders and stay silent. I'm making my boundaries clear, and I dare anyone to stop me.

"What the hell is with you and this closet?" Isobel breathes at me, narrowing her eyes. I narrow mine back, not answering her.

They walk around the island and through the door, and I wait until they're completely out of my bedroom before I walk to Melody who's standing there with her arms folded, looking upset.

"Hey," I say, pressing a kiss onto her lips, then her temple. I wrap my arms around her in a hug. "I didn't hear the elevator open, baby. I am so sorry." I pull back and lean down to make eye contact with her, seeing she's seriously embarrassed. "I know you're shy, and I never would have kept going had I known they were there." My eyes flicker between hers, seeing they're tear-filled. "Do you believe me?"

Please believe me.

"Yes," she says quietly, folding her arms across her torso.

I reach over and grab a light cardigan off a hanger and pull it over her shoulders, knowing she's feeling too exposed right now.

"I think I need to have a talk with them about some things." I heave a deep sigh and press my fingers to my eyes, trying to rub the tension away. "You're more than welcome to join us, *or* you can stay in the bedroom, and I'll send them away when I'm done. You shouldn't feel the need to mingle with them after what just happened, love. But I'll leave it up to you."

I pull my hand away and fold my own arms, waiting for her to let me know what she wants to do.

"I'm okay to go," she says in a quiet voice. "I mean, I'm going to have to get over it sooner or later. Rather it'd be sooner. I just hate that they know what I sound like when I orgasm." Her face flushes bright red, and it takes everything in me to keep from chuckling.

I lift her head back up to meet my eyes. "You sound beautiful, baby." I praise her. Tilting my head, I arch a brow and drink in her pretty face greedily. "Did you know you were multi-orgasmic?"

She gasps, trying to pull her face away, but I tighten my grip. *"No,"* she complains in a strained voice, wiggling against me.

I do chuckle this time. "You came for a very long time, too. You were squeezing me so good, baby. We're going to need a repeat of that as soon as they're gone. Because they robbed me."

Her brow scrunches together. "Robbed you? Robbed you of what?"

I keep my eyes on her as I pull her dress up slowly, sliding my fingers into her panties until I feel her bare pussy. I reach lower, clasping her clit and pinching it.

It's thick. Swollen from earlier.

Sensitive.

I scrape my nail across the hard, sensitive bud and revel in the feel of her juices slicking out and coating the tips of my fingers.

I lean in, placing my lips to her ear. "Of seeing just how many orgasms I could force out of you. Of seeing how long I could push you before you marked my back and begged me to stop. Of what you sound like when you're hoarse from it, screaming and crying until you're nothing but a limp, desperate and quivering pile of need, so sensitive that just the feel of my breath on your skin sets you off. Of what you look like when you can't take anymore, and I keep going anyway."

"Oh, Mase," her breath hitches in her throat but she presses closer, molding her curves to my body. "You're so damn selfish for thinking you were the only one that was robbed."

She nips my ear with her teeth, and I'm rock hard, straining against my pants.

"Ohhh, you fucking little bitch," I snarl, yanking her head back by her hair. She whimpers, and I feel her shaking against me. "We're not done," I say down at her, seeing her eyes wide open. "The second I kick them out you better run as fast as you can, sweetheart. Because when I catch you, I intend to finish what I started before we were so rudely interrupted."

"I can run faster than you," she whispers back defiantly.

I recoil my head, offended. "No, you can't."

She's *not* faster. We're neck and neck, having raced each other many times.

"Yes, I can."

"No, you can't."

"Yes, I *can."*

I roll her clit hard, mercilessly manipulating it until her fingers dig into my shoulders and her legs begin to shake. "I'm the only one who gets this feisty attitude? Huh?" I question her.

At her silence, I pull my fingers out of her panties and make her watch me suck them clean. I let her hair go and smack her ass hard, sending her stumbling to the door.

Though she's embarrassed, I'm glad she's going to be by my side while I lay down some ground rules with my brother and his over-protective wife.

I set the wineglass down on the table with a clink before handing Melody her glass.

"Thank you," she says, taking a small sip.

"You're welcome." I pour Isobel a sparkling water and Hendrix and myself a scotch, sliding his over to him.

I don't drink mine, not yet. I don't even sit down. I stand behind Melody's chair and place my hand on her shoulder, squeezing. She stiffens and then tilts her head up to look at me, but I look at them instead, addressing Hendrix.

"I know that we haven't been the best of brothers, for reasons that we don't need to discuss right now, and for a lot of years I caused you grief and was just generally a huge asshole most of the time, but I think have more than proved myself to you *and* to our father, whether he wants to talk to me about any of this or not."

Hendrix folds his arms and gives me a slow nod, his face so serious you'd think he was in a board meeting. Melody's hand comes up to cover mine on her shoulder, and she gives my fingers a squeeze.

"I am in love with Melody," I say quietly. "I haven't been with anyone else since I saw her almost four years ago. Hendrix didn't tell you, Isobel," my gaze slides to Isobel where she meets my gaze boldly. "Because he thought I didn't know what I wanted. That I'd get bored and move on after a while, but I knew. I knew clear as day that Melody belonged to me, and I belonged to her. He wasn't trying to keep you in the dark about anything."

Isobel turns her face to him when he turns to her, a look passes between them, and I just know without either one of them saying anything, that they've been fighting over us.

"I'm going to need you to cut off that Amex card, sell the car that you bought Melody that you store at your house, cancel her country club and SoHo memberships, and any other thing you pay for. Cut off her phone service, and limit your phone calls to her to no more than two times a week." Isobel's eyes almost pop out of her face, but I continue, unbothered. "And whatever other allowance you give her is done. Melody's my responsibility now," I finish.

Hendrix sits back in his chair and shoots back his whiskey. "Done," he says.

I pause at his words. He just gave me his respect, for probably the first time ever.

Holy shit.

I grin, and he gives me a grin back.

Isobel cracks her head over to look at him. "Hendrix!" she hisses. "Are you going to let him just-"

Hendrix turns his head slowly and pins her with a look that has my balls drawing up, because, damn, I take back my words about him going soft.

He's still got it.

Isobel's eyes go wide, and then she turns to place her gaze to the table in front of her. King meets my eyes, and for a minute, all of our sibling rivalry, our fights and bickering falls to the background as a new understanding passes between us.

His eyes slide to Melody, who cradles her wine to her breast and stares at him back. "Do you love him?" Hendrix asks. Isobel's eyes rise to look at Melody, too.

"Yes," Melody says.

"Do you want this?"

"Yes, thanks for asking."

I smile, squeezing her shoulders.

"Do you trust him?" The words fall off his lips and hang in the air while all the oxygen sucks out of the room.

My heart skips a beat before pounding into overdrive, a muscle twitches in my jaw, and I damn near stop breathing because... I've never had anyone tell me they trust me before.

Melody pauses before tilting her head back up to look at me. The back of my eyes prick, and I swallow hard, not wanting to cry in front of Hendrix or Isobel.

"With my life," she says, giving me a sweet smile. "I trust him with everything."

I nod. Despite my best efforts a tear falls down my cheek, and I push away from her, scrubbing a hand down my face. "You guys have to go." I say briskly.

"Huh?" Isobel says, scrunching her face up. "But the dress!"

"You'll see it the day after tomorrow, Izzy," I say, walking to the front. "I'll call you tomorrow, Hendrix, but I need you to go."

"What? Why?" Isobel says in an incredulous tone, trying to get out of her seat. Hendrix pulls her up by her hand.

"You heard him. Let's go, little demon," he says.

"B-But-" she stammers.

"I'm happy for you, honey," he says, leaning down to give Melody a hug. She stands up and throws her arms around him, and they rock for a second while I stand with the door open trying not to cry. "Give your sister a hug, and let's go woman," Hendrix says sternly.

Isobel gives Melody a hug before Hendrix bends and picks her up bridal style, pregnant belly and all. "You know," he says, carrying her swiftly past me. "They got the right idea. We haven't ever fucked in an elevator before."

Isobel's face goes bright red, and she buries her face in Hendrix's chest. He glances over his shoulder as he makes his way to the elevator. "I'll be looking for that phone call, Mase."

Turning, I look over to see Melody staring at me from the threshold of the dining room.

I slam the door, locking it.

"Why aren't you running yet?"

CHAPTER 24

SEX

I CAN SEE THE second she clocks the seriousness on my face; she drops her wine glass on the table and turns on her heel the second my shirt hits the floor.

She yelps, running to the hallway and tearing around the corner. Her bare feet slap the hardwood floor with sharp taps, driving my arousal to feral heights as we enter into a cat and mouse game that she knows she's going to lose.

We both know it.

Shivers roll down my spine when she throws a panicked look over her shoulder, and she sees me in close pursuit.

We crash through the living area at almost a breakneck speed, and Melody vaults the couch like a fucking gazelle and stumbles, recovering quickly as she moves fast working her way to the piano, getting it between us. She lets out a little giggle as I go to round it, and then she walks in the opposite direction. Her chest heaves as she breathes hard. Not because she's tired out; no, because she's turned on by the chase. By me.

"I'm going to have so much fun fucking you, sweetheart," I say, moving a little faster.

"If you catch me," she says with a little grin. Her dark skin is tinged red, and her lips are stained red with the wine from earlier. She's drop dead sexy.

Will be even sexier with my cum smeared on her face.

The tension between us mounts as we stare each other down, walking circles around the baby grand.

I lunge forward, ready to end this game

"Massoonn!" she screams, laughing and backing up as I pull myself up by one arm and launch myself over the piano, sliding across the smooth surface.

I love showing her I just don't give a fuck sometimes.

Her eyes widen, and she turns before my feet even hit the floor, racing to the opposite end of the penthouse. Her huffs of breath cause my dick to strain against the zipper of my pants, but I ignore the momentary discomfort as I fly down the hallway in close pursuit.

We turn sharp corners and go past room after room until we find ourselves at the end of the penthouse in a huge library and half-study that so far I don't think she's seen before.

She pauses, panting lightly as she turns her head to look to the side, probably to see if there's another door to go through.

Nothing.

There's nowhere else to go.

I take advantage of Mel's stillness and snatch her up, smiling when she squeals as I lift her by her waist and spin her, tossing her over my shoulder. "Gotcha, butterfly," I say, landing a hard slap on her ass. "You never could outrun me, but it's fun to see you try."

"Let me dooowwnnn!" she yells, pounding against my thighs with her fists.

I ignore the blows, walking to the corner of the study to the right of the fireplace and set her down, keeping a hand on her wrists as I open a cabinet and pull out a low stool, placing it in the middle of the fireplace, though it's not lit. As I stand up, I drag my hand up her leg, gripping her dress and pulling it up with me as I advance up her body.

Pre-come leaks from the tip of my cock as more of her glorious skin is revealed to me.

"What are you pouting for?" I say, ripping the dress over her head and tossing it across my desk. My eyes immediately zero in on her beautiful breasts, and I can't help but reach forward and cup one, rubbing my thumb over her pebbled nipple. Her eyes go hooded, and she sways into my touch; her lips part and her tongue darts out to wet her bottom lip.

"I'm not pouting," she says quietly, moaning when I tighten my fingers in a gentle pinch, rolling and plucking at her nipple. Her scent sharpens in the air between us, and I bring my other hand to her nape, squeezing to stabilize her when she sways again.

"We're getting ready to test how strong these legs are," I say, trailing my hand down her stomach and to her mound where I go even lower, twisting my wrist and thrusting two fingers inside her warm, wet pussy, seeing her nostrils flare slightly as she sucks in a sharp breath. "Fuck, you're tight," I growl, pumping my fingers in and out for long minutes until her legs are shaking. I pull my fingers out slowly and hold them to her lips, smearing her cum on her mouth. Before she can lick her tongue out again, I lean in, sucking her lips into my mouth. When her taste is gone I pull away and jerk my head towards the stool. "Step up, and spread your legs."

She glances down with a nervous expression and steps up, bringing her about eight inches taller.

I eye her, undoing the button on my pants and shoving them down and off, tossing it over her dress, and then place my hands on her hips as I step forward and slide my aching cock through the seam of her pussy.

"Now, you can thank Henny and Isobel for this, since we were so rudely interrupted earlier."

Her eyes meet mine warily, and I press deeper, scraping against her clit until I find her entrance and slide in a few inches. Deep enough I know I've hit her g-spot. I reach further behind her and gather her ass cheeks in my hand, bunching the flesh in my grip and pull her back, and then yank her back on me, our skin slapping together sharply. She traps a moan in her throat.

Her eyes widen, and she sucks her lip between her teeth.

I repeat the movement, every thrust dragging my shaft continuously along her clit, and I really wish I had piercings on top to make this even better for her. She tilts her head back and closes her eyes, her long hair tickles my forearms and wrists as she exposes her pretty neck to me.

"Melody," I say sharply. She drags her head back and her eyes pop open, meeting mine. Her gaze is so lustful a zing of pleasure draws my balls up tight, and I slow the pace of my thrusts in order to get control over myself. "We're going to be here for a while, so hang on to me baby," I say, leaning forward and pressing a kiss to her swollen lips.

She loops her arms around my neck, pressing her breasts to my chest and nuzzles into my neck, settling into me. Trusting me. I press my lips to her ear and glance at the clock on the mantle.

"Mason!" Melody pleads in a hoarse, strained voice, but I don't let up. "Mason, *please stop!"*

The room is filled with the sounds of our flesh slapping lewdly. Sweat is dripping down my body, her body; her toes are curled around the edge of the stool, and there's a small pool of her excitement built up on the surface between her feet. I'm so fucking turned on that I've been edging her for over an hour. I haven't given her one orgasm.

It's cruel, I know. But I wouldn't deny myself this for anything, even at the threat of her wrath.

My forehead rests against hers, my arms are rock hard and burn from constant flexing and contracting. I couldn't move us because I didn't want to break this intimacy between us. Fearing it might fucking kill my ass to part from her. For the last twenty minutes I've been bearing the brunt of her body weight to keep her standing upright, and the pain I'm in right now is worth it.

She's worth it.

I turn my head slightly, my gaze roaming her face. She's flushed, her eyes are glazed over. Her breaths saw in and out of her lungs: some hitched, some breaths almost barely existent.

Her ass is bright red from my ruthless grip on her where I yank her off me and jerk her forward on and off my cock only deep enough to stimulate her g-spot. She whimpers and trembles in my hold. Her arms have loosened from around my neck, and she weakly clutches at my shoulders, almost spent.

I stop the hard thrusting and spend a second catching my breath. My chest heaves, and my pecs are as hard as my arms. The veins stand out in sharp relief, which I can tell she likes very much as she stares at them excessively. I pull out of her slowly, catching her when she makes a weak sound and sags.

"Brace your hands on the mantle," I say.

I turn her so her back is towards me and keep my hips firm on hers until her hands get in place against the dark wood.

Raising my hand, I push her hair to her front, running my hand down her spine. "Your skin is like silk," I praise her. I caress her slowly, until I get to the waistband of her panties. Bending down, I take a gentle bite out of the swell of her ass cheek, tightening my teeth until she raises up onto her toes and yelps. Standing back up, I smack her ass harshly, watching the flesh bounce as a red handprint appears, marring her tan colored flesh.

Putting my hands on her hips, I pull her back slowly so she's leaned forward, bracing more of her body weight on her hands and then notch the tip of my cock in her entrance. I wince. She's swollen from constant friction for so long. And hot. Her heat sears me. I clench my jaw hard and snap my hips forward hard at the same time I yank her back completely onto my dick for the first time since we started, sinking deep into her in a thrust so hard she lifts off the stool several inches and just hangs there helplessly.

The scream that erupts from Melody's throat is unreal.

She scrambles to move her hands to the top of the mantle and grips, moaning and sobbing as she orgasms so hard it almost sends me over with her. Her pussy clenches down so tight onto my dick that my world narrows down to nothing but me and her. The library fades away, leaving the slight curve over her back, her hair, and her ass in a tunnel vision meant to set my body on fire.

I hold her there for a moment before I pull all the way to the tip and just fuck.

I let her body have it, unapologetically.

"I don't care about the whining," I hear myself snarl at her almost as if it's not even me talking. "I don't care about your pleading, and I definitely don't care if you can't take anymore because you're going to." I lean forward, nudging her soft curls out of the way and putting my lips to my ear. "We're making up for all the time that was taken from us. You with me?"

"Y-Yes," she says weakly, grasping with her toes on the surface of the stool. I drop her a couple inches until she finds purchase, and then I fuck this woman with everything in me.

I fuck her until my back burns with pain from every thrust, until my thighs are stone hard, and my hips are tight. Until my feet lose purchase on the floor and growls erupt from my throat, so loud that they almost drown out her whimpers and moans of pleasure.

My balls draw up tight, and a hot shiver of pleasure rolls up and down my spine. I'm taking her so hard that I know I'm going to have to be sweet with her tomorrow. On our honeymoon.

My and Melody's honeymoon.

I snarl, fucking her even harder at the thought of making her mine. I zone out, single mindedly focused on our pleasure. I bend my knees and pound, her cum splashing between the two of us as she's in a constant state of orgasm.

"Mason, oh my god, please baby, I'm *b-begging you! M-Masooon-nnn!"* her sobbing voice sends me over the edge, and I thrust into her one last time and shiver as the tip of my cock literally explodes inside of her.

I tilt my head back and groan, grinding deep into her, soaking up the rhythmic clasps of her pussy. We collapse at the same time, hitting the floor on our knees and rolling over to the side, both of us breathing hard. I wrap my hands around her and pull her tight to my front, closing my eyes against the floaters obstructing my vision.

I hold a hand to my eyes and press, taking a deep calming breath as my thundering heart rate starts to slow.

"We're getting married tomorrow," she pants, her breasts beat wildly against my forearm.

"I know," I say, pulling my hand away from my face and rubbing it down her arm, soothing her.

"Isn't there some rule that says you aren't supposed to see your bride the night before, much less fuck them?"

I roll to my back, pulling a knee up and taking a deep breath. "I spent almost four years waiting for you. I could give a shit less about a day," I grumble.

"Even if it's our wedding eve?"

I feel my lips twitch with amusement. "Even then, butterfly. You think I'm going to keep my hands off you just because of a superstition?"

"It's not a superstition."

"Okay. Old wives' tale, then."

She lets it go.

We're both quiet, listening to the gentle chime of the clock above us. "What's it like being married, do you think?" she asks quietly.

I roll my head back over to look at her.

She meets my eyes, and though hers are heavy lidded with pleasure, I know her well enough to see that anxiety she always wrestles with swirling around in there as well. I take her hand, bringing the back of it to my lips.

"Marriage is obviously different for everyone," I say slowly, treading lightly because she spent her whole life not seeing an example of marriage until my parents, and then her sister. "But, that's why we need to trust each other to make our own path. It's okay that we may not have all the answers, or know what we're doing all the time. But, I promise to come to you, if you promise to come to me?"

Melody blinks nice and slow, before a smile spreads across her face. "Deal." She holds out her pinky finger and I chuckle, taking it with mine and pulling her to me for a harsh kiss.

"Want to have breakfast instead of working out tomorrow before the wedding?" she mumbles against my lips.

"As long as it's naked, and in bed."

I pull her up, pick her up bridal style and carry her to the bathroom, placing us both in the tub and laughing about the stunned look on Izzy and Henny's face when they caught us having sex.

CHAPTER 25

OUR SOULS LINGER

"OH MY GOD," I whisper, so nervous.

I sit in front of the vanity and blow a gentle breath, fanning my hand in front of my face to keep the tears away. My eyes are drawn to the flurry of activity behind me. My mother and Teresa are wrestling Mariah into her flower girl dress, and Isobel is bent over awkwardly with a steamer, obsessively going over the satin fabric even though there's not a wrinkle to be found.

"Be still girl, or I'm going to smear it," Karissa whispers, holding her tongue between her teeth as she swipes my eyeliner on, *brown,* because I know Mason doesn't like me to wear a lot of makeup, and I want to please him today. Just like he likes to please me.

So, I met in the middle and did a more natural look today, but still having Karissa play up my eyes with different browns and rose colors on my eyelids.

"Sweetheart," my mom huffs, standing up straight and smoothing her mother of the bride dress down. "I can't wait for you to see the reception. It's beautiful."

"I bet it is," I say, reaching over to tear off a small piece of croissant and pop it in my mouth following it with a sip of mimosa.

It's all I wanted: a croissant, a mimosa, and the song "Going To The Chapel" playing. Which we did on the way to the beautiful cathedral we're being married at. We're having an intimate Catholic wedding with a priest and communion. It was all Mason requested.

"All done," Karissa sings, swiping the brush over my cheeks with one last flourish before backing away.

I turn to my mom who clasps her hands together with tears in her eyes. "Oh, you're so beautiful, honey," she says in a quivery voice. I give her a smile and eye her dress. It's a beautiful dark-purple satin, off-the-shoulder number with a draping pattern that accentuates her hips and legs. Her dark skin gleams under the lights, and her locks is pinned up in an elegant updo. She looks positively royal.

"You're beautiful, too."

Standing up, I go to give her a hug, knowing this wedding was extra special to her because she didn't get to see Isobel's. I look over at her, putting the steamer away and fussing over my dress. She's still hurt over her and Mason's interaction a couple days ago, and this is the first time we've talked or seen each other since. She met us here at the cathedral and hasn't looked me in the eye yet.

I grab the sash of my robe and fidget, walking over to where she stands and put my hand on her shoulder. "Hey, sis," I say, waiting until she meets my eyes to give her a smile. "You look beautiful, too."

Isobel's eyes soften.

Seeing her break out into a reluctant smile, I walk into her and wrap my arms around her, leaning over her round tummy and rubbing her back. "Thank you for everything you've done for me, sis. All the sacrifices you've made, some I'm sure I don't know about. You're the reason I met Mason." I sniff, pulling away and wiping a stray tear that falls down my cheek.

She shrugs her shoulders and gives me a sassy eye roll. "Well," she says, clearing her throat, "all I've ever wanted was for you to be safe and happy."

I nod, giggling. "He makes me very happy," I whisper behind my hand.

Izzy snorts and holds her hand to her mouth, her eyes sparkling as she looks at me with wide eyes. "Yeah, I could tell."

We're in the middle of laughing when Hendrix's voice interrupts us.

"Ladies, you all look so beautiful!" he says, walking through the wooden door and then closing it behind him. He's holding a tray of what looks to be swirling purple and pink drinks and something else in his hands.

"King," Isobel gushes, leaving my side to go to him. She stands up on tiptoe to give him a peck on his lips, and he smiles down at her.

Out of the corner of my eye I see Karissa visibly preen as Isobel steps away from King to attend to Mariah, who's trying to throw rose petals around everywhere. She walks up to King and smooths her hand down her beach blonde waves, letting her hand caress down her breasts for a second before she reaches forward and snags a drink off the tray.

"Thank you, Mr. King!" she sings, twirling away with a dramatic hair toss and walks back over to the vanity.

King gives her a little once over before walking towards where I'm standing by my dress. "Melody you look angelic!" he says, giving me a smile.

"Thank you, Henny." I eye the drinks, seeing there's also a long stemmed white rose as well and a note. "What's all this?"

"Compliments from my brother," he says, putting the tray down on a lone table. "A drink he had specially made called The Melody, a rose, and a note for you." He hands me a drink and then reaches into his pocket pulling out a box. "Oh and... he was worried about your lack of something blue, so he sent me to give you this."

My fingers fly to my lips at the beautiful aquamarine, emerald cut cocktail ring nestled in the velvet box.

"Oh, Hendrix," I breathe. "This is beautiful."

He nods, pulling it out of the box. "May I? He wanted to see you wear it at the altar."

I nod and hold out my right hand, letting him place it on my ring finger. I burst into tears, and it sends Karissa into a fit. She flies over to me with a tissue and pushes at Hendrix's chest.

"No, no, we can't have her crying! I just perfected her makeup!" Karissa scolds, dabbing at the corner of my eyes with the tissue.

Hendrix frowns at her, taking a step back and then cautiously holding the handwritten note out to me. I take it, trying and failing to get control over my sobbing.

"He said he wants an answer, and I'm to bring it back to him. So, if you could just-" he sidesteps Karissa who's shoved her hips at him in a dramatic movement, leaning into my face with a brush to go over my face again.

"Karissa," I scold, narrowing my eyes at her. "Hang on a second."

I open the note and read it.

Mel,

I need this in writing so I forever have proof.

Do you agree to marry me? Circle one.

Yes No

And just like that I burst out laughing, chasing the tears away.

Hendrix peers around me trying to see what it is.

"Do you have a pen?" I ask.

He reaches into his inner pocket and pulls one out, handing it to me. I draw a heart around *yes* and then write 'you dork' next to it. I give it back to Hendrix with a smile.

The next couple hours happen in a whirl. We have a traditional catholic wedding, and it's so beautiful it's going down as a day I'll never forget. He wiped a tear away when I walked down the aisle, his face full of emotion. Not just his eyes. I'll never forget it. Just like I'll also never forget the way Mason looked at me as he slid my wedding ring on my finger.

The way his lips felt on mine as he kissed me after we said "I do."

I laugh the short drive to the reception venue, the cans bang after our car as we drive along and he holds my hand the entire way. He carries me bridal style into the reception, and my eyes widen at the explosion of purple and white flowers everywhere. They're hanging from the ceiling and in massive floral arrangements on the perfectly decorated table scapes.

Our name is lit up on the floor.

And there are butterflies flying around.

"Oh my God," I breathe, looking at Mason excitedly. "There's butterflies!"

He smiles playfully, giving me a deep kiss. "That was my request, love. I wanted you to see yourself everywhere today."

I melt as he sets me down, and we commence to having so much fun. Which is quickly dampened when we get to the part of the night when it's time for the father and bride dance. I feel that tug of sadness that's been eating at me lately deepen, the only thing that puts a cloud over our day.

I glance at Mason, silently imploring him to get us out of here, but he just smiles and leans forward to stand me up, promptly handing me over to Hendrix. After the tumultuous past few days we've had, I feel guilty at how I've spoken to him when I glance into his eyes. But when I do, I see nothing but love and forgiveness in his.

I hope he sees the same in mine.

Smiling shyly, I take his hand, and we walk out on the dance floor, where he spins me around until we're interrupted by Richard who taps Hendrix's shoulder and takes me into his arms next. I'm almost in tears I feel so cared for. After our dance, I'm back in Mason's arms.

"When I get you to Italy, I'm going to lay you down, spread these gorgeous thighs of yours and spend some time finding the honey that's in honeymoon. I'm going to eat you up, girl. I hope you're ready."

I burrow deeper into his neck, giggling. "Mason!" I gasp. "You're so bad."

Mason nuzzles the top of my head. "I'm ready to go. We've got a flight to catch."

I turn worried eyes to where my sister stands with Hendrix and our parents. The only request his mom had was we stay for a reception.

Mason turns my face to him. "Hey," he says softly. "Can we have a day where it's just about us? And we don't worry about anyone else? Is that okay, butterfly?"

I smile. "That sounds fine with me."

CHAPTER 26

You're In Love

I ROLL MY LIPS, and my skin flushes as Mason opens the door to our private suite within the palace walls he'd rented for our honeymoon. His eyes are hot on me as I step inside, and I linger within the foyer as the door clicks behind me loudly. Locking out the security and amplifying how alone we are. My toes curl in my heels as anxiety rears its ugly head, making me feel discombobulated.

It is the first time we've been alone since the wedding.

My eyes flicker around, barely able to see the beautiful space with its high ceilings and gilded wainscotting, as it truly hits me for the first time that I am married, and I have *no idea* what to do with a man.

I've never been around one longer than a few hours at a time, and I've certainly never cohabitated with one.

Mason insisted on a two week honeymoon, and I'm terrified.

I clench my fingers together as my stomach heaves with emotion. Mason steps beside me, and I almost jump out of my skin as his warm broad hand settles against my back, and he presses his lips to my temple. "Go freshen up while I bring our bags into the room and unpack them."

Jerkily nodding my head, I turn and walk down a hallway and find a powder room. Though it's not a full bathroom, I shut myself inside and sit on the lid of the toilet and pull my phone out of my purse, finding my text thread with my sister and typing out a message.

Help! -Mel

?-Isobel

What's wrong? Did you make it okay? -Isobel

Yes, we made it just fine. I'm just nervous... -Mel

Nervous? You guys already slept together.... I'm confused. Make it make sense. -Isobel

I roll my eyes, huffing out an irritated breath.

NO, listen! I don't know the first thing about being married. What am I supposed to do with him, Izzy? -Mel

Turning my head, I lean towards the door as my ears strain, picking up the muted sounds of Mason moving around the space on the other side. There's a bang followed by a rough, cut-off curse that forces a shiver to roll down my spine.

What do you mean what are you supposed to do with him? -Izzy

She sends the message with a few horrified face emojis.

I'VE NEVER BEEN MARRIED BEFORE. WHAT THE HELL AM I SUPPOSED TO DO?! -Mel

How the hell am I supposed to know? -Izzy

I scrunch my face up, typing furiously.

You've been married for four fucking years, Isobel! What the hell are you talking about how are you supposed to know? You're almost half a decade in and you don't know? -Mel

A knock sounds on the door, making me jump. "Melody, what's going on? Are you okay in there?"

"Yes, I'm fine," I answer, walking to the sink and running the tap on cold. I put my fingertips under the water and then press them to my eyes, huffing a breath so deep it hurts my lungs.

There's silence from the other side of the door, but his footsteps don't recede, and stubbornly I keep the tap running.

"I'll be out in a minute!" I call out loudly, washing my hands just to buy myself some time.

Opening the door of the bathroom, I step through and push a lock of hair behind my ear, giving him a small smile.

"Hi," I say, feeling shy.

He gives me a devilish smile, reaching for my hand and pulling me to him. I smooth my hands up his chest, and when he crooks a finger under my chin, tilting my head up for his kiss, my knees tremble a little as he spends long seconds licking into my mouth. He groans and pulls away, smoothing his thumb across my bottom lip.

"Let's sit down. We've been traveling for a while."

He turns, heading towards the couch in the living area, but I linger a bit behind, dragging my feet. He sinks into the couch and watches me as I meander over to the drinks cabinet instead and pick up the little welcome card to distract myself. But the wedding ring on my finger shines up at me, highlighting my new marital status and amplifying my anxiety.

"Melody, you're shaking," Mason says in that slow, assessing way of his. "Why're you so nervous?"

I wet my lips, putting the card back down and look to the side, meeting his eyes. "I uh...um..." I trail off, unsure of how to word it. I don't want him to think I'm stupid. Or possibly make fun of me.

"Um what, Mel?"

"I don't..." I take a deep breath and will my hands to stop trembling. Turning to face him head on, I nibble on my bottom lip, wringing my hands. "I don't know the first thing to do with a man."

His brow arches, and then he gets a wicked smile on his face. *"Oh, butterfly."* He hums deep in his chest, and the sound travels straight to my clit, making me clench my thighs together. "Don't know what to do with a man, *huh?* Sounds like a serious problem. Come sit on my lap so we can talk about it." My eyes slide to the seat next to him. But he shakes his head, drawing my attention back. "Sit down, or I'll sit you down."

My lips part on a shocked inhalation of breath, and my thighs tighten in response; however, he just sits there patiently with his head cocked to the side, staring me down.

"Okay, Mason, I'll come," I say softly, feeling my shyness ramp up even more at the hungry expression on his face.

I somehow will my frozen feet to move, and Mason makes an appreciative noise in his throat as he leans back into his seat and spreads his legs as I come closer.

"That's a good girl," he murmurs as I swing a leg over his thick thigh before settling down and pulling my other leg up.

His hands find the back of my thighs and then smooth up to my ass, plumping the flesh in his hands. He gets a knowing, sly look on his face as he squeezes harder, rocking me on top of him. I feel the color rise in my face, and he notices, based on how his lips curve at the edges. He moves his hands to my shirt, pulling it off me, and then unhooking my bra. Tossing that to the side, too.

His eyes fall to my naked breasts, and I fight the instinct to cover them with my hands, keeping them flat on his chest. "There's a difference between me and any other man that's out there, Mel," he says in a slightly rougher voice.

"Oh?" My voice quivers.

"I've waited for you. *Starved* for you." His eyes rise to mine, and I suck in a deep breath at the intensity in his gaze. "Every second that I was forced to deny myself your touch, your taste, *your presence* tortured me and bonded me to you in a way that is only special to me. I'm the only one in the world who knows what that particular ache feels like, so no, you *don't* need to know what to do with a man, butterfly" he says, leaning back and releasing a slow, deep breath as he rests his head on the cushion of the couch behind him.

I squirm on his lap, his words quickly overwhelming me. I wet my lips, determined to be brave despite how thoroughly his words have not just turned me on, but have turned my heart inside out.

"I don't?" I manage, my voice soft and slightly unsure.

His grin is so sexy. "No, sweetheart. You only need to know what to do with *me.*"

My heart skips a beat as his eyes pin mine. Unable to find the words, I just scoff, my gaze lowering from his.

Mason palms my cheek with his broad hand. "I wouldn't lie to you."

My eyes rise back to his. "You....you won't want me to leave after you figure out just how little I know about life? About.... being with someone. Marriage?" I half-whisper, a bit ashamed.

"Leave me?" he asks with a chuckle. Leaning forward, he presses his lips to the side of my breast. "Ahh, you're so very cute for thinking you could have slipped through my grasp after all these years I've spent providing for you, waiting for you, keeping you untouched for me."

My lips part. *"What?"* I scoff. "What do you mean *untouched?"*

"Why do you think I was so angry that you might have slept with Leo?" Mason pulls away from my breast to stare at me with a patient expression. His hand travels slowly up my thigh and then palms my right ass cheek, squeezing firmly. *"Hm?"* He tilts his head, his eyes flickering between mine. "I have paid off every so-called boyfriend of yours to leave and never come back. I indulged you in your quest for companionship so that you could have that experience, but I drew the line at anything intimate." His eyes darken, letting me know he's serious. "I let you play, but I didn't let *them* play with what was mine."

The fingers on my ass dig in harder as he dips his head, taking my right nipple between his teeth and tugging lightly. Throwing my head back on a sharp cry, I squirm in his lap as my fingers sink into the soft waves of his hair, and he nibbles and sucks at me leisurely, as if we have all the time in the world.

My heart races as my pussy swells with blood and need, dripping into my panties. My desire for this man is razor sharp, always has been.

Forever will be, I think.

I trail my fingertips from his hair down his shoulders and to the hard slabs of his chest where I smooth my hands over him, blatantly exploring. His skin is devoid of hair and completely smooth to the touch.

"Mason, what are we going to do for two whole weeks?" I ask breathlessly, tensing up as he tightens his teeth slightly harder. *"Mason!"* I yelp, flinching on his lap.

He lets my nipple go with a grunt, moving to latch onto the other one where he makes me wait for him for long, torturous seconds. "We're going to shop, eat, and swim. But aside from that, I plan on crawling between your legs and showing you exactly how badly I've wanted you. We've got four years to make up for, and I'm going to fuck this pussy raw every chance I get," he says in a harsh voice.

My eyes widen. "Mason, you're so *dirty,"* I admonish, feeling my face heat up with a blush at his words.

His hand moves between our legs, the clink of his belt signaling he's undoing his pants. He moves my skirt out of the way, his knuckles scraping against me intimately as he hooks his fingers into my panties, tugging them to the side.

"Lower yourself onto me," he says with a growl that makes my belly clench.

I rise up onto my knees, curling my fingers around his shoulders as he works to line his cock with my opening, and as I lower down, the burn of him stretching me out causes my legs to tremble.

"Oh!" I gasp, grimacing. Riding him is very different than him taking me. My pussy spasms, rejecting his thickness.

"Pause for a second," Mason murmurs, his other hand searches beneath my skirt until he finds my clit, and he rubs firmly, rolling it between his fingers and flicking it. My eyes slam shut, and I toss my head back. Whimpering, I gyrate my hips side to side in a feeble attempt to elude his fingers and the pleasure pain of him stretching me out. "Go slow. There's no rush. We've got time," he says.

I become even wetter, and I slide down until I feel the first piercing.

"Ahh!" My eyes fly open as I half-scream in shock as a warm wetness envelopes my nipple in a tight suction. My nails dig into his shoulders at the same time his hand tightens on my ass, pulling me back off to the tip and then firmly pressing me back down on him until the first piercing slides inside me. I shake, and my body mists with sweat.

Helpless moans escape my throat, feeling almost dizzy with arousal.

Mason pulls me off of his beautiful, thick cock, and repeats the movement over and over again until I'm finally at the last piercing. Tears of pleasure are swimming in my eyes, distorting his face. "On your feet," he says.

I pull my knees up until my feet are under me and we lock eyes. His face is flushed, his brow is lowered, and his jaw is clenched. He pinches my clit, and I inhale sharply as I sink the rest of the way onto him with an audible smacking sound, orgasming the second he grinds the base of his thick dick inside of me.

"Oh *f-fuck, I'm cumming!"* Shocked, I bite my lip as my head bows, and I shudder and jerk through my orgasm.

Leaning forward, Mason's arms band around me, one wrapping high on my back and his other forearm encompassing the width of my ass easily. As I pant and squirm atop him, he licks a slow lap up my neck to my ear as he pulls me off him almost comically slow. He pauses when only the tip of him is lodged tightly inside me. Shivering with the after effects of my orgasm, I let out a little whine as he raises an arm to gather my hair into his fist and then pulls my head back to look into his face.

"You're the only one who's ever truly seen me, Mel," he says quietly, pressing me against his chest so hard I can feel his heart beating against mine.

My throat slightly burns with how he's stretching my head back. His hard chest scrapes my nipples with every inhale we take, and our flesh throbs around each other. It's the most intimate encounter I've ever had in my life.

"You're worried about what to do with me?" He reaches a hand up and smooths his fingertips across my brow softly. "All you have to concern yourself with is looking at me with these beautiful, brown eyes as if I'm the only one in the world for you." His hand lowers to my heaving chest, his gaze tight on me, not letting me look away as he presses his hand over my heart. "And all you need to remember is how much I love you. And if you can manage to love me even half as much, then we'll be okay."

I stare at him, tears filling my eyes. "Okay," I whisper. "I think I can do that."

His lips curve into the widest smile I think I've ever seen, and he pulls me to him, burying his face into my neck and wrapping his arms around me tightly. "Thank you, baby," he says, pressing his lips against my skin.

But he shouldn't be thanking me. No, I should be thanking *him.*

Because Mason's saved me.

Time and time again he's come to my rescue. In so many different ways. I could never repay him back for all the times he's shown up for me. So if all he wants is for me to love him, well then, that's easy, because I've never *not* loved him.

I've always been in love with him.

And I always will be.

CHAPTER 27

Open Up

THE NEXT MORNING MASON'S got me folded double in the center of the bed, going out of my mind with pleasure.

"Look at it," he rasps, his usually elegant voice is strained and hoarse from calling my name and growling his pleasure for hours on end.

I give him a tiny head shake. "N-No, Mason," I plead in a small voice, feeling my heart begin to pound heavily in my chest.

He makes a low, deep sound in his throat, wrapping his hand around the base of my neck and tilts my head down. I shiver at the sight of his cock only three fourths of the way inside me. My lips stretched impossibly wide. He fucked me so good yesterday that I'm swollen, and he's having a hard time getting all the way in.

"I keep warning you and warning you not to challenge me, and you just won't. Fucking. *Listen."* He exhales a breath as his abs tighten, and he slides those last three inches deep inside of me mercilessly. Splitting me wide.

I screech, clenching my ass as I try to recoil from him, but he's got me pinned to the mattress with his big body and there's no where to go. His hips press into mine heavily, and he pulls out, the piercings rubbing against my sensitive flesh as he pulls out almost to the tip and slings his hips forward in a harsh tempo, making me watch the entire time.

It doesn't take long. My face pinches up, and I cry out as I'm attacked from every angle by pleasure so intense I see stars.

We struggle against each other as I orgasm. My pussy spasms as heat explodes throughout my body, and he grunts as I come all over him like a waterfall. My juices slick everywhere, wetting us both. Satisfied, he lets my head go, and I fall back to the pillow, shuddering and moaning as I'm just so tired.

He's barely let me sleep. We've barely eaten.

He brought me to Italy to fuck me to death, and we've got twelve more days of this to go.

"That's not f-fair," I whimper, wiggling my hips side to side as he keeps himself pressed inside of me.

"What's not fair about it?" he says in a low voice. "You said I couldn't get all of me inside of you, so I merely showed you just how wrong you were." His eyes rise to mine, which are watering. I haven't been dressed since he took my clothes off when we got here yesterday. "When I tell you that you're going to take all of my dick, Melody, I don't mean half of it or a third of it; I mean *all* of it."

He rolls his hips against mine, and I shake my head, whimpering as he begins to fuck me, nice and slow. His pace letting me know we're going to be at this for a while, despite him pretty much being inside me for the last twenty-four hours.

He fists his hands into the mattress on either side of my head and holds himself up, his muscles bunching impressively as he circles his hips and thrusts leisurely.

"You're not tired?" I ask breathlessly, letting my knees drop open and relaxing into the feel of him fucking me.

He tilts his head, giving me a slow smile. "No, baby. And neither are you. And you want to know why?"

I nod.

He bends, pressing a soft kiss to my lips. "Because you're whatever I want you to be," he purrs.

Three hours later we're basking in our private cabana, poolside, watching the other residents milling about in their swimsuits. I can't help staring, because there's a lot of people walking around in the nude.

I wanted to try, but Mason didn't let me.

I've been teasing him mercilessly about how tender his dick must feel, because I know I'm little miss throbbing city over here.

"You know," I say, tucking my arm behind my head and pull a leg up. "Like the time you were nailing that board and smashed your thumb and couldn't use it for like three weeks." I giggle, relaxing in the pool with Mason while we eat our gelato. Beyond the pool, the ocean is beautiful. The sky is clear.

The people walking around are gorgeous.

He quietly clears his throat before he grins, and I wish he didn't have his sunglasses on so I could see the mischievous look in his eyes.

A group of three women roughly my age walk by, and they openly eye Mason who's scooping out a spoonful of gelato without a care in the world, not even noticing them, completely focused on our conversation.

"So what are you trying to say?" he asks in a snarky voice, making me snort on another giggle.

"I'm saying your dick doesn't feel like how I'm guessing your thumb felt?"

He chuckles, and the girls slow in their steps, one even looking over her sunglasses at him.

"Girlie, your legs are amazing!" The one in the back says, staring at me rather stunned. "What's your workout routine like?"

Mason turns his head to look at them, but then immediately turns back to his gelato, taking a bite.

"Oh thanks," I smile shyly. "I run like, ten miles a day-"

"You have to find you a man to wrap your legs around, and that'll give you a great start-" Mason talks at the same time I do, his voice laced with amusement, holding up an arm when I gasp and throw my balled up napkin at him. One of the girl's jaw drops.

"Mason!" I whisper yell. "G*et-don't listen to him,"* I say in an exasperated voice, raising my brows and shooting him a "will you shut up" look when the girls giggle before moving on. He just grins and puts another bite in his mouth, chuckling to himself. "I can't believe you!" I say before peeking around.

That's when I realize Mason and I are actually garnering a lot of attention.

"Mason," I hiss, tugging on his hand. He takes off his sunglasses and rolls to his back, putting his head on my thigh. "Mason, there's a lot of people looking at us!"

"So? We look good, and we work damn hard for it. As long as they're not trying to touch you, let them look," he says wryly. I eat another bite of the gelato and then absentmindedly play with his hair. "We're leaving soon."

I frown, tilting my head down to look at him. "But we just got here like an hour ago. We haven't even swam. Why do we have to leave so soon?" I twist my lips as he tilts his head up to look at me, giving me a "really?" look that makes me roll my eyes. "Mason, we have to spend a little time out of the palace."

"And this *is* a little bit of time." He turns his face to kiss the inside of my leg, just inches from my pussy, and I can feel myself heat up from more than the Mediterranean sun.

"So, what's with the tattoo?" I ask, motioning to my name etched in his lower stomach. "When did you get it?"

"The day after your eighteenth birthday."

My brows rise. "And I never knew."

He smiles, I'm sure feeling very clever. "Nope."

"What else didn't I know? Were you fucking anyone?"

He smiles. "The last time I fucked anyone other than you was three days before I met you."

"How much did you spend paying my boyfriends to go away? And where did they go?"

He grins. "Two hundred and fifty thousand dollars per guy-" I gasp, outraged, "and where they went?" He shrugs a shoulder and gets an amused look on his face. "Who knows. As long as they didn't go inside of *you,* they could have fallen off the face of the earth for all I cared."

I scoff, scrunching up my nose. "Selfish. Anything else I don't know?" He suddenly goes quiet and I put down my cup of gelato, turning a bit. "Mason?"

"Enough questions. My turn." He turns to look at me. "When did you know you loved me?"

It hits me in my feels, and I flop back down on a huff of breath. "When I saw you leave your dad's office one day. You guys had gotten into an argument and I'd followed you out. Remember? When we all had just gotten back from doing the charity house build?"

He nods. "Hmhm."

Slowly over the last five days of us officially being together little things have come out along the way, like the tattoo, how we'd wanted each other for a while, Hendrix knowing, Mason fighting for me to have a semblance of a life but... now we're able to get to the really good stuff.

"I gave you a hug, and it was the way you put your arms around me... I think. Because for so long you'd always been there for me, but up until that point I hadn't been there for you in the same way. I felt like I contributed to our relationship, and that you'd needed me just as much as I needed you. And from there... I spiraled slowly I think..."

He gets a little grin on his face, but he remains quiet for a minute. "The day I met you I went and talked to my Uncle about getting the loan for my business. And then I went and bought the cufflinks that you see me wear all the time."

"The M initials?" I whisper. My heart beats fast and my brows scrunch together. *Can't be.*

Just about every time I saw him, he had them on. My mind races, at how every time we were together, he'd been pining for me just as much as I did him.

"Yep. Everyone thought M was for Mason, but-" he turns his face to me and then reaches out a hand and trails his fingertips across my brow and then down my cheek. "But the M was really for my butterfly."

Oh wow.

His words hit me right in the heart. I blink past the tears in my eyes and nibble my bottom lip.

"I love you, Melody," he says softly, his eyes boring deep into mine.

"I love you, too, Mase," I choke out, leaning forward to take his lips in a soft kiss.

We don't even make it into the pool; he packs us up and then we go back to the bed that we barely leave for the rest of the trip.

CHAPTER 28

HONEYMOONS

OVER THE LAST TWELVE days of our honeymoon, I've more than made up for the time we'd been made to spend apart. And as I tighten a hand on her ankle where I've got her knee bent back to the mattress, I groan with pleasure at how wet she is as I swivel my hips against hers. How beautiful her pussy sounds as I'm fucking her and how delicious her skin tastes under my tongue.

I swallow, relishing the sweet taste of her still inside my mouth.

Her pussy's so good, I would have happily waited four more years for this if I'd known this was what I'd be rewarded with, I think.

My eyes drag across Mel's face, eating up all her beautiful expressions.

The shadows dance across our bed and the wall next to us, the only light in our suite from a lamp set on dim in the very corner of the room; its wattage is barely strong enough to reach our bed, though the soft lights from outside make up for it so we're not completely in darkness, or silence, as sensual music fills the air around us.

I worked hard to plan the perfect honeymoon, even down to the ambiance, needing to make up for the years I'd been unable to wine and dine her the way I would have done had things been different. Years that sex wouldn't have even been the goal, or even mattered, because.... I don't *just* want to fuck her.

I want to penetrate her down to her soul.

Circling my hips nice and deep, getting her attention back on me. Her eyes flick to mine and widen, that beautiful pouty mouth of hers quivers.

A wince of pleasure shifts Mel's features.

"Ohh!" she sucks her bottom lip between her teeth and bites down on a whimper. I move against her slowly, swiveling my hips, being tender and sweet with her after our rough fuck from yesterday. Her cunt's swollen, locked around my cock in a vice grip that's tighter than usual, though she's not complaining.

I swivel an expert shift of my hips, grinding against her clit. The corner of my mouth tugs up in amusement as she traps a desperate scream in her throat, swallowing it down so hard she almost chokes on it.

I tilt my head. "You can scream, baby," I encourage her in a level voice. I drag my hard cock through her, tilting just a little more to the right, taking advantage of my curved cock and pressing against the side of her pussy for a different angle and pressure. She does scream, now. It's sexy, hoarse. "Does that feel good?" I chuckle against her neck. My hips rise and fall against hers in a steady tempo. She's locked her legs high on my back; her hands smooth down my shoulder blades, her nails slightly scratching me as she tilts her head back, whimpering. I nip the sensitive skin of her neck, making her gasp. *"Tell me it feels good."*

"Yessss...." she trills in a hoarse voice. "Yes, Mason, *yesss..."*

My heart beats wildly in my chest, but not because of *my* pleasure. No. Because of *hers* and of her obvious enjoyment of us coming together like this.

Her enjoyment of the simple act of making love with one another.

Her head turns to the side, and her eyes shut as she huffs out a breath of air. "God, you're so *beautiful,* Melody," I say, tightening my lips and fighting every instinct in me to pound into her.

I force myself to keep my thrusts short, only pulling out halfway before rocking back in her firmly. She counters every thrust with a roll of her hips, and feeling her participating despite how obviously I'm wringing every drop of pleasure from her body has me moaning my own ecstasy into the air around us.

A lock of her curls sweeps across her face as a gentle gust of wind filters through the open patio doors, fluttering the curtains next to us and cooling the sweat that's coating my skin. I groan, fisting my hands in the sheet under the pillow on either side of her head, relishing the contrast of the cool air against my wet shaft every time I pull out of her body.

Her lips tremble, and her eyes open wide, meeting mine in a helpless expression as the color goes just a bit redder in her cheeks, letting me know she's close to another orgasm. I flex my ass, grinding deeply into her, causing a shocked sound to escape her parted lips. She tightens her ankles and then bucks up into me, causing me to groan again-this time in frustration as I move my weight to my knees and reach for her legs, bending them towards her shoulders and doubling her over. Opening her up just a bit wider for me.

I shudder as her pussy clamps down somehow even tighter on me.

Bending, I take a straining nipple in my mouth, relishing the velvety texture and the little ridges of her areola against my tongue. Feeling her flinch, I roll it gently between my teeth before sucking it. The sheet falls from my hips, tangling around my calves instead.

"Oh p-please," she whispers, the desperation in her voice forces me from her breasts with a soft sucking sound. I meet her eyes, letting one of her legs go to run my knuckles down her cheek, sliding my hand to the nape of her neck and gripping softly. My fingers tangle in her sweat dampened hair that shows me she's suffering.

As am I. The restraint I'm exercising is costing me dearly, but hurting her already tender pussy would cost me even more. So I go slow, my back burning, the muscles in my arms and chest flex tightly as I worship this beautiful, sensitive wife of mine.

The bed rocks with us, her swollen tissues suck and tug on my piercings, causing tingles of pleasure to glide up my cock and draw my balls up tight. I let out a rough exhalation of breath, slowing my pace even more. Causing Mel to grab onto my forearms hard. My gaze immediately locks onto the ring finger of her left hand, the glittering princess cut diamond, my proof of ownership of this woman.

The song switches, and I adjust my knees and my pace to match the tempo of the music. Melody's visible frustration is immediate.

"No, Mase!" she says in a quivering voice. "Fuck me *harder,*" she whines, causing my eyes to slide to hers.

I firm my grip on her legs as she digs her nails in and attempts to buck against me, her cute feet bob in the air, the charms of her ankle bracelet tinkling with her movement.

I say nothing, my only response is to lean more of my body weight into my thrusts. The dull, smacking sound of our flesh colliding making me feral, and making her mouth drop open as she looks down between us.

My eyes slide down her body as well, taking in the sight of her breasts bouncing, the muscles in her abdomen flexing, and down to her clit. The fingers of her left hand leave my arm to slide across her mound to her clit, rubbing furiously. A grin tips my mouth, and I watch fascinated as she plays with herself.

Still I say nothing, content to watch her do whatever she wants to herself.

A desperate whine sounds out between us, affecting me so badly my hips falter, and my eyes snap up to hers to see her brows are furrowed, her mouth is pursed into an adorable pout, and her eyes are closed. Her pussy flutters around me, her hand moves faster before she lets out a half scream and tears her hand away, arching her back off the bed and shoving her breasts in the air as she orgasms hard. I maintain my thrusts, not giving in even as her belly tightens.

Her pussy twitches around me again just as a stream of her juices erupts from between us, flowing down her mound, across the trembling muscles of her abdomen, and slicking in the crease of her breasts.

I make a rough sound in my throat as her fingers claw into the sheet under us on either side of her hips, and the sight of her knuckles going white sharpens my own pleasure to a painfully perfect edge.

I'm not ready. This is our honeymoon, and I wanted to take my time with every time we fucked over the last two weeks; I wanted this to last longer, wanted to spend hours inside her.

I mean I have, but... it's still not enough.

My chest heaves, and a trickle of sweat moves down my neck. Heavy, hot breaths escape my nose as my body responds to hers, my skin pulling tight as my temper rears its head. *I'm not ready.* My eyes narrow as I pick up the pace, slapping my pelvic against hers and increasing my pace as red hot irritation momentarily tinges my vision.

"Fuck," I growl. *"Fuuccckkk."*

"Mason!" she cries out, pushing me over headfirst.

Her wetness flows over my shaft in a warm waterfall, her cunt twitches hard before squeezing and fire explodes over my skin as my own orgasm hits me. I growl, smacking one last time into her sweet body as my cum flows out of me and into her hot channel. I grind my teeth, the primal feeling of me orgasming in my wife heightening my pleasure. I tighten my hand on her nape and her knee as I bend down and take her other nipple into my mouth in a slight punishment because she forced me to come before I was ready.

I latch on tightly, causing her moaning to crescendo into a full on scream.

Her hand slaps against my chest as she jerks against me, smearing the juices that were on her fingertips on my skin. I pull away from her breast, grab her wrist and wrap my lips around the wet tips of her fingers, sucking them clean of her taste as I relax my weight into her trembling body. Staring deep into her wide, shocked eyes.

"We're not done," I warn.

I move my lips to her collarbone, kissing my way up her neck until I get to her lips, where I silence her whimpers and panting gasps for air with a lazy, slow kiss I make last forever. Until I recover, harden, and fuck her all over again like I wanted to the first time.

"So what's your uncle like, Mase?" Melody asks, drawing my attention from the dresser where I'm busy clasping my watch and trying to pick out a pair of earrings for her. She's seated at the little vanity by the window, struggling with her eye liner.

"Truthfully, I don't know much about him," I respond, settling on a simple pair of emerald studs and a delicate gold bracelet.

"Really?" she says in a shocked tone before scoffing, pulling out a makeup wipe in an agitated movement.

I hum. "Really. He doesn't come around much."

"Why not?"

Her voice sounds weird, I turn my head, seeing she's leaned two inches away from the mirror and her mouth is open wide as she concentrates. She grumbles, fucking up the wing again. I scrunch my brows and fold my arms, leaning a hip against the dresser as I watch her smooth the wipe against her skin and take a deep breath before picking up the eyeliner pen.

"He and Father have some sort of... beef."

She turns, putting curious eyes on me before going back to the mirror. I grab our beaded matching bracelets that we'd gotten from the vendor in the market yesterday and pull mine on the same wrist as my watch. I pull out my phone, texting Dante and Stephen that we're almost ready and to meet us outside of our suite so we can head out to the cars together.

Sensing she can't do her makeup and hold a conversation at the same time I keep talking. "You know, we were never really told other than something happened between Father and him that they can't get past." I elaborate, walking towards her and place my hands on the back of her chair, leaning in as she takes another makeup remover wipe and scrubs at her eye. I tsk my tongue and turn her gently, stepping between her legs and reaching for the liner.

She arches a brow at me, recoiling her face and pinning me with an incredulous stare. "What are you doing?" she asks sharply as I tilt her head up and to the side, pulling the cap off and tossing it to the vanity table.

"Doing your liner for you since you can't seem to manage it," I say, getting closer and putting the tip of it to the corner of her eye.

"Have you ever done this before?" she says with amusement, blinking.

"No. Now be still and close your eyes for me."

As she does, I begin to stroke the pen carefully across her eyelid, going slow. "You know," she says quietly, "I wonder if it has something to do with the missing journal from their archives." Finishing the wing she likes so much, I pause. Pulling back, I frown at her as she opens her eyes and swivels her head to look in the mirror.

"Hey! You did it, and it looks so good, too." She gets a wide smile; however, I can't enjoy it, curious about what she's talking about. "There are three missing journals, actually: your parents', your grandfather's, and your Uncle William's."

"Oh," I say absentmindedly. "Well, my parents just don't want us to see how raunchy they were, so they closed it off from us kids. As far as my Uncle, he never took a spouse so he wouldn't have one," I pause, helping her off the little bench and taking her hand in mine as we walk to the door to head down to the cars awaiting us outside. "That I know of, I mean. He dropped out of the family about four decades ago, and when he was here four years ago he never mentioned any cousins of mine so... I guess not."

"Well, that's sad," she says in a mellow tone. "He didn't wan't to come to our wedding?"

I shake my head, giving her hand a squeeze. "Nah, he told me once a decade was more than enough. He said he'd be more than happy to meet you on our honeymoon."

"Four decades," she breathes. "Mason, that's a long time to not have your siblings, your nieces and nephews. No spouse and no parents either? The poor man must be fucking lonely," she says as we take a grand staircase down to the lobby, our security tailing us in discrete clothes.

As we slide into the back of the car, she puts on her sunglasses, protecting against the Mediterranean sun. I hand the driver my uncle's address and click my seatbelt on. We ride in silence for a bit, and I hold her hand as we both take in the beautiful coast.

"It's so pretty here," she states quietly, looking out the window. "I'd love to live somewhere off the water one day. What sea is this?"

"It's the Adriatic Sea. William's got a place near here about fifteen minutes away that butts up to the water, so I'm told."

"Jesus," she scoffs, turning her head to look at me. "Italy's a pretty far place to relocate."

I hum. "It is. Hendrix gifted Vi a villa somewhere near here. We're supposed to drop in and check on it at some point."

Our attention is riveted to a pair of iron gates that open easily, letting us onto a property that hosts a sprawling villa. The car bumps over cobblestones, and when it comes to a stop, Melody and I climb out to the sight of Uncle William standing on the front steps. Dressed in a pair of beige colored pants, a white shirt, and leather dress shoes, he leans against the white-washed stone of his villa with his hands in his pockets, looking way more welcoming than I'd ever seen him in the States around us.

"Uncle," I call. Taking Melody's hand I toss her a glance and smile down at her as I pull her up the steps. "How are you?"

When we get to the top, he immediately pulls Melody into his arms. "Buongiorno! Look at the blushing bride. You're so beautiful, just like your mother," he says in a boisterous tone that's reminiscent of my father's.

Her mother? My brain picks up on that little bit of information, storing it to go over it sometime later.

I feel a rather interestingly lighthearted joy at the sight of William. He looks calm, even peaceful, dare I say it, in his element. With not an ounce of stress that usually marks his face when he's around my parents. He lets go of Melody to eye me.

"Mason," he says, pulling me in next. I go a bit more cautiously than Melody did; nonetheless, William doesn't act like he notices, patting my back and fixing his smile onto me. Dare I say he's the more outgoing brother? "How's being married?"

I smile, my mind immediately going to us making love last night. I clear my throat and look down at Melody, whose lips are twitching as she tries to beat back that wide smile I love so much.

"Well," I say. "You won't hear me complaining one bit."

William gives me a knowing chuckle and turns us, gesturing for us to go ahead of him through the red stained double doors. As we walk through the white, open concept foyer, he turns to Melody. "I hear you have an appetite for books?" he asks.

This time her smile does break free.

"Yes, I *love* them."

"Well, then." He takes her by the shoulder and then bends down as if he's sharing a juicy secret. "If you go down that hallway, you'll find an extensive collection of books I doubt you've seen in the States."

Melody's practically salivating. "Really?" she half whispers, taking a step forward. Pulling up short, she turns her head to look back at me. I walk forward, placing a kiss on her lips and press gently into her lower back.

"Go," I say. "William and I should probably talk a while anyways. I'll come get you for lunch if you haven't found us by then." She laughs and then takes off in the direction of the library, and I turn eyeing my uncle who's watching me thoughtfully. *"What?"*

He shrugs, giving me another good-natured chuckle. "Nothing much, but oh, to be young again."

He pivots and leads me through the home and into a cozy, yet expansive den where the four double doors are opened, letting the breeze and mist of the sea filter into the home. I can't help but be anxious now that we're alone. Other than the time four years ago that I'd come to him desperate for a loan to start up my finance company, I don't know much about the man. I never get a chance to see William, so, when Melody told me she'd wanted to honeymoon in Italy, I took the opportunity to get to know my elusive uncle.

Correction: *ostracized* uncle.

I step across the red bricks inlaid in the floor and take in the space, my eyes immediately going to a framed quote above the fireplace.

Assemble the shattered and broken pieces of yourself, safe in the knowledge that even scars can catch the light.

A jolt runs through my body at the words.

Seeing me staring, his eyes slide to the quote before flickering back to mine.

"It's there to remind me every day that the world doesn't wait, Mase." He turns back to the hand painted quote on the wall. "Even when we need it to," he says softly. "It's choosing to understand the raw truth about life: it doesn't wait until you're ready to break you down and strip you of your innocence and your preconceived notions of what love is... *or what family means.* It's choosing to understand that life will break you down, and you have to get up and find that drive within you to keep going anyway." He turns, his eyes pinning mine. "That's why I gave you that money to start up."

"You saw something in me my own father didn't," I say harshly, that pain of choosing to go at it alone those first two and a half years without the protection of my family name throbbing in my chest.

Even though I eventually formed my own sector under King Dynasty, I wasn't allowed in until my father deemed I was ready.

Uncle William's eyes soften; he folds his arms and shakes his head on a deep sigh. "I saw a man who needed someone to take a chance on him. A man who just wanted to survive. But I know what it's like to survive, Mason. And I knew that if you were just let out of your corner long enough, that you might have half a chance of *thriving.*"

His eyes rise to meet mine. Emotion rolls through me, causing my throat to tighten and my eyes to prick with unshed tears, and his voice softens with his next words.

"But...I also saw a man who desperately needed forgiveness and understanding. Something I was never granted."

CHAPTER 29

The One That Died

Back at home in New York, I bite my lip, the letter in my possession burning a hole in my pocket. I pull it out as Mason rolls our luggage through the foyer, and I can't even wait for him to put his wallet on the sideboard before I'm bursting at the seams with anticipation.

"Have you seen this?" I say the second we're back in our house and out of earshot of the security.

"Seen what?" He glances down curiously at the piece of paper I'm clenching in my fingers. My hand shakes, just knowing I've hit the jackpot of all jackpots with this letter. A small part of the missing piece of the King Dynasty archives I'd been studying. But a piece nonetheless.

I thrust it at him, eager to get answers. "How come you've never told me about this before?" I say accusatorially.

"About *what,* Melody?" he says sharply tilting his head. "Jesus, you're practically vibrating."

"Your aunt Stephanie!" I pause at the perplexed look on his face. "The...the second," I whisper, feeling stupid. Suddenly hit with the knowledge that I might have unknowingly stepped into something bad.

"Who?" His eyes meet mine sharply. "What are you talking about?"

I falter, feeling my face pale. "Um..." My fingers tighten, wanting to rewind the last minute of time so I can tear the paper up and act like I'd never seen it.

I have no such luck. Mason takes the paper from me, opening it slowly. I blow out a calming breath in a feeble attempt to still my racing heart as his eyes widen at the beginning contents referencing Richard and William.

"Where did you get this?" he asks. At my silence his eyes go back to mine. "Melody?" I wring my hands as his voice lowers. *"Did you steal this from William's library?"*

"No!" I snap. "I'm not a thief. I made a copy of it. He's still got the original."

We stare at each other for ten very long seconds before he turns, stepping further into the den, then sitting down on a seat. He puts his elbows on his knees and reads silently, still as a statue. His brow furrows, and he sits back in the seat with a rough exhale, scrubbing a hand across his jaw as he holds the paper higher. When he's finished, his hand falls to his thigh, and he just stares off towards the glass windows.

The second morphs into a full minute of teeth-clenching silence.

"Mason!" I grit out, reaching forward and shaking his arm. He turns his head and looks at me, his eyes roaming my face thoughtfully. "Well?" I ask hopefully.

"I didn't know anything about this," he says in a hollow, almost disembodied voice. "I didn't know I had an aunt....Father's never mentioned any of this." His face is tight with distress, and I knew I was right to wait until we were home before I sprang this on him.

"I'm sorry, Mason," I say quietly, rubbing his thigh, not knowing what to say.

What a horrible family secret.

He shifts in his seat, reaching to pull his phone out of his pocket.

"What are you doing?" My voice is hesitant, hoping to God he's not calling his father.

He works fast, swiping into his phone and clicking a number. "Calling Hendrix." My brows rise at the sound of the phone ringing over the speaker.

"Hey, Mase," Henny answers. "It's good to hear from you. How was your honeymoon?"

"It was amazing, Hendrix, but uh..." Mason trails off, bringing a hand up to scrub down his face. "Hendrix, who's Stephanie?"

"Who?"

"Stephanie."

"Mason, don't be a jerk. You can say the name a million times, and I still won't know what you're talking about. How am I supposed to know? The only Stephanie I know of works in HR at King Dynasty," he pauses. "Fuck," he says in a rough tone. "Am I being blackmailed or something? Goddamn it, Mason. Whatever she's saying, it's not fucking true! Do you hear me?"

Mason sighs, digging his fingers into his eyes and just breathes for a second. My lips tip into a frown and worry fills me at how serious of a situation we're in.

"Mase...." Hendrix says. *"Are you okay? What the fuck is going on?"*

"No, uh...." Mason scoffs. "Hendrix, I don't know how to tell you this, man..."

There's silence on the phone, and the sound of the door closing loud almost makes me jump. "What happened? Is it Melody?"

"No."

Hendrix pauses. "Is it *you?"*

Mason's jaw clenches. "I think we need to get Teresa on the phone, Hendrix."

"Oh my God, Mason." Hendrix bites out a curse. "Well, hurry up! Only you could have my ass cheeks clenched like this."

Mason huffs a humorless laugh, not responding to Hendrix's comment as he works to dial Teresa on speakerphone. It doesn't take long for her to answer.

"Hey, bro," Teresa says brightly, and in my mind's eye I can picture her beaming smile. "How was your honeymoon? Did you have a lot of sex?" she asks suggestively, and I put my hand over my mouth, blushing, but even her ribbing us about fucking doesn't break Mason from his stoic demeanor. He just clears his throat and glances back down at the letter in his hand. "Well, come on, don't be shy. Tell me all about it," she says in a chipper voice. "It's not like I watched you guys do it like *Hendrix* did," she cackles, snickering and snorting.

"Hey!" Hendrix butts in, sounding offended. *"You weren't supposed to tell him that we told you that."*

"Hendrix, is that you? What are you doing on the phone?" Teresa says in a shocked voice before going quiet. "Oh my God, what *are* you

doing on the phone? We've never had a three way call before. Mason, are you okay?"

"Yeah, I'm okay... but we need to have a talk. Melody stumbled across a letter in Uncle William's library. One that *isn't* in Father and Madre's library."

They all go silent for a few seconds before it's broken by Hendrix. "Well?"

"Is it bad?" Teresa asks, concerned. "Can you read it to us?"

"Yeah, it's pretty bad, I think. What are you guys doing this evening?"

"Why?" Hendrix asks hesitantly.

"Because we're probably going to want to go to King compound and talk with Father about this."

My eyes widen as both Hendrix and Teresa curse now.

Mason takes the letter, and in a strong voice, begins to read:

To my sons,

Richard and William,

The past few years have been heartbreaking, yet comforting, knowing that we are now safe together as a family. Even though it was at the expense of your beautiful sister, Stephanie II. Her murder at the hands of your father is something that I don't know I will ever heal from. And though your father pulled the trigger and successfully killed Stephanie, I know that the two of you will forever also bear the memories of him turning the gun on you two as well, and I will carry the weight of that consequence on my soul for the remainder of my life. I couldn't protect Stephanie, but I thank God that I was fast enough to save the both of you.

I want to apologize to you both for spending so long under your father's abuse. I thought that you two would be protected from his wrath if I bore the brunt of his stress and ire. I see now that it was the wrong move. I want to take the opportunity to remind you that even though I failed as a King, as a wife, and even many times as a woman, my most hurtful failure, and I believe *impactful* failure, has unfortunately been my role as your mother. I have failed you three in ways that I don't know if I'll ever be able to make peace with.

Naively, I thought by running King Dynasty, and following in the footsteps of your grandfather, that our family's success and reputation would protect me from the world's cruelty. And so, when I fell in love with your father, I did so without an ounce of caution. And, consequently, fell into a trap I couldn't see my way out of. Especially within the way we snare our spouses.

To put it simply, I was stuck. Your father became abusive, a *monster,* all in the name of power. And when he was done breaking me down, he moved to your sister. And I wasn't fast enough to save her. It is my hope that even though your father attempted to thwart King Dynasty's powerful legacy, and shatter the remnants of our family, that the two of you will come together to rebuild this family's legacy into something more powerful than ever before. Always put each other first.

Do not let anyone come between the two of you. Choose your spouses *wisely.* Make sure you take the time to ensure they are worthy of this place within this family, within your heart, and within your life. Look to each other for love and understanding. This is how we honor your sister, Stephanie.

This is how we avenge her death.

Your mother,

Stephanie King I

Eerie silence cloaks us in an oppressive blanket as Teresa nor Hendrix say anything, and neither does Mason.

"Let's meet at Father's in an hour," Hendrix says simply, not elaborating enough for me to get any clue of what he might be thinking or feeling, hanging up without another word. Mason bites off a curse and shakes his head.

"Wow," Teresa exclaims in a shocked tone.

"I don't think this is the end of the secrets, Teresa," Mason turns his head to the side in a frustrated move. "Melody mentioned our parents' documents are missing from the archives."

"Well, they're s*upposed* to be sealed, right? Only to be opened upon their deaths."

"Okay, so explain to me why *this* letter is not in their archives either. This is William's copy. *Where's Father's?"*

"Well..." Teresa trails off. *"I mean...that's not something I can see Dad wanting to keep, Mase."*

Mason's brows rise as a shocked look clocks his features. "Teresa, he's not supposed to remove anything from the archive. It's in the code."

"Mason, it's none of our business! *You know what happens when we press Father too hard."*

"Yeah... but don't you want some answers, Teresa?" Mason questions in a hard voice. "Don't you want to know this business between William and Father? And why keep the fact we had an aunt a secret? Why didn't they tell us, Teresa?"

"I-I don't know, Mason, but I'm sure there's an explanation for it. We need to at least give him a chance to explain himself," Teresa says rapidly. "Calm down. We'll meet up at Father's, and I'm sure he'll be more than willing to answer any questions we have. I'll see you there." She hangs up, and Mason's eyes, hard and full of resolve, slide to meet mine. Which I'm sure is full of trepidation.

"Will you come with me?" he asks.

My lips part on a sharp inhalation of breath. "Of course, I'll come with you, Mase. I'll always be here next to you." Despite my best efforts, my voice shakes. This man has proven to me time and time again that he's here for me no matter what, and I'll be damned if I let him go face Richard's potential wrath alone.

"Do you trust me?"

I blink, tilting my head and regarding him quietly. "Yes," I say.

His chest rises and falls with his breathing and I can tell that the Mason that's being presented to me is one that took him years to evolve into. "Good," he says. "Because between you and me, I feel like we're on the cusp of something that's going to alter this family forever. And I don't know if I want to be a part of it, baby. And when I say it's time to go, we're going."

Goosebumps erupt across my chest and arms at his words.

"Okay," I say quietly, reaching a hand out to squeeze his. "As long as we have each other." I slide to my knees in between his legs and raise my hands to his face, pulling him down to me. I kiss him slowly, thoroughly. Needing that intimacy and wanting to show him that no matter what happens we will have each other. Even through the ugly times.

He makes a sound deep in his chest as his tongue touches mine, and he pulls me into his lap as he sits back against the cushion, forcing me to straddle him while he palms the back of my head and kisses me deeper. "You'll always have me, butterfly. I ain't going nowhere."

A tiny thrill courses through me, because it's the first time I've believed anything without a shadow of a doubt. This man won't leave me, and he won't break me.

CHAPTER 30

WHO ARE WE

EXACTLY AN HOUR LATER we pull onto the pea gravel circle drive behind Hendrix's vehicle. It's an ungodly late hour, as we hadn't even gotten home from our honeymoon until ten, and it's now nearing midnight. I put the car into park, my eyes drawn to the rearview mirror where the headlights of our security flash behind us, followed by Teresa's Land Rover and her security tailing her.

Melody places her hand on mine as the muffled sound of doors slamming interrupt the silence, and she squeezes against me, causing me to look at her. As our gazes clash, she gives me that almost mischievous smile that I've come to know so well. She clears her throat and then leans forward, her perfume enveloping me in a comforting cloud.

"Don't worry, baby," she says, now stroking her fingers down my cheek. I nuzzle into her touch, finally feeling for the first time that I don't have to face Father's wrath alone. "This time, you've got *all* of us behind you."

"Thank you, love," I say, leaning forward to place my lips to hers.

Just then a knock sounds at my window, startling her and making her pull away. I fight to not roll my eyes and open the car door, stepping out to Hendrix who's got his hand out and a stern, no-nonsense look on his face that's usually present in a King Dynasty board room.

"Hey, Henny," I greet, reaching into my back pocket.

I pull out the letter and hand it to him just as Teresa walks to us, leaning in to give me and Melody a hug, who'd just appeared on my other side. The security's footsteps crunch on the pea gravel as they form a circle and step to the side to give us a minute to group ourselves.

Hendrix reads quietly to himself, and Isobel steps out of their car with her cell to her ear.

"Yeah, Mom, I'll let you know as soon as we're headed home." She leans in to hug us next, leaning in from the side so as to not press into her pregnant belly. "Yeah, okay. Okay. *Mom, don't worry; we've got it!* Love you, too. Bye. Hey, you guys. Sorry to see you like this so soon after your honeymoon," she says, giving Melody a once over.

"Hey, Iz," Melody greets quietly, shrugging her shoulders. "It's alright."

"So, what's the game plan?" Teresa asks, her eyes bouncing between me and Hendrix.

"Well," I say, "I figured since Melody's the one who found the letter, I should start-"

"No." Hendrix shakes his head, folding the letter back in half, meeting my gaze. "No, Mason, I think it's best you let me start off. You know how Father....gets...." he trails off, clearing his throat and flicking his eyes to Isobel and Melody who have adopted similar, worried expressions at the reminder of Father's temper. They haven't been on the end of it, or really seen much of it to be honest.

I have a feeling they won't be able to say that after tonight.

"If you insist." My voice is clipped as I slide my hand in Melody's and grip tight. "Let's go get it over with."

As we make our way to the front door, it swings open as our parents' butler, no doubt tipped off by our security team, welcomes us to the home. "Mr. Kings, Mrs. Kings," he reclines his head at us. "Please come inside. I have alerted your father of your arrival, and he is waiting in the study."

He turns to lead the way, but I pull ahead with Melody in tow.

"No need to accompany us, Jefferies; we know the way," I say. "Thank you."

An eerie, uncomfortable feeling swells inside me the further we journey down the hallway. The lights seem lower than usual, giving the home a rather oppressive feel. It's in direct contrast to the cheery brunches we attend where there's plenty of light and servants milling about to laugh and chat with.

I briefly wonder if this is how it feels when we're not present at King Compound.

Wasting no time I push through the door to Father's study, Melody's hand tightens around mine as both Father and Madre come into view. As our eyes meet, something tells me to keep quiet, so I don't even bother to open my mouth to greet him. I wait until both of my siblings and Isobel pour into the study behind me.

A bright fire is going to the side of the room, and I fight to keep my muscles from clenching. I hate Father's office, and for the last three decades of my life I've done everything I could to stay out of here. A visit to Father's office meant one of two things: an ass whooping or a promotion. And considering I just started officially working for the family two years ago, well.

Enough said, right?

So the fact that we're all in here right now makes my skin crawl. As does the look in his eyes. Madre stands next to him, dressed in a simple gown covered by a robe, letting me know she didn't even bother to change into regular clothes. It eats at me that she can't even let us be alone with him for any length of time in here. And has always inserted herself between us and Father, as if we needed her for a buffer.

Well, I guess *I* did.

Caution mars his features. Highlighting, at least with Hendrix and I, how he always treated us in a business sense first. Never letting us close. The loosest he lets himself get is during holidays or the birth of one of our kids, other than that, he always has a guard up. And where I thought he once favored Hendrix, after two years within the family business, I've seen that he's also held my brother slightly away from him as well.

Hendrix and I are no different. He's just more respected because he'd been the more responsible one.

And in a way my heart breaks for Father, because if what I'm gleaming from that letter is correct, his own father was abusive to the point he killed his sister, and then attempted to kill him as well. My heart tugs as empathy for Father bleeds in alongside the spite that has lived in my heart for so long that it only began to abate when I met Melody.

To know that his abuse led him to make him not even bond with his own sons. To set us apart and not let us close.

"Fuck," I mumble, feeling a headache gathering between my eyes.

Suddenly this seems like a bad idea.

Father's eyes roam us slowly where we stand staggered but still on the other side of the room.

"Children," he drawls slowly. "You all never visit me like this unannounced. Is something wrong?"

He puts his pen down and then places his elbows on the desk, pinning Hendrix with a sharp stare.

"A bit, Father, a bit," Hendrix says, stepping forward. "We'd like to know about Stephanie the Second and what happened to her."

I groan quietly to myself, because he could have worded that so much fucking better.

A tug pulls Father's lips down, and he blinks once in surprise. But he doesn't say a word to acknowledge him, even when Madre's head snaps to look over at him. Her fingers clench together tightly, and I know deep down in my soul that tonight isn't going to go the way Hendrix expects it to. Right now, the formidable Richard King looks like he's been struck mute.

Madre inches her way closer and lays her hand on his shoulder, but he looks a bit lost, as if he can't even tell she's there.

Seeing he's still not answering, Hendrix lays the paper on the desk in front of Father, crossing his arms and then taking a step back. If I thought the room had plunged into frigid temperatures, that was nothing compared to the icy tundra we're now all wading in at the sight of Father's eyes nailing themselves onto the paper.

Father's face turns to stone as his body visibly stiffens. My blood pressure rises because I know that stance; I know that look in his eyes. The temper that comes after is a fearsome one. My fingers clutch

Melody's harder as he opens his mouth to speak, his lips a thin, stern slash against his chiseled face.

"For my kids to show up here, unannounced, in a bid to ambush me in my own home-"

To my surprise, Hendrix takes a step forward out of Isobel's reach. However, I bring Melody even closer, tucking her under my arm. "Father, no one is trying to ambush you" he says. "We just want to know-"

Father stands up from his chair in such a harsh movement that it knocks over onto its side, and Mother puts her hand on his bicep, looking up at him with wide, brown eyes.

"Richard, you don't have to be angry. They don't know, much less understand-"

"Where did you get this? Did you break into my vault, Hendrix?" he snaps in a hard voice that causes my neck and chest to warm, turning that cold gaze to Hendrix now, and Melody moves as if she were to speak, but I tighten my arms around her in warning.

"It was me," I lie, ignoring Melody's small gasp, and Hendrix turning to face me. "I took it from Uncle William's library when we were in Italy."

I avoid locking eyes with Hendrix like the plague.

"Mason," Melody whispers, tugging at my hand, but I studiously ignore her as well. I will do anything to protect her, including lying to my father.

Father's face flushes red. His eyes fill with betrayal, but I stand my ground.

"What the hell do you mean you were at his house?" he shouts, leaning forward to slam his palms to the desk before bringing a hand up to point at me. "How dare you betray me like this! You know he and I don't talk-"

"Yes, and that's exactly it!" I say, interrupting him. "You and William don't have a relationship, but we don't know why. We deserve to know the truth about why our family is so fractured!" Striding to the desk, I snatch the paper up and hold it aloft between us. "Is *this* the reason why, Father?"

Drawn out seconds pass as I wait for him to answer me.

"Well?" Teresa steps forward now, her arms folded tightly around her torso. "Daddy, why have you never told us about Stephanie, or of our grandfather killing her *-almost killing you and William too,* i-it sounds like?"

The paper trembles in my hand; however, I stay silent. We all do.

There's a palpable hush that has descended upon the room. Energized by what seems to be a truly sickening family secret that looks like it affects Father very much. His chest heaves once, and his eyes flicker around between all of us in a moment of nervousness that is as rare as it is discombobulating. Oddly enough, this small slice of vulnerability chills me to the bone.

The sight of it makes me break out into a cold sweat while simultaneously stoking the fires of my own anxiousness.

Something's not right.

He glances away as his fists clench. Madre steps into him once more, but before she can say something, Hendrix speaks up. "Father, we just want to know. It's okay; you can tell us."

Seeing Father is still hesitating, I try to find my way in, thinking to help nudge Father to mend the divide between him and his brother.

"When I went to see William I saw a man who has been unjustly cut from this family's love and resources." Lowering the paper back to the desk, heat crawls up my neck as his eyes snap to mine, the vulnerability bleeding out to be replaced by fury. "I saw a man who is alone, and broken-" My voice rises as Father rips away from Madre to round the desk towards me, but I still keep my ground even when Hendrix hurriedly steps between the two of us. Isobel cries out as Father roughly shoves Hendrix to the side, and then I feel Melody's fingers fall from my arm as Teresa snatches her away from me. *"I saw a man who deserves forgiveness!"* I shout.

Father yanks me up by my shirt, lifting me to my toes and giving me a rough shake.

"You know nothing about what is unjust, or who has had to suffer from the decisions of others!" he snarls into my face, his own becoming redder with every passing second. *"You, who have had every privilege granted to you-"*

"What goddamn privilege?" I shout in his face, shaking. "What the fuck is privilege when your own father can't fucking stand you-"

"Father, *let him go,"* Hendrix says, stepping to our sides and then putting a hand over Father's. But it only makes him clench down even harder on me, narrowing his eyes as if he didn't even hear my words, continuing as if Hendrix isn't right next to us.

"You, who have known a life of luxury, what the hell would you know about being alone, of being broken?" he snaps, starting to shake now. "Of not having love? *Huh?* How dare you fix your mouth to tell me that man needs forgiveness when you don't know what that fucking bastard has done to me! I lost a family. *My entire family.* And the one person that remained, *the one person* who was supposed to walk by my side through life turned around and stabbed me in the back like it was nothing! And I was left to shoulder it all alone. Do you know what it's like to have your sister killed in front of you in cold blood-"

"Richard, let him *go!"* Madre shouts, her hands now over Hendrix's to try and loosen his tight grip. Her face is flushed, and tears are sliding down her cheeks as her small hands grasp futilely at my father's harsh, unforgiving grip.

My eyes go back to his and tears fill my eyes at the pain that's in his. Isobel steps to his other side, as does Melody, and Teresa stands on the other side of Hendrix until we form a tight circle. But he doesn't let up, looking me deep in the eyes.

"You're just like him," he whispers. "You'll betray me, just like you betrayed your brother."

The hair on the back of my neck stands on end, because the truth is in his eyes. This is how he feels about me deep down inside.

Hendrix tightens his grip even further. "Father, you know as well as I do that wasn't Mason's fault. He was taken advantage of-"

It's appreciated, but not needed at the moment. My eyes narrow at Father.

"You compare me to the man, but then won't even tell us what the hell happened between the two of you so we can make that decision for ourselves," I say in a level tone, but yet my heart races at the venom within his eyes. "Think what you want about me, I don't care anymore. But I will not bow down to you just based on your *fucking word.*" My voice rises. "If you'll hide this from us, then what *else* are you hiding? Who are we, Father, if we keep these kinds of secrets from each other? Because it certainly isn't a family. This is not how you raised us! *This is not the King Dynasty way!*"

Father's eyes narrow as he lets me go, and Melody immediately squeezes against my side again. However, I stand my ground. His gaze turns to us all. "Your uncle is a *snake.* He will wrap himself around you and squeeze every drop of common sense out of you if you let him."

When he turns his eyes to me, I get the feeling that warning was more for my siblings to guard themselves against me.

He turns his back on us and walks through a hidden door, leaving us alone with Madre who looks bewildered and beside herself.

"Children, I-" she gasps, bringing a hand up to wipe a tear off her face. *"I am so sorry for your father."*

"Madre, what is going on?" Hendrix implores, stepping forward and taking her hands in his. "Why won't he discuss this with us? Mason's right; we deserve to know what really happened. Or, at the very least, why he's hiding it from us?"

Madre looks up at him with eyes wide with worry, and perhaps even fear?

"Mijo, some wounds run deeper than others." She holds a hand up when Teresa goes to interrupt. "And it is not my place to tell, but yes... it was bad. It was truly horrible what happened, and even after all these years, your father still bears the brunt of that wound." Her eyes flick to me, turning even sadder. "I know your father gets angry, but his anger is fueled by unimaginable hurt. A hurt that I'll even admit might be something he may not ever get over. So, I'll have to ask you all to... to please stop pressing him for answers he's not ready to give." She trails off, and we all stand in silence, not sure what to say.

She brings a hand up again, wiping at her eyes.

"Is he going to be okay, Madre? Are you?" I ask softly.

Madre nods. "Yes, mijo. I'll go check on your father and make sure he's okay." She walks towards us, stretching her hands out and ushering us towards the door. "It's time to go. Go home and get some sleep. I will call all of you tomorrow."

She finishes escorting us out of the house and stands in the doorway while we get in our cars. No closer to answers than we were before we came.

Closing the door I lean back in the seat and put my fingers to my eyes, blowing out a breath. A tap on my window has my head swinging to the side. Hendrix is motioning for me to get back out of the car.

Opening the door, I keep my eyes averted from his as I step back out into the chilly night air.

"What?" I grit out, ready to go home and hole up in my closet and lick my wounds like I always do.

Hendrix steps forward into me, clasping me in a hug so hard I tense up. One hand clasps between my shoulder blades and the other tightens on the nape of my neck, holding me so hard I can feel him trembling.

"You listen to me," he grits out in a thick voice, his breath warm in my ear. I keep my arms tight to my sides, slightly alarmed and not really trusting it. "I don't care what he says, you are not worthless. Do you hear me?" My throat clogs up and tears prick the back of my eyes. *"Do you hear me, brother?"* He shakes me once.

"I do," I manage.

"Do you *believe* me?" His voice is hesitant, worried. I pause for a few beats too long because he tenses up now and pulls away, looking me in my eyes. I'm determined to remain stoic, not willing to break down in front of him. *"Mason?"*

I give a jerky nod.

It's the best I can manage.

"I love you," Hendrix says, letting go of my nape and stepping sideways so Teresa can envelop me in a hug, and then Isobel.

Everyone's in tears, and I just don't know how we're going to come back from this.

Everything's shifted, changed.

I'm silent the entire way home, and as much as I don't want to close her out, I go into the closet which has been my solace for years, lay on the bench and let myself cry. For myself. For Father.

Mourning the death of a fictitious relationship I'd always craved, but now I know we'll never have.

And for the life that I'd worked so hard to be worthy enough of so I could bring Melody by my side, now crumbling away.

CHAPTER 31

Hard Truths

"Mari." I half turn, looking towards the corner of the bedroom where Maribel stands with her back to me in a floor-length pale gold nightgown, looking out the window.

Her dark hair spills down her back, molding to her curved waist and flowing over her lithe arms. At almost fifty-nine, time has been very kind to her, and if you didn't know her you wouldn't be able to tell she was a day over forty.

The wind whips against the window pane as if the elements themselves can't help but to mirror the anxiety and anger that radiates off her in waves so strong they reach to where I stand on her side of the bed waiting for her, but it's a futile effort. She's not coming.

Her arms are folded, and she doesn't even bother to acknowledge I've called her, much less I'm even in the room.

"Mari?" I call again.

Finally she turns her head to the side to look at me, and as our eyes meet that stare of hers pierces me down to my soul. "How. Dare. You," she whispers through trembling lips, something akin to hate swims in her eyes, and I balk at the fervor of it. It causes me to feel hot, and my heart to freefall into my stomach.

She's never looked at me like this before.

"I'm sorry, honey," I plead, needing her to reassure me. *Needing* her understanding, because for so long she's been the only one who's seen the depth of my hurt. The only person who's witnessed how the strain of shouldering King Dynasty alongside my mental and emotional anguish has eroded my sanity and left me broken at the worst, and at my best, depleted.

But I think I've reached the end of my rope with her.

I roam her features greedily, as always. Her usual bright eyes are dulled, her face is washed out and there are bags under her eyes.

When did that happen...

I swallow uncomfortably.

"I don't want your *'sorrys,'"* she says in a hard voice that shocks me. Her jaw is tight with tension, and her eyes are filled with pain. She turns to face me, keeping her arms folded, and her brown eyes narrow in a look that's becoming more familiar than her understanding. "I've been hearing some version of 'I'm sorry' for forty years, Richard!" she snaps, making me wince. *"When are you going to stop saying sorry?!"*

I blow out a heavy breath, turning from her to shove an agitated hand through my hair and grind my teeth.

I know she's right. She always is. My heart thumps painfully as I futilely fight the feelings of anxiety and unrest that have plagued me for years. But now those emotions are compounded with my children demanding answers from me about horrific things, trauma, that I've tried my entire adult life to scrub from my memory. Maribel's been the only one who's kept me sane, normal.

If I lose her, I'm as good as gone.

But I can't lose her. She's the love of my life. Though she's kept me sane I love her. Need her. Cherish her.

"Those are our kids!" she half-yells, tears welling in her eyes and her face flushing a deep pink as her breath catches in her throat.

"What do you want me to do?" I say wearily, rubbing my hand across my jaw.

She walks over to me, her bare feet tapping the hardwood floor and her eyes searching mine, but I'm reluctant to meet her gaze.

"I want you to fix this!" Her eyes remain hard on mine, but her voice quivers. "I want you to fix *yourself!* To heal yourself, Richard. *If you aren't careful, your father, sister, and brother aren't going to be the only family members you've lost. Go to therapy!"*

I avert my face, inhaling a deep breath as anger floods my system.

"I've been asking and asking you-"

"Therapy isn't going to bring them back, Maribel!" I snap in a rough, loud voice, feeling my face warm as I finally meet her gaze and feel every muscle in my body tighten. "I can't relive that night. I won't. That night almost killed me! And if I'm forced to dissect it, I might not come back from it!"

She turns her face away, rubbing her fingers across her brow as she wets her lips. "I won't keep talking to you about this. Asking you- no- *begging* you to-"

"I'm your husband, and we took vows to always be here for each other," I yell, my voice strained as my throat begins to clog with emotion.

"You're my husband, but you are *ruining our fucking family!"* she yells, her face turning a deep red now, and a vein in her temple stands out. A tear falls down her cheek, but when I raise a hand to reach for her she steps back. "No!" she hisses, taking a deep step back. *"Don't touch me."*

"Maribel!" I say, feeling my face contort with pain. She never removes her touch from me or disallows me to touch her. Furthermore, her words hurt. They slice deep, touching that part of my soul that I don't think will ever be healed.

My hand falls to my side, and I take a deep breath, willing my emotions into check so I don't lash out at her. I know I'm deserving of her wrath. There's truth in her words, but I can't. I physically can't bring myself to do what she's asking of me.

It hurts too bad. Can't she see it?

I scrub a hand down my face, willing myself to stay calm. But the heat and tremors come anyway despite my best efforts. I swallow bile, wrestling with the looming panic attack threatening to break free.

"That's your son!" she yells, pointing to the door that leads to the study we just came from. Shame fills me at her mentioning Mason. "That's your son, and you treat him like *trash."*

"I am not a bad father," I growl, but the tears come along with the self-doubt, with the pain of her words, because it's true. My lips tighten as my body lights up with emotion so strong the hair on the back of my neck and arms stand up.

Her eyes narrow. "You are *barely* their father," she says in a tight voice laced with venom.

My face turns to stone, and I inhale a ragged breath, but she keeps her eyes tight on mine. My hands begin to tremble, and my face begins to perspire, but I bite the inside of my cheek hard to take my attention off it, fighting off the panic as the shame of her words eats me damn near alive.

"The only one of our children you act like a father to is Teresa, *and you know it. And I am tired, Richard,"* her voice cracks as more tears flow down her face, but I don't dare reach for her right now. "You told me if they somehow found out, that you'd discuss it with them. But the moment you had the opportunity you somehow made it worse. Our son told you that he felt like you couldn't stand him," she whispers, hurt lacing her tone. Her chin quivers with emotion. *"Don't you see how badly you're hurting him?* And I'm left to pick him up *every time."* She points a finger at me, narrowing her eyes. "To hold the broken pieces together while *you* get to wallow in your self-pity, and we all tiptoe around you because you can't be bothered to do what it takes to fix yourself."

"Mari, I-" I cut my words off, unable to express how I'm feeling. "I was ambushed," I say weakly. "And he brought up *William.* Mari, you know what that does to me. *You know how I feel about him and what he did-"*

"I don't care any longer." She holds up a hand and sniffs. "That is my son! I birthed him. *Twenty eight hours in labor, in case you forgot.* And I will not sit here and watch you treat him this way. The way you talked to him tonight was despicable!"

"Mari, I'm not-"

"You have stewed in your anger for four decades now and the time for excuses are over." She pulls her five foot one frame straight and pins me with a stare. "You don't want to go to therapy, fine. You don't want to let your sons close, fine. You don't want to tell anyone what happened to you, and leave everyone guessing and closing yourself off *then that's fine. You* do what you have to do Richard, but I'll be damned if I stand by you while you hurt *him or* our other two children."

"Where are you going?" I ask, but she presents her back to me, striding across the rug of our bedroom towards the door. "Mari!" I shout. "Mari, please!"

She doesn't answer me.

I blink, feeling my own eyes well with tears, but I can't bring myself to move to her.

"Don't leave me alone," I whisper, but she's already on the other side of the room, heading out of the door. "Mari, don't leave me." My voice cracks just like my heart, but I have no energy to fight right now. She slips through the door without a backwards glance, and my knees buckle.

I sink to the floor, my hands clenching into fists and I gasp as I dive headfirst into a panic attack. One of the worst I've had in years.

All I can see is my father shooting Stephanie point blank in the face. Her blood splattering all over the room. All over me.

Momma screaming as her only daughter, her first born slumped over lifeless on the living room rug.

William coming around the corner yelling, and Father swinging the gun on me, too. The sound of the bullet as it went off, but momma rammed her body into him and it missed my head by mere inches. Two more gunshots as he aimed wildly at William and me, despite her attempts at stopping him.

My nails catch on the rug as I grasp at it, trying to claw my way out of this hell that feels like it'll never leave me.

Me flinging myself into William and getting him out of the room, screaming at him to run while I went back to find my momma, rolling around on the floor, fighting with him. The gun just feet away while he punched her in the face, flinging her off so that he could reach for it. But I got it first.

My eyes flicker, searching for Mari's help, but she's gone. A tear rolls down my face, followed by another one as the memories become sharper, clearer.

Almost as if I was back in that room with the feel of the steel gun in my hand. I squeeze my eyes shut, but my other senses pick up the slack.

The smell of the smoke as the bullet released and hit Father in the head.

The sound of his body when he hit the floor, so close to Stephanie their fingers touched. The lifeless look of their blue eyes as the blood pooled between them.

I shudder, bringing my hands to my face to try to scrub the memories away. But they won't leave like Maribel just did.

No.

Out of everyone and everything that leaves me, the memories won't go. Gripped tightly around my psyche, planted deep. So deep that no amount of culling has helped because, like with all things invasive, they come back, even if I think they're gone. But they'll never be gone.

The memories and the pain of that night are here to stay.

CHAPTER 32

MY TEARS ARE YOURS

"MASON?" I CALL SOFTLY, knocking on the closet door. "Mason, can I please come in?"

My heart races, and tears prick my eyes at the sound of him weeping beyond the door. I crack it open, not waiting for a response, and my eyes widen at the sight of Mason sitting on the bench on the other side of the room, elbows on his knees, his phone in one hand and his forehead in the other, crying so hard he's shaking.

Big heaving breaths fill the air, and I swipe a tear off my own cheek as I advance closer. His pain is my pain, always has been. However, I've only ever seen the strong Mason, never the broken down and hurt boy that lives inside of him. And everything in me wants to heal what's broken.

To make him whole again.

"Mase?" I call softly, reaching out for his phone.

He doesn't answer me.

As I pull the phone away, the phone lights up to show me a picture of him and his dad when he was much younger, probably around eleven years old, laying a floor together. I put the phone to the side, and my heart beats wildly as my fingers brush against his hand, seeing blood smearing his fingers, and noticing he's clutching something else within his grasp.

"Oh honey, you've-you've hurt yourself. Let me see." He lets me pry his fingers apart, and I gasp at the mangled paperclip wrapped around his forefinger so tight it's cutting off his blood circulation. *"Oh my God. Masey!"*

"Go away, Melody. I don't want you to see this," he says in a raw voice.

My fingers fly to it, unwinding it from his finger and rubbing the raw skin. I lean in, nuzzling my lips to his jaw and running my hands up his arms. I snuggle in deeper, forcing his head back and straddling his lap slowly. I pull his head to my chest and stroke a hand down his hair and another down his back.

"You can cry, my love," I sniff, crying also. "You can tell me."

"He hates me, Melody."

My heart skips a beat at how tortured he sounds.

The blood turns to ice in my veins, and I shake my head because it simply isn't true. "No, Mason, he doesn't-"

He pulls back, his face red and damp with tears and his eyes swimming with misery as he stares into mine.

"Melody, all that man has done his entire life is push me away. He doesn't respect me. He thinks nothing of me. *Nothing!"* he spits. "All he cares about is Hendrix and that *stupid fucking company!"*

"No, don't say that!" I gasp sharply. I put my fingers to either side of his cheeks and lean my forehead to his. "Mason, he loves you. Richard loves you!"

"No," he gasps, clutching at my hips so hard I wince. "No, he doesn't."

"Mason, he loves you so much. I know he... he approaches you with a tough love style. But he *does* love you." I rock him slowly, feeling his tears soak my blouse. "When we fence, he's brought you up. He not only loves you, but he's also proud of you."

He pulls away from me, his eyes flickering between mine. Sad. "Then why doesn't he *tell* me, Melody? Why does he treat me like this?"

I wet my lips, feeling a shiver race up my spine. "Mason, he's been hurt."

"I'm hurting, too."

"I know, baby."

"I'm hurting, Melody."

A little line appears between his brow, causing my heart to tug painfully.

Oh God.

I press my lips to the top of his head while he cries into my chest.

We stay there so long until my legs go numb, and he's staring off to the side because he's so exhausted. But I keep stroking my fingers through his hair, rocking him gently side to side. Eventually I convince him to stand up. I wash his face and put the covers over him, waiting until he's fast asleep to do the one thing that soothes me during times like this.

I reach into my nightstand for my diary.

> Dear Diary,
>
> There's too much pain in this family. Someone's got to do something. Maybe it should be me. I have no clue if I'll succeed, but I'll never live with myself if I don't at least try.
>
> M. King

The next morning I wait until Mason is at work and ask for Stephen to drive me to King Compound. Doubting myself the entire way. By the time we pull up on the pea gravel, I'm suddenly worried that despite my best efforts to do my part to repair their relationship, I'll make a monumental mistake and cause it to become worse.

I hand my jacket to Jefferies to hang up, following him not to Richard's office but instead to a rather lovely den with a roaring fireplace and the most beautiful view of a perfectly manicured lawn. Pausing in the threshold, I glance around at the tasteful dark maroon walls and taxidermy deer heads mounted on the wall with swords and medieval axes, and fight the overpowering feeling of nervousness as Richard's eyes pin on mine.

"Mel, how are you, sweetheart? Maribel's not here right now; she's out for the evening. Some women's charity thing she heads that she couldn't get out of."

"Oh, I'm not here to see Maribel. I'm here to see you. I wanted to check on you, make sure you're okay." I journey deeper into the room as his eyes, though sad, flicker with a spark of warmth. He sits in a leather chair, with an old photo album open on the table in front of him alongside a letter. His eyes slide back to it.

Forcing myself to sound assertive, I clear my throat, bending to give him a kiss on the cheek before sitting in the chair closest to him and curling my legs under me.

"I-I'm sorry to come by unannounced-again," I wince, "but may I speak with you, please? It's really, really important." I pull a throw blanket over my lap, showing him that I intend to stay for a while.

"Sure, honey." Richard turns tired eyes to me. "I'm sorry for losing my temper last night, Melody. I hate for you to see me like that. It wasn't my finest moment."

Sympathy arises in me at how haggard he looks. Aside from probably not having much sleep last night, he doesn't look mentally well right now. I reach a hand out to him, placing it over his and stroking my thumb across his fingers.

"Can I..." Averting my gaze I hesitate once more; however, the look of pain that was in Mason's eyes last night drives me on and brings my eyes back to his. "Can I talk to you frankly? Not just as the Melody that you know right now, but... but as a little girl who's lost her father?"

Richard's eyes widen and he leans in, his fingers wrap around mine. "Of course, you can, Melody. You know that."

I swallow hard, deciding it's now or never. "You're going to lose him, papa," I whisper, feeling a tear trail down my cheek. His lips tighten, and he takes a deep breath. "And I don't want to see Mason live a life that I have to live. Not having a father. The only difference is I don't have a choice. My father is dead. You aren't."

Richard's eyes flicker from mine to land on the photo album, and as I look over, I see an old photo of what looks to be Richard's parents, Richard as a teenager with his unmistakable brow, a younger William who looks a bit like Hendrix, and a beautiful blond girl roughly sixteen or seventeen who has to be Stephanie. I squeeze his hand again.

"She's beautiful," I whisper. "Your sister."

"Thank you," Richard says roughly, clearing his throat. "I haven't brought out these photos in almost three decades."

Rolling my lips, I put my other hand over where ours are joined. "Richard, I'm the one who found that letter. Not Mason." His eyes cut to mine, but I stand my ground. "He lied and said he's the one who found it because he was worried you'd be angry with me-"

Richard shakes his head. "No, Melody, I wouldn't have-"

"He doesn't think you love him." I say in a rush. not wanting to lose my nerve. Richard goes very still, recoiling his head slightly and furrowing his brow. "He cried all night last night, and I've never seen him cry like that before."

Richard swallows hard. Glancing away. "I love him. Very much. But..."

There's a long pause as he takes a minute to find the words.

"But?" I press.

"It's complicated, Melody."

I tilt my head. "Love's not complicated, papa."

When his eyes turn back to me, the pain in them is so reminiscent of Mason's that it takes my breath away. "For me, it always has been."

"It doesn't *have* to be," I say determinedly. "Not with Mason. He just wants to know he's doing something right. To see you look at him with pride. I *know* you're proud of him! You've told me a couple times when we've been fencing. So, why can't you tell *him* that?"

"Because every man in my life has hurt me. When I extend myself out, I get bitten in the end."

"So you're going to make Mason pay for that?" I ask, squeezing Richard's hand. "I know he's disappointed you at times, papa, and

maybe hasn't done everything by the books, or how you wanted him to, but what those *other people* did to you is not his fault. And you shouldn't hold him accountable for it."

Richard pulls his hands away to scrub them down his face on a deep exhale. He folds his arms across his chest and looks into the fireplace.

"Papa," I sink to the floor and go to my knees. "I don't have a father, and every day it hurts... but at least I don't have to live with knowing that there's a chance for reconciliation, and he's too stubborn to give in. Don't do this to him. Tell him you love him. *Tell him you're sorry.* Hell, tell him whatever you need to to begin to fix this. But this *is* fixable."

I stand, digging into my pocket for the mangled paperclip I'd kept from last night. I hold it up, the dried blood on it glows in the light of the fireplace and I bend, placing it on top of the picture of his family.

Richard's eyes nail themselves on the small piece of metal.

"He has dozens of these spread all over his office, in his pants, in his jacket, and at home. He uses it to ground himself, and to remind him to keep control and be calm. If you'd just let him in, you'd see that he's safe, and you can trust him." I step forward and bend to wrap my arms around him, ignoring him stiffening against me. "I'd give anything to have a second chance," I whisper in his ear. "Take yours while you still have the chance."

Pulling away, I leave him, striding out of the den and nodding at Stephen to let him know I'm ready. A heart wrenching, guttural sob sounds from the other side of the cracked door, and I fist my hand, forcing myself to be strong. On the way home I contemplate telling Mason about my visit, but then decide against it just in case Richard doesn't extend an olive branch, then there won't be any feelings hurt.

I just have to know I did my best. And I'll always do my best regarding Mason.

Back at home, I go straight in the kitchen, thinking of doing something to sweeten up Mason's day. So, I take out the ingredients to make homemade peach cobbler cinnamon rolls. It's a new recipe that I haven't had a chance to perfect yet, and I'm still trying to learn my way around our kitchen, but there's no time like the present.

I keep thinking about my talk with Richard, wondering if there was something else I could do or say that would have gotten through to him.

The peaches and syrup mixture is boiling on the stove, and I'm rolling up the dough on the counter when my phone dings with a message. Thinking it's Mason, I wipe my hands on a tea towel and grab my cell, opening it to see a message from Karissa.

Hey bestie! Whatcha doin' tonight? Can you come hang out? Kari

I frown, reaching forward to turn off the stove and move the pan from the hot burner. After Mason being so upset last night, I don't know if it'd be wise for me to leave like this. I bite my lip, taking a couple minutes to slice the dough into three-inch thick medallions before responding.

Hi Kari, where are you trying to go? -Mel

To the Lazy Tiger, the new club downtown. It's a networking hotspot. I figured you'd come out, spread your wings a little. Maybe find something to interest you to get out of your funk. -Kari

I frown.

I haven't been in a funk, Kari. I've been on my honeymoon. Big difference. -Mel

Yeah well, the honeymoon is over. Now it's time to hit the ground running and figure out what you want to do with your life. Unless, you're content with being a kept woman, and if that's the case hell ya! -Kari

I roll my eyes, swiping out of our thread and pulling up Mason's number.

"Hi, my love," he says, his voice low. "Everything okay?"

"Yeah," I say breathlessly, heat crawls up my neck at his sexy tenor and I melt, a little like the syrup mixture I'm pouring on the cinnamon rolls as a matter of fact. "I'm okay. Are you okay?"

He chuckles. "Yes, I'm okay; it's just a busy day. I miss you." He pauses as I slam the oven door shut and fiddle with the buttons. "What are you doing?"

"Nothing!" I squeak, thinking I should have been a bit more stealthy about his surprise.

"Nothing, huh? Sounds... interesting."

I clear my throat. "So um...when are you getting home?"

His response is quick. "Probably not for a few hours still. Hendrix asked me to come up to his floor to see him when I get off, and I unfortunately have a late client." He heaves a deep breath. "He insisted on staying late. Why? What's up?"

"Oh, uhm, Karissa asked if I could come out to this new networking club tonight."

"Sounds fun. Take Stephen with you."

I roll my eyes.

"I can see you, you know."

I raise a brow, flicking a look around. "What do you mean *you can see me?"* I ask sharply, glancing around the room.

"We have a smart house, baby," he says. "I've been watching your ass jiggle the whole time you've been making those delicious cinnamon rolls. Tell me, why am I just now learning you know how to bake?"

"Mason!" I whine, stomping my foot, glaring into a random corner. "Your present was ruined!"

"Aww, turn a bit to the left and tilt your head up love."

I do.

"Hi," he says. "You can't see me, but I'm waving at you." I snort, shaking my head. "I'm so sorry, baby, but I just can't help watching you. You're so perfect."

Tsking my tongue, I head towards the bedroom and straight into the closet. "Okay, well, can you at least talk to me for a second? I haven't heard from you almost all day."

He chuckles. "I texted you when I first got to the office, again before lunch, and another time in the afternoon."

I grumble. "I know, but I got used to having you all to myself for the last two weeks." I flick through the garments on my hanger, pausing at a red dress.

"We're going to have each other for the rest of our lives, butterfly. No, you'll be uncomfortable in that one. It's getting cold outside. Pick the blue dress. The one with sleeves."

My eyes widen and I turn around, searching for a camera I already know I'm not going to see.

"Are they in the bathrooms, too?" I'm met with eerie silence. *"Mason!"* I snap. "You had better not be watching me go to the bathroom!"

"No, damn. You're no fun," he grumbles. "No, Mel, they're not in the bathrooms."

"Say you swear."

"What are we, five years old?"

"Say it!"

He heaves a heavy sigh. "I swear, baby. Sheesh."

I put the phone on speaker and strip down to nothing, taking my sweet time pouring myself into my dress sans bra and panties. Mason's breathing deepens on the phone."Fuuuccckkk, Mel. Look at that body."

I blush, my irritation withering away to nothing. "Tell Henny hello from me," I say, pulling up my and Karissa's texts.

I'm in. I'll meet you there at seven-thirty. -Mel

Yay! I can't wait to see you, Bestie. -Kari

Mason grunts. "Forget him. I'm more concerned with what you're going to say hello to when I get home."

My heart skips a beat, and I inhale sharply. "Mason, you're sweet treat isn't enough?" I giggle.

"Is your sweet treat your hot mouth wrapped around my cock?"

"No."

"Is it my tongue in your pussy?"

"No."

"Is it you bending over our bed and spreading your ass-"

"Mason!" I shriek, covering my face with my hands. *"Stop it."* My cheeks are so hot they feel like they're on fire.

"Well then, there's your answer," he chuckles again. "You know, for as much as I fucked you over our honeymoon, I didn't expect you to still blush like that."

I scoff. "Okay, well, *I do,* greedy."

He's very greedy. We fucked no less than three times a day for two weeks. Sometimes five.

He hums into the phone, the sound traveling down to my clit and making me wet. I'm seriously considering canceling with Kari, but I don't want to be that young wife who abandons her friends just because she's married.

"The interesting thing that no one tells you about greed is that the more you get, the more you want. I'm a little worried for your pussy, honey. Because I just don't know sometimes. I thought our honeymoon might make my desire for you somewhat tolerable, but instead, it made it worse."

"Mason, no one could ever accuse you of being a man of few words, you know that?" I say with a half laugh. Still finding it hard to believe that not even three weeks ago I'd been doubting his feelings for me.

"Well, we'll put that theory to the test tonight. Because when you get home, I don't plan on doing a lot of talking. So go. Have fun, drink a little, but not too much. And come home in a good mood."

"Yes, sir."

He goes silent.

"Mason?"

"Hang up the phone before I change my mind."

I giggle. "Yes, my love. I'll see you tonight."

"I love you."

"I love you, more."

"Not possible. Bye, baby."

"Byeee."

I get off the phone and do a little wiggle, imagining him laughing. I sashay my way out of the closet and leave once the cinnamon roll peach cobbler is done. Ready to have some fun and try to figure out what I want out of life.

CHAPTER 33

WHAT WE ARE TOGETHER

I *dare* you to fuck him in one of the empty bathroom stalls, girl.- Kari

THE TEXT COMES THROUGH as I'm sitting in my study. Since Melody's out I'm taking advantage of her absence, getting some things done for work and listening to some jazz, minding my own fucking business and just generally having a great time eating a hot cinnamon roll paired with ice cream when I open the message from Melody's friend Karissa. I freeze when I read it, and my blood runs cold.

What the fuck?

I frown, confused, going over to Melody's text thread trying to figure out what the hell is going on. But I don't see anything from her. I debate on messaging her back; however, a minute later another text comes through.

> Who cares? You're so young Melody. Live a little! Mason will never know. -Kari

I clench my jaw so hard a tooth protests, and I launch myself out of my office chair, calling Stephen.

"Yes, sir?" he says. A loud hip-hop beat filters through the phone making my blood pressure rise to what I'm sure is stroke-inducing levels.

I pull on my jacket, grabbing my wallet and keys and head out the front door. "Stephen, what the fuck is my wife doing right now?"

"She's talking with a few people at a table here at the club."

"Where's Karissa?" I snap.

"I'm sorry, sir," Stephen says, sounding hesitant. "I uh...I wasn't aware I was supposed to keep you apprised of her whereabouts when she isn't with your wife otherwise I would have called you, but she left the club about forty minutes ago with a couple guys she met here."

My phone dings with another text, and I pull it away from my ear to check it.

It's enough to let me know that I'm somehow getting texts that are meant for Melody, but they're being sent to *my* phone instead of hers for some reason. I have no clue what Melody's saying back.

> Come on. He's *rich*. All rich men have a mistress, and then the woman gets her own lover to cope. Wouldn't it be so fun to beat him to the punch? -Kari

Stepping into the elevator I smash the down button and pray that God grants me mercy and steps in to keep my temper in check. "Who's at the table with her?" I ask Stephen. "Is there a man there?"

I shoot Melody a quick text.

Baby, you okay? -Mase

"There are three men here, sir."

I freeze. "Is she flirting with one of them?"

"No, sir, she's being her regular, friendly self," he says.

Melody? -Mase

The bubbles pop up immediately, but the trip to the ground floor feels like it takes two years off my life because it's so slow.

Hey, sorry I didn't respond by the way babe.
I'm at the Lazy Tiger Lounge, what's wrong?
Are you okay? -Mel

I step off the elevator and head to the parking garage.

"I'm on my way to come get her. Call me if anything happens," I say, hanging up on him and pushing through the door into the concrete garage. I pull out, seeing Dante trailing me.

The drive also feels like it takes forever, even though it's only half an hour to the club in Friday night traffic. I hit every light, and by the time I park illegally outside of the club, I am seething, having read two more fucked up messages from Melody's trashy whore of a friend, along with a picture of her sucking off two men with jizz all over her face.

I bypass the line, ignoring the various party goers cursing me out and walk straight on in.

I clock Stephen right away, and he nods his head in the direction of the curtained off VIP booth. Melody's curly hair is the first thing I see through the flimsy gauze material, her silhouette unmistakable.

Making my way through the crowd, I push off a woman who runs her hands across my shoulders seductively, keeping my eyes on my wife. My chest tightens hard from being so pissed, but I keep my temper under check because as far as I know, Melody didn't do anything wrong.

But I'm not exactly going to sit around and give her the chance to, either.

I flick the curtains to the side, meeting her eyes immediately when she looks over in surprise. As do the other five people in the booth.

"Mason," she croons, getting a smile on her face. "What are you doing here? I thought you had some client business to take care of?" she says, turning her face up to me when I lean down to kiss her.

Though her lips are sweet as sin I don't deepen it, not wanting to embarrass her in front of whoever these people are. Pulling back quickly, my eyes roam down her body, seeing her legs crossed and her cradling her half filled drink in her hand.

"I decided to join my wife," I reply, sitting down on the cushion next to her. I lean back in the seat and cross an ankle over my knee. Pleased when her hand immediately goes to my thigh.

"Everyone, this is Mason, my husband," Melody says cheerfully, introducing me to an aspiring doctor, two lawyers, a wall street banker, and an engineer.

I'm sure there's a joke in there somewhere if I cared to look.

"Pleasure to meet you," I say in a clipped tone.

I give the bottle girl my order and make myself comfortable, picking up quickly that Melody is having a good time talking with them. Noticing right off the bat she's asking way too many questions about their jobs. I'm ready to haul her out of here so I can discuss the texts with her, but her talk with me about not being sure what she wanted to do with her career forces me to sit still and let her make connections.

But I'm still irritated with her friend, so I don't add anything to the conversation.

Twenty minutes in, the engineer looks at me curiously, leaning past Melody to catch my gaze. "Hey, don't I know you from somewhere?"

"Maybe," I say, swirling my drink in my glass. "Depends."

The wall street broker looks over. "Yeaahhh, I know you. You're Mason King. With King Dynasty financial. I've seen you walking the floor before at Wall Street." His eyes slide to Melody who takes a sip of her drink and keeps quiet. "You didn't say your husband was *Mason King."*

"Sorry, Lance, it didn't come up," she says simply, shrugging her shoulders.

Usually when people figure out who I am, it's party over so I stand, holding my hand out to Melody who takes it immediately, finally sensing I'm just not in the mood. "Have a great night," I say, waiting until she waves goodbye and puts her drink down to pull her firmly with me and out of the club.

"Mason, why did you even come?" she questions. "You didn't seem like you enjoyed yourself at all."

I click the fob on my car and watch it beep. Opening the door, I gesture for her to get in and then close it back. Rounding the vehicle, I snatch the parking ticket off the windshield wiper and slide into the driver's seat, waiting for Dante to flash his lights before I pull off.

"I came because of this," I say, letting more of my displeasure seep through my tone. I pull out my phone and open it to Karissa's texts and place it in her lap.

I'm met with dead silence as she scrolls through.

After a few minutes she puts my phone in the holder under the radio. "How did you get those? Are you having my texts forwarded to your phone?"

I frown, glancing at her quickly. "What? No," I snap. My voice is rough with irritation. "They just got sent to me."

She scoffs.

"You don't believe me?"

"It's just fucked up, Mason. It doesn't look good."

"No, *that,"* I half yell, pointing at my phone. *"That's* what doesn't look good, *Melody.* Why the fuck was she sending you those texts?"

Melody looks over at me with an uncomfortable expression on her face. "I don't know, okay? This is how she acts sometimes, she just.... she likes to play around."

"No, Melody," I breeze through a yellow light, forcing Dante to run a red. "That's not playing around. She's fucking bad news. What if all I had gotten was the picture of her and jizz all over her face and you saw it? *Huh?* You would have thought I was cheating with the bitch!"

"Okay, okay, I'll talk to her," Melody says, but I'm *so* unhappy.

I don't move to take her hand like I normally do, because in my head I'm making a decision that I know is going to test our relationship. She doesn't say another word to me.

She's quiet while I stew the rest of the way home in my anger.

And what's worse is the true reason as to *why* I'm angry. Because I had a friend once upon a time who almost cost me everything. And in the end, he didn't give two fucks about it. Guilt and betrayal that's four years old sours in my stomach as fresh as if it happened yesterday.

I need her to listen to me, because I don't want her feeling the way I feel.

She's quiet on the elevator ride up to our apartment. I clench onto the paperclip in my pocket until my fingers go numb. It's when I decide to break the silence between us, knowing I'm starting a fight.

"I don't want you seeing her anymore," I tell her quietly, watching her closely as she walks by me and through the front door into our home.

She dumps her purse on the side table against the wall, and instead of kicking off her shoes like she normally does, she heads straight into the den, ignoring me. I clench my jaw and place my wallet and keys next to her things before following her.

The lights illuminate our living area even on the dimmed setting.

The twinkling lights of the city shine through the expansive windows, but I can still see her reflection in the window.

I discard my jacket, draping it across the back of the couch and then sitting on the arm. I lean forward, placing my elbow on my knee, rotating a paperclip in my fingers. "Hey, Mel, am I talking to myself here? Did you hear what I said?"

"I heard you. I'm just wondering what the fuck me still hanging out with Karissa has to do with anything?" she says, giving me an annoyed look and snatching up a bottle of vodka off the drinks cart. She pours herself a shot, then makes me a drink, handing it to me and then stepping away to pour herself a chaser.

"She's a bad influence," I snap, placing my glass on the end table with a careless thunk. "And you need to end that friendship before something bad happens. I don't want you around her, Melody."

"That's not for you to say, Mason," she snaps back, taking a step forward and folding her arms, looking down at me. "She's my *best friend.* And she was drunk! Those text messages weren't even meant for you."

"Your *'best friend'* who left you with a man you didn't even know weeks ago to go fuck her so-called boyfriend instead of staying with you when she *knew* you two had been drinking," I snap back, leaning forward in my seat, pinning her with a stare. My voice rises with my irritation. "Your 'best friend' who encouraged *you* to fuck someone else, the *minute she got you away from me!* She's a fucking slut, Melody, and I don't want her around you, or around *me* for that matter."

"I never would have fucked him, Mason. I love you!" she yells, her face tight with anger. "Why can't you trust me?"

Her eyes are wild as she looks at me, and her chest heaves with her irritation.

I haul off the arm of the couch, pissed off.

"It's not you I don't trust; it's *them!"* I emphasize, pointing an arm towards the floor to ceiling windows where a million people litter the city below us. "That man would have fucked you like you were nothing, and-"

I cut my words off, seeing something different flash across her face. She tries to hide it, though. She averts her eyes and folds her arms across her torso and takes a tiny step backwards.

"What was that?" I say, tilting my head curiously and stepping forward, gaining back that space she put between us and then some. "Mel?"

Melody blushes, tilting her body a little and rocking herself. "Nothing!"

"Nothing," I scoff, nodding my head and looking to the side. Rubbing my jaw I turn my face back to her. Contemplating her demeanor.

I walk a slow circle around her, staring at her from all angles and making sure she hides nothing from me. "There's that fucking word again," I say, tsking. "I think I might need to give you a little education on it, so that maybe you can start using it correctly." I come to a stop directly in front of her, clearing my throat.

She blushes even darker, and her nipples get hard, poking through her dress.

"You want me to fuck you like you're nothing? Is that it?" I ask, tapping my hand on my arm as I force myself to wait. "Answer me."

"Yeah," she says, flicking her eyes to me and licking her lips. "Maybe. Does it turn you off that maybe I'd want you to fuck me like I'm nothing sometimes? I know you're more than capable." Her eyes leave mine to skim down my body, making my skin burn with need. "You walk around everybody else arrogant, *cocky,* pissed off. Like you have a chip on your shoulder." Her eyes flick back to mine, and I go very still. "You give everyone *bad boy Mason.* Well, when is it *my* turn to get him?"

My cock twitches, and I feel that heavy feeling of arousal that's always inside me concerning her illuminating a bit brighter, needing to be satiated. "Your turn?"

"Yeah," she says with a bit of attitude in her tone. "I want you to force me to come over and over-"

"I already do that-"

"And I want you to wrap your hands around my throat and tell me how good it f-feels, and tell me that I'm your slut, and then I want you to fuck me until I fall apart..." she trails off, blinking as if she's stunned she even said all of that. Getting that embarrassed look on her face that I love so fucking much.

I keep my cool. "Hm," I grunt, narrowing my eyes at her. "Are you even aware that you've got no fucking clue what you're asking?"

Her chin lifts and the fire in her eyes is addicting, making my own flame spark. Her bravery only strokes my arousal.

"Yeah, I got an idea. I've watched p-porn," she stammers, making my lips twitch with amusement.

"Ahh," I sigh, putting my fingers to my lips and rubbing. "Honey, porn only shows you so much."

She rolls her eyes and scoffs. "Yeah, well, I guess I'll keep on dreaming then." There's a tense silence where she looks to the side, visibly switching tactics. "I'll let you know what I decide regarding Karissa. I'm going to bed."

I snatch her arm up, hauling her to me. She yelps and struggles against me, but I just tighten my hold on her. "I already told you what to do regarding Karissa, Melody."

"You can't tell me what to do!" she snaps.

I walk into her, fast, pushing her backwards until the backs of her thighs hit the end table. Her eyes widen, and she stumbles, falling back onto it and bumping the lamp to the floor with a loud crash. I bend down into her face, wrapping a hand around her throat and squeezing, ignoring her gasp.

"I'm done coddling you," I say in a rough voice. My tone is clipped, my speech rapid. I'm obviously shocking her, and I don't give two fucks. She wants bad boy Mason, then that's who she's going to get. "I will give you all the leeway in the world, but when I ask something of you, I expect you to fucking show me some goddamn respect, *wife.* You will not talk back to me right now, and you will not bring that whore into my house."

I let go of her throat and slap her across the face. Not hard, but hard enough to know I mean business.

Melody's head snaps to the side, and her eyes flutter shut as she struggles to gasp for air, clutching at her throat with her hands. I let her suck in a full ragged breath before I throw her to the rug beneath us. She rolls to her stomach, but I use my foot and nudge her onto her back.

"You're going to learn your place tonight," I say, looking down my nose at her. "I'm not going to just fuck you like you're nothing; I'm going to break everything you are into little pieces and hand them back one by one *only* when it pleases me to do so."

She cries out, putting a trembling hand to her belly.

Stepping forward, I straddle her torso and then sit straight down onto her chest, being careful not to crush her. Her wide eyes meet mine, fearful.

Lustful.

I say the one thing I didn't think I'd ever find it within me to say to her.

"There's *nothing* about you that pleases me right now. So, it might take a hell of a long time for you to put yourself back together again. You want bad boy Mason so badly? You gotcha, sweetheart. You can have him."

I unbuckle my belt and pull out my cock.

CHAPTER 34

WHAT'S NOTHING, BABY?

"YOU WANT *BAD BOY* Mason?" Mason huffs quietly, almost like he's speaking to himself. "I'll give you what you want."

I wiggle under him as he yanks his belt off, the whoosh of it making my eyes go wide.

"Wait-" I stutter, suddenly afraid he's going to hit me with it.

But he pays me no mind. "There's no waiting," he says harshly. "You want to be a slut for me so bad? I'm getting ready to train you how to be what I need. Get ready, because you're jumping in headfirst, butterfly."

He takes his belt and wraps it around my neck.

Oh my God, I feel those butterflies fluttering around inside my stomach. Nerves mix with that nasty, wanton desire that I need for him to do this to me. To fuck me. *Use me* like I've only ever dreamed he would.

"Teach me! I want it, Mason!" I whimper desperately right before he tightens the belt and then winds it around his forearm, gripping tightly. Though I have enough room to breathe, I choke slightly as he undoes his pants and pulls out his cock. It's hard, dark and swollen. Glistening wet at the tip with pre-come. The bars of his Jacob's ladder gleam under the lights of the den and, not able to help myself, I lick my lips.

"I'm such a whore for you," I admit, glancing up at him, then back to his cock.

A spark of pride glints in his eyes as he looks down at me. "Keep your eyes on mine," he says.

I drag my eyes up the V of his pelvis. The sharp planes of his muscular abdomen and thick chest, which is stone hard with tension, until I'm staring into his chocolate eyes. There's a dangerous, rough tint to his voice. Carefully veiled with his usual arrogant elegance, but I know it's there.

My pussy clenches hard, and I buck up my hips impatiently.

Mason sits a bit more on me to still my movements, making me struggle for my next breath. The fire in his eyes burns brighter as he pulls the belt slightly, arching my head off the floor. "Someone's a greedy girl," he rasps. He takes his dick in his hand and then slaps me in the mouth with it. I squeal at the hot velvet feel of him knocking against my lips hard. I part my lips, intent on letting him in, but he slaps me again.

And again.

Sharp taps against my lips that sting slightly.

I stick out my tongue, but he slaps that too. I know my mouth is going to be bruised and sore tomorrow.

Irritated, I pull up another inch and suck the tip into my mouth then tighten my teeth around it. A harsh growl escapes Mason's lips, but he digs a thumb between my teeth, loosening my grip before standing and forcing me up via the belt around my neck. He only lets me get to my hands and knees before he pulls me, leading me a few feet over to the couch before he sits down heavily and spreads his legs.

His cock juts out from his body lewdly. The veins rope around his shaft and the sheer thickness of him makes my pussy even wetter, dripping down my thighs.

He pins me with a stare. "You want to be my whore, huh?" he says, reaching over to grab his drink off the table. He takes a deep swallow before putting it down and then grabbing an ice cube out of the glass. He pulls on the belt firmly, bringing my face closer. "Open," he says.

He pops a couple of ice cubes in my mouth. It's cold, uncomfortably so. I suck on them, and then I flinch as he holds another cube of ice to my lips, rubbing around and around until water is dripping down my chin and splashing on my breasts. My mouth is good and numb, freezing.

He notches the tip of his cock in my mouth and then jerks the belt *hard*, pulling me all the way on him. I gag this time and screech around how thick he is.

Mason pulls me off him, then firms his grip closer to my neck and begins to firmly push and pull me off him. I suck hard.

"Sheathe your fucking *teeth,"* he snaps. "You bite me again, and I'm biting back."

Obediently, I sheath my teeth and then pull my cheeks in harder. He growls, bouncing me on and off his lap. I moan, digging my nails into the fabric of his pants at his thighs, but he doesn't let up. He jacks his hips up, meeting me before I'm even to the base of his shaft, making sure I get every inch.

My neck burns, my throat burns. Saliva and his pre-come slick down my chin and smear across my cheeks, mixing with the tears running down.

And it's so *good.*

My arousal slicks down my thighs and drips to the floor underneath me. The smell of us invades my senses, making me even more horny for him.

He tugs me off him harshly before I'm ready, and then pushes me onto my back on the ground once more. His arm bands around my waist, and he lifts and flips me quickly until I'm on my front and my chest is pressed to the floor. He takes the belt off my neck and then pulls my arms behind my back, tying my wrists together.

"You want to be treated like nothing; then I'm going to show you what that looks like," he grits out. He pulls hard, making me rise off the floor and settle my weight onto my knees. My shoulders stretch, Mason's grip on the belt holding me elevated. "By the time I'm done with you, you're going to know what the fuck *'nothing'* means, too."

"Oh god, Mason," I complain, my eyes flickering until they land on our reflection in the window. Seeing my attention diverted, he turns us to face it head on.

My breasts are in full view as he holds me up, shiny and streaked with my saliva. My nipples stick out hard and long, drawn up tight with my lust for him.

He lines his dick up with my pussy and then slams into me with a thrust so hard my knees come off the floor, and my arms jerk as I'm forced into a deeper arch somehow. I come instantly at the feel of his thick length spreading me apart.

Jesus, his cock is so fat.

I throw my head back in a scream that echoes off the glass and marble around us.

When he lowers me, my legs are like jelly, not able to hold myself up onto my knees at all. My legs spread into a deep split, but he jerks the belt. "Get the fuck up on your knees, slut."

I scramble against the floor, struggling to draw my knees up under me. Still inside me, Mason rises slowly, adjusting himself until he's in a deep squat behind me. He leans back slightly, uncoils the belt once and then begins to fuck into my body so hard that I lose my breath.

He pounds hard, so hard I open my eyes wide in shock, seeing his face set in a stern expression as he looks down at my ass recoiling with every slap into my tender pussy.

Mason goes on and on, battering into my body. He pulls all the way to the tip and then slams back in until my knees lift off the floor again. I shriek, yanking against his hold. But I'm not even granted an inch.

"What's the matter, baby?"

"Nothing," I cry out, overwhelmed but not daring to tell him after how much I've needed this.

"Correct. Now crawl."

My eyes snap to meet his in the glass, and I tremble.

"Crawl," he orders, dragging the word out slowly.

I shuffle forward on my knees, and he begins fucking me again. Every few thrusts, I shuffle forward a little more, until we make it to the other side of the living room. My pussy clenches tight as I fight him, even holding my breath. My lungs burn, and my muscles lock in place as I attempt with everything in me to fight this next orgasm.

"Oh, you're cumming whether you want to or not. *Put your leg up on the table and bend forward,"* he says harshly. "Open yourself up for me. I'm not in deep enough."

My heart pounds hard and heavy in my chest. *"You're already in as deep as you can-"*

A sharp crack rents the air, and I scream feeling my right ass cheek explode with pain. He spanks me several times in a row, until the heat spreads up my back and down my thigh. He leans forward until his lips are at my ear. I pant, feeling another orgasm rise swiftly. "Did I ask for you to say a fucking word, slut? I told you to put your fucking leg on the table. *Now do it!"*

I whimper and shuffle further to the table, and then lean on my left knee, raising my leg and propping it up. Mason immediately starts pounding again.

And yes, he could get deeper.

"Fuuucccck," I wail, my mouth dropping open as he thrusts in a steady, hard tempo.

"Look at that," he growls. "Such a nasty fucking whore for me. Letting me fuck you all over our living room."

Despite my best efforts, my orgasm slams into me, but I'm stuck.

I flinch, screaming. "Masooonn!" I yell. "I cannn't! I cannn't."

He lets up the slack on my arms, letting me lean forward a little, still fucking me through it.

"What's the matter?" he asks in an indifferent tone, almost as if he was asking me what I wanted in my coffee.

"I can't take it, Mason," I gasp, "I can't take-"

He snatches me back up, until my back is to his front. "The word you're looking for is *'nothing,'* slut. Because there's nothing wrong with you. You've only had two orgasms, *so* I don't want to fucking hear it. *Don't be fucking weak.* Now crawl, this time to our bathroom."

He reaches over and snatches his phone up, pressing a few buttons.

"What are you doing?" I whimper.

"Don't worry about it," he says, with a wicked smile tipping his mouth. He slides it in his pants pocket, and then firms his grip on the belt around my wrists.

I cry and come, cry and come the entire way to the bathroom. I shuffle until my knees are raw, and when I try to stop, he holds me in place and gives me another orgasm. By the time we make it halfway, I'm shivering with pleasure. By the time we make it to the bedroom, he lets me place my forehead on the floor, screaming with something like my fifth orgasm.

Weak, just like he doesn't want me to be.

"Crawl," he enunciates slowly.

It's then I hear the running water coming from the bathroom.

We make it slowly, my knees getting a temporary relief from the hardwood floor as they now sink into the plush carpet of our master bedroom. The burning comes back though as we enter the bathroom where the floor is marble. He leads me to the clawfoot bathtub that's steaming with fresh water.

I stare at our reflections, and he stops thrusting.

My body is dripping sweat, my hair is matted, and my mascara is running. Relief fills me as I realize I'm about to get clean. He's granting me mercy. My pussy spasms. He sits high and hard inside me still. I don't care, as long as I get in the tub.

"Now, sweetie, do you happen to know the definition of what 'nothing' means?"

I hesitate, feeling the blood drain out of my face. "Like-like the official Webster definition of nothing?" I ask quietly, my eyes flicking, trying to think of the official answer.

"Yup. What's the definition?"

"Uhm," I wet my lips. "I don't...I don't know..."

"Hold your breath," he says, shoving me in the water. I suck in a quick breath right before he plunges my head in, and I flinch as he starts those slapping thrusts. I orgasm quickly, squeezing my eyes shut and forcing my lips shut tight, fighting my bodily instincts to suck in a sharp breath at the pleasure.

He yanks me back out, and I cough and sputter, gasping on a ragged inhalation of air. He rolls his hips slowly, making me feel every thick inch of him.

Oh my God.

"The definition of *nothing* is having no prospect of progress, of no value," he says, putting his hand to the back of my head. "So, to make sure you understand what 'nothing' is you're staying under until you have no air in your lungs. Suck in another deep breath, and make it count."

I get exactly three seconds to suck in a breath of air before he pushes my head back in.

The water flows around my head and weighs my hair down, and he starts thrusting again. With his other hand he reaches around and pinches my nipple, tugging mercilessly.

I flinch in pleasure, squirming against his touch, and struggling as I'm not able to breathe. My lungs burn, as does my pussy. He thrusts, moving his hand to my clit and scraping his fingernail across it. It shocks me so bad I scream despite my best efforts, and huge bubbles of air float to the surface.

He doesn't let me up, though, so I close my mouth to keep from choking, but my eyes are wide open. My heart slams into my ribcage as I stare wide-eyed at the bottom of the tub as panic begins to set in.

I jerk against the belt on my arms, bucking into him.

I put my foot flat on the floor and push, but he tightens his hold on me.

Right when my body gives in and I'm about involuntarily suck in water, he yanks me up. I cough, and inhale air desperately into my burning lungs, wheezing for air at the same time I orgasm. The air fills my lungs, the relief filling me from head to toe as sharp as my orgasm, and I scream weakly.

Water cascades around us, wetting my body, and the floor underneath me.

"M-Mas-" I gasp, not even able to get his name out right.

"Fun fact, butterfly," Mason growls in my ear. "The opposite of nothing is *everything*. And that's what I'm prepared to give you: everything. And in case you haven't noticed, I don't particularly care for that word. So if I have to hear it, you're going to damn well know how to use it, and how it feels to *be it.*"

He pulls me up, my hair dripping, and walks me to the bedroom where he undoes the belt, freeing my wrists and throws me on the bed sopping wet. He crawls in with me, and I'm seriously wondering how much more I can take.

"Mason," I whimper, "pleaasseee..."

Mason says nothing, just kneels between my spread legs and spreads me wider for him.

Tilting his head, he opens his mouth and a string of saliva drips from his mouth and to my pussy. He ignores me, his face the picture of concentration, a muscle clenching in his jaw as he works to notch his thick tip back to my opening.

"What's wrong?" he finally asks, keeping his head tilted down as he slowly pushes forward. "Talk to me while I'm feeding you my cock. I asked you *what's the matter?"*

His eyes snap to mine, making my pussy clench with just one hot look. "Nothing," I answer, my lips trembling.

"That's right baby, *correct again.*"

"What are you doing to me?" I say breathlessly, tilting my head back as he presses a little deeper. *"Mason?"*

He stills a third of the way in on a half laugh. "I'm fucking the shit out of my wife. I know it's a bit unbearable right now, but what are you going to do to stop me?" he says, cutting his eyes to me.

"Nothing."

He smiles nice and slow. "That's right baby, *and that's a good, good girl."* His fingers travel down my body to my clit where he grasps it, rolling and rolling until my eyes roll into the back of my head. I come again with a sharp cry.

"That's one piece of you back. Now, we've got the rest of the night to work on the others."

I whimper, staring up at him helplessly as my eyes well up with tears of acute pleasure that blur his figure before they slip down my cheeks, affording me a crystal clear view of his face before blurring again. That burning sensation settles into my core and flushes throughout my body, making my nipples, toes, ears, and fingers hot. The sign that the hard orgasm is coming, the one that tightens its grip around me and refuses to let me go.

I moan, whimpering as I clench my muscles, hold my breath, and try everything in my power to fight back against it. But it's no use. I stare deep in his eyes as the crack starts slowly, before splitting me right down the center of my being. I suck a sharp breath through my nose and clench my teeth against the scream trying to bubble up my throat as my entire being implodes.

I flinch, my knees jerking against his tight hold. My body's only outward reaction to the little death I'm experiencing.

A wicked smile curves his lip on the right side. "What do you need, baby, hm?" Mason asks, giving me hard, slapping thrusts that sting and go on and on and on.

"Nothing," I sob, tears continually falling down my face with how hard my orgasm is taking over my body. An orgasm that hasn't stopped since it started who knows how long ago now. He lets his grip on my legs go to move one hand to my pussy where he rolls my clit, and one to my nipple where he plucks and rolls it between his fingers.

A high keening noise escapes me as I flood the space between us. The sounds become wetter, sharper, and my legs splay open wide as I don't have the strength to hold them up on my own anymore as he batters against my pussy.

It burns, it's so overpowering.

Mason's hands leave me to wrap around the crooks of my knees, pushing them so far down into the mattress that my hips are elevated off the bed, granting him full access to my aching pussy.

And he's owning every bit of it.

The pleasure slices sharp through me, cutting deeper and deeper with every collision. I stare up at him mute, helplessly, while he so thoughtfully gives me what I told him I craved. And I fall in love with him somehow even more.

"I can't hear you," he snarls down at me, pounding into me with no mercy. Sweat slicks down my neck and in the valley of my breasts. My hair is heavy, the curls damp with sweat. He tilts his head, leaning down further to get into my face when I begin to thrash my head, caught up tight in this insane orgasm that feels like it's going to kill me. *"Butterfly, I said I can't hear you,"* he grunts with the next heavy roll of his hips, letting me know I need to look at him.

I turn my face back to his sucking in a sharp breath.

"Nothing!" I scream hoarsely, a long drawn out wail that almost takes my voice.

"That's right, sweetheart; that's the right definition of that word. *Finally,"* his voice loses a little of his roughness but his thrusts don't.

He keeps them hard, fast, our skin slapping loudly. The bed is shaking. The headboard banging. My fingers curling into the sheets and tugging as I arch deeply for him. Whining when he bends to suck a sensitive nipple into his mouth. The wet heat of him is almost too much, and black tinges my vision as he pushes and pushes until I can't take anymore.

Not letting up until I, in fact, give him everything.

Instead of nothing.

CHAPTER 35

Peaches Are Good

Wrapping my arms around her I bring her close to me. "Shhh," I shush her gently, pressing my lips to hers in a chaste kiss, cradling her against my chest.

It's the next morning. I let her sleep in, and she woke up moaning, writhing under the covers.

Last night was the longest I've ever seen her come. It's also been the hardest I've pushed her body since we've been married. I stroke my hand down her hair, and though her arms are wrapped around me, I'm sensing a withdrawal I'm not sure I'm comfortable with.

"Would you like a bath?" I murmur. Her head shoots up to mine and her eyes widen. I bite back a grin, smoothing a fingertip over her lips. "A *real* one."

She lets out a relieved breath and then nods her head, staying quiet. Seems I've fucked all the sass out of her.

Five minutes later she's in the tub and I bring her a glass of water and a Tylenol. "Thank you," she whispers hoarsely.

I watch her carefully as she takes the medicine, seeing her nipples, slightly red from me sucking on them half the night, poking out of the water. Not able to help myself, I dip a hand in and cup her breasts, fluttering my thumb over the tip and tilting my head at the way she bites her lip and whimpers when I roll it ever so gently between my fingers.

"You did so good last night," I praise her, seeing her sink further into the tub. She draws her knees up until they poke out of the water. My eyes nail themselves onto the bruises there, and I take my hand from her breast and rub them gently. Her head turns lazily to the side, and she meets my eye. I move my hand up to her tender neck, the skin slightly abraded from my belt. It's not wintertime yet so she won't get away with wearing a turtleneck. I twist my lips. "We're all supposed to go to your mom's place today."

She heaves a deep sigh, her eyes turning to the water in front of her. "Yeah, I remember. I'm supposed to be bringing the chocolate chip cookies."

The air becomes silent and thick with tension. I bring my eyes to her and place a finger to her cheek, turning her to face me. "Melody, are you okay with what we did last night?"

Time itself almost stops as I hold my breath, waiting for her reply. Her eyes snap to mine, and she holds my gaze for a few beats of time, a flush coloring her cheeks. She looks away before wetting her lips. "I loved it," she replies tentatively. But I know her well enough to know by now that it's only shyness that's causing her to sound like this.

I reach out, pulling her to face me again. She tries to jerk away, but I grip her tightly. "No, don't look away. Not for this." I wait until her eyes meet mine again. "Baby, I know that you're shy, and I love that so much, I really do, but I need you to be brave and do this one thing for me. Have this *one* conversation with me, and then you can go back to being shy. I just need to know. Are you sure?"

Her eyes search mine, her fingers tremble on my wrist, but I don't let her break my eye contact.

"Because I fucked you really, really rough, baby. *And if I h-hurt you-"* My voice catches as emotion takes me over. *Fuck, I'll never live with myself.*

"No," she says sharply, reaching out to put her fingers on my hand. "It actually hurt so good." Her voice trembles with nerves. "I asked for it. I *wanted* it, Mason. Everything you did felt so good." She rubs her fingers on my lips as her own tremble. "So right."

Leaning forward I press my lips to hers. "We should have had a safe word baby. That's my bad," I mumble against her lips. Pulling back I allow her shy look and even her sinking further into the tub until the water covers her chin. "Pick one."

"A safe word?"

I nod. "Yes, baby. If you want to have sex like how we did last night, then this is the only way I'm comfortable. So, I need you to pick one."

A line appears above her brow and she thinks hard. Suddenly, a smile crosses her face. "Peaches."

I put a hand to my mouth to stifle my urge to laugh. "Allright. Peaches it is." Chucking her under the chin, I stand and remove my sweatpants, stepping into the tub behind her.

I chuckle low in my throat at how hard Melody's blushing as we stand outside Donna's front door, waiting for her to open it. I hold the platter of cookies in one hand, keeping Melody tucked under the opposite arm and playing with her fingers.

I'm leaning down to her ear, about to tease her about how she almost levitated off the bed last night when I playfully licked her ass when the door opens, forcing my spine to straighten. I wipe the sheepish look off my face quickly, but I think Donna still saw.

"Baby!" Donna's joyful smile never fails to be contagious. We're all smiles as she steps into Melody and wraps her up in a hug, then me.

"Hey, mama," I greet her. She squeezes my arms and slaps my bicep playfully. "I see you, you can try, but you'll never be able to out muscle me."

I laugh. "I wouldn't even dare, mama."

I don't bother telling her the only reason I'm so defined today is because I spent all night using her daughter as a piece of workout equipment.

"Well, don't stand outside like strangers. I really need to get you guys a key, don't I." She's all smiles as she ushers us into the house. It's a stone one-story Mcmansion on a very prestigious side of town in a gated community. Isobel wanted her to move in with them, but she put her foot down, to Hendrix's happiness. The woman is clean, and I always smell bleach whenever I come over. Tonight's no different, though there are other scents mixed in.

"Hmm, smells like tacos?" I guess.

"Yes, and I got stuff for buffalo chicken dip, too!"

I flick her an amused look, seeing Melody fiddling with her jacket that's currently covering up the state of her neck. "Oh man, mama, you spoil me."

She really does.

"So who's all here?" Melody asks.

"Everyone. You are the last ones to arrive, *as usual,"* she stresses, making me chuckle. "Here, give me those. I'll put them in the kitchen. You two go say hi to everyone. They're in the living room."

She takes the platter of cookies from me, and I nod at Pablo, the security guy Hendrix gave her four years ago and never took back. He sits off the foyer area, doing something on his tablet. Stephen joins him, and I have half a mind to dismiss him for a bit. But the last time I did he'd explained that he and Pablo are good friends, so I leave it optional whenever we're all together.

We walk into the living room hand in hand, and Father is the first one to catch my eye, surprisingly enough.

"Hey, son," he says, "How are you?"

Did the world stop turning or something?

I arch a brow and wet my lip, unsure. "I'm okay, Father; how...uh...how are you?"

He nods, giving me a small smile. "Doing okay. Doing okay."

Well, that's fucking odd. I blink, my eyes sliding to Hendrix who has a minute frown on his face. I bend down to Melody's ear. "Is Father seriously going to act like the last time we were all together we weren't at each other's throats?"

"Who cares," she whispers back, "just go with it."

She steps out of reach to bend down to give Isobel a hug who looks like she's about to pop open all over the living room. My eyes rise, before flicking to Hendrix again. No fucking wonder he looks like death.

"Hey, uh, Izzy. When are you due, hermosa?" I ask, bending down to kiss her cheek.

"Yesterday. I was due *yesterday,* Mason."

I ignore her irritated tone and grin. "Really? Shouldn't you be in the hospital then?"

She rolls her eyes. "No, jerk, I have two more weeks to go."

"Ohhh." I sit, pulling Melody down next to me when she's done giving out hugs. "So are you going to the Balducci-Scognamiglio wedding this Sunday?"

"I plan on it. I have to go..."

I nod. "Maybe the baby will come early and spare us all the hassle of going."

Father gives us all a stern look when we look too happy for his tastes. "We will do no such thing. We're all going to the wedding to express our gratitude and solidarity, and the baby is coming exactly when he's supposed to. *End of."* Father motions with his hands like that's the legitimate end of it, and I can't help laughing, bringing his eyes to mine.

"So, how's life?" he says, flicking his eyes to Melody, who has adopted a rather strange smile. She tugs at the hem of her jacket again.

"It's fine," I toss to Father, glancing around and not seeing mama. "Hey, where's Madre? Did she not come?"

He gets an uncomfortable look on his face that makes my eyes narrow. "She's in the kitchen with Donna."

His eyes go a little wary as he turns his head to look towards the kitchen door, and for a second he looks a little lost. I throw a look at Hendrix who just gives me a small shake of his head in a *'don't say shit'* look.

"Ah." Bending down to Melody, I nudge her arm. "Baby, just take it off. I can tell you're hot."

She shakes her head. *"Nu-uh. I'm okay."*

"Dinner's done!" Donna yells from the kitchen.

Everyone gets up to make their plates, and by the time it's our turn, Melody's face is bright red, and she's got a light sheen of sweat on her face.

It isn't until we sit at the long dining room table that Madre leans over, saying, "Honey, you're *sweltering.* Take your jacket off."

I roll my lips, seeing she's not holding hands with Father like she normally does. I peek at Teresa who's glancing at where their hands are usually linked with a small frown on her face.

Melody throws her a fake smile. "I'm fine-"

"Oh, for fuck's sake. Take the goddamn jacket off before I have a heat stroke, you *stubborn bitch,"* Isobel snaps, causing Hendrix to choke on his food.

"Isobel!" Father exclaims sternly, his eyes wide. "Was that necessary?"

But I feel sorry for her. She looks insanely uncomfortable, and her face is red as well. Sporting a scowl and fanning herself with a collapsible fan looking like she might, in fact, actually have a heat stroke.

"I'll turn the air down," Donna says, getting up and disappearing down the hallway.

When Melody gets over the shock of her sister's outburst, she unzips her jacket and then slides it off breathing an audible sigh of relief. But then all hell breaks loose right as Donna sits down and opens her mouth to say something, but my mother's shocked gasp causes her to glance sharply at her and snap her mouth shut.

"Mija, what's happened to your neck?" Madre asks.

Father's eyes go wide before flicking to mine, then back to Melody. Then back to me. Then to Hendrix, and back to Melody again.

"It's nothing," she mumbles, putting her hand to the abraded skin. With her other hand, she picks up her wine glass and sips it as everyone stares at her in shock. *And then at me....*

I keep my gaze impassive. Though I want to grin remembering how it felt to put my belt around Mel's neck. I chuckle, trying to cover it with a sip of my drink.

"Melody, maybe you should get that looked at," Donna says, leaning in to get a better look and squinting her eyes. "That might be a rash."

"It looks like you got bit by something. Mason, why didn't you take her to the doctor?" Isobel asks in an accusatory tone, curling her lip at me and looking like she's about to leap across the table at me.

Hendrix gives Isobel a warning shake of his head, telling her to stay out of it. Except Teresa leans in next, and Melody visibly stiffens. I put my hand on her thigh, leaning in as the women all start bickering about what kind of rash it might be.

"Baby, calm down-"

But it's no use. Melody slams her palms into the table, the move so reminiscent of Isobel's tantrums that I instinctively snatch the knife from in front of her. And mine.

"I like rough sex, *okay?"* she shouts, giving us all a glare. My eyes slide to hers in disbelief. *"It's none of your business! Now stop asking me."*

Oh the irony.

I can't help but put a hand to my jaw and chuckle. "Damn," I whisper, clearing my throat.

The table goes so silent you could hear a pin drop. I put my hand on her back, letting her know it's okay. She stares in shock at the plate in front of her, and just when I'm sure she's about to get up to run away, a rough sound at the end of the table gets our attention.

To my utter shock, Father laughs. He's hunched over his plate, holding a napkin to his mouth and roaring into it. He carries on and on.

Everyone stares as Father completely loses it, tears streaming down his face, laughing so hard that even Madre is staring in shock. We all gawk, never having seen him laugh like this before.

Hendrix and Teresa trade looks before meeting my eyes, and Teresa starts giggling, leaning forward to pat Father on the hand. His face is bright red, and it only gets worse as everyone else joins in.

Mariah looks down the table, chewing on a mouthful of food. "Mommy, what's rough-"

"No! No, no, no, no!" Isobel shouts over her, and Hendrix gets an irritated look on his face, tossing his napkin to the table and then putting his hands to his face and scrubbing.

And this time it's *my* turn to dissolve into laughter. Except like Father, I don't try to hide it.

When we leave, Teresa gives us stern instructions on how to dress for the long awaited Scognamiglio-Balducci wedding, wanting us to come as a united front and not embarrass her with colors that don't correspond. The uptight witch.

And Father gives me a hug.

CHAPTER 36

A DIFFERENT PATH

TWO NIGHTS LATER I sit up in the middle of the night, out of a dead sleep, with my heart pounding for some reason.

My chest tightens, as does my cock at the scent of Melody's pussy on the air, hearing a needy whimper disturb the pristine quiet of our bedroom as her need ignites my own. I stay quiet, listening to the lewd wet sounds of her playing with herself.

She's been so mortified over what happened at her mom's that she hasn't let me touch her. It was all I could do to get her to sleep in the same bed with me.

Turning my head, I feel the sheet moving as her hand moves up and down between her legs as she works to finger herself. Her knees are bent back under the covers, and I make out the motion of her hand rolling her nipple. She goes back and forth between the two, and they're currently poking against the sheet.

"Climb on top of me," I say. She sucks in a sharp breath and goes still, but her panting betrays what she was doing. "Yeah, you're caught." My cock tightens so hard it aches, forming its own heartbeat. *"I said, get. The. Fuck. On. Top. Of. Me."*

She moves fast, rolling over and straddling me clumsily.

Desperate, I rip the sheet from between us and snatch up her hand, inspecting it. Three of her fingers are soaking wet. I suck them into my mouth, grip her hips hard with my hands, and then snatch her up 'til she's hovering over me.

I tighten my teeth on her fingers the second I slam her down all the way onto my dick.

Fucckkk, she's so wet and tight.

Staring up at her through the darkness I growl through her fingers, lifting her up and slapping her back down again repeatedly. She throws back her head on a silent scream, her free hand clawing into my chest, but I fuck her harder, digging the soles of my feet into the mattress, jerking my hips up and mercilessly fucking her through it.

I let go of her fingers and rear forward, latching onto her right nipple and tugging with my teeth.

"No," she whimpers. "No, Mason, no!"

I suck harder, rolling us so she's on her back, and then bend her legs back until her knees are pressed against the mattress and her hips elevate off the bed, fucking her so deep I'm bouncing off the back of her pussy. Her brows furrow, her mouth drops open, and her gaze lowers to where we're joined.

"Uhnn!" she whimpers, squeezing her eyes shut and then trying to recoil her hips.

I snatch her back with a displeased grunt and circle nice and slow, until I see her eyes roll into the back of her head, and she stops breathing.

"That's the spot, huh?" I whisper, tilting my hips and pressing hard. "And after you tried so hard to keep me from it." She clenches her jaw, and her legs try to jerk straight, but I keep them hooked in the bend of my elbow, fighting her body's resistance. Melody gasps, seizing up as I massage it over and over again. *"Jesusss,* the sucking sounds of your pussy drive me crazy."

My back begins to burn. Sweat slicks across my skin. But I keep on, letting myself go crazy with the joy of pleasuring us both.

"Oh god, oh god, oh god, oh god," she whimpers.

"Hm, baby?" I taunt, leaning down into her ear. "Open that pretty mouth and tell me what's the matter."

I flip her to her front, drag her hips up, and on my next thrust I circle my hips nice and deep. She lowers her head to scream into the pillow, but I grab her by her hair and yank her head back. Pounding into her.

Wet slaps echo throughout our room to join the sound of her disjointed screaming as I work our bodies together, keeping her bent in a deep arch.

I spread my knees, shoving her legs apart further, and the screaming stops as her body flinches in shock as I get in even deeper. Her fingers claw into the bedsheet so hard her knuckles turn white, and her knees spread even further for me.

"Tell me!" I shout.

"It feels good-" she gasps raggedly. "Mason, it feels-*it feels..."*

I grunt, smacking hard into her body over and over. "It feels like I'm hittin' that spot you don't want, doesn't it?"

She moans.

"Doesn't it?"

"Yesss," she wails.

I chuckle. "God, baby. I so enjoy fucking you. I don't know why you'd deny me this. Because you're shy?" I tut, fucking her even faster. "I thought I proved the other day that I'll fuck the shyness out of you. *Did I not do a good enough job?"*

Though I need her approval, she doesn't answer, so I slap her ass hard, the sound echoing. *"Answer me."*

"You did! You did, Mason."

I pull out of her before she can come again, toss her onto her back, and step off the bed, dragging her to the edge until her head hangs off. She's panting and has tears in her eyes, but she opens her mouth and sticks out her tongue. I slap it with my cock once before putting it into her mouth and pressing deeper.

Letting go of my shaft, I palm her breasts and roll her nipples between my fingers, tugging. When I get to the ring of her throat I pause. A tingle wraps around my balls, shooting up my spine and down to the tip of my cock.

"Fuucccck," I groan.

Rolling her nipples, I see her abdomen quiver, her legs bend back and I lean forward, letting one of her nipples go to slip my fingers through the lips of her pussy as she takes me down her throat.

"You're so pretty, baby," I praise her, pulling my hips back and then thrusting back in gently. I part her warm, wet flesh, seeing her clit protruding. I flick it, and she stiffens up, her mouth suctioning even tighter around me. "It's swollen." I flick it repeatedly until she squirts against my fingers and her juices coat her inner thighs. *"Very* sensitive." I bend, sealing my mouth to her clit, groaning as her taste floods my tongue and ignoring her when she jerks hard against me.

I scrape it gently through my teeth, nibbling as I pull my cock all the way out of her mouth as she bucks hard against me.

"Mason," she sobs with her orgasm, jerking her hips against me. I give her a sharp slap to the back of her thigh and suck even harder, not letting her have any reprieve. "No!" she gasps. "No, wait! *Mason, I can't t-take anymore-"*

She screams as I turn her back around, haul her hips off the mattress, and slam back into her. Her lips tremble, and her eyes are wet with tears of pleasure.

"Seems like to me you're taking it just fine, Melody," I say in a rough voice.

And she does.

She takes it very well over the next hour, in fact.

***

A week later, I fall to my back on the bed, sweaty, with my chest heaving. I wouldn't fuck her hard tonight; her pussy's been too tender.

"I'm quitting college."

Turning my head, I glance at her with my brow arched. *"Oh yeah?"*

Melody nods. "Yeah."

I wait for her to elaborate, but she just stares at the bedroom ceiling, contemplating. I move my arm, finding her fingers and gripping them. Giving her patience so she can work it out for herself.

"I know that the plan was for me to go back next session," she says hesitantly, *"but..."*

I roam her face, seeing she's uncomfortable and hesitant. "But?" I ask softly.

"But I don't think school is working for me."

Her voice is small, and I can tell she's scared to share this with me so I tread lightly, letting her know I'm with her no matter what.

"I get that," I say. "It's not for everyone." Turning on my side, I prop myself up on an elbow and rub my hand down her arm. "I'm okay with whatever you want to do, love. If you need time to figure out what you're passionate about, that's fine. It's not like we're hurting for money."

She turns her head to look at me, with a wary expression on her face. "I don't wanna..." she trails off, her cheeks tinge pink.

"Want to what?" I enquire softly, now rubbing my hand down her hair.

She turns to me, propping up on her elbow so we're almost even. "I don't want to freeload off you."

I chuckle and move a couple inches closer. "Baby, I hate to break it to you, but," I arch a cheeky brow, lowering my voice to a whisper, "we're *rich.* If you want to freeload off me, you can. And you're my wife. You're *allowed* to." I give her a bright smile. "Actually, I encourage it."

She rolls her eyes at me. "Oh, come on."

I laugh. "I'm serious. I'm man enough to admit that it turns me on when you spend my money. That's what's got me through the last four years, knowing I was providing for you, even if you didn't know it."

She bites her lip, bringing her gaze back to me. "So all this time it really was you, huh?"

I nod. "Sí. That was the stipulation Hendrix and I agreed on."

"It seems kinda unfair, don't you think?"

"What do you mean?"

"Well," her eyes flick to my lips then back to mine. "You had to wait, *and* you had to pay a bunch of money for my upkeep."

I smile, leaning forward and giving her a soft, slow kiss. "And every time I got that monthly bank statement, it was like Christmas morning while getting to riffle through and see what you treated yourself to that month." I pull back. "Lots of drug store purchases, though."

She blushes. "Well, a girl gets her period every month."

I nod. "Hmm."

"Mason," she draws a fingertip down my chest, biting her lip nervously. "Can I ask you something?"

I grin at her, relaxing into the bed and enjoying just being with her. "You can ask me anything."

Her eyes flick to mine and then narrow slightly. "What do you be getting up to?"

"When?" I frown, my mind immediately rolling through what I do during the day.

She blinks. "When you take those late night phone calls."

My heart rate picks up, not expecting her to ask that. I clear my throat and capture her hand with mine, bringing her fingers up to kiss them one by one. "Just work stuff, honey."

"At night, though?" She arches a brow.

Oh God. Here we go.

Laying on my back, I scrub a hand across my jaw before sitting up and draping my arm over my knee, looking down at her. "I'm involved in..."

I sigh, squeezing my eyes shut before averting my face.

"Yes?"

"I'm the financial advisor to the man who helped get Isobel back," I answer, bringing my gaze back to her.

Melody's eyes widen. "What?"

I nod. "Yep. That was the price our family had to pay."

I. The price *I* had to pay.

A little line appears in between her forehead. *"The mafia?"* she sputters. An incredulous look crosses her face. "You're involved with a criminal organization, Mason?!"

The urgency in her voice gives me pause. Anxiety trickles up my spine and makes the hair on the back of my neck stand on end. "Well... yes and no."

She sits up now, too, holding the sheet to her breasts. Her dark hair is a mess of waves cascading down her shoulders and arms, but I keep my hands to myself for now because she's looking a bit... wild. And not because I just fucked the shit out of her. She scrunches her face up in clear irritation.

"What the *entire fuck* do you mean *yes and no?"*

Wetting my lips I turn a bit to face her head on, keeping my posture as loose and open as possible. "I'm technically not in the mafia, butterfly. I take charge of Luca-"

"Luca?! *Oh!"* she says in a shrill voice, her eyes going wide. *"Oh okay,* so we're on first name basis with the fucking mafia, now?"

"Yes, he likes to be called Luca." I continue patiently as if she didn't interrupt me. "I handle Lucien Scognamiglio's businesses that aren't wrapped up in the mafia. There's no money laundering, and everything is completely above board and legal. I oversee the financial operations and advise him on stocks. *That's it,* okay? I promise."

I damn near hold my breath as her eyes flicker between mine as that line between her brows never goes away, and I note -with displeasure- that she only recently developed that after she'd got with me.

Melody nibbles her lip. "I don't like it," she whispers.

I avert my gaze, staring at my hand instead. My fingers twitch as if I'm twiddling an imaginary paper clip.

"I know," I say softly. "I don't like it either, to be honest. There's no time limits on my commitment to him. I have to take his phone calls whenever he calls. I'm obligated to him, Melody. I'm sorry." My eyes turn towards hers. "But this is why I warned you about Karissa, Mel. A person who I thought was my friend betrayed me and used me to get information on Isobel, and that's why she was kidnapped by her father. And now, this is my penance."

Her eyes widen, and I can see the wheels in her head turning at my admission.

The silence grows between us. Right when I'm sure I'm to be rejected, she reaches a hand out for mine, taking it in a soft grasp. *"Our* penance." My eyes widen, and she flutters her thumb across my knuckles. "To have and to hold, remember?"

My heart beats wildly in my chest, and an overwhelming need to cry takes over my senses, heightening my vulnerability. But I know it's okay, because Melody and I have always been able to be vulnerable with each other. Good and bad. Pretty and ugly, we're always us.

"You promise?" I rasp.

"I promise."

Tears well up in my eyes as she leans forward and wraps her arms around me. I'm a little shocked and don't move right away, but when I get my muscles unstuck, I band my arms around her and pull her as tight as I can to me. We settle back down to our sides, our limbs wound tightly together as we kiss. Unhurried, as if we have all the time in the world.

"I hope you really love me," she says quietly into my mouth.

I frown, pulling away to look at her. "What do you mean? Of course I do."

"Because I've decided to end my friendship with Karissa... You're right, she's not a healthy friend, and I keep making excuses for her." Her lips tighten. "She's the only friend I have, Mason."

"Wrong," I say, putting a hand to her cheek. "You've got *me,* butterfly."

She gives me a tentative smile, and presses her lips to mine. Although I'm feeling alone, too, due to the issues with my family. And she knows it. Right now, we sort of seem like a ship without a sail.

I clench her tighter against me, needing our connection, and kiss her deeper.

Pulling away, she meets my eyes with nothing but warmth, love, and understanding in hers. "We'll find our way, Mase." The reassurance in her tone does a lot to make me feel confident, as does her running a hand through my hair. "As long as we have each other, I think we can do anything."

And you fucking know what? She's damn right.

So goddamn right.

CHAPTER 37

MAFIA INVOLVEMENT

Joaquin is driving me nuts. -Henny

Why? -Mase

Because he doesn't want to marry Amelia. And now, he won't stop calling me to bitch about her. This is why I didn't want to get involved in the mafia, because of this shit right here. It's way too much drama. -Henny

I thought you didn't want to get involved because of an inflated superiority complex. -Mase

Don't be a dick. All he does is talk about her. -Henny

We're not technically in the mafia, yet look at how much drama *we're* in. -Mase

What are you whining about now, Henny? -Teresa

Lol! -Mase

I. Do. Not. Whine. -Henny

Yes you do. Fucking liar. -Mase

I am trying to run a fucking empire here! See how much patience you have when you head almost four hundred thousand employees and bear the responsibility I do. -Hendrix

Awww, don't do that. Don't change your name because you're mad. We're sorry. -Teresa

Pft. Speak for yourself. And by the way, in case I never told you before, I am NOT sorry for you. -Mase

Gee, Mase. Thanks. -Hendrix

Tee, can you please come get Isobel for a night? I'm so fucking tired I can't think straight. -Henny

Oh so you're 'Henny" for Tee, hm? -Mase

Sure, I'll come get her at 2p for a girls night. Mase, stop being a jerk. Jerk.-Tee

Sure, but can you please get Melody too? It'd be good for her to get out of the house. -Mase

Doesn't she have school? -Henny

Yeaaa....about that...-Mase

What do you mean "about that?" -Henny

We'll be by tomorrow to discuss it. -Mase

Okay. See you. -Henny

Peace. -Mase

Bye bye. -Tee

CHAPTER 38

WHAT DO YOU MEAN?

"WHAT THE HELL DO you mean, Melody?" Isobel snaps, shifting her weight in the seat at the dining room table. She smoothes her hand down the sleeve of her tan, cashmere sweater, playing with the tank watch Hendrix gifted her for their first anniversary before throwing an irritated look to Mason, then bringing her gaze back to mine. *"You can't just quit school-"*

"Yes I can!" I snap, slapping my hand on the table.

"Respecfully, Isobel, that's not your decision to make!" Mason backs me up, tossing back the rest of his whiskey.

I can't blame him, really. I love her, but Isobel's been more insufferable lately, and it's draining.

Even after an evening and night of pampering she still has that stick up her ass.

"Look, sis," I say, leaning forward and taking her hand in mine. "I love you, okay? You know I do. And I know you've been more like a mother to me than a sister for my whole life, but I need you to be my sister now. *Please?"*

Isobel presses her lips together and squirms uncomfortably, throwing a look to Hendrix, but he ignores her, his eyes keeping mine while he takes a deep breath with his arms folded over his chest as he takes a second to respond. Moreso soaking in the information than reacting to it.

"Isobel," Hendrix says quietly, turning his face to hers. A blossom of hope erupts in my chest at him siding with me, and I almost can't believe it. "It's time to take a backseat, little demon. They've got it."

Her mouth gapes open. *"What?"*

"You heard me. We have our own kids to raise, Izzy. And besides, they need to bump their heads a little, make their own choices. I think it's time we just chill out for a bit. Because how we've been handling it is obviously not working." He arches a brow, turning to look at me. "I believe you can find your own way, Mel, and I'm sorry if we got in the way of that. We were wrong. You know that we'll always be here to support you though. Both of you. No matter what."

Isobel blinks rapidly, looking stunned.

I peek a look at Mason, not quite trusting it.

He looks just as stunned as she does, his fingers rotating his empty crystal glass over and over. Instinctively, I can tell he's not sure to trust it, either.

From our conversations, I've come to really see just how complex and *off* their family dynamic has been. The family secret that Richard won't discuss has been weighing heavily on all of our minds, and I've heard Mason and Teresa on the phone late at night talking about it which lets me know it's got everyone in a whirlwind.

It's brought up a range of questions: about why Richard won't get close to the boys, and how he holds us girls so close, as well as how that might be affecting the men. I've paused mine and Richard's fencing practice, not feeling comfortable continuing while everything's so tense between us all.

I don't want to hurt Mason by flaunting the ease of Richard's and my relationship in his face, deciding instead to move forward as a unified front. Us against them, if you will.

I hate it has to be this way, but he's my husband first and foremost.

"Thank you," I whisper.

Isobel nods, tightening her lips. "Well, is there anything you're interested in besides running?" she asks softly, brushing her hand down her wavy, deep auburn hair. Another little blossom of hope sparks in my chest.

"Well..." I smile, looking over at Mason. "I've really been baking a lot lately. And Mason's suggested maybe opening a shop." I furrow my brow, taking a quick sip of my tea. "But I don't know about that. I have no clue how to start a business or-"

"Well, *we do."* Hendrix interrupts in an excited tone. "Whenever you're ready, that is..." he trails off, looking rather sheepish.

"But that's the thing," I huff a deep breath. "Even if I did, what does baking have to do with King Dynasty? My business would add no value to your company whatsoever. And I don't even know if I'm really good enough to-"

Mason holds up a hand. "Wait, stop. I'm going to pause you right there. You have the skill, butterfly. But I think what might be smart is to do it for awhile -with no pressure from any of us- and see if you think it's something you'd be comfortable with in the long run."

Hendrix nods, agreeing. "You're young. No one's going to deny you the time you need to figure it out. Deciding on a career is something no one should feel rushed into." He puts his eyes to Mason, who just slides a hand around my waist and presses a kiss to my temple.

I nod. "Well, thank you."

"No problem, sis. And besides, you *could* make that a part of the King Dynasty if you wanted to. We have office buildings and conferences all over the world. An in-house bakery business that caters to those events would be beneficial, *and busy;* if that's something you'd be interested in, that is. Everyone loves a good cookie or croissant," Hendrix adds.

Chewing my lip I look over at Mason, who's staying quiet, letting me decide for myself. "I, uh... I think I'd feel better if I took my time. Let me see if this is something I can see myself really loving before I commit to anything."

"Sure."

Hendrix, Isobel, and Mason nod, and now it's my turn to squirm in my seat. "Henny," I say hesitantly, wetting my lips nervously as anxiety causes me to flush hot. "Can I tell you something?"

His brow lowers, getting a concerned look on his face as he leans forward, bracing his arms on the table top. "Sure, Mel. You know you can talk to me about anything."

My eyes fall to the empty plate in front of me. Tears well in my eyes as I let myself be vulnerable, realizing the four of us are turning a crucial point in our relationship and wanting to show them that I can change, too.

"These last few years have been really hard," I bite out in a thick voice, wiping a tear off my face with the back of my hand. "I've been feeling really lost, I guess. And hurt because I don't have a dad. And I just want to tell you how much I appreciate you stepping in and filling that role for me." I sniff. "I'm sorry for crying like this, but it's been so hard seeing your family deal with all of... *this.* All the stuff that you all are dealing with, and it's been making me think more about our family situation *a-and my father.* I wish I had a father to fight with, and he's d-dead." I sniff again, my fingers trembling. "So I just wish you all could figure this thing out, you know? Because fighting isn't worth it."

"Oh, Melly," Isobel's chin quivers as tears fill her own eyes, but she doesn't come to me to smother me like she normally does.

Hendrix's eyes widen, and a look of shock crosses his face before he carefully conceals it behind his everyday mask. Everyone goes quiet, and Mason's fingers tighten on my shoulder as he, too, stays silent.

"You know it's my pleasure, Mel," he says in a soft voice. "I love you, sweetheart." A tear falls down my cheek, and he stands up, rounding the table and pulling me in for a hug. "Come here."

I squeeze him back, taking the familiar scent of him in. However, for the hundredth time I wonder what my actual dad smells like. What would he sound like.

He reaches forward and clasps Mason hard on the shoulder, and they share a long look that I can't decipher.

Hendrix returns to his seat, and we switch the conversation to other things. Catching up on the day to day stuff. Mason and Hendrix's relationship seems easier and a lot less forced, as is mine and Isobel's. Though I can tell she's not happy with me quitting college.

But I feel heard. And, most of all, respected.

"You're doing a bit much today, aren't you?" I glance at my mom, who's busy doing bicep curls in the mirror of her in-home workout gym.

"Well, I gotta do something to work off that honey cake you brought over, Mel," she huffs through a curl that looks unnecessarily painful. "Your sweets are wayyy too luscious for me to let sit on my hips like that."

"So, what exactly is Isobel being honored with at this wedding?" I ask, running on the treadmill next her.

Physical fitness is about the only thing I think mom and I have in common. Though I love her to death, we're not exactly close because of her absence when I was growing up due to her working under the table for money so we wouldn't be discovered by Isobel's father.

Isobel took over mothering me because mom was gone so much until I was about fourteen when Isobel was able to help with money from her interior decorating business. And even though I lived with mom after Isobel moved in with Christopher, Isobel only really disappeared when we worked out.

She was there to take me shopping for clothes, only relenting to mom's outfit restrictions. Was there for every parent teacher conference right alongside mom as if she was the second parent and came to every track meeting. She only missed one time when she had the stomach flu.

Mom's eyes flit to mine in the mirror.

"Apparently with the wedding alliance between Amelia Scognamiglio and Joaquin Baluducci, she and the King family are being granted protection from both the East and West coast mafia. It's a very big deal because it includes protection from the other mafia families within the states. A tall order, if you ask me."

"That's nice." I hit the button upping my speed, and clocking the disturbed look on her face.

Mom *disdains* the mafia. I'm shocked she's even going.

Mom nods, putting the weights down and taking a drink of her protein shake, wiping her face with a towel. I eye her well-defined body, wondering for the first time why she feels the need to keep herself toned like this. Just like she always needed everything neat and orderly. When she *was* around when I was growing up, she didn't leave much room for spontaneity.

Everything in our home had a place, and we didn't have much. Hardly any art on the walls. We never really went out to do much of anything fun. Our free time together was spent doing physical exercise because I ran a lot for school. So, that's how we ultimately bonded.

"She needs it, because they're going to forever be a target," she gasps, wiping the back of her hand to her mouth and then bending to grab her curling bar.

I think my arms would fall clean off if I did even half of what she puts her arms through. She won't stop after the curls either. She'll step over to the pull up bar and put her security man to shame with the amount of pull-ups she can do.

I'm impressed she's not bulky, though; she's toned and lithe like an arrow. But don't let her punch you. She broke Hendrix's guard's nose one day when they'd playfully made a wager that her arms were all show, and she couldn't actually hit.

She can.

"So, how's it going with Mason?" she asks, failing to hide the hurt in her voice.

I run for a few seconds, watching her arms contract and flex before answering, fighting the guilt that I just don't feel close to her no matter how hard I try. I come here every other week to workout, I call once a week to check in, but I can't feel close to her for some reason, and it really bothers me.

"It's nice."

"It's nice," she parrots back, almost to herself. And I hear her asking herself in her head why I won't give her more. It makes me sad because I don't think I'm capable of giving more. But I try anyway, though it makes me uncomfortable to do so.

"Yeah, it's nice. We've decided to not have kids."

Her brows raise. "No?"

"No. We don't want them in this life like this," I explain. "With all these expectations of kids and stuff."

"Ah. I get that, I think."

"I quit school."

Her eyes fly to mine. "Really? What happened?"

"It's just not for me."

"Oh. What did Izzy have to say about that?" Her voice is hesitant.

Her eyes tighten, and I see it for the first time, maybe a hint of jealousy that Isobel took her spot? Is that it?

Does she resent Isobel?

I have so many questions, but don't dare bring it up.

"She didn't like it, but she took it in stride."

Mom bends, setting down the bar and then stepping over to where I'm running, patting me on the arm. "Well, you'll find your way, love."

As expected, she moves to the pull-up bar on the other side of the room, effectively ending that conversation. Despite my effort, we fall into silence, focusing on our workout routine, not having much else to talk about.

A minute later it hits me like a ton of bricks. It's not that she doesn't *want* to talk. It's because she doesn't have a life to talk about.

I hit the button to stop the treadmill three miles short of my goal and step off, stretching my hamstrings. "Mom," I call out, watching her pull herself up effortlessly on the bar.

"Yeah, honey?" she huffs.

"Get off that thing and let's go find something fun to get into."

She jumps down, turning around and smiling brightly. *"Yeah?"*

Her excitement makes me feel bad for a moment, seeing she just wanted an invitation. It's when it also hits me that my mother has respected Mason's wishes and has done what she can to not meddle, to give us space, making me melt even more.

"Yeah." I smile, linking my arm with hers and giggle as we make our way out of the room. "Let's get out of here for a while."

CHAPTER 39

HERMOSA

Hi my love, are you almost ready to go? I just got my hair done. Dicky and I are will be there in two hour to pick you up. -Maribel

Donna? -Maribel

Mari, will you be too disapointed if I don't go? -Donna

We talked about this, quierida. We will be by your side all night. No one is going to hurt you. You got this. -Maribel

And besides, William is really looking forward to seeing you again. -Maribel

But you know how I feel about the mafia. -Donna

I know sweetheart, but we're all being honored tonight. You, us, and Isobel. It'd look bad if you didn't go. -Maribel

But...-Donna

Nevermind. I am on my way now. We will have a nice relaxing drink, and then the men will pick us both up. -Maribel

CHAPTER 40

A Mafia Reception

What is he doing? I think, narrowing my eyes curiously.

My attention for the last five to ten minutes has been monopolized by a tall, statuesque man with dark-brown hair. He's leaning a shoulder against a stone pillar on the perimeter of the reception hall, occupying the same side Mason and I are standing on, talking with one of his friends.

The man's a handsome guy, from what I can tell by his profile.

He was walking by us when he looked over, distracted by the sound of my mother's laughter. He paused mid-step, and has been cemented in place ever since. Not moving. And that was over five minutes ago.

"Melody, have you heard *anything* I just said?" I jump as Mason's elegant, slightly accented voice disturbs me from staring.

"What? No," I answer absentmindedly, pushing my flute off at him, refusing to look away from the fascinating man who's a few feet away. "Why won't he just *ask* her already?" I mumble to myself, folding my arms and tapping my toe.

My eyes slide to where mother stands with William, who's leaned in rather close, putting another glass of wine in her hand. But *he* hasn't asked her to dance yet. My face breaks out into a wicked smile, and I decide to stir up some trouble. Someone's going to ask her to dance tonight if I've got any say in the matter because after my epiphany the other day while we were working out, I've made it my mission to make my mom's life as full as possible.

Starting with getting her laid.

"Careful, Melody, that's your third glass of champagne," Mason warns me.

I hiccup, rolling my eyes. "Whatever, I'm off to frolic in the drama."

"What drama?" he frowns, turning his head to eye the crowd.

"There's always drama at wedding receptions," I tease. "I'm convinced it's all part of the fun. And speaking of..."

"Where are you going?" he asks, tightening his fingers on mine when I take a couple of steps in the Italian man's direction.

"I'm going to get my mom a dance!" I shoot over my shoulder, wagging my brows at him.

Mason gives me a sly smirk, letting my hand go and giving me a wink. "Don't stay gone too long. I'll be looking for you."

I turn. making my way through the guests and mosey on up to the man who'd stopped dead in his tracks at the sight of my mother. There's two men nearby who look hard at me, and I'm versed enough to know by now that he's got his own security. However, they leave me be, and I turn my attention to him.

He's quite good looking for an older guy. He's so enraptured with staring at my mother that he doesn't even realize I came to stand behind him. Poor guy.

He looks love sick.

I lean into him, tapping him on his arm. "She's single, and her name is Donna," I whisper. "Go ask her for a dance."

His eyes snap to mine, then widen. As do mine at the intensity within his brown irises. He recovers quickly, his face morphing into a cautious, yet hard mask, reminding me once again that I'm in a room full of powerful men. I'm a little stuck looking at him, wondering why he seems so familiar to me. He turns to face me head on in a smooth move.

"Maximus," he says, holding out his hand, and I take it.

"Melody."

Maximus' eyes flick down my face for a second before turning back to resume his prior stance.

"So, how do you know she's single?" He has an Italian accent, and I'm enraptured by the richness of his voice. He waves a hand towards my mom and smiles warmly, and I decide right then and there that I like him.

"Oh, I'm her daughter." I half-laugh at the look he gives me, pulling my hand away and lacing my fingers behind my back.

"You're not Isobel. Can't be," he say sharply, giving me a thorough once over.

"No, I'm not Isobel." I giggle. "Isobel's my sister. *See?* She's over there." I point to the thick crowd where Isobel stands with Hendrix and Joaquin and his new wife with several security on standby in case anything happens.

I frown, seeing Amelia still hasn't relaxed since they said 'I do' at the alter. She stands next to her husband in her gorgeous white dress, looking a bit like a beautiful deer caught in headlights.

Maximus glances briefly over to where Hendrix is blocking a part of her face. "Nonsense," he says softly. "I'd know Isobel if I saw her."

My brows raise, and I snort.

"*Well, obviously not.* See, she's right there." I point again. "Gosh, if you pull out a paper and pen maybe I could draw you a family tree," I joke.

Maximus' eyes widen as he steps a little closer and squints, following where I'm pointing. He goes silent, and I flick my eyes to his, understanding his conundrum. "I know, I know she looks young, but she's grown, I promise." I laugh, placing my hand on his arm, feeling free with him. "Mom, Izzy and I all do, but she's actually seven years older than me."

"No, that's... That's not..."" He trails off looking confused. His eyes turn towards me, and he holds my stare unblinkingly for a few heartbeats. Eventually his wets his lips and frowns, tilting his head. *"How old are you?"*

"I just turned twenty."

His eyes widen, and it's dead silent. Uncomfortably so for several long, drawn out seconds. His head turns back to Mom and William, and a tingle makes its way up my spine at the look that comes over his face as he continues to stare at my mother.

"Is...is something *wrong?"* I ask hesitantly.

Suddenly I feel like an idiot. What the fuck am I doing trying to set my mother up with a man in a place that's crawling with mafia members? I nibble my bottom lip, feeling stupid.

"If you'll excuse me, Melody," Maximus says in a clipped tone, striding away from me, headed towards my mother who's laughing at something William is saying to her.

The security guys follow, and I frown, looking over my shoulder to see Stephen a couple feet away, and Mason twenty feet away, walking towards me. I whip my head forward again, and pick up the skirt of my dress to haul ass behind Maximus.

I think I manifested the drama unfolding, and it happens as if in slow motion.

William looks over first, seeing us headed towards them. His eyes narrow as he grabs my mother by the elbow and gestures with his drink towards Maximus, who's moving with more purpose than I've ever seen another person have. Mom's brow furrows in confusion, then she looks over, her mouth dropping open as she locks eyes with Maximus, and her drink slips out of her hand.

I'm about fifteen feet away when I hear the crystal shatter to the floor at her feet. But what happens next draws me up short.

"Donnatella?" Maximus says in a strained voice, stopping just shy of the glass shards.

Donnatella?

My eyes snap to Mom, but she's stuck in an insanely intense battle of let's-see-who-can-blink-first with Maximus. Looking like she's not even breathing, frozen still as a statue.

"It's so lovely to see you again after all this time. You haven't aged a day."

Mother stares like a deer caught in headlights, and in the corner of my eye I see Richard striding towards us with Maribel on his arm, both of their faces drawn tight with worry.

Mason's hand slides around my waist to pull me in, and he bends to my ear. "What's going on?"

"I don't know," I whisper back. "I don't know what's going on. I just met this guy, and now he's calling my mom Donnatella!"

He frowns. "Maybe he's got her confused with someone?"

I inch closer as Isobel and King come up beside us, and Isobel has a strange look on her face. She stares hard at Maximus.

Leaning into Mason she whispers out the corner of her mouth, "That man looks familiar for some reason." She glances up at Hendrix, who's already alerting their security to move in closer. "Honey, was this man there when I was rescued?"

"No," Hendrix answers quickly, shaking his head.

"Do you mind telling me who that woman is right there?" Maximus steps back and turns to point at me. His gaze suddenly slides to Isobel, who's eyes widen in shock, before coming back to mine.

"I'm *Melody. I just told you-"* I reply, but Mom takes a step back and then turns and runs in the opposite direction. My brows rise as Mason and I share a look.

"Melody, I have to tell you something-" Mason starts, but Maximus' loud curse interrupts him, and he runs after her, as does William.

Then Richard and Maribel.

My heart pounds hard, seeing the various guests milling about nearby all turning to stare at us.

Hendrix lifts Isobel into his arms and literally hands her to a security guard behind him, tearing after the two men like his heels are on fire. Mason and I glance at each other before taking off as well, ignoring Isobel calling out for us to wait.

Mason and I are faster than Maribel and Richard, passing them in what looks to be a private hallway away from the main reception area.

I hear them before I see them. Their raised voices lead us to a secluded room in the back of the reception area meant for storing extra tables, clothes, and chairs. We burst through the door, hurrying in, seeing Mom, Hendrix, William, and Maximus standing in a circle, and so much security you'd think we were preparing for a terrorist attack.

We pause just outside the center of the room, linking our hands together.

Maribel and Richard comes in behind us, as does the security carrying Isobel, who looks terrified out of her mind.

"Hermosa!" Maribel calls out, running to Mom who is shaking her head and crying, not letting anyone near her. Richard and William stand on either side, trying to touch her. But Maribel runs directly to her and flings her arm around my mother who's barely standing on her feet. "Who are you? *What do you want?"* she says to Maximus.

Mason hauls me to his side so hard it hurts. I gasp, and Mom sees me, becoming more upset.

"Get her out of here!" Mom yells. *"Richard, please!"* she turns to Richard, grabbing onto his arm.

"Oh my God, am I in danger?" I ask Mason, digging my nails into his arm.

A trickle of fear morphs into something so big and heavy it causes my knees to knock together. Fuck, I'm so *stupid.* Laughing and telling this stranger every fucking thing about us. Pointing out my mom, my sister and Hendrix.

Fuck, what the hell is wrong with me?

"Who is she, Donnatella?!" Maximus' voice is stern, no-nonsense. His brow is low, and his face bright red with anger as he points all his frustration on my mother, who looks like her knees are buckling as Maribel wraps an arm around her waist.

"Maximus, this isn't the time or place-" Richard starts, but Maximus turns his head to him and pierces him with an indifferent look.

"Stay out of my way before I have you shot, Richard," he snarls.

"Maximus," Mother cries, taking a shaky step forward. "Please, not like this."

Mason stiffens against me, snapping his head over to look at Hendrix, who makes a low sound in his throat then slides his eyes to Mason, then to me. I tear my eyes away towards our parents, who are literally the center of the fucking drama I was *just* romanticizing about not even twenty minutes ago.

"Melody," Hendrix and Mason say at the same time, but before they can speak, Richard turns towards me, locking eyes with Mason before snapping his fingers.

"Security, remove my children. All of them. *Now,"* he snaps.

I watch stunned, as every security guard in the room turns, stepping towards us and begins to herd us back towards the open doors behind us but I push back, struggling against Stephen and Dante. However, I don't struggle for long as Maximus' security flans us from the back, preventing us from retreating.

The next thing I know, everyone's pointing guns at everyone, and Hendrix gets in the face of the security guard directly in front of him. One of *ours.*

I look at Mason, seeing he's squaring off with Dante and Stephen as well. "If you know what's good for you, you'll back the fuck off," he growls.

"Maximus!" Mom cries, sobbing now.

"No one's leaving here until I have answers. *Is that my daughter?"* Maximum asks, making my heart skip a beat.

My brows rise, and an eerie hush falls over the room as everyone turns their heads to look at me, even the security.

"No, m-my father's dead," I say, swallowing hard. "Mom told me my dad was dead." But I stare stupidly over Stephen's shoulder, locking eyes with Maximus, who's turned to look at me. *"My dad is dead,*

Maximus..." I trail off, feeling goosebumps erupt on my skin as I take in his face a little differently.

Looking into eyes that are shaped like...

Mine.

My lips part, and my heart beats wildly in my breast as I see the leashed anger in his eyes. Then, anger morphs into pain, and he takes a deep breath that hitches in his throat as his eyes visibly well up with tears. As do mine when he advances closer.

"She'd be about the right age," he says softly. Though his voice isn't raised, his tenor carries throughout the room regardless. His eyes flicker across my face slowly, as step by step brings him closer to me. "She has my cheekbones, and she stands a bit like me." My lips quiver as I see his eyes are filled with tears. "And she looks.... *you look* a bit like my mother."

In my peripheral I see my mom sink to the floor and I sniff, feeling a tear fall down my cheek. Mason's hand squeezes mine tightly as Maximus puts a hand to Stephen's shoulder and pushes him away gently. He stands in front of me, before putting a hand to my cheek and pressing.

My eyes close as something settles in my chest.

Dad...

"You're so beautiful. *And funny..."* His voice is choked up as he chuckles through his tears. "That joke you made about the family tree. I guess we'll really need to make one now, huh? Come here, kiddo. Can I give you a hug?"

He tugs at my wrist, and I step into him, letting him wrap his arms around me. I nuzzle into his neck, inhaling his scent. My tears flow down my cheeks and wet his suit jacket as his smell seeps into my consciousness. He smells safe.

Like home.

"Dad," I whisper, squeezing him harder.

His arms band around me, pulling me so tight that I feel his chest swell. "Daughter. I am so, so sorry."

I smile into his neck, pulling away and sniffing again as his hand comes to my face, his thumb wiping a tear from my cheek gently.

"Let her go! You can't have her!" Mother's scream makes my ears ring, and she launches off the floor to run at Maximus. However, William grabs her from behind, hauling her into the air. Maximus pulls away from me, turning to the side and watching as Richard and Maribel crowd close, flanking them. "I won't let you take her from me."

He strides to her, and he puts his hand to her cheek, getting close. "I loved you. Why the hell would I do something like that to one of our daughters?"

My brow rises at the look, so intimate that I avert my face to peek a look at Mason, who's pressed against my side and watching the events unfold. My eyes go back to them, though, riveted at the sight of my parents together.

Mom sobs, her lips trembling. "Claudio... Claudio s-sold I-Isobel..." she cuts off, bowing her head and crying, not able to get the rest out. Maximus' eyes go wide, and he turns so fast it makes me dizzy.

"That was *you?"* he half-whispers, locking eyes with Isobel, his olive-toned skin going white as a sheet.

Isobel nods, her eyes still flickering back and forth between his. He comes closer, tilting his head, putting his hand on his chest. "Izzy, do you remember me at all? I'm Maxy!"

We're all locked in a tense silence, and her mouth drops open as it apparently clicks.

"Maxy?" Isobel wiggles, struggling against Hendrix until he puts her down. Her chin trembles as she takes a few wobbly steps toward

Maximus and then flings herself at him, belly and all, causing him to stumble back a couple steps. "It *is* you! *Maxy!"* she shouts.

"You all are bad people," Mom whimpers. "All you do is *h-hurt* us!"

Maximus turns back to Mom, reaching forward for her again. "I'm not a bad person, Donnatella." He sinks to his knees in front of her and cradles her head in his hands. "I got you out, remember?"

Mom's chin quivers as she stares up at Maximus defiantly.

But my brow furrows as something clicks now for me, too. Isobel and I are the only ones who look shocked. But no one else does.

They look at us with pity.

"Wait..." I interrupt as it finally hits me, and my being fills with hurt and betrayal. "You *knew?* You knew he was alive?" I snap, everyone turns towards me as I take a couple steps closer to my mom. *"You knew my father was alive, and you didn't tell me?!"*

Her watery eyes turn to me. *"Melody, I'm sorry..."* she says, standing back to her feet.

My head snaps to the side as Isobel gasps, grabbing at her tummy and looking down. My eyes widen at the sight of water splashing on the floor between her feet. *"Shit!"* she says, bending at the waist.

"Fuuuck," Mason breathes, sliding his hand into mine.

"Yeah," I huff. "Fuck is right."

CHAPTER 41

SWEAR YOUR LOYALTY

FOR THE TWO WEEKS since the wedding, our lives have been fraught with tension from both sides of the family.

We've all been walking on eggshells.

Melody hasn't been talking to anyone because we all knew her father was alive and kept it a secret. It took *days* for her to speak to me after she found out I knew about her father and didn't say anything. Those first few days I was in hell, sure as shit she was going to leave me, wondering when the divorce papers and her wedding ring were going to show up on my desk.

William has stayed behind in New York, not retreating back to Italy because apparently he's been seeing Donna since our wedding, and because Hendrix and Isobel just had a new baby. He's been staying with us because he's not welcome at Father's house for that extended of a stay.

Melody's been spending a lot of her time with her father who rented a home about ten minutes away. Trying to get to know him and attempting to distract him from going to Donna's house, because she's afraid he'll get into it with *William* over her. However, according to Donna's security, Pablo, William hasn't even been allowed in her house. Neither has Maximus.

Lucien gave Maximus extra time off his duties in New York to connect with us. The revered mafia boss finds all of this rather hilarious, the asshole. Not only has Donna not let Maximus in, she also hasn't been speaking to him either.

It just gets more convoluted from there. More communication has been coming through our security teams than from us as a family.

Richard hasn't been talking to William. Isobel hasn't been talking to anyone, which is understandable, because of the new baby. But from what Hendrix tells me, she hasn't even been speaking to Donna because of how bad this secret has hurt Melody.

I haven't been speaking to Father, but that's really nothing new.

It's all fucked up. Apparently two weeks of this is all I can take, and I decide I can't live like this anymore, so I call an emergency family meeting with Father, Teresa, and Hendrix, bringing William and Melody along with me.

Later in the evening we walk into Father's office, and I shake the feelings of deja vu off as Father pins his eyes hard on me while we file in through the double doors. His eyes narrow when they get to William, but slide back to mine. Ice crawls down my spine as his entire demeanor changes, and the air in his office becomes tense, stifled with secrets and long repressed emotion.

"Why is *he* here?" Father snaps, referring to William.

"Hello to you, too, Father."

His eyes pin to mine, narrowing. "Oh, cut the crap, Mason. *Why is he here?"*

"Because I brought him here, Father." I sit in a chair across from his desk, pulling Melody down into the chair next to mine. She keeps her eyes averted, still hurt.

"I told you I didn't want to discuss it," Father snarls, his eyes cold as ice.

"I'm not here to discuss whatever '*it*' is," I say, spreading my legs and clearing my throat, waiting until both Hendrix and Teresa take a seat in nearby chairs. William elects to stay standing, perching himself near a tall window to my right. "I'm here to discuss my role going forward, and my personal interests. William is here because I would like him to be a part of our family. And if 'our family' only means Melody and I, well..." I trail off, looking at her. She's a bit paler than normal, all the stress of everyone fighting wearing her out. "I just wanted to let you know that we *will* be moving forward with a relationship with William."

Father scoffs in disbelief, sitting back in his office chair and folding his arms. "Who is your loyalty to, boy? Because it's clear to me that it's certainly not to King Dynasty!"

"Fuck King Dynasty," I say harshly. I maintain his gaze, not even bothering to raise my voice. "My loyalty is to *Melody."*

A hush falls over the room, and I feel Melody's nails dig into my forearm, but I stand my ground. Hendrix stiffens in his seat next to Teresa a few feet away, giving me a look but remaining silent.

"My loyalty is first and foremost to her," I say, my voice raw with passion and self-assuredness. "It is not to that fucking *company,* or even to this lifestyle that all I've seen witness it do is threaten to stifle us or smother us. *It is to her!"* I shout, leaning forward and pounding my fist to my chest as my voice echoes throughout the room. Madre's eyes widen, but I keep my eyes firmly on Father's. "And I *need* to take her away from this. I will not stick around here and watch whatever happened to you, whatever sickness haunts this family, eat her up. Melody won't be collateral damage. I'm withdrawing from King Dynasty New York headquarters, effective *immediately."*

Father stares at me stunned.

"Until you come to terms with your secrets. Until this family works out whatever bullshit has them all divided, Melody and I are stepping away." I hold my palms up and shake my head, letting him know how serious I am.

William leans forward. "Richard, we need to talk. Maybe it's time we discuss this with them."

Father stands up so fast his chair topples over. "You say a single fucking word to my children, you snake-"

"Brother, you know momma wouldn't want us fighting like this," William implores, spreading his arms.

"Then you should have thought about that before you-"

"It was a goddamn accident!" William yells, his face flushed. "And I am sorry-"

"Enough!"

Williams eyes turn sad. "I have paid my price, Richard! For forty years I have paid and paid! How much more do you want from me?" he says bitterly, his face red as he steps forward, fisting his hands.

"I want you gone!" Father roars.

"I have been gone!" William shouts back, his voice cracking as anger twists his features. "Richard, let it go, okay? You have three kids. A wife! You run a fucking global empire. I moved to the other side of the world, left everything behind, and I only come back when it's *deemed*

necessary. Let it go, brother. We're getting old, and it's time to move past this. *Momma and Stephanie-"*

Father points a finger at him. "Don't you dare speak of them to me!"

"You act just like father!" William shouts, his eyes welling with tears. "You try to remove yourself from that fucking time in our lives like it never happened, *but you act just like him!"*

I suck in a sharp breath and let go of Melody's hand to stand up hastily as Father moves to round the desk, but Madre runs in front of him quickly, throwing herself between the two men.

"Richard, c-calm down, my love."

"You are dead to me!" he shouts over her shoulder, pinning William with a death stare.

"Daddy!" Teresa gasps, her hands coming up to cover her mouth, as does Madre and Melody. Father and William stare at each other past Madre, their eyes locking and years of tension implode in the room.

"Get over it, Richard. Please," William implores, holding his hand out. "I am *begging* you. Forgive me. I know I said you're acting like him, but you are *not* Father."

Father's eyes leave William's to pin me, and the pain in them chills me to the bone. He looks at me as if he doesn't even see me.

"And Mason's just like *you.* No wonder he'll pick you over us. Abandoning his own *father."* His eyes go to William's again as the color in his face deepens. "Genetics are funny, aren't they?" His eyes go back to mine as he turns towards me. "If you leave out that room don't even bother coming back because if you do, I am done with you, too."

"Richard!" Madre gasps, her face contorting with pain. *"No."*

The blow of Father's words reverberates through my being, and the crack that's always been there effectively shatters the rest of the way, leaving me in a thousand pieces so sharp and jagged I know I won't ever be put back together the same way again.

I say nothing.

Remaining silent as the part of my heart I'd been carefully nurturing my entire life to maintain hope that we could have a relationship finally dies. All because of whatever this thing is that happened before I was even born. It cost me.

And it's deposit slices deeper than you'd think.

"Get out!" Father shouts, casting everyone a furious look before turning his back on all of us. "All of you! *Get the hell out of my goddamn house!"* He turns, snatching away from Madre who's openly crying, sobbing into her hands as he retreats through a hidden side door in the wall.

Father has never left Madre in tears like this.

I pull away from Melody, eyeing Hendrix who's expression looks torn between thunderous rage and concern and walk over to her, wrapping my arms around her slight frame. Pressing my lips to her temple in what I pray isn't a final kiss.

"Te amo, mamá," I choke out. "No matter what happens just remember that, okay?"

She throws her arms around me, sniffing into my shirt.

I let her go, turning and holding up my hands as Hendrix reaches for me, shaking my head in a warning to not be touched. I only need one person right now, and I hold my hand out to her.

Melody steps forward and takes it, trembling fingers and all. We lace our fingers together and walk out without another word to anyone.

Effectively closing the door on this chapter in our lives.

CHAPTER 42

DEADLY SWEET

Three Weeks Later. Los Angeles, California

LISTENING TO THE SOUND of our feet crunching along the pea gravel, I also listen patiently as Dad shows me the gardens outside of his property while he talks. I relish the feel of his arm around me as we walk slowly, my brain being even slower about processing everything he's telling me about our family and its connections.

"I'm Lucien's uncle," he says, patiently.

"And I'm Lucien's cousin?

"Yes."

"And Lucien's the Don?"

"Hmhm."

I pause. "One of the five Dons in the country?"

"Yes."

"And he married *his* cousin to one of the five Dons, Joaquin, who is also Hendrix's best friend."

"Yes. But she's *your* cousin, too."

I nibble my lip. "When am I going to meet him?"

He shoots me a look and grins. "I'm not ready to share you just yet."

"Oh, that's sweet." I melt, giggling. "And who are *you* in all of this?"

"The underboss."

"Right under Lucien?"

"Yes."

I glance up at him sharply. "You've killed people?"

A wince crosses his face. "Yes."

"Ah." I stare ahead, keeping my arm twined around his as I glance at the beautiful foliage in the distance and try to imagine my dad killing someone. I'm a bit surprised that this doesn't bother me the way it probably should.

I guess I'm silent for too long because he gets an uncomfortable look on his face and blows out a heavy breath.

"Mel, I know it's a lot..."

"So I'm a cousin to the Donnn," I drawl, my brows furrowing as I look up at him. "That seems like it might not be a big deal, though?"

He frowns. "It's actually a very big deal. Amelia is your first cousin as well, and Lucien married her off to protect her and to ally the two families. You probably would have been treated the same had you grown up in this family."

"Sooo what you're saying is I'm a mafia princess?" I snort.

Wild.

Seeing as I'm not distancing myself from him, he gets a relieved smile on his face, his eyes turning even more warm.

"Well, only if you want to be, I suppose," Maximus chuckles, tucking me under his arm as we stop to admire a hedge of dogwood.

I laugh lightly. "I don't know what I want to be. That's the problem." I lean forward, pressing my nose to the petals and smelling. We turn and continue our journey.

He hums, keeping his eyes on our feet as we round a corner and under an archway of climbing roses, meandering through a beautiful piece of his garden where the various plants are designed in almost a maze, keeping you moving through so you can take in all its beauty.

"It's okay to not know what you want to do, Melody. Part of the joy of life is figuring it out as you go along."

I nod, wrapping myself even tighter around his arm as we journey deeper through the gardens. It's a few more minutes before he speaks, his words coming out hesitantly.

"How's your mother?"

I scrunch my nose, still feeling the sting of betrayal. But thanks to some time and distance, it's lessened. "Well... I guess she's okay."

Truth is, I've barely talked to her in the weeks since the fiasco at the Balducci wedding.

He grunts lightly. Putting a hand to his nape, he squeezes, now staring straight ahead. "Is she still talking to that William guy?"

"Ummm..." I say slowly. "From what Izzy has told me, their relationship has been something that's been driving a thorn deeper into the King Dynasty family dynamic. So it's a little touchy there, I suppose."

He looks at me. "What do you mean?"

"Her and Richard's wife, Mason's mother Maribel, are very close. But William and Richard don't get along. There's a very, very old family secret and some other drama that's severed their relationship," I pause. "It's part of the reason Mason and I are out here, actually. Mason wants a relationship with William. Richard doesn't like it and has disowned William. It's *so* complicated. We needed some distance from it all."

"What's the other drama?"

I shrug a shoulder. "Who knows. Richard won't talk."

"Richard sounds like a hard-ass," he mutters.

"Hm, Richard's not a bad man but..." I trail off, twisting my lips as I find a way to word it. "He's got a lot of trauma behind something really awful that happened in the family, and it's caused him to be wary of men. Including the ones in his family. I feel really bad for him..."

"Sounds bad, sweetheart," he says quietly, clearing his throat. "You know I, uh...I don't get along with one of my brothers either. Lucien's other uncle, not his dad," he corrects on a deep, heavy sigh. "Though we haven't disowned him, we *are* just merely tolerating him. Family ties are tough, Mel. They're never perfect. Especially in our world." His eyes find mine and he gives me a little, sad smile. "But we're happy to have you, sweetheart."

I smile back, feeling shy. Still not quite believing that I have a father, much less a whole family to get used to. And I'm *welcomed.*

"I don't need perfection," I say quietly, giving his arm a squeeze.

He nods. "Well, I'll do my damndest, honey. That I can promise you."

We walk for a few more minutes before he talks again. Over the last few weeks of getting to know him, I see that our mannerisms are very alike. The silences between us are comfortable, neither one of us feeling pressured to fill it with chatter.

"I think the pie is done. Let's head back inside?"

"Sure," he says, turning us effortlessly down another path. If I hadn't had him with me I'd be downright lost. I can barely see the top of his house through the hedges we're walking through.

"Dad, are you still in love with my mom?" I blurt out, not able to help myself.

You'd never know he was bothered by my question by looking at him. He stares ahead of us, always looking forward it seems like. He's silent, taking a second to soak in my question. And I let him.

"I am."

My heart thumps painfully at the two simple words that mean the world to me.

I tug on his arm, digging my heels into the ground and forcing us to a stop. He tilts his head to look down at me. *"Well, then go after her!"*

His eyes flick between mine before he looks away, and tightens his arm, making me resume walking next to him. "It's not that simple, Melody."

"But it is-"

He tuts, shaking his head. "Melody, no, sweetheart. It's not. She has a deep mistrust of the mafia because of how she's been hunted down, and now with what happened to Isobel..." he trails off, getting a sad look in his eyes. "I don't want to traumatize her, sweetheart. Maybe it's best she just pursue a relationship with William."

I huff a breath. Knowing that if she's with William, then mom probably won't be around Maribel and Richard. Maybe even Isobel...

"It's so fucked up," I say quietly, pushing the door open when we make our way to the back of the house. The security flank the door, remaining quiet as we go through. "You *love* her."

"Love's never been for me, I don't think."

I keep my comments to myself, preferring to ruminate on it for a bit before responding. We take our shoes off in the mudroom and hang up our light jackets before heading to the kitchen. Dad inhales and grins.

"It smells amazing," he compliments me with a pat on the back.

"Thanks, and it smells done."

I pull a strawberry pie out of the oven, glad to not have a million eyes on me. Dad has thankfully dismissed the household staff today, only leaving us with security, and we've spent the time bonding over cooking and baking.

He cooks; I bake.

We sit at the island, sharing a bottle of Italian wine from his vineyard, and talk about anything and everything. After an hour I trust I can cut the pie without it falling apart, and I slide a piece onto a saucer plate for him and hand him a fork. He takes a bite and groans, his eyes closing as he swallows.

"Wow, Mel." I grin as he takes another bite, getting a thoughtful look on his face. "Hey, this tastes a lot like the pie at Deadly Sweet."

"What's that?"

"A bakery. Pretty prolific one, too."

"A bakery?"

"Yes, I go once every other week. That's all I allow myself," he chuckles. "Gotta keep the girlish figure, you know."

I choke, laughing and holding a napkin to my mouth. *"Shut up,* you don't have a inch of fat anywhere, silly!"

We both laugh, and Mason comes through a door behind Dad, dragging a hand through his hair. Our eyes meet, and my laughter dies on my tongue, dissipating at the look in Mason's eyes when our gazes clash.

"Hey, you," I say softly, gesturing at the pie between dad and me. "I made a strawberry pie. You want a slice?"

"I'd love some, baby. Hey, Max," Mason claps Dad on the shoulder before rounding to the other side of the island where I sit, and I accept his kiss graciously. Not rejecting him in front of my father.

Behind closed doors is another story, however.

I would have thought the constant rejection of anything intimate between him and me would have caused him to blow up at me, but it hasn't.

He's exercised a lot of restraint these past three weeks.

"How's my nephew?" Dad asks gruffly, putting another bite in his mouth.

"He's fine. Always fine," Mason says. "I have to meet with him tomorrow night about something important, apparently." He reaches forward, grabbing a saucer and scooping out not one but *two* big slices of pie. My eye go wide, and he sees. *"What?* I need my strength."

"For what?" I giggle.

"Later." He arches a brow, and I look away sharply.

Our sex life has been a little fucked up since I found out he knew my father was alive, and it's been pretty stagnant since we've moved in with Dad temporarily while we've been house hunting these last three weeks.

"You know, Mel, I'm pretty sure I saw a help wanted sign for an additional baker when I was there last week," Dad says, raising a brow and taking a sip of water.

"What are you talking about?" Mason asks, his eyes flicking from Dad's to mine.

"A bakery that's hiring for a new baker."

I blink rapidly. "But I don't have a degree, or any formal training-"

"Doesn't matter, sweetheart," Dad interrupts. "Take some advise from your old man. If you want something out of life, you go grab it by the bullhorns. Dominate it."

Mason grunts and laughs, throwing me an amused look.

"Okay," I say. "Well, then let's go."

Dad's brow arches.

"What?" I tease. "Afraid of fucking up your girlish figure?" I laugh, shaking my head when Mason throws me a 'what the fuck' look. "I'll tell you later," I say quietly.

"Nah, I could go for a brownie actually." He stands up, throwing his napkin down on his plate. "Let's go. It's a little under an hour away."

"Hey, uh, is there any possible way we can leave some of the security behind?" I ask hopefully. "I doubt I can get a job with a bunch of men flanking me."

Mason and Dad trade a look. "Surely we can ask them to stay outside?" Mason asks, collecting our dishes and taking them to the sink to soak.

"Yeah. I doubt anyone will try to kill you at a bakery," I say wryly, rolling my eyes.

Dad gets an amused look on his face and then grins. "Let me talk to my man, Mario. See what I can manage."

He turns on his heels and then walks out of the kitchen, leaving Mason and me alone. I join him at the sink, meaning to rinse while he fills the sink with hot sudsy water.

"I miss you," he says quietly, not taking his eyes off the saucer he's washing.

My eyes well up with tears, those three words making my already heightened emotional state even more distressed. Because I've needed him desperately, but he hasn't forced me into anything. Giving me time and space.

The bubbles trail up his arm, and the water steams between us as we work together. Our arms brush, and guilt swamps me at how I've been denying him sexual intimacy because I've been hurt. He's left his family and moved us all the way to the other side of the States so we could make a new life for ourselves, and I repay him by shutting him out.

Chewing my lip, I tilt my head up to look at him. "I'm sorry," I whisper.

His eyes meet mine, the sadness in them melting to desire. "I'm sorry, too, butterfly."

Standing up on my tiptoes, I press my lips to his, moaning as he deepens it slightly. The dish he was washing splashes at he drops it in the sink, and he turns to me, putting his hands on either side of my face and pulling me into him. Soap gets on me, but I don't mind, craning my neck back and parting my lips more for him, stroking my tongue along his.

His cock swells between us, pressing tight into my belly. "Make love to me?"

Dad comes back into the room, clearing his throat, making us pull away reluctantly.

"Tonight," Mason whispers against my lips.

We both turn to face him, and I'm blushing so hard I feel faint, forgetting just how badly Mason's kisses affected me. My heart thumps heavily in my chest, and my breasts swell against my bra, my need making itself known.

Dad's lips tip in a grin as he looks between us, arching a brow. "Can we go?" he drawls slowly. "Or do y'all need to go take a nap or something?"

I gasp, slapping my hand to my mouth and turning back to the sink, hurriedly washing the other dishes.

"We're fine," Mason chuckles, tucking me under his arm when I rinse my hands and shut the water off. I take the towel he gives me and dry my hands with it, throwing it to the counter when I'm done.

"So, an hour away you said?" I squeak, clearing my throat and turning to head to the mudroom for my shoes.

"Yup. Almost, anyways." Dad laughs, and ten minutes later, we're in an armored SUV, driving down the coast headed to what I hope is going to be a new beginning for me.

My hope is thoroughly crushed as I stand outside, flanked on either side by Dad and Mason looking up at the bakery in front of us, my mouth gaping.

It's not just a bakery. It's a bakery/factory that takes up damn near a quarter of the block. Its storefront is beautifully decorated with white paint and pink shutters. The pink neon sign *Deadly Sweet* is in a beautiful cursive, featuring a cartoon cupcake. Swirls and various sweets are written in white and pink on the store window, and several iron tables and chairs with umbrellas are lined outside on the patio, which is filled to the brim with customers and servers bringing out elaborate desserts.

It's so girlie it's comical, but despite how sweet it looks, it's a *massive* business.

Beyond the storefront, you can see a white building attached. It has its own production factory.

I'm instantly intimidated.

"I can't apply for a job here," I hiss to my dad. "Look at this place!" I moan, putting a hand to my forehead. *"And we drove all the way here too."*

Dad puts a hand to my back, looking down at me. "Since you've been with me you've made a desert every night. And not only are they *good,* they are comparable to everything I've eaten in here. I wouldn't have brought you otherwise."

I look into his eyes, feeling some of my unease melt away as he looks at me with so much kindness it's hard to believe he's an underboss to the most powerful Don in California, and I can see why my mom fell in love with him all those years ago.

I huff out a breath, steeling my resolve, and squaring my shoulders. "Okay, here goes nothing."

Walking inside is like something out of a movie. I can't believe the difference in stepping off the sidewalk and into the store. I'm immediately hit by smells of all kinds, and the place is enormous. The space is big enough for at least thirty circular white tables, with pink chairs and all of them are packed full.

My eyes roam, seeing an entire wall to the left is nothing but frosted glass freezer doors with cakes, pies, custards, and different flavors of ice creams. At the register are at least three clerks who man the store next to a glass display of cookies, muffins, donuts, biscuits, pastries, brownies, and puddings.

There are three lines of people almost to the back where we stand.

The opposite wall is a stretch of wall to wall glass panels with what looks to be party rooms beyond, and I see a group of girls dressed up, posing in front of an impressive selfie wall made of flowers and greenery taking pictures.

Jesus.

Glazed white round tables break up the customer tables throughout the space and decorated with what I would assume you'd find in Willy Wonka's chocolate factory. Candy of all shapes and sizes dominate these tables, reaching high almost to the ceiling. Each table is a different color scheme.

There's even a little melted chocolate fountain bar.

I shiver. "It's cold in here," I say nervously, catching the eye of a woman walking towards us who was delivering a pair of comically tall sundaes piled high with whipped cream to a table.

She looks to be about thirty, and so pretty she could be a barbie doll. She reminds me of the African American version of Karissa she's so perfectly put together. My eyes fall to the chunky bangle on her wrist, and her ears decorated with beautiful earrings. She's in front of us in no time at all, giving me and Mason a curious once over before putting her attention back to my dad.

"Maximus!" she trills, smiling brightly as she steps forward and wraps her arms warmly around him. Mason and I stay silent, just watching as they greet each other. She steps back and gets a teasing scowl on her face and hits him in the arm, surprising me. "I haven't seen you in a *month, you asshole.* Where have you been? I thought you'd gotten yourself in trouble and I was going to have to come rescue you!" she says in a sharp tone.

Though it's obvious she's teasing, I frown. Wondering if Dad's a player.

"Ah, Charayl," he drawls, getting an amused smile on his face. "Do you really think you would have found me?"

Her eyes narrow. "I'm quite confident."

He chucks her under her chin, making her nose scrunch. "Just as sweet as ever," Dad says playfully. He steps back, turning and gesturing an arm towards us. "I want you to meet my family. This is my daughter, Melody, and her new husband, Mason."

Charayl's brows go up, and she side-eyes Dad before stepping forward and holding out her hand to Mason and me.

"H-Hello," I say shyly, shaking her hand and then tucking a lock of hair behind my ear. "I was sort of here for an application..."

She turns her face from me dismissively, looking at Dad. "You didn't tell me you had a daughter, Maximus," she says in an accusatory tone. "You've been coming to me for almost *eight years now.* What else are you hiding from me?" Her eyes dart around quickly. "And where's your people that you usually roll with?"

She's perceptive, and tough. Damn.

Dad laughs and crosses his arms. "I just wanted to have a bit of privacy with my family today. Is that alright with you, my dear?"

She rolls her eyes before putting them to me and looks me up and down. Though she looks as sweet as her shop, goosebumps erupt along my skin at how intimidating she is.

"Melody, go behind the counter, snag a brownie, and eat it. When you're done, go to the back and bake me a creme bruleé." she says in a no-nonsense voice, her eyes turning sharp. My brows rise, and I toss a look to Dad, who's reached for a menu off a table, only to have it snatched up by Charayl who tsks at him and scrunches her nose. "Are you kidding me, Max? Don't be so fucking insulting. *I know what you order."*

I huff a little laugh, unsure. Tightening my lips when she shoots me another sharp look and just stares. Her eyes are eerie, making my toes curl. *"Did you hear me?"* she asks, blinking.

I jerk, shoving my purse to Mason who's pulled out a chair next to Dad and made himself comfortable.

Winding through the customers, I head to the front of the store, and slip behind the counter. The clerks spare me exactly one glance as I walk to the little sink and wash my hands before grabbing a little piece of wax paper, reaching in and grabbing a brownie. I step to the side, and watch as the customers flood in, filling each of the three registers at least ten people deep.

The first bite I take almost floors me it's so luscious, and I know right then and there why she had me do this. If I can't deliver at this level, then there's no point in even trying. Despite the sweetness in my mouth, I feel sick. I've only made creme bruleé one time, and that was a year ago.

Fuck.

"Okay, I can do this." I whisper, swallowing the last bite and heading through the steel door that leads to the massive kitchen, finding an apron and pulling my hair back. Not one of the at least twenty women moving around the bakery kitchen blinks at my presence, and I grab a huge mixing bowl and make myself at home.

Two hours later I got the job with a sixty thousand dollar a year salary.

Wow.

CHAPTER 43

I Need You

"I CAN'T BELIEVE I got the job!" Melody whoops as she steps out into the night air. Max and I both laugh as her joy is infectious.

She talks our ears off about it the entire drive home, wondering what all she's going to start off baking. Her first day is Monday next week. She goes on and on and on from the backseat, her face lit up in the light of her cell as she no doubt looks up recipes on her phone. Sure enough, a YouTube video begins to play with a technique on how to make a rum soaked cake with a complicated sounding filling.

Thankfully Maximus keeps her occupied because I'm slowly being cooked to death in the driver's seat. Getting uncomfortably hotter one degree at a time until I'm in a oven of red-hot lust with seemingly no relief in sight. I swallow thickly against my dry throat, not even sure I could talk if I wanted to.

One thing I've noticed, Maximus is a very patient man. He's patient about everything. Driving, holding a conversation. He moves with ease through the world, a man unbothered.

I don't share these characteristic traits.

So, I gun it a lot faster than I normally would. Because I need to fuck her.

"Make love to me?" she'd asked earlier in the day, and it's been way too long since her request.

What if she doesn't remember? So yes, I've got to get us home.

We pull onto Maximus' property in record time, and I jump out into the cool night air, ignoring his quizzical look at me as I round the car to their side and open her door. Pulling her out.

"Goodnight, Max," I call over my shoulder, pulling her along with me, still droning on about some recipe.

As soon as we make it to our bedroom I close and lock the door and take her phone, tossing it onto the dresser and slanting my mouth over hers, ceasing her talking with a deep kiss.

"Stop talking, and take off your clothes," I rasp, pulling away from her and stride to the terrace doors and open the curtains.

I throw the doors open to our terrace on the ground floor, filling the room with the perfectly humid night air that smells like lemons, thanks to the abundance of citrus trees planted throughout the property. When I turn, she's already slipped the straps of her dress off her shoulders.

My eyes darken as it pools to the floor at her feet.

My cock, already stone hard, throbs and tightens even more as she steps out of the garment and makes her way slowly to me. Her white-tipped toes tease me, as does the little ankle bracelet she wears.

My eyes rise to the perfect triangle of her bare pussy, and I'm momentarily stuck in place, not sure whether to sink to my knees before her or pick her up into my arms.

My hands twitch at the dilemma. That's how fucking wrapped around her finger she's got me.

"Mason, are you okay?" she asks, her eyes going wide.

I can see why, because I can't move. Her beauty has me paralyzed.

"No. I don't like it when you keep your body from me, butterfly," I answer, my eyes flicking to hers. "I've been suffering, love."

Not that we've been together long enough for her to know that information, but still, I try to make her see just how badly she affects me when she withholds from me emotionally, sexually. It destroys me from the inside out because she's my safe place.

Without her, I am nothing.

Wetting her lips, she gets a rather sheepish look on her face, ducking her head and then pulling her arms across her torso in a bid to hide from me.

"I'm sorry," she whispers. "I just got so upset."

Nodding, I clear my throat. "That's alright, baby, but... I missed you. So, I'm going to fuck you all night, or at least until I feel better. Because I was upset, too."

Her eyes rise slowly to meet mine, but she stays silent as I flick her hair behind her left shoulder, spanning her ribcage with my hands and bending down to take her nipple in my mouth, sucking hard. Her hands fly up to my hair, and she stands on her tiptoes with a moan, arching into my mouth.

I pick her up easily, making her wrap her legs around my waist. "Are you wet?"

"Yes," she gasps. "Shut up and fuck me, Mason."

"Oh, you're getting fucked. You don't even need to ask, baby."

I pull away from her breast and straighten my spine, looking down into her eyes as I line my cock up with her warm, wet entrance and lower her on top of me. Her pretty mouth parts, letting out an even prettier gasp of air. I grab her ass with my hands and pull her onto me slowly, rolling my hips into her and beginning to rock us.

Everything in my body shifts back in alignment as we become one for the first time since we've moved here to Cali. I missed her so much, and my eyes prick with the force of my emotion. As do hers.

Her eyes well up, and she nibbles her bottom lip, her eyes going hooded with desire.

"Mason, please be gentle tonight..." she says, tilting her head back as I begin to move us, slowly. Purposefully.

Overcome, I place my forehead to her chest and just hold us together. Not moving, or trying to race to some finish line. Breathing. Settling. *Feeling.* Just existing and merely wanting to connect with my wife.

"I'll be gentle, so don't worry," I whisper against her skin, licking her from her breastbone up her throat until I get to her mouth and kiss her like my life depends on it. I roll my hips into hers lazily, taking my time. Just like I'm going to ride her tonight, nice and slow.

Her body becomes dewy, and a flush enters her face and travels down her neck to her chest. Her pink lips part as her brows furrow, and I can tell she's immediately regretting her request by the way her throat bobs, and her beautiful brown eyes go to mine. I know her well enough by now to know when she wants more.

"No," I say, tilting my head. "We said slow, Melody."

"Harder!" she whimpers, beginning to squirm against me.

I shake my head, chuckling. Walking towards our bed I pull back the sheet and lay her down "No. We agreed."

It's hours before I stop, both of us boneless and spent. And even then I keep my cock lodged inside her balls deep, unwilling to part from her. We sleep tangled up in one another. Exactly how I crave.

As one.

The next afternoon, Melody yelps, gulping as the tattoo needle strokes across her flesh and tears of pain well in her eyes, threatening to overflow. *"Oww,"* she complains.

I smile, gripping her free hand as the tattoo artist stays bent over her hand where she's having my signature tatted from her wrist to the base of her thumb.

"Almost done," I murmur, giving her fingers a kiss.

She gives me a shaky smile. "Does it look good?"

I look down, grinning. "It looks perfect."

"I start Monday morning at the bakery," she says in an awed voice before getting a little goofy smile on her face.

I chuckle into my fist, my eyes lighting up at her joy. I doubt she even notices this is her twentieth time saying that since she got the job two days ago.

"It sounds like a dream come true, baby." I indulge her, egging her on in her happiness. The only other subjects I've heard her speak in this kind of tone about have been track and, well....me.

My heart skips a beat at the knowledge that there's a person in this world who loves me for me. Despite my flaws, my sarcastic wit, and oftentimes overpowering temper. My fucked up family. She loves me in spite of it.

And her love is more than I could have ever asked for.

The tattoo artist finishes, smearing her with gel and then wrapping her tattoo in plastic. We pay, walking out of the shop and strolling down the sidewalk to our car, pretending to not see Dante and Stephen tailing us a few feet behind. There are a couple more men milling about with their eyes on us, courtesy of Luca, but I don't tell Melody.

Her phone rings, and she pauses, stepping to the side to dig in her purse for it. Holding it up to her ear she gets a wide smile on her face. "Hey, Daddy."

I swear, her dad coming along was the unexpected plot twist we all desperately needed. Taking advantage of the break, I pull out a cigarette and light up, my brows furrowing as she blinks and gets an irritated look on her face.

"You did what?" she says in a hushed, furious voice. Her mouth sets in a hard line, and I reach forward to touch my hand to her arm. She steps closer. *"She's there?" Uh oh.* Her jaw clenches. "I don't want to talk to her, Dad. Yeah, I know it's been over a month. *I'm not dumb!*"

I blow out a plume of smoke, ignoring the judgmental look of a woman passing by.

Melody scrunches up her face and huffs a deep breath. I pull her into me, wrapping her with both of my arms and rocking her while she finishes her conversation.

When she hangs up, I snuff the cigarette out and then throw it in a bin, taking her hand as we resume our walk to our car.

"What's up?" I ask, but I don't need to. I already know.

She squints against the setting sun on the horizon. "Mom's in town. She's at Dad's."

I scoff and open her car door, letting her slide in. We've got a new car with the top down to really embrace Cali life. "Let me guess, she just showed up?"

"Yes."

"That doesn't sound like your mom, love."

I climb in the driver's side, starting it and looking in the rearview mirror until I see our security smoothly pull out, holding up traffic for us to pull in front of them.

"I know."

"Are you going to talk to her?"

Her mouth tightens in a line, and she turns her face away, looking at the waves crashing along the coast as we drive past. "Well it'd be really fucked up of me if I turned her away after she flew all the way here. But if you're asking me if I'm going to accept an apology... I don't know."

I nod, taking her hand and kissing her knuckles.

Twenty minutes later we arrive at Maximus' place, and she gives me a pointed look as we park right outside the front. "We need our own house," she grumbles, looking put out for the first time since we've moved here.

And that's saying a lot because she was mad at me for those first few weeks until we made up.

"We've been looking. You've told your dad that, right?"

She nods, and though Maximus denies it, I feel we've outstayed our welcome.

Despite all the space, it'd be nice to have our own place. I squeeze her hand and open the car door. "Let's get this over with. We can soak in a nice tub with some wine when it's all over. But we need to get this over with."

I know I'm one to talk, having ignored Hendrix's and mother's calls since I've been here in California, but as her husband, maybe I need to start leading by example. I suck in a deep breath when she closes the car door with a slam and put a hand to her shoulder.

"Hey, butterfly," I say hesitantly, catching her eyes. "Do you think..." I trail off, suddenly losing my nerve.

Her eyes widen, and she puts a hand to my cheek, caressing me. "Do I think what?"

"Do you think maybe we can call my mother after we talk to yours? Maybe tonight?"

She gives me a sad smile, standing on her tiptoes to press her lips to mine. I wrap my arms around hers, deepening it. "Of course we can."

I nod, and we make our way into the house and through to the den where Maximus stands across from Donna, who's looking rather teary-eyed. Pablo's sitting next to the baby grand in the far corner of the room, out of earshot with his face averted.

Melody twists her lips as Donna turns and catches her eye.

Donna's face contorts as she sniffs, her eyes slightly bloodshot. She smooths her hands down her royal-purple silk dress and takes a few hesitant steps towards us. Tears stream down her face before she lets out a gasp and full-on runs to us, colliding with Melody, who buries her face into her neck and squeezes her hard, now crying, too.

"I'm so, so sorry, honey," Donna sobs. "Will you please forgive me? Don't hate me forever; I can't stand it!"

Stepping away cautiously I shake my head, fighting against the sting in my eyes. Wishing more than anything I could have a moment like that with my father, but it doesn't seem like that's in the cards for me.

Leaving them to it, I make my way over to Maximus and cast him a look, my brow rising, seeing his eyes are red-tinged as well, like he'd been crying.

"Are you okay, Max?" I ask gruffly, folding my arms and turning to the side a bit, averting my face from the two women. I see Melody pull away and then step away from Donna, whose face falls as Melody shakes her head and holds up a hand.

"Hmhm," he grunts, clearing his throat before turning and walking completely out of the room, through the accordion glass doors and into the gardens outside the den.

My brows rise at his sudden departure. Damn.

Hearing the women crying, I pull out my phone and text Hendrix.

Melody's rejection and Donna's tears affect me more than I care to admit. The fact our family is so fractured in so many different ways cuts me deep and causes me to make concessions where I can. And I think I can start with my sibling.

I'm sorry I've been ignoring you. Let's plan some time this week to talk. I have a lot to catch you up on. Please give Izzy, Mariah and the baby our love. -Mason

CHAPTER 44

M&Ms

I WAKE AROUND FOUR o'clock in the morning and look over at Mason sleeping soundly on his back with an arm bent and tucked behind his head. He's nude. The sheet only covering his cock, leaving the rest of the well-defined muscles of his physique to my gaze.

At one point in time, not that long ago, this very vision had been a mere figment of my imagination. A craving.

His broad chest rises and falls evenly with his breathing, and right when I'm about to climb on top of him, his phone lights up on the nightstand, and I reach over to grab it, not wanting it to wake him up.

He's been making himself available to me, my father, and now Lucien, and I want him to get his rest.

Naked, I swing my legs over the side of the bed and walk over to the chaise lit up in moonlight by the window and sit, pulling the throw pillow into my lap. Checking that he's still sleeping, I open his phone to see a text from his mother. They'd briefly talked when I was falling asleep after we made love, but I was so tired I couldn't tell you what was said.

I should put the phone away, but Maribel's words draw my attention.

Mijo I'm so sorry, mi amor. Please forgive me. -Mami

My eyes widen and I cast a quick glance to Mason who's still dead to the world, before going back to his phone. I tentatively scroll up, curious as to what was said before this. I gasp, putting my fingers to my lips. Maribel's temporarily been staying with my mother! Apparently, she moved out of King Compound shortly after we moved to California.

And one of the texts was her asking him to please not tell Hendrix.

Oh my god.

A quick look at Mason's phone log shows dozens of missed calls from Hendrix and even Richard along with fifteen voicemails from Richard that Mason hasn't listened to. My fingers itch to play one; however, there's only so much sleuthing that I feel comfortable doing. And though I believe Mason shares everything with me, this is a horrible invasion of privacy.

No, we'll tackle this together when he's ready.

I place the phone down gently onto his nightstand, giving him a kiss to his lips before tiptoeing out of our suite and heading to the kitchen where I go into the big walk-in pantry and grab a mason jar. Spying a giant bag of M&Ms, I pour them all in the mason jar before sealing it with the aluminum lid and then make my way back to our bedroom, seeing him stirring.

It's five minutes to five, about the time we normally wake up and start our day.

I crawl back into bed and have almost just managed to slip completely under the covers seemingly undetected when Mason's voice rings out.

"Melly? Why are you up, baby?" he rasps.

I bite my lip and flop to my side on a huff of breath. "Because I've been thinking."

He groans lightly. An intimate, deep sound that causes heat to curl tight in my belly. *"About what?* More baking tips?"

I giggle, circling his nipple with my fingertips. "No," I breathe, leaning in to press my lips to his chest and up to his lips where I give him a smacking kiss. "I've been thinking about sweets."

"Same difference." His eyes pop open, and he scrunches his nose at me.

I laugh. "No, listen. Sit up." I scramble to my knees and click my nightstand on low and grab the jar of M&M's and face him, sitting back on my heels and biting my bottom lip.

He sits up slowly, the sheet falls away revealing ripping muscles. His eyes are hard on the jar nestled between my breasts, and he holds out his hand. I take it, shuffling forward.

"Are we starting a new tradition of sharing a jar of M&Ms before we get up for the day?"

I laugh. "No, silly. But, uhm..." I trail off, glancing down at the sheet between us and lowering my voice. "I'd like to try something. Something just for me and you?" My eyes go up to his, and I see him watching me carefully.

He reaches forward and tucks my hair behind my ear.

"Go on."

"I've been thinking about what you said. How you don't like me to cut you off emotionally, and..." I take a deep breath. "I was thinking, during the times when you and I are mad at each other, we go to the M&M jar and each feed one to each other, to remind us to be sweet."

He tilts his head, giving me a sexy grin. Reaching forward again, he slides his hand up my forearm until he grabs my elbow and pulls me even closer. His eyes go hooded, the sheet tents with his erection, and it in turn makes me aroused that he doesn't think my idea is silly. Rather, he likes it.

"M for Melody?" he rasps.

I nod. *"And* M for Mason."

He chuckles, taking my mouth in a deep kiss and then lowering me to the bed and placing his hard body on top of mine. The jar falls to the side as my legs wind around his hips, and I kiss him back with everything in me, sinking my hands into his hair and rolling my hips into him.

"I love it, beautiful," he whispers. "Thank you for being so sweet to me."

The day is a bright one full of sunshine and chirping birds.

A few hours later I find myself walking through the massive Italian villa on the Scognamiglio estate. I glance nervously at Dad who looks at ease and in command as we journey through the hall flanked by security. I look over my shoulder, seeing Stephen trailing the two other men, feeling bad for him.

I actually want him closer.

Stopping Dad with a hand to his arm, I turn and look past the two men that are always with him. "Stephen, please come walk next to me."

"Yes, ma'am."

Dad arches a brow but waits patiently while Stephen eases between the two mafia guards and stops at my left-hand side. Trying to get used to the amount of security that's been an ever present nuisance since our plane touched down three weeks ago has taken a lot out of me, and instead of wishing Stephen gone like I had while we were in New York, I crave the familiarity of him by me.

We continue on past wooden doors flanked by gas lantern sconces until we get to an arched recessed double door at the end of the hall. Dad pushes us through, and then ushers me in ahead of him. I smile, seeing Mason sitting in the seat across from the big desk, but draw up short at the incredibly intimidating man on the other side who cuts his eyes to me and gets a devilish grin.

"Ahhh, cousin," he says, standing up.

"Hi," I say shyly, taking in how tall he is, his olive skin, striking features, dark brown hair and sharp eyes. He looks like a mafia boss, indeed. Broad.

And where he can't physically fill up a room, his energy does. It's a bit scary.

I peek at Dad before shifting my weight on my feet.

Lucien tugs his suit, smoothing one hand down his abdomen before casting a curious look at Mason, who just gets this wicked grin on his face and then scrubs his hand across his jaw, trying to hide the mischievous glint in his eyes. I warm because I know that look.

I just know they were talking about something inappropriate.

Hopefully *not* the marathon night of lovemaking he made me endure the night before.

Just for that, I'm taking his ass on a long early morning run tomorrow. Lucien comes up to me and places his hands on my shoulders, giving me a light squeeze before bending down to kiss both of my cheeks.

"Bellisima!" he says loudly, chucking me under the chin and then standing back a couple feet, giving me a thorough look up and down. He tsks. "Do you know how close we were to getting married?"

"U-Uh..." I stammer, frowning and throwing Dad and Mason a look. *"No."*

He chuckles, grinning at me as he walks past and sits back down in his seat. "Would have been incredibly fucked up finding out we were cousins after the fact." He makes a face. "Jesus, that would have been a mess."

Making my way to the seat next to Mason, I sit down gingerly, looking around his office while he picks up a pen and starts flipping it. My eyes clock a ugly as hell looking rabbit on his mantle, and it makes me think of Charayl because of the rabbit necklace she wears.

He waits a few heartbeats before clearing his throat softly, bringing my attention back to him. "How're you finding California, Mel?"

"Oh, it's beautiful. I'd wanted to go to college here, but I was forced to stay in New York."

He smiles. "What a shame. You look like a Californian. New York is so..." He flicks a look to Mason before bringing his eyes back to me. *"Nasty."*

I tighten my lips and nod. Not exactly sure how to make small talk with a mafia Don.

"So, why has it taken you so long to come see your big cousin?" He gives me a blinding smile with his perfect teeth and I grin, looking at Dad.

Maximus chuckles. "That's my fault, Luca. I just wanted to have her to myself for a while. Thanks for indulging me."

"Well," he scoffs, looking to the side and tossing his pen down on the table. "That's what family is for, am I right?"

The men trade a look and I twist my lips, feeling nervous and eager to say something, *anything.* "Do you like sweets?" I blurt out.

He arches an amused brow. "I do, why?"

"Well, Mr. Scognamiglio, I'd thought about bringing you a desert, but wasn't sure which one you'd like."

Lucien smiles. "Oh please, Mel. We're cousins, call me Luca. And I love, *love* a good brownie."

I give him a small smile back. "Okay, Luca. I'll remember for next time."

"She's quite the baker!" Dad boasts, looking down at me with pride. "I've already gained four pounds since she's come to stay."

Lucien's smile broadens. "I love sweets. They're my guilty pleasure." He leans forward and lowers his voice to a whisper. "Especially peaches and cream cheesecake. Bring that next time, will ya?"

"We can still hear you," Mason drawls in a bored voice, rolling his eyes.

Luca smiles and sits back in his seat, adopting a sudden, stoic look. "Anyways, I thought it'd be best to inform you two together that I will be having to place you under our security detail-"

"Uhm, why?" I half laugh, throwing a 'back me the hell up' look at Mason. "There's no need. We have our own, and Dad's place is crawling with security guards."

He lets me finish my sentence, even giving me a second or two after speaking just to see if I've said all I needed to say. And that's nice to see, honestly.

"Because you're the cousin to the head of a very powerful family, and the wife to a member of another very powerful family, and the daughter of a man who many want dead." He makes a cutting motion with his hand. "Three strikes, *you're out.*"

I pout. *Well, damn.*

He tsks. "Aw. Come on, don't give me that face. Unfortunately we all have to make concessions."

My brow arches. "And what's *your* concession?"

His eyes go to the ugly ceramic rabbit and turn a bit sad. "Giving up on having true happiness."

Everyone goes a little quiet before the tense silence is broken by the guard coming from outside and leaning down to whisper in Luca's ear. He nods dismissively. "Thank you, Blane. You may go."

"Am *I* free to go?" Mason asks in his usual bored tone.

Luca sniffs and stands up, brushing his hands together. "If you must, friend. Thanks for going over the numbers with me. I'll mull over your advice and let you know what I decide tomorrow. Go. Enjoy the night."

Dad and I stand up, and Mason tosses Luca a look before his eyes slide to me, showing me the lust in them.

My cheeks warm, and I look away sharply, avoiding Luca's knowing stare. Yup, they were talking about us fucking.

Great.

CHAPTER 45

CONSIGLIERIE

MELODY ALMOST KILLED ME on our five o'clock morning run this morning. On the fucking *beach.*

The soft sand tore my ass up.

I'm typically pretty in shape, but not right now. Right now I think I'm going to *die,* and Luca's ridiculously fucking amused face makes me want to lunge across the table at him and fuck him up for looking so smug. Except I *can't,* because Melody made it her personal mission to shred my quads for some reason.

She's embraced Cali life like a champ; her hair is lush, and her skin is glowing because she's always outside doing something, like picking fruit in her father's gardens or taking his two dogs for a run along the coast.

And the sex we've been having has been better than it was in New York, somehow.

Luca chuckles and twirls his pen, throwing it up in the air and catching it. "Oh, man. I feel so bad for you, actually."

My eyes snaps to his. *"I couldn't imagine why,"* I say as sarcastically as possible.

"Because you look like dog shit." His eyes raking down my body judgmentally. "Seriously. What the fuck's wrong with you?"

"My daughter."

My head snaps to the side before I can answer, seeing all six-foot-two of Maximus striding through the door. If I didn't know his age, there's no way in hell I'd guess he's fifty-five.

"Uncle!" Luca drawls, chuckling. "Your daughter, eh? You mean my sweet, innocent cousin *Melly?"*

Though they're cousins, I narrow my eyes at his new nickname for her.

"Innocent? She might be sweet, but innocent she is *not,* and don't let her fool you," Maximus laughs, patting me heavily on the shoulder before lowering himself in the seat next to me.

"Hey, Max," I greet him, my hands going back to my thighs.

Luca gets up and then walks to the door to the right of us and slides the glass into the wall, opening the space up to the outside before taking out a tin of cigars. I reject it, pulling out my cigarettes, packing them quickly and lighting one even quicker.

Fuck, I might need *two* smokes.

Luca raises a brow, trading a look with Maximus before bringing his eyes back to mine, but I don't care. I suck in a deep drag and let out a long, low groan. *"Fuuucck,* that's good."

Luca snorts. "Anyway, I need to talk to you, Mason."

I take another drag, and flick the ash in the ashtray. "Shoot." His entire demeanor changes, making my body tighten up as his face darkens and his posture goes ramrod straight. It's such a difference from his attitude not even just three seconds ago that I pause bringing the cigarette to my lips and just stare. "What's wrong with your bipolar ass?"

Luca's mouth tightens, and even though the air suddenly becomes chilly, my aching thighs prevent me from taking this seriously. "My consigliere has betrayed me, leading me to need to replace him."

"Your concera whata?" My brow raises as I lower my hand and grip my thigh hard.

"Consigliere," Luca enunciates slowly, as if I'm stupid. Which is actually how I feel because nothing is sinking into my brain at the moment.

"It still doesn't quite ring the bell you think you're hitting, friend," I say wearily, rubbing my jaw with my hand. "Besides, why's this any of my business?" I fight to roll my eyes, and clear my throat instead, looking over at Maximus who's staring between me and Luca quietly. "Max, *every time* your nephew calls me in here, it's for something that could have been an email. Did you know that?"

Maximus' lips twitch, and he brings up a hand to scrub along his jaw, trying yet failing to hold in his chuckle. His eyes glint with amusement as he tosses a wry look at Luca who's resumed tossing that pen back up in the air. I swear, this man can't take anything seriously. My thighs cramp, and I grimace.

"It's your business because you're replacing him."

My brow rises as I flick my eyes to his and then to Maximus who just threads his fingers together and sits calmly. "I'm *what?"*

"Replacing him."

"I heard you, dumbass-"

"Then why did you ask-"

I hold up my hand, narrowing my eyes and blinking. "Luca, isn't the consigliere your *third?"*

He nods, getting an amused smile on his face. "Yes." His brows furrow as he tilts his head at me. "You do realize that you can only get away with calling me a dumbass because you're family, *right?"*

I roll my eyes. "What about my brother?"

He shrugs his shoulder. "That's above me, now." Meaning, in other words he couldn't give a fuck. It makes me smile. I love Hendrix and all, but he can eat grass.

Intrigued, I flick the ash before taking another drag, holding his stare the whole time. "How do you know I won't betray you?"

He chuckles, standing up swiftly from his chair and tugging the lapel of his blazer before rounding his desk. "Follow me," he says curtly.

As Maximus and I stand, I snatch up the ash tray, bringing it with me as we walk out of his office, winding through the halls of his home until we reach the stairs that lead to the basement. Reaching another door, a guard opens it, and I look inside seeing stone instead of the sheetrock of the basement. We descend those stairs, too, and the temperature plummets.

"Fuck," I complain. My thighs protest, and I grumble, taking another smoke and flicking the ash again before setting the little tray in a recessed hole in the wall of what looks to be a dungeon. This shouldn't shock me, but it does. I'll admit it.

The man has a real life dungeon with lanterns; seven stone rooms with iron bars and little prison toilets take up the dank space.

There are several men milling about down here. The usual mafia type: tatted, wearing all black, stone-faced, huge, menacing guys who seem to be in love with the idea of silence because no one here hardly talks. Joey stands next to one of the rooms, the iron bars are open, and the sound of flesh pummeling flesh and agonized groans of pain sound out.

I stand silently next to a stoic Maximus, minding my own business, watching while Luca shrugs out of his blazer, unbuttons his cuffs, and then pushes the sleeves of his white button down shirt up his arms. He holds out his hand, his thick forearms flex as he crooks his fingers, and a guard steps forward and places a glock in it.

He checks it, racking the chamber, and waves me closer.

I frown, stepping forward and looking into the cell where his current consigliere sits in a wooden chair, face completely rearranged to the point I could only tell it was him based off his tattoos on his chest. With no last words, or any warning whatsoever, Luca points the gun at his head and shoots him point blank. No questions asked.

I take a drag of my cigarette, then flick it to the floor, crushing it with my foot. Point taken. "Hm."

That's interesting.

His head turns and he meets my eye. "You going to betray me?"

I frown. "Nope. Wouldn't even think about it, brother."

He smiles. *"Good. You start now."*

He must see the look in my eyes because he gets an amused look on his face and turns, putting his arm around my shoulder and steers me back the way we came. "Well, maybe we can start after you fucking fix whatever my cousin did to your leg, eh?" He chuckles as we walk and then side-eyes me. "You know you're family now, right? That wasn't a joke. You're one of us."

I bite back a smile and scoff a chuckle. "Yeah, I feel that."

And for the first time, I really do.

CHAPTER 46

WE'RE HOME

TWO WEEKS LATER, MELODY and I are ten minutes away touring a fifteen-million-dollar property that just came up for sale.

"It's gorgeous!" Melody's eyes go wide as we take in the estate situated on almost eleven acres of land.

We're standing in the backyard, trying to take it all in. There's so much, though. The place has eight bedrooms, thirteen bathrooms, a cellar, a game room, a tea cottage on the property, a pool with a little guest cottage, and even a playground. But it's the abundance of citrus trees and the gardens that have her sold.

That and the community, which feels private enough that we could live a semi-normal life if we really wanted to.

I hum, tucking her under my arm as the sun sets, situated perfectly between two palm trees side by side.

She leans into my side and puts her lips to my ear. "Masey, can we afford this? I only make sixty thousand dollars a year."

Shit, she's cute.

I chuckle quietly and kiss her ear. "That's how much your one wedding ring costs, love," I whisper.

Almost, anyways.

"I'm serious, Mason!" she grumbles, casting a nervous look around the beautiful courtyard we're standing in. It's miles away from our penthouse that I called my home for over two years back in New York, but I'm okay with us coming closer to the ground now.

I scoff, rolling my eyes. "At this point, just stop asking, honey. Just always assume the answer is yes."

She shakes her head, pulling away from my arm to walk deeper into the property, leaving me alone for a moment.

When she walks down a couple of stairs leading to a sunken garden and disappears behind the hedge, I turn, putting my hands onto my hips and craning my neck to see the house from the back. It's reminiscent of Maximus' home in the classic Italian villa style. Melody adores Maximus' house. So the moment this one went on the market I booked a viewing.

The realtor sidles over to my side, and crosses his arms, craning his neck up too. "She sure is a beauty."

I nod. "Yep. We'll take her. Cash."

He snaps his head over to look at me. *"Cash,* Mr. King? It's fifteen million dollars!"

Turning my head to pin him with a stare, I raise a brow. "Did I stutter or something?"

He fixes his face quick and then shakes his head. "No, sir. I apologize for my rudeness. If you'll just get Mrs. King, we can head back to the office and go over the paperwork."

"Sure. Be right back." I turn, and make quick work of finding Melody. She's already deep in the grounds picking a grapefruit, it looks like.

"Look, Mason!" she shouts, waving at me with the hand holding the dark orange fruit. She points, shielding her eyes with her hand. "See, it's a little vineyard! Isn't it cute?" She turns, her hair whipping around her as she points in another direction, but I only have eyes for her. "And look, there's a little garden house and a pool over there, too!"

As if she can't contain herself, she jumps up and down. Happy.

Finally fucking happy.

Her joy jolts through my body, making my body tight and my heart warm up. Because this is how she *should* have been feeling this whole time. Content and at peace. And I'll do whatever it fucking takes to keep her right here in this very spot where her eyes light up, her smile almost blinds, and she looks around her with so much wonder it's healing to behold.

I run to her. "It sure is, baby," I say, picking her up. She wraps her legs around my waist as I turn her back to the house, beginning to walk back the way we came. "It's our own little slice of paradise!" she says happily, beaming up at me.

My paradise lies between her legs and in her heart, but I keep that secret to myself as I smile back down at her, passing the relator who raises his brows as we walk by.

"Mr. King, are we leaving?"

"We'll be right on out." I open the sliding doors that lead from the outdoor living area to the den, and keep walking through until I find my way to the master.

"What are we doing?"

"Christening the house," I say, pushing her against the wall and lifting up her dress.

One swipe of my fingers to her pussy tells me she's ready for me, and I move her panties to the side, undoing my pants and pushing them down while I seal my mouth to hers, stroking along her tongue.

Fuck, she tastes amazing. Always does.

"Mason, the realtor is *waiting,"* she mumbles against my lips, pulling away and giving me comically wide eyes that shoot pointedly towards the bedroom door, turning red.

"Come'ere," I say, bringing her face back to mine and kissing her harder. "I don't care; I need you." I hitch her leg around my hip and thrust firmly, sending her up the wall. I wait until her eyes open and meet mine before smiling. "We're about to be homeowners, baby. Can you believe it?"

She smiles warmly as I carefully press into her, tilting her head up for a kiss as I begin to rock us, beating my hips against hers in a fast tempo, racing us to the finish line. The realtor knocks on the door, calling for us so we can leave but...

It doesn't matter because sounds of love are in the air, and I won't have it disturbed for anything.

CHAPTER 47

EPILOGUE

Two Months Later

"How many did they lay?" Mason asks softly.

I hum as I open the little hatch top at the side of our chick inn, and he presses his front to my back as he works to peek impatiently over my shoulder as I raise the wooden top.

I look inside, holding my breath. "Five *-no, six!* Trixie is laying now!" I say happily as I reach into the straw and grab the chicken eggs and place them carefully in the basket he holds towards me.

This is our morning routine: we get up for a five o'clock run, do a little harvesting in our small garden, then we check the eggs before we start our day with work. It's a very fulfilling life, very different from the one we led in New York.

The chickens cluck as they walk around, picking at the feed and vegetable scraps Mason threw out for them.

We close the pen, and I look down as our beagle Betsy runs up to us, excited and whining for pets. Mason bends down and scratches her behind her ears as our other dog, a golden retriever, runs off after a bird in the distance. I wrap my arm around his waist as we make our way to the back of our house across the expansive grounds of the property and look up at him.

"I love you."

"Not as much as I love you." He bends down and kisses me slowly, not breaking our stride as we make our way into the house, and then place the eggs into the fridge.

"I'm about to head in." I eye him as he sits at the breakfast table and changes out of the boots he wears when we're outside in the gardens or the chicken coop, and puts on a pair of nice shoes. "Am I going to see you in time for dinner tonight?"

He glances up sharply and gives me a wink. "You can bet your pretty little ass on it. What are we having?"

"Egg drop soup and lo mien." I giggle, shaking my head as I try to evade his hands and head to change my own shoes.

Six hours later I'm in full swing at the bakery, teasing my boss Charayl about her non-existent love life. As I always do.

I tried to set her up with Stephen, but she just won't do it for some reason. She rolls her eyes, unbothered by my teasing, and shoves a big plate of steaming brownies topped with vanilla ice cream and warm caramel glaze to me. I grab it carefully.

"Help me take this out to the table," she says in a weary voice, no doubt sick of my teasing.

She picks up the other two plates, and I follow her out to the customers, where they are sitting patiently waiting for their desert. We stand and chit chat with them for a while. Charayl is amazing at customer service, and it never fails to amaze me how she knows everyone. And not only does she know them, she actually remembers the little details about them and always has follow-up questions.

Her brain is a bit intimidating, but under her tutelage I can tell I've grown a lot. I'm not quite as shy and feel a lot more confident in my abilities.

Right as we're turning to walk back to the front, the little door bell rings, and I turn back to greet whoever is walking in. But seeing it's just Mason, I break out into a wide smile and laugh because I just knew he wasn't going to go all week without seeing me until dinner time.

"Babe," I laugh, walking to him and giving him a hug, reaching out to playfully slap Luca's arm as he walks in behind Mason along with three of his men. *"What are you doing here?"* I ask in an accusatory tone.

"Well we had to come for the cinnamon chocolate chip cookies," he says in a sexy, thick accent that let's me know him coming here wasn't all for the cookies. I mean, *maybe* a cookie, but not the dessert type.

I roll my eyes. "Sure you did."

He gives me a wicked grin and lowers his voice. "Come on, butter-fly-"

"Don't you 'butterfly' me!" I whisper futilely in his ear. "I'm not leaving early just so you can fuck me!" He chuckles, and I turn to my cousin, seeing he's been quiet this whole time. "Hey, Luca," I call, but he's not paying me any attention.

My brows furrow at seeing him standing still in place as a shocked look melts away to an amused one, and a grin tips his lips. "Hello, Rabbit," he says in a low tone, and I frown, pulling away from Mason to turn to look behind me, seeing Charayl looking like a deer caught in headlights.

My brows rise. *"Charayl?"* I call slowly, seeing her struck mute.

I've never seen my sharp-as-nails boss struck stupid before. My eyes cut to Mason who just shrugs and brushes his hand down my hair. "Guess that explains that ugly as fuck rabbit statue on his mantle," he breathes, making me giggle.

Seeing Charayl just blinking at him I smile. "I guess so."

I walk over and bump her lightly with my hip, trying to snap her out of it. "Charayl, meet my cousin Lucien."

Her head snaps to me and her eyes widen. *"Cousin?"*

I nod. "Yep!"

"Charayl, would you like to come to our house for dinner tomorrow? We're hosting," Mason says.

"We are?" I ask, failing to play it cool. It's not effortless for me like it is for him.

"Hmhm. Remember? You wanted to test out the new jam you made from our berries."

Oh, yeah!" I say, smiling. "So, dinner at our place tomorrow. I'll text you the address."

But Charayl's not paying attention, and neither is my cousin. Her and Luca are too busy eye-fucking or something to listen to what we're saying.

"Okayyyy," I trill, deciding to leave anyway because this is a little awkward. "Gotta go. See you tomorrow." I say to them both, then Mason and I walk out the door, leaving them to whatever is happening.

"Talk to your mom today?" I ask as we walk down the sidewalk towards our car.

"Yeah, she's been staying with your mom."

I wince, "I'm sorry."

"No need to be sorry." He cuts his eyes to me. "How about you, love? Have you returned your mother's calls this week?"

"No."

He nods, looking ahead as we meander slowly. "I think maybe you should think about that, butterfly. Being upset is one thing, but holding a grudge this long is another."

I breathe in deeply, knowing he still hasn't made amends with Richard, who stopped calling when he saw Mason wasn't going to answer.

"That was a big secret, Mason," I say sadly. "I don't know how to move past it."

He puts his arms around my shoulder and presses his lips to my temple. "Together, Melly. We'll move past it together. I believe in us. Don't you?"

I nod. "Yeah, very much so."

We get in the car and drive in silence, not needing to talk any more about it, and as I look past the palm trees and to the bright aqua water crashing against the sandy beaches, I firmly believe we will get past it. It'll just take time.

I squeeze his hand, thankful to have the love of my life at my side to go through this with. Because patience and the passing of time is something neither of us are strangers to. So, we aren't scared.

As long as he's by my side, I know there's nothing to be scared of.

CHAPTER 48

EPILOGUE II

"HM," I FROWN AT the open laptop on the patio table in front of me and take a sip of my coffee, watching the latest celebrity news anchor just word vomit all over my family's legacy. I'm only watching it because it's not usual for our family to be splashed over celebrity sites as we're solidly business, not celebrity. Every now and again I might see Teresa on during a broadcasting of some major fashion event. But nothing like what I'm looking at now. *"Typical."*

"As of two days ago, a simple trip to the lobby of the revered King Dynasty building shows Mason King's finance plaque is still firmly in place next to the other businesses spanning across forty-five floors. Mason King is the youngest son of Oligarch, Richard King, and brother to current CEO Hendrix King. If you try to visit his former business, you will find the floor non-operational as Mason King now resides in California with his new bride, Melody King. A simple google search shows an LLC opened under his name; however, the finance business is only but a third of what Mason ran while he was stationed in New York. King Dynasty has sustained a *staggering* three-hundred-and-fifty-million-dollar loss in revenue since his departure."

I whistle, shaking my head. *"Damn,* that's pretty steep."

My eyebrow rises when a picture of my older brother and Maribel flashes on the screen.

"As if things weren't bad enough, there are also reports that Richard King and his wife of forty years are on the cusp of a divorce. Subsequently, it has not escaped our notice that Richard King's younger brother, William, who is the current Communications Director of a charity in Italy, has taken a leave of absence and is back in New York. One brother moves out, while another moves in. Does this spell disaster for the King family, and what does this mean for New York society? As we know, the King Dynasty reach spans across *both* business and politics, with many of the city's influential voters and heavy hitting donors to political campaigns often mirroring the Kings." I shake my head on a muted curse. *This* is why our family is being featured on a celebrity news outlet.

Fuck.

Scrubbing my hand down my face, I wish more than anything I could pick up the phone and call Richard. Mother would be utterly *horrified* at the King family making these sorts of headlines. I can see her rolling over in her grave right now as our family seemingly rips apart at the seams.

Unraveling the very threads she almost killed herself stitching together with her blood sweat and tears, rebuilding King Dynasty after the horrific death of her husband and the senseless murder of my sister.

My heart squeezes painfully at our misfortune splashed across every major news outlet. The stocks consistently going down. Acquaintances I haven't heard from in years crawl out the woodworks as news of my stay creeps into the other wealthy families' homes, and rumblings of an imminent coup is billowing like smoke from glowing embers just waiting to ignite with real fire.

This is the *last* thing I need: for Richard to feel like I'm trying to trump Hendrix and take over.

I reach over for my cup of coffee but pause at the sound of the doorbell.

Seeing as I don't have staff here, I rise from the seat, tossing a heavy linen napkin left over from my breakfast on the table, and carry my coffee with me through the sliding glass doors into the penthouse.

I frown, reluctant to go see who it is since I'm not expecting visitors. Today's not the best day as I'm a bit homesick for Italy and the feel of the Mediterranean sun, so I came out here for breakfast and a bit of warmth and relaxation. I don't care to break it for an unexpected guest.

Since they now live in California, Mason and Melody graciously loaned me their place to use while I'm stationed in New York, and I've made every second I've been here these last two months since the Balducci wedding count. Whether it's visiting with old acquaintances, or attempting to heal my relationship with my brother, I've done what I can to keep my mental health strong.

But Donna's constant rejection has been wearing at it.

The concern over my brother's mental health hasn't been helping, either.

What's worse is it's piled on top of all the issues between us, and so not only do I have to deal with Donna's rejection, I'm dealing with Richard doubling down on his disdain for me. And now with Maribel gone, he's also suspicious I'm trying to take her from him, as if it were forty-one years ago all over again.

With so much familial strain I've been nervous at spending too much time with Hendrix, much less have enough time to get to know Mariah...

God, this family is in shambles, and I desperately wish I knew the magic phrase to fix us.

Answering the door, I pause briefly in shock. Attempting to mask it as the one person I hadn't expected to come calling comes into view.

Maximus.

Not wanting to show him my displeasure, I raise a brow and step to the side, letting the underboss in and closing the door behind him. He walks in leisurely, like he owns the place. And I guess as Melody's father he would feel like it. He rakes a hand through thick, deep brown hair as he hesitates just inside the foyer, taking in the portrait of Melody and Mason posing on a beach, laughing.

I told Mason it was an odd spot to put such a picture, and he replied by saying they hung it there to always remind them to come into the house happy. The boy is wicked but sickeningly sweet sometimes, and I'm so proud of how far he's come in life.

"To what do I owe the pleasure of your company?" I ask wryly, seeing as he's not going to talk first.

He turns to face me and tilts his head. "Are you not going to offer me a seat?"

"And why should I?"

"Well, for one, it's polite." He gives me a knowing smile. "And two, because we have things to discuss. Obviously."

I scoff, folding my arms and spreading the stance of my feet just a bit. "I have nothing to discuss with you."

"I beg to differ."

I lower my brows, but he just stands there seemingly unaffected. Holding his stare, I gesture with a hand to the kitchen where there's a small breakfast table, wondering at his lack of security.

"Where are your people?"

"Out in the foyer," he says lightly. "May I have a coffee?"

My face hardens. "Do you plan on being here for a while?" I ask in a bored tone in an attempt to let him know he's not welcome.

"However long it takes." He gives me a charming smile, and I bristle at how open and at ease he is, because deep inside I want to break his face open for having had Donna first. He's part of the reason she won't trust again.

He and the world he's connected to.

Striding over to the counter I pour him a cup of coffee, leaving it black, and then set it in front of him with a clank against the glass table top. He picks it up, takes a sip, and sighs appreciatively. "Perfect."

I'm sure it is, dick.

"Can you get to the point? I have an entire day waiting for me, and I don't want to waste it looking at you." I sit across from him and cross my arms, informing him with my body language that I'm over it. Whatever *it* is.

"I spoke with Donna-"

I scoff, shaking my head. The audacity.

"And she told me that she was seeing you. I wanted to ask you if that was the truth."

"It is not, no," I say simply. "Now, if that will be all?"

"No, that will *not* be all." He gives me another one of those smiles, and I take a deep breath, searching for calm. "She said she was seeing you, and I had every intention of informing you that I wanted to get you out of the picture."

I laugh, glancing at him in amusement. "So, you're here to kill me?"

He takes another sip and sits back, eyeing me. "No. She wants you, William. So I wouldn't dream of it."

"Thats interesting, because she has rejected every attempt for me to get close to her. The furthest she has let me in is a coffee date."

He nods thoughtfully, rubbing the rim of his cup with a forefinger. "Not only is she scared to move on, she's also fearful of the mafia." He eyes me for a second, seeing too much. "And there's the little matter of you being Richard King's *brother*. Of course she's not letting you in. I haven't had any luck either, if that makes you feel better."

I tilt my head. "So you came here to ask for my help? How bold of you."

He shakes his. "No, I came here to see if you'd be willing to indulge me in something."

Staring at him for a minute, I fight feelings of uncertainty. Thanks to my brother's verbal lashing, and emotional and physical ostracism, I often find it hard to be in men's company. And I don't trust his patience or how careful he's being with his words. I feel the walls I've spent years keeping erect begin to shudder slightly with the way Maximus is so calmly regarding me.

No yelling... no evil looks, even though it's so very plain we want the same woman. Is this to be my fucking life?

Am I cursed?

Raising my brows, I take a sip of my coffee, regarding him quietly. "Go on."

"I can tell you from experience that Donna's a brat."

My inner dominant stretches and then stands to attention. Heat crawls up my neck, and a shiver flows down my spine at his words.

Because brats are my absolute *favorite* to play with. My pleasure is slightly dampened at the reminder that he's had her first. Had a child with her.

"That's what's wrong with her," he continues. "I think she's had too much leeway. A woman like her craves a firm hand and sure guidance."

My cock thickens, and I almost purr with desire, imagining Donna under *my* hand, because if only this man knew what I was like in the bedroom. My tastes. I could get that woman to scream, to sing out her pleasure. Scream it.

I've imagined the woman under me more times than I care to admit. To the point I feel insane with the need.

Fucking feral with it.

And I refuse to leave New York until she lets me have it.

"She's flailing, not sure which direction to turn. Scared to make a decision one way or another. So..." Leaning forward, he braces thick forearms on the table and levels me with a stare so serious that if I hadn't had the background I do with my monster of a father and a stoic, no-nonsense brother, I'd be cowering. "I say we make her choose."

"Between *us?*"

He nods. My interest is piqued. I stare at him for a second, seeing his demeanor is open. He's serious.

Well, what's a friendly competition?

"It'll never work here in New York; she's got too many places to run. Too many resources with the King family."

He nods. "Well, we'll have to take her somewhere if we're to do this the right way."

I smile. "I live in a different country. Does Italy sound stimulating to you?"

"Maybe in the beginning. She won't want to be that far from the girls and the babies for that long, I wouldn't think." He thrums his fingers on the table top. "I've got a property out that way. It's unoccupied at the moment because I've been busy with my nephew, but I can have it staffed and running soon. Roughly around three weeks, give or take."

"Hm." I avert my gaze to the floor-to-ceiling windows, contemplatively.

"Who gets her first?"

I throw him an irritated look. *"Whoever manages to get her first."*

He clears his throat and then sips his drink. "So, how dirty are we willing to fight?"

A wicked grin tips my lips. "Dirty as I want. Has anyone ever told you how the Kings procure their spouses?" I ask slowly, bringing my eyes back to his.

He gets a wicked grin and shakes his head. "No, but this sounds really interesting."

I smile back, elated at a challenge. "You got time?"

Crossing his legs, he sits back and takes another sip of his coffee. "I got all the time in the world, friend." His eyes narrow. "Only one problem, though: She's a fighter; from memory I can tell you she hits hard, like a man."

Leaning forward, I feel a wicked smile curve my lips. "That's never bothered me any. Does it bother you?"

He sips his coffee and a muscle clenches in his jaw. "Never. I like 'em rough."

"As do I." I chuckle and tip my cup at him. "May the best man win."

CHAPTER 49

More To Enjoy

INTERCONNECTED WORLDS

The Billionaire's Assurance Series

Colin and Olivia's story:

The Pain We Nurture (Book 1)

The Pain We Allow (Book 2)

Coming 2025: Sarah and Alexander's story

Will You Reach For Me (Book 3)

Unmasking Me Series:

Lola Unmasked part. 1

Lola Unmasked part. 2

Coming 2025: Lola Unmasked part 3

Christmas Novella:

Surrender At the Snowflake Inn

The King Dynasty Series:

The Heir

The Spare

Coming Soon: The Reign

Psychological Thriller

In You (2025)

CHAPTER 50

ACKNOWLEDGMENTS

I HAVE SO MANY people to thank that I don't even know where to start. But firstly, my family: I love you all to the moon and back. I couldn't do this without your patience, your understanding, and support.

To my readers; your value to me is immeasurable. I adore each and every one of you. I wish you could see how much. You give me the motivation to keep going.

To my betas, my alphas, my ARC team; thanks for being there every step of the way, even when I bounce back and forth seemingly crazy, it's because of all the characters inside my head wanting to get out. I hope you enjoy seeing their creation, as much as I love creating.

To D.W. Cole, Cheryl, and Tia Fanning, I hope you know I'm just as much in your corner as you are in mine. Thank you for helping me to break out of my cocoon, this story was healing for me to write.

To Traci, Brad, Ashli, Kelly, Tris, Mari, Melody, and Danni who stood side by side with me every single step of this book, and encouraged me to keep going, and to not give up even when I was discouraged, I couldn't do this without you either.

To my editor Traci, you are a lifesaver, through and through.

To a certain Prince and Duchess, who may never read the book that was inspired by their love story; with every breath I take, and every word I write, I will always spread the word that Love Wins.

Until the next book.

Best,

S.K. Presley

www.ingramcontent.com/pod-product-compliance
Lightning Source LLC
LaVergne TN
LVHW010626110826
845149LV00014B/2789
9798999635068